Come Home With Me

Recipes for Romance: Book Three

by

Suzie Peters

GWL
PUBLISHING

First Published in 2018
by GWL Publishing
an imprint of Great War Literature Publishing LLP

Produced in United Kingdom

ISBN 978-1-910603-64-2 Paperback Edition

GWL Publishing
Forum House
Sterling Road
Chichester PO19 7DN

www.gwlpublishing.co.uk

Dedication

For S.

Chapter One

Tess

"It'll be okay." Ali's voice sounds reassuring, but I still feel scared. I turn and smile at her, and notice that Sam's looking at me as well. His eyes voice his unspoken concern and I try my best to look happy.

Don't get me wrong; I am happy. Well, I'm happy for them at least. Sam's good for Ali. They're good together. He makes her happy, and she hasn't felt like that for a long while, but none of that stops me from feeling worried about the step she and I have just undertaken – to sell up and move three thousand miles to begin a new life in a completely different country.

The aircraft levels out and, after a little while, we unfasten our seatbelts and an air of relaxation settles over the passengers. Well, most of the passengers. I'm anything but relaxed.

When I left the safety of our grandmother's house three years ago to start my course in History and Comparative Literature at St Mary's University in London, I didn't really know what I was going to do once I graduated. I had some vague idea of writing, perhaps, or maybe a research position. The very last thing I saw myself doing was emigrating to America, and facing a completely unknown future.

Of course, that all came about because my sister took on a job in the States at the beginning of the year, to refurbish a restaurant, and while she was there, she fell in love with Sam. And then he proposed her. She didn't accept straight away, even though I knew she wanted to. What she did was to call me, and tell me about his proposal, and then ask me to move to the States with them... because Ali and I have been pretty much inseparable since our parents were killed in a fire over thirteen years ago. The idea of living in a different country, away from the things, and customs, and people I know really frightened me. But the idea of living on a different continent to Ali terrified me more. So, when she called me a few days ago to tell me that she'd decided to accept Sam's proposal, I had to say I was okay with moving to Connecticut with them. What choice did I have?

At the time, she and Sam had been down at our house in Dorset – a beautiful seaside cottage named Waterside, that had belonged to our parents and that we'd inherited when they died. Our grandmother had arranged for it to be let out years ago, and a series of tenants have called it home since then, but the most recent ones didn't pay the rent, and when our managing agents sent them a reminder, they took off, leaving a false forwarding address, and completely trashing the place.

Ali and Sam spent a couple of weeks fixing up the house and then we took the heartbreaking decision to put it up for sale, because Ali and I both agreed that we didn't need the hassle of having bad tenants again. Parting with Waterside was never going to be easy and, in a way, I'm glad that Ali dealt with it all. I've always had a particularly soft spot for the cottage, and I'm not sure I could've faced it. That said, Ali tends to deal with pretty much everything anyway, so I don't really know why I was worried.

Once that was done, they came back to London and I had my first real chance to see them together as a couple; and I knew straight away that Ali had made the right choice.

I'd seen them together before, but only very briefly, when Sam followed Ali back from the States. It turned out they'd had a big fight over there and Ali had flown back here to help me out with the problem over the house, without even telling him. So Sam had jumped on the next flight and arrived on our doorstep just a few hours later. To say the atmosphere between them was frosty would be the understatement of the year, but even then, I could see they were meant to be together and when Ali announced she was leaving for our house in Dorset, Sam said he was going too... and I kind of helped them on their way. It was the only thing to do, especially as Ali was being a bit childish about the whole thing. She wanted to be with him; she'd even admitted that to me. And yet she was putting up roadblocks. He'd hurt her, that much was obvious, but the guy had flown three thousand miles, just to apologise. I think that warranted a little credit…

In any case, it's clear they're perfect for each other, although from what I've gathered, Sam had some persuading to do, especially when Ali found out that he'd been married before, and hadn't told her. I'm glad I wasn't there when that happened. I imagine it wasn't pretty…

Still, they worked it out eventually… And so it is that we're all on a plane to America, having also put our London flat up for sale, thus cutting all ties with home, England, the past, and our parents.

I feel a sting of tears behind my eyes and close them, pretending to be asleep.

Actually, I could do with some sleep. The last few weeks have been hectic and exhausting. I had to finish my ten thousand word dissertation, which I handed in last Friday. I don't think I've ever read so much, or made so many notes, in my life, but I got there in the end. Then Ali and Sam got back from Dorset on Saturday, and that's when the planning really kicked in. The first thing Sam did was to book us on flights for today – Tuesday – which gave us three days to pack, and arrange for the shipping of all the things we want to have with us in America, which mainly consists of books and mementos of our parents. We're not taking any furniture; we're having it moved to Waterside because the house is virtually empty after all the damage that was done and it'll probably sell much more easily if there's furniture in there. Then Ali spoke to our father's solicitor, Miles Kingston – well, I suppose he's our solicitor now – and arranged with him to put our London flat on the market. He's also going to handle the removal of the furniture to Waterside, and make sure everything gets shipped properly to America. I have no doubt he charges us for what he does, but he's an old university friend of our father's, so I imagine he helps out because he wants to, rather than because we're paying him.

Once all of that was done, all that was left was paperwork, sorting out my visa and other annoying, fiddly things that took a long time to organise, like getting my university to accept that I wouldn't be attending graduation and was leaving before the semester officially ended, even though there were no more lectures to attend, and nothing else to hand in. For some reason, it seemed to be a big deal. Almost as big a deal as arranging to have our mail forwarded overseas. That was more complicated than we'd expected too.

Now, when I look back at the whirlwind, I'm not surprised I'm feeling so tired…

Apart from being woken up for food and the occasional drink, I think I slept through most of the flight in the end, and Ali woke me about twenty minutes before we were due to land.

Now, we're on our own. Sam's not with us anymore because he doesn't have to go through immigration, which seems be taking an incredibly long time. Ali takes charge and tells me what to do and say, and I obey. Despite sleeping on the plane, I'm still too tired to question anything.

When we come out, Sam's waiting for us and, looking at Ali's face, I can see how reassured she feels to see him. I have to admit, I am too. He seems to be very at home here, even though we're in an airport arrivals hall. Of course, he's not hard to find; at his height, he towers above most other people, and he steps towards us the moment he sees us.

"Everything okay?" he asks, taking Ali's hand.

"Yes, just fine," she replies.

Our cases are all stacked on a trolley, which Sam commandeers and he guides us towards a crowd of people who are awaiting various flights.

"Ed and Rob are both busy at the restaurant," he explains to both of us, "so they couldn't come pick us up. But Rob arranged that Jackson would meet us." He looks around while we're walking and then nods his head. "Over there," he adds, and changes direction just slightly, guiding us towards a man with short blond hair, probably just under six feet tall, who's holding up his hand.

"Hey," Sam says as we draw closer.

"Good to see you, boss," the other man replies, then looks at Ali. "And you, Ali," he says to her, leaning down and kissing her cheek.

"Hello, Jackson," Ali replies.

Then he turns to me.

"This is Ali's sister, Tess." Sam makes the introduction.

"It's a pleasure to meet you." His eyes sparkle as he smiles and moves a little closer than feels comfortable. "If you need anything, just ask for me. My name's Jackson."

Right at that moment, Sam grabs him by the sleeve of his jacket, yanking him away.

"And that'll do," he says, gruffly. "Here, if you wanna be useful, push this." He offers the trolley to Jackson, who takes it sheepishly. "Whose car did you bring?" Sam adds.

"Rob told me to bring yours."

Sam nods and smiles. "Good. I'll drive home." He turns to Ali. "See, I told you. I don't like to be driven."

She shakes her head, smiling back at him.

"Are you okay?" Ali asks me and I nod just once.

Sam and Jackson sit in the front of the car, which is a relief, being as I'd dreaded Ali wanting to sit with Sam and me being left with Jackson for the journey, which Ali's informed me will take over two hours.

"You can sleep some more, if you want to," Sam says, looking at me in the rear-view mirror.

"I've already slept for hours."

"Hmm, but you've had a very tiring few days," Ali replies. "Besides, the secret to dealing with jet lag is to try and stay up late tonight, so make the most of getting some sleep now."

I take her advice and, using her shoulder as a pillow, I settle down to sleep again.

"We're here." Ali wakes me, just as Sam switches off the engine.

"Where's here?" I look around. We appear to be in an underground car park.

"We're beneath the hotel a few doors up from the restaurant," Sam explains. "I have an arrangement to park my car here."

"Oh… okay."

Sam and Jackson get out and open the doors for Ali and I. Jackson takes my hand, helping me down from the car, which is a Toyota Land Cruiser and feels enormous on the outside, although looking around the car park, it doesn't seem so big. All the vehicles in here look much bigger than the ones at home.

"Thank you," I say to Jackson, staring down at our hands. He seems reluctant to let go, but Sam calls him to the boot of the car and he goes, releasing my hand, thank goodness. Ali comes around to me and gives me a smile, linking her arm through mine.

"Don't worry about Jackson," she whispers. "I think he's a bit smitten."

"Really?" I look up at her. She's a couple of inches taller than me… well, three, if we're being absolutely accurate.

"Yeah. Get used to it." Her smile widens and she leads me to the back of the car, where Sam and Jackson have unloaded the cases.

"Do you want some help?" Ali offers and we both step forward.

Sam gives her a look and a slight smile. "Hardly," he replies and he and Jackson pick up all the bags between them and we start towards the lifts.

"Why can't we help?" I whisper to Ali.

"Because that's how it seems to work over here. It's like opening car doors."

"Women don't open car doors?" I ask, bemused.

"They do, but men like doing it for them. Well, nice men do anyway." I nod my head. "You'll get used to it," she adds.

Will I? I wish I felt as sure as she does.

We go up to the ground level and out onto the street, where I'm struck by the height of the buildings, and the noise of the traffic. The pavement is wide – much wider than at home – but the noise feels overwhelming. Even though I'm used to London, I usually spent most of my time there in the tube, avoiding the busy streets, or in lecture halls, or in the library, or in our flat. I didn't go out much, except with Ali.

She obviously feels me flinch against the noise and tightens her grip on my arm.

"We've only got a really short walk," she says quietly, guiding me along the pavement.

She's not wrong. Within a couple of minutes, we arrive at the restaurant.

"It looks lovely," I say to her, honestly, taking in the grey paintwork and trimmed bay trees at the front door. "I mean, I don't know what it looked like before, obviously, but it looks lovely now." This is what Ali came here for originally, to make over the restaurant and, as usual, she's done a magnificent job.

"Thanks, Tess," she says, smiling at me.

Sam manages to unlock and open the door, despite the encumbrance of the bags he's carrying, and we pass through into a beautiful interior. The wall on the left is covered with small framed photographs, which are too far away for me to make out what they're of. There's one at the back though, which is easily identifiable. I'd know it anywhere. It's a huge picture that covers the whole wall, featuring a view of Positano in the evening, with the village's lights reflected in the bay below. Ali's put in spaced white vertical lines every so often, which break up the photograph, without spoiling the effect. There are several waiters and waitresses, currently laying up tables with white linen table cloths and sparkling glassware and cutlery, but they all stop and come over as soon as they see Sam.

"Hey, boss. Good to see you back."

"Where have you been?"

"We were starting to forget what you looked like."

He smiles at them and nods his acceptance of their greetings, then looks around at everyone gathered before him.

"Where's Rob?" he asks.

A dark-haired man answers. "He's in the kitchen, boss."

Sam nods. A couple of people are talking to Ali, saying hello and asking how she is, but Sam gets her attention and she goes over to him, taking me with her. "We'll make the formal introductions another time," he says, looking at me, "but this is Ali's sister, Tess."

Everyone says 'hello', or 'hi', and I nod my head, unsure how to respond.

"And now," Sam says, "I'm gonna go see if my two brothers have wrecked my kitchen."

They all laugh and make a space for us to pass through. Sam leads the way towards the back of the restaurant, going into a corridor and then through a set of double doors on our right. He holds them open until Ali and I are on the inside of a huge kitchen area, then he lets them close and turns around, dumping the cases on the floor.

"What the fuck do you call this?" Sam says loudly.

Everyone in the kitchen stops and turns, and then the noise level shoots up as they all come over and start talking at once. I feel myself tense and curl inward. There are too many people here for me and I wish I could be anywhere else. They're all greeting Ali too and she's pulled away from me, into the crowd, just as I become aware that Jackson is still with us, although I don't really know why.

"Are you okay?" he asks. I'm sure he only means to be friendly, but I don't know him.

"Yes, thank you." I move away from him slightly, even though it means getting closer to the crowd.

Just at that moment, I notice two men walking towards us from the very back of the kitchen. They look almost identical. One's wearing all black, and has short dark hair, which is spiky on top. He comes straight over to Sam and slaps him on the back, making a joke. Sam pulls him into a hug and then away from everyone else and they talk for a few minutes. Sam looks a bit angry, but then his expression clears and they seem to be okay again. The other man hangs back a little while this is going on. He's wearing chef's whites and has longer hair. It's just as dark as the first man's, and he's got brown eyes and a square, clean-shaven jaw. I guess these two must be Sam's twin brothers, Rob and Ed, although which one is which, I don't know. The one with the longer hair waits for his brother to move back and then steps forward and hugs Sam affectionately. They whisper something to each other and seem a lot closer than Sam and the other twin were.

The twins then turn to Ali, and I notice the one in black looks embarrassed, although I don't know why. He hesitates and then says he's sorry.

"Why?" Ali asks, looking at him.

"That dumb text message. I didn't realise Sam hadn't told you about Amber," he says. His accent is nice. It's soft, not as harsh as Jackson's.

"It's not your fault," Ali replies. "He hasn't been threatening you, has he?"

The man shrugs. "Not with anything I can't handle."

The man in the chef's whites is staring at them. "Is anyone gonna enlighten me?" he asks and I catch my breath. If I thought the other twin had a nice voice, this man's is breathtaking. It's beautiful and intoxicating and for a moment, I'm mesmerised, just staring at him.

"I might do, one day," the other man replies, and then they both step forward and hug Ali together.

I've got no idea what that conversation was about, but I can ask Ali later, and eventually, they break up the hug and Ali turns them around. She's about to introduce us when someone laughs loudly behind her, the noise level shoots up again, and I flinch. I wish I didn't feel so nervous all the time, but it's been like this ever since Mum and Dad died; any loud noise, and I become a nervous wreck. I try to hide it, but it's there, and it infuriates me.

The man with the longer hair, in the chef's whites turns around to face everyone else.

"Okay guys," he says, his voice deep, but still calm . "Let's give Sam and Ali a chance to catch their breath, shall we? Take some time out and be back here at five-thirty. Okay?"

They all make approving noises and slowly disperse, and then he turns back to me. And he gives me such a smouldering look, I wonder why it makes me shiver.

Ed

"I guess it depends how long Jasmine's gonna be away for," Rob says to me, and I lean back against the countertop in the dessert section of the kitchen and look across at him. He's currently propped up against the wall by the door, and I've gotta say, he looks exhausted. It's not surprising really. He's been helping me out in the kitchens for the last few weeks, while Sam's been in England, as well as doing all his usual admin and meetings, and working front of house at lunchtimes. He's had to do that, because our normal head waitress, Jasmine, hasn't been in, since her daughter got sick. Rob's girlfriend, Petra, has been helping out too, but the hours are clearly starting to get to him.

"I know. But Sam's back today. That'll help."

He shrugs. "I've still gotta cover the lunch *and* evening sessions out front," he points out.

He's right. Normally, he only works in the restaurant in the evenings; he doesn't cover the lunch session, unless we're really busy. Jasmine does that, which leaves Rob free to do all his other work in the office. I've got no idea where he's found the time to get all of that done over the last three weeks.

"Once Sam's back we can—"

"What the fuck do you call this?" Sam's voice rings out from the other end of the kitchen and we both look up to see him standing there, larger than life.

"Well, talk of the devil," Rob says.

He has some idea of how relieved I am to be handing back control of the kitchens to our big brother. I've hated these last few weeks and I can't wait to let Sam have the run of the place again. Actually 'hated' isn't really a strong enough word. I've gotten more used to it as time's gone on, but in the beginning, when he first announced how long he was gonna be away for, I was literally sick with fear at having to manage the kitchens for so long without him. I was throwing up in the bathroom at home, grateful that Rob was so preoccupied with Petra, he didn't notice. I told him fairly early on that I was struggling, but blamed it on tiredness rather than the crippling fear that was eating into me at just the thought of having to run another service. So now, just seeing Sam at the other end of the kitchen is enough to soothe my nerves.

Having Sam back is about more than that though… For the last few weeks, I've lived in even greater fear that he'd decide to stay in England, or at least move over there on a permanent basis, once he'd worked out the logistics of doing so. We know how much he loves Ali and we all know that Ali has a sister, and that moving here was always gonna be a big ask for her, and it occurred to us – well, it occurred to Petra – that Sam might decide to move to England, rather than ask them to move here. That prospect filled me with absolute dread. Obviously him moving away would leave us with a huge hole in the restaurant, but my main worry stems from the fact that Sam's been my rock, my support, my hero, if you like, for the last nine years or so, ever since our dad made clear his disapproval of my decision not to follow him into the main kitchen, but to pursue my own dream of working in pastry instead. I've come to rely on Sam and the thought of trying to work without him… well, it wasn't something I even wanted to contemplate. It still isn't. The other reason I feared him going was that we're a team. We're a family. We fight, we bicker, but we also laugh. We laugh a lot, and deep down, we love each other. Okay, we're an incomplete family, because our parents don't speak to me or Sam, but the three of us are tight. We're about as close as a family can get, and I can't think of anything worse than breaking that up, by one of us moving so far away from the others.

I haven't really had the chance to talk that through with Rob, being as he's been living at Petra's for the last couple of weeks, but he knows me well enough to gauge how I feel. We're not twins for nothing.

Rob gives me a smile and we both step out into the main kitchen area, where Sam's now been surrounded by all the other kitchen hands and chefs. Ali's there too, saying hello and smiling at everyone. God, it's good to see her again, especially looking so happy.

Rob goes straight over to Sam and slaps him hard on the back, and before I can move in to greet him, Sam's pulled Rob into a hug and taken a couple of steps away.

I can't hear what they're saying, but Sam looks madder than hell.

They talk for a few minutes and then Sam's face clears and, if I'm being honest, he looks more concerned than anything else, and finally he smiles and I heave a sigh of relief. The last thing I needed today was for Sam to start a fight with Rob.

Sam looks over at me as Rob moves away, and I just go up to him and hug him. He returns the hug, patting me on the back gently.

"You brought her home," I whisper.

"Sure did." He pulls back a little and, as far as I'm concerned, his smile makes the last three weeks of stress, fear and hard work worthwhile. "And thanks," he says.

"What for?"

"Covering for me. I really do owe you."

"You owe Rob too."

"Yeah, yeah. I know." He grins and we step away from each other, and I turn and Rob and I go over to Ali, who's still kinda surrounded. Once she sees us, she breaks away and comes over.

"I'm sorry," Rob says. I turn to look at him. I've got no idea what he's talking about.

"Why?" Ali replies, clearly as confused as me.

"That dumb text message. I didn't realize Sam hadn't told you about Amber." He hadn't? He hadn't told Ali he was married before? What an idiot... but how does that involve Rob, or a text message?

"It's not your fault," Ali says. "He hasn't been threatening you, has he?"

Rob shrugs his shoulders. "Not with anything I can't handle."

I look from Rob to Ali, and back again. "Is anyone gonna enlighten me?" I ask.

"I might do, one day," Rob replies and then rolls his eyes. I hate it when he does that, and decide to leave it for now. I'm sure I'll find out soon enough. We move forward and hug her together, before Ali pulls back and looks at us both, then turns us around. And that's when I see her sister for the first time.

My skin's tingling and my mouth's gone dry, although the rest of my body feels numb. She's beautiful… she's clearly terrified of something, but she's beautiful.

So this is Tess… I take in her long, wavy dark blonde hair, her porcelain-smooth skin and her delicate pink lips, but I'm most drawn to her eyes, which are huge, and blue, and perfect.

Ali moves away from us and takes a step toward her sister just as one of the guys behind us laughs really loudly and I notice Tess flinch and pull back, her eyes widening even further. Sam might be back, and it might be his kitchen, but he's not doing anything about this, so I'm going to… I turn around and face the group.

"Okay guys," I say. "Let's give Sam and Ali a chance to catch their breath, shall we? Take some time out and be back here at five-thirty. Okay?" I think it's best if we have as few people out here as possible. Tess is clearly frightened enough already. She doesn't need this.

Everyone starts moving away and Sam comes back over toward us, just as I turn back to face Ali and Tess and, as she looks up at me, our eyes meet and I actually feel myself falling into them. It's a weird sensation, but I like it. I like her too.

"Rob, Ed," Ali says. "This is my sister, Tess."

We both step forward, although Rob gets to her first.

"I'm Rob," he tells her. "People say it's hard to tell us apart, but it's not. I'm the good looking one."

She smiles, shaking his hand and her head at the same time. "Do you say that to everyone?" she asks, and I notice how soft and quiet her voice is.

"Yes, he does," Ali replies. "All the women he meets, anyway."

"Hey," Rob says. "I'm a reformed character."

"Doesn't look like it to me," Sam mocks.

Everyone laughs and Rob moves to one side as I take his place and offer her my hand. She takes it and we shake.

"Hello," she whispers. "So, if he's Rob, you must be Ed."

"Yes. It's good to meet you."

"You too."

Our eyes are locked, and now I'm this close I can see hers are a darker shade of blue than I thought, her lips are fuller too, and her skin's flawless... oh yeah, and I can't breathe.

"Did you have a good flight?" I ask, because I can't think of anything else to say.

"I slept through most of it," she replies. Her quiet voice suits her. She's shy, guarded, and based on what I've seen so far, I'd say very easily frightened. All my instincts are screaming at me to protect her – from everything and everyone.

"How's it been?" Sam's voice interrupts my thoughts and I look over and see him staring at me. At the sound of his voice, Tess pulls her hand away from mine and the feeling of loss is almost overwhelming, to the point where I have to take a moment before replying to Sam.

"We've coped," I manage to say.

"You've told me Rob's been working in here. So, how's it been out front?" He gives me a long, slow stare, then turns to Rob. "Has Jasmine been helping out?"

"No," Rob replies. "In fact, Jasmine's not been here for the last few days. Scarlett got sick. She's in the hospital."

Sam pushes himself upright and goes over to Rob, standing in front of him. He's obviously concerned. "What's wrong with her?" he asks. While they're occupied, I take the chance to look at Tess again. She's staring down at her hands, which are clasped in front of her. She looks kinda lost and I wanna take her somewhere quiet, away from everyone else, maybe hold her hands and stop them shaking so much...

"They think it's Lyme disease," Rob explains.

"Isn't that the thing you get from ticks?" Ali asks.

"Yeah," Sam replies, turning back to her and going to stand by Tess, while glaring at me once more. For some reason Sam seems to be bothered by me paying her too much attention, so I focus on him instead, while Rob explains what's been going on with Jasmine. After a few moments, Ali nestles into Sam, and rests her head on his shoulder. I guess they're all pretty tired, and he puts his arm around her, pulling her close, before he puts his finger underneath her chin and raises her face to his, kissing her, just gently. I glance at Rob and notice that he's smiling, and I'm not surprised. Sam's never been one to display his affections in public, so that was kinda nice to see.

As Rob finishes explaining about Jasmine, Tess looks up again. "Is she okay?" she asks. "The little girl, I mean?"

"She's getting better," I reply quickly. "They're hoping she'll be out of the hospital in a couple of days."

"And Jasmine?" Sam asks.

Rob looks over at him again. "I've told her to take all the time she needs," he says. "And I've told her we'll still pay her… She was worried."

Sam nods his head. "Good." He seems to hesitate, then adds, "If Jasmine hasn't been here, how have you managed out front?"

I glance over at Rob, because I don't know how much he wants to tell Sam about Petra. We haven't talked about it – again, because I've only seen him at work since he and Petra got together, so there hasn't been the time. Between running this place and his sex life, we've both been too busy. "It's been fine," I say.

Sam looks from Rob to me and back again and then opens his mouth. Knowing Sam, he's probably going to yell at Rob, or me, or both of us.

"I need to speak to you," Rob puts in, before Sam can even speak. "You and Ed."

I wasn't expecting that. And I don't think Sam was either and we exchange a quick glance.

"I'll take Tess upstairs," Ali says, taking Rob's not very subtle hint that this conversation needs to be between the three of us. "We're both really tired. We could do with having a coffee and putting our feet up for half an hour."

Sam hands her his keys. "Okay," he says, "let yourself in. You know where everything is." He pulls Ali into a hug and whispers something to her.

She leans back, looking up at him, and says, "That's fine with me. I think I'd prefer it that way. I don't want a fuss." She nods at Tess.

"Sure?" he asks.

"Yes." She kisses him on the cheek, then turns to Tess and offers her hand, which Tess accepts. "Come on," Ali says. "Let's leave them to it."

I take a step forward. "Do you need any help with your bags?" I suggest. I don't want Tess to leave – or if she has to, I want to go with her.

"It's fine." Sam's beside me in an instant. "I'll take them up later."

I hide my disappointment as well as I can, although I'm aware of Sam watching me, even as Tess and Ali go out through the kitchen door.

"Okay…" he says as soon as their footsteps have faded on the stairs up to his apartment. "What aren't you telling me?"

"It's nothing bad," Rob says quickly

"It honestly isn't," I add, defending him.

"Now I'm really worried." Sam looks down at us, his expression slightly threatening.

I don't know what to say and I feel like the ball's in Rob's court. He asked to speak to us, so he needs to start this off. He sucks in a deep breath. "Petra's been helping out," he says, looking at Sam.

"Petra? The photographer?" Sam's surprised.

"Yeah. She'd done some waitressing before and she offered to lend a hand," Rob explains.

"But who's been running the restaurant?" Sam asks.

"Petra."

"And she's been doing a really good job of it," I say quickly, because Sam seems doubtful about the whole thing. "She's a real hit with the customers, and all the other staff really like her."

Sam looks at me for a moment, then nods his head. "Okay."

"There's something else…" Rob adds and Sam focuses back on him again."Petra and I are together."

"I'm not entirely surprised by that." Sam's smirking now, although how he had any clue about Petra, I have no idea. Unless Ali told him that Rob texted her, asking for Petra's contact details and he's put two and two together, and actually made four, for once in his life.

"Yeah…" Rob continues, "but what might surprise you is, she's got a four year old daughter, called April, and… she's married."

Sam stares at him, his face darkening. "Petra's married?"

"Only on paper," Rob replies. A look passes between them, and I wonder if it's got anything to do with their earlier conversation when Sam arrived. There's a lot going on today that I don't understand, but to be honest, the only thing that interests me right now is Tess and whether she's okay. "Her husband didn't treat her very well…" *What?* I listen up and move toward him. He didn't tell me that bit, and I wonder how long he's known… "And he left her before April was born," Rob says. "They didn't divorce at the time, because they couldn't afford it. But they're getting divorced now…"

"Because of you?" Sam asks him.

"Because her husband wants to re-marry," Rob explains.

Sam nods. "Sounds like you've had an interesting couple of weeks," he replies, his face clearing, and a smile forming on his lips.

"You could put it that way…" Rob hesitates, like he's nervous, which isn't like him at all. "The thing is, I have a favor to ask of both of you."

Sam stands up straight and crosses his arms. He's a couple of inches taller than Rob and I, and he knows this makes him look more intimidating. I'm just waiting to hear what Rob's got to say, because I don't have a clue.

"I doubt you're gonna like this," Rob begins, "but please just hear me out… What Ed said is completely true. Petra's really good at running this place, and she is a hit with the customers… So, I was wondering how you'd feel about her carrying on here, working with me, maybe a couple of evenings a week."

Sam turns to look at me and I notice there's a slight twinkle in his eye. He wants to have some fun with this, and I've got a good mind to let him, for once. This makes sense of Rob's conversation with me earlier. He was clearly trying to sound me out about Petra working here in the future – although why the hell he couldn't just ask me, I don't know. Rob sighs. "I know we've spent a lot of money on this place the in the last couple of months," he says, sounding a little desperate now, "but I really want this, guys. I'm in love with her, and it's gonna be real hard not seeing anything of her from breakfast until midnight. If we can just do this…"

I'm useless at this kind of thing. He's my brother. Even more than that, he's my twin. I can't watch him suffer, even if Sam can. "Oh, put him out of his misery, Sam." I smile across at him.

"Of course she can work here," Sam says, going over and slapping Rob quite hard on the back. "And I do get the whole thing about missing her during the day. That's why Ali's gonna be working in the kitchens whenever she can. I don't wanna miss out on seeing her either. I'm real happy for you… although what that poor woman sees in you is beyond me. And what she's doing letting a reprobate like you near her daughter is anyone's guess, but if this is what you want, then you got it."

I love it when Sam's like this. He can be a miserable grouch sometimes, but when he's happy, when he's being kind and generous – which is the real Sam, the one before his ex-wife messed with his head – he's a great guy to have in your corner. I should know; he's been in mine for years now…

"You say that," Rob continues, "but just wait until you meet her…"

"I've already met her…" Sam replies. "Well, I've seen her, anyway. She was here at the opening."

"No, I mean April," Rob explains. Even I haven't had that privilege yet. "She'll have you eating out of her hand within minutes… And being as you'll both be her uncles—"

Uncles. I knew he was gonna ask Petra to marry him, but I hadn't thought about being an uncle. I also didn't think he'd own up to Sam about the proposal… not yet anyway.

"Whoa… wait a second." Sam's staring at him. "Does this mean the divorce isn't entirely for the other guy's benefit? Are you saying marriage is on the cards? The whole ready-made family, and everything?"

"Maybe." Rob shrugs.

"Only maybe?"

"Well, I haven't actually asked her yet."

"But you're going to?"

Rob nods. "It's been a little busy around here the last few days…" He looks over at me and I give him just a hint of a nod. Last weekend was real dramatic for Rob, after Petra's ex – well, her husband, I guess – came into the restaurant and Rob saw them together, being a little more intimate than he felt comfortable with. He and Petra argued, and that was when Rob found out that the guy he thought was her ex is actually still her husband. I think they came close to breaking up over that, but they dealt with it and I guess he doesn't necessarily want Sam to know about it, which means he won't hear it from me. My nod to Rob is just me letting him know that.

Sam turns away from both of us and goes over to the countertop. "It doesn't take that long to propose, you know." He looks at us, smiling. "I think it took me a matter of seconds to propose to Ali…"

"You… you proposed to Ali?" Rob manages to form a sentence, because I can't.

Sam's nodding and grinning at the same time. "Yeah. And before you say anything, I know we haven't been together that long, but this is nothing like Amber."

"We know that," Rob says. "Ali is nothing like your ex."

"No. She isn't."

"I take it she accepted?" Rob's trying not to laugh now.

"Of course she fucking accepted," Sam says, glaring at him. "It took her three weeks, but she said yes."

"Three weeks?" I can't imagine Sam waiting three weeks for anything.

"Yeah. It was a tough decision," he explains.

"I can imagine," Rob jokes.

Sam stares at him and murmurs, "Asshole," under his breath, although we both hear him. "She wasn't just accepting me," he continues, speaking normally again. "She was accepting moving here too, and that meant moving Tess." He looks at us both, but focuses on me. "That's a long story." It's clearly a story that involves Tess, so I'd like to hear it, but he's obviously not going to tell us, and he stands upright again, yawning and stretching his arms above his head, before he looks down at Rob once more. "I hope you're okay covering one more night in here," he says. "Because I have no idea what time of day it is, so I seriously doubt I should be put in charge of anything that we're expecting people to pay to eat."

Rob shakes his head, smiling. "It's fine. We expected that. Petra's coming in tonight."

"She is?" Sam asks.

"Yeah."

"What time?"

Rob thinks for a second. "She's coming in a little before six. She wants to spend as much of the day as she can with April."

"Okay," Sam says. "I'll come down and meet her."

"Be nice to her." There's a warning note in Rob's voice.

Sam walks over toward the double doors, bending to pick up the bags, but then turns back and smiles. "I'm always nice," he says, then he goes out and we look at each other, just as we hear him call out, "Well, I am now."

Rob seems worried now about Sam and Petra meeting and, without even looking at me, he goes out into the restaurant to wait for her.

Left to myself, I wander back toward my own area of the kitchen, the space Ali created for me as part of the refurbishment, where I can do what Sam tells me I do best – namely make desserts. I can't help smiling to myself as I flick the convection ovens on, ready for tonight's service. The last few weeks have been hard work, and kinda lonely, if I'm being honest, and I'm looking forward to the fact that Sam's back and, after tonight, I won't be responsible for this place any longer. I'm really glad that he's brought Ali back with him too, and that they're engaged. They're right for each other, and she belongs here. On top of that, she's a damn good pastry chef. She worked with me for a while before she went back to England, and she's got talent – real talent. So I was glad to hear Sam say she'll be spending some time down here again. Not only can she cook, but she's good to bounce ideas off of.

I'm also really pleased that Rob's told Sam about Petra and that she's gonna still be working here too. Him asking us about that, rather than just doing it and telling us about it afterwards, tells me he's learned his lesson. He brought Ali over here to work on the restaurant without checking it with me and Sam first, and while that may have worked out well in the end, it was kinda ugly to start with. This time, at least he asked. We may be a team, but Rob and I have never disputed the fact that Sam is in charge. We both kinda like it that way and I know Sam will have appreciated Rob asking, rather than just doing, even more than I do. Just with that one gesture, it feels like the pieces of our jigsaw are really back together for the first time in ages. I mean, I obviously miss Rob, now that he's moved out of our apartment, but we're still together at work, and he's happy; happier than I've ever seen him, so I'm okay with that.

As I get into my own section and make a start on this evening's prep, I'm still smiling. And I know why. I may be happy for my brothers and their girlfriends, and I may be happy that Sam's back, and the three of us are together again, but I've got an even better reason for smiling to myself…

Her name's Tess.

Chapter Two

Tess

I slept terribly.

I suppose it's not that surprising. I'm in a strange bed, in a strange room, in a strange flat – or apartment, as they seem to say here – in a strange city, in a strange country. Not only that, but the time difference is playing havoc with my brain and my body. I feel sick a lot of the time, but Ali assures me that it's just jet lag and it'll pass soon, once I get settled. So that'll be sometime never then, because I can't imagine ever feeling settled here.

"Good night?" Sam asks, dishing up scrambled eggs on to the plates in front of us. He's wearing shorts and a tight t-shirt and it's hard to avoid the way Ali keeps staring at him. I feel a little awkward and wonder if I should take my breakfast into the living room, or my bedroom and leave them alone for a while.

"Yes, thanks," I lie, eventually remembering to answer him. I don't mention the nightmare that woke me at just after three. Ali will only worry.

"Sure?" He looks down at me.

I nod and he turns and puts the pan back down on the stove, before coming and sitting down at the island unit with me and Ali. They're sitting together, holding hands and I'm opposite them by myself, and I wonder if this is how things are going to be from now on; if I'm going to feel like the spare part in their lives forever.

We start eating and, despite the nausea, I have to admit, Sam makes really good scrambled eggs.

"This is delicious," I say, swallowing down my first mouthful. I hadn't realised I was this hungry.

"Better than mine?" Ali asks, taking a mouthful herself and smiling at me.

I stop chewing and look at her, and she smiles, and then laughs. "It's okay," she says. "I know Sam makes the best scrambled eggs."

He chuckles. "Why, thank you, ladies," he says. "Wait until you taste my pancakes."

"I already have," Ali replies. "And they're very nice."

"Nice?" Sam grins at her. "Nice? Is that the best you can say?"

Ali smiles. "Okay. They're the best pancakes I've ever eaten. They're almost as good as your fish and chips, your pasta, your pizza, your beef stew…" She lowers her voice to a whisper. "In fact, everything about you tastes just perfect." She looks up into his eyes and he cups her face in his hands.

"No, you're the one who tastes perfect," he murmurs quietly, although it's loud enough for me to hear. I have no idea what they're talking about, but the look they exchange is positively combustible, and then he leans down and kisses her and, for a while I focus on what's on my plate, wishing I could get up and go somewhere else, but knowing that if I do, it'll just appear that I'm embarrassed – and while I am, I don't want them to feel that they can't be themselves in their own home.

"Do you have any plans for today?" Sam's voice makes me jump and I look up from my plate. They're both staring at me.

"No. Not really. I was going to start unpacking, but other than that…"

"You should come down into the restaurant at lunchtime, and meet everyone," Sam suggests.

"Really?" I can't think of anything I want to do less, not after yesterday. There were so many of them, and it was far too loud. "Are you going to be working all day?" I ask him, trying to cover my awkwardness.

"Yep. Back to the grindstone for me." He looks at Ali. "I think if I asked my brothers to cover for me for anything more than about five minutes, they'd probably walk out and not come back."

"Come down anyway," Ali says to me.

"You're going to be down there too?" I hadn't expected that.

"Yes." She nods. "I'm going to see if I can help Rob out a little bit, just while Jasmine's away. I can't run the restaurant for him, but I might be able to help out with some of the admin." She looks up at Sam.

"You're too good to him," he says, and I get the feeling this is something they've been discussing in private.

"He's been good to you… and us," she replies. "And he looks exhausted."

"Only because he's not getting enough sleep."

"Exactly," Ali says.

"But that's got nothing to do with this place, and everything to do with Petra keeping him occupied." Sam smirks.

"Even so," Ali says, smiling. "Give the guy a break."

"And Ed?" Sam says. "Doesn't he get a break?"

Ali leans into him. "Just having you back is enough for Ed. I'd have thought you could have worked that out for yourself."

Sam looks at her for a moment, then shakes his head and smiles. Whatever he says, I can tell he agrees with her; and he likes what she does for his brothers. It's part of who Ali is, and I imagine it's one of the many reasons he loves her so much.

I've spent the morning unpacking my clothes and moving them around my room, until they seem to be in the right places. It's a lovely room, with an enormous iron bedstead against one wall, a comfortable chair over by the window, a chest of drawers and a wardrobe, and two bedside tables. Two of the walls are exposed red bricks, and two are painted white; the floor is oak, and there's a beautiful, huge painting of a coastal scene which hangs opposite the bed. I spent a lot of last night sitting up and staring at it, trying to feel more relaxed. It helped… I mean, I still didn't sleep, but I wasn't as scared as I might have been, because I could pretend I could hear the waves crashing on the shore, and that I was at Waterside and that, if I opened the curtains, I'd be able to see the sea. Of course, when I opened the curtains this morning, I saw the buildings opposite and the street below, and instead of waves and seagulls, all I heard was traffic and car horns. It was a harsh reality check.

The last thing Sam and Ali said to me before they went downstairs earlier was to repeat that I should go down at lunchtime to meet everyone. I don't want to, but I know if I don't, one of them will probably come up here to find out why I haven't, and then I'll have to explain how scary I find this whole situation. Ali will understand, and probably feel guilty for bringing me here. Sam probably won't understand, so he'll tell Ali, and she'll still feel guilty for bringing me here. Whatever happens, if I don't go down, Ali will feel guilty, and I can't face that.

So, knowing the restaurant opens at twelve today, I go downstairs at quarter to, because I can't expect to meet these people if they're in the middle of serving their customers.

I get to the bottom of the stairs and close the door behind me, then go along to the double doors that lead into the kitchen, because this is really the only room I know, and I'm not going out into the restaurant by myself.

I push through the double doors and stop in my tracks. It's even noisier in here than it was yesterday. Everyone's busy, getting ready and I wonder if this wasn't a really bad idea.

"Leo? Where the fuck are you?" Sam yells and I jump. A man goes over to him. "What do you call this?" Sam asks him, showing him something in a bowl. The man replies, although I can't hear what he says, and Sam shakes his head. "No it isn't," he says loudly. "It's nothing like it. It's too liquid. Do it again. And get it right this time." He turns and his eyes lock on some other hapless creature. "What's wrong with you, Casey? I've been back here less than a day, and already you're being a fucking idiot." I knew Sam could probably be intimidating, but this…? I turn and go back out through the doors, standing in the corridor.

"Hey…" Sam's voice beside me makes me jump, even if it is much softer now. "Are you okay?"

I turn and look up.

"Yes, thank you."

"I didn't see you come in. Did you hear all that?" He stares down into my eyes and I nod. "I'm sorry," he adds.

"It's okay. You're working."

"No, right now, I'm yelling." He smiles. "Were you looking for Ali?" he asks.

"Yes."

He moves around me and opens the door that's directly behind me. "She's in here," he says. I poke my head into the room and see Ali sitting behind a desk. She looks up and a smile forms on her lips.

"Is everything alright?" she asks.

Sam's ushers me into the room and follows, closing the door. "I think I just scared your sister to death, but other than that, yeah," he says.

"What did you do?" She gets up and comes around the desk to me.

"It's nothing," I interject. "Really."

"I was yelling at a couple of people in the kitchen," Sam explains, ignoring me. "And Tess came in."

Ali's face darkens and she turns to Sam. "Tell me you didn't shout at her." Her voice holds a warning note.

"Of course I didn't," Sam replies.

"He didn't." I back him up.

Her face clears again and Sam touches her cheek with his fingertips. "There's no way I'd yell at either of you. I nearly lost you…" And I remember their fight was over the fact that Sam shouted at Ali in the kitchen for no reason. "I'm not making that mistake again," he adds. "And I know that yelling at Tess would be worse than yelling at you, in your eyes, anyway."

"Yes, it would." She looks up at him, but she's not angry anymore.

"Besides, I told you I'd look after both of you," Sam says.

"I know." Ali leans into him and they hug briefly, before she turns to me, smiling again. "You're gonna have to learn to ignore Sam when he's working," she says indulgently.

"Or I could just learn to moderate my behaviour," he replies.

Ali looks up at him. "And have your staff think you've gone soft?"

He shrugs. "Better that than scaring Tess every time she walks past the door."

I look up at him. "You don't have to change anything on my account. Really. I'm fine."

Sam checks his watch. "I've gotta go," he says, then he looks at me again. "And I am sorry I scared you. I didn't mean to."

"I know."

He goes out through the door and I turn to Ali. "I don't want him to feel like he's gotta behave differently around me," I tell her.

"I'll talk to him," she says, taking my hand and bringing me around to the other side of the desk. "But for now, I need your help."

"You do?" I can't imagine what she could possibly need my help with, but I wait for her to sit down and stand beside her, waiting.

"Yes. I do. I've finished all the work Rob needed me to do," she explains, "so, I thought I'd do some things of my own."

"Oh. Are you looking into setting up your own business here?" This was something Ali discussed with me when Sam first asked her to marry him and move here, but I'd have thought she'd wait until they were married first.

"No," she replies. "I'm gonna leave that for a while. Right now, I need to start looking at wedding venues."

"Really?" I'm surprised and I've never been very good at hiding my emotions from Ali.

She looks up at me, and nods to a chair that's over by the wall. "Pull that over here," she says. "This could take some time." I grab the chair and drag it over, sitting beside her. "Sam and I have decided to get married as soon as possible," she says, twisting in her chair so she's facing me. "So, we've set the date for the last Saturday in June."

"But… but that's only eight weeks away." I'm staring at her, with my mouth open.

"I know."

"Is this what you need my help with? Planning the wedding?"

"Yes. There's so much to do... starting with the venue." She pulls her laptop forward. "What do you think of this?" She shows me a website. The venue is the clubhouse of a boat club, right alongside a river. It looks like it was built in the 1930s, although whether that's authentic or not, I don't know.

"Where is it?" I ask her.

"It's about twenty miles south of here," she says.

"So it's feasible."

"Yes."

"Have you shown Sam yet?" I ask.

"No."

"Don't you think you should?"

"Just tell me what you think first."

I click on the track pad and go to the gallery, which is full of photographs of a few other weddings they've obviously hosted. I've got to admit, they all look beautiful. Informal, but beautiful.

"It's very you," I say eventually. It is.

"It's the closest thing I can get to a beach wedding, without actually dragging Sam's entire family to the beach," she says.

"I take it he's got a lot of family...?"

"Oh yes."

Great. I force a smile onto my face. "Is it available on the date you've chosen?" I ask her.

She looks up at me. "That's the thing. When I found this place, I didn't think it would be. I thought that would be too much to ask... so I called them to check. And they've had a cancellation..."

"For the last Saturday in June?" I ask.

She nods her head. "I know we don't believe in fate, but..." She's staring at me. "It's got to be, hasn't it?"

I nod. "It looks like it."

She picks up her phone and dials the number that's on the screen.

A few minutes later, with all the arrangements made, she puts her phone down again. "We'd better go and tell Sam," she says.

"Now? In the middle of a lunchtime service?"

She takes my hand and gets up. "It'll be fine. His bark is significantly worse than his bite. Trust me."

I'm not sure I want to know about Sam's bite, but I follow her out of the room and into the corridor. She closes the door and then stops and faces me.

"I meant to tell you earlier," she says. "I'm gonna be working in the kitchen in the evenings."

"Oh." I suppose I should've expected this, but I'm still a little surprised.

"It's just that, if I don't, I won't really get to see Sam very much," she explains.

"I understand."

"And you're okay with that?"

"Of course." I'm going to be spending my evenings sat upstairs by myself, and to be honest, I could've done that in London, or Dorset, or anywhere else on the planet for that matter. But I want Ali to be happy, so I smile, trying to make it look as genuine as I can.

We go into the kitchen together and she goes straight over to Sam. He stops what he's doing and she leans up and whispers something to him. He smiles and nods.

"Monday?" he says.

"Yes. Four o'clock. Is that okay?"

"It's fine."

"We just need to take a look around and, if we like it, we can book it."

"Okay." He looks over at me. "You know about this?" he asks and I nod. "You've seen it?"

"Yes."

"You approve?"

"Yes, I do."

"Okay." Sam smiles at me, then looks back at Ali, pulling her into his arms. "Guess you'd better find yourself a dress then."

She leans back, staring up at him. "Among a hundred other things, yes."

He bends down and whispers something to her and she nods and kisses him briefly, then comes over to me. "Let's go up to the apartment," she says and takes my hand again, leading me out of the kitchen, through the door and up the stairs to Sam's apartment.

Once inside, we sit down in the living room, facing each other on the sofa.

"What's wrong?" I ask her.

"Nothing."

"Oh right… so you just dragged me out of the kitchen and up here for no reason."

"No, but nothing's wrong. I just need to ask you a question."

"Okay…"

She takes a breath. "Will you be my maid of honour?" she asks.

I stare for a moment, and then feel tears pricking behind my eyes. "O—Of course I will. I'd be privileged."

She throws her arms around me. "Thank you," she whispers, and I think we both know she's not just thanking me for agreeing to being her maid of honour. I knew, you see, when she told me that Sam had proposed and that he wanted her to live here with him, that my decision was going to be pivotal to her happiness… and that's why I agreed to come here. When she called me to say she had to marry Sam, that she couldn't be without him, I knew what my decision had to be. The idea of living without her terrified me, but I'd already worked out that Sam wouldn't be able to move to the UK; it wasn't really an option… he's got too many ties here. He belongs here, and Ali belongs with him. I also knew how hard it would make it for her if I said 'no' to coming here too. I knew how torn and guilty she would feel. So I said 'yes'. She's my sister, and I'd do anything for her. Because I love her.

We spent this afternoon looking at bridal dresses on the Internet – most of which were horrendous. The end result was that we had a really good giggle, and that Ali has found a couple of small boutiques she wants to try, and that she's got a reasonable idea of what she likes and what she doesn't… and that I'm relieved it's her having to make the choice and not me.

The evening service starts at six-thirty, but Ali and Sam need to be downstairs about an hour before that. We eat early and they go down, and because I don't really know what else to do, I go down with them. I recognise a few of the staff from when we arrived yesterday, but most of the people who were here at lunchtime seem to have gone home. Ali explains quietly that only a very few of the kitchen staff work both sessions – like Sam and Ed do – and, unlike Sam and Ed, they don't do it every day. It seems much quieter in here this evening, and when I notice Sam watching me, I wonder if the peace has been arranged for my benefit.

"Do you want me to show you around properly?" Ali asks. She's wearing whites herself, and I'm reminded that I haven't seen her dressed like this for years.

I check out the embroidered name above her pocket.

"What's this?" I say, pointing it out.

"Sam got Rob to arrange it for me, as a surprise," she says, smiling over at him. He smiles back, and winks at her, then she links arms with me and leads me straight down to the back of the kitchen, where there are two separate areas. "I had these put in," she explains, pointing to the one on the right first. "That's where they prepare all the gluten free dishes, so they're separate from the rest of the kitchen." She turns slightly, and we move to the other area. "And this is where Ed works," she adds, and we go into his space.

He's leaning over a food mixer, which is turned on, so he hasn't heard us yet, and we stand and wait for a moment until he switches it off.

"How's it going?" Ali asks, and he turns, his eyes focusing immediately on me, not her.

"It's going fine," he says, and I notice again that, while his voice is very deep, it's also soft and quiet.

"What are you making?" I ask him.

"Espresso Gelato."

"So… coffee ice cream." I smile at him.

He smiles back. "Yeah. But so much better."

I step toward him. "What are you doing now?"

"I'm whisking the egg yolks and sugar together in this bowl, and then I'll add the milk and coffee in a minute." He nods toward the hob where there's a large saucepan of milk simmering.

"Why do you have to use such a big food mixer, if you're just whisking up egg yolks and sugar?" I ask him, looking into the bowl. It doesn't look like he's been mixing them for very long.

"Because I'm lazy," he replies, smiling. "And because I have to do this on a fairly industrial scale, every day, or every other day. I've got far better uses for my right arm than hand whisking eggs, when there's a perfectly good machine that can do it for me."

"I see."

"Can you just excuse me a second?" he says and reaches over to grab the pan of milk.

"That didn't boil," I observe.

"It wasn't meant to," he replies, and I watch while he adds it to the eggs. "If the milk's too hot, you'd just end up with fairly disgusting sweet scrambled eggs."

"But how did you know it was ready?"

"Experience," he says. "When I first started, I used to leave a thermometer in the pan, but I don't bother anymore."

He picks up a bowl of dark liquid from the back of the work surface and already I can smell the deep aroma of coffee.

"Is that just normal coffee?" I ask as he pours it into the bowl.

"Normal coffee?" He turns to me, grinning now. "I think Sam would probably char-broil me if I used normal coffee in anything. It's really strong espresso." He thinks for a moment. "I guess it'd be the equivalent to a triple shot, in terms of strength."

"You want your diners to stay awake all night then?"

"Can't hurt," he says, smiling at me as he pours all of the mixture back into the pan that the milk was simmering in.

"What happens now?" I ask him.

"I have to stir it until it thickens, then chill it and then it goes into the ice cream maker." He nods toward the back of his area, where there's a large machine sitting on the work surface.

"And this will be ready for tonight?"

"No. This will be ready for tomorrow night."

I stand beside him and watch as he stirs the mixture. "How thick does it have to get?"

"So it coats the back of the spoon," he says, holding it up. "We're nearly there."

"It's very precise, isn't it?"

"Yep. That's pastry cookery for you." He glances out to the main kitchen. "Out there you can take more risks. In here, it's all weights and measures."

"And coating the backs of spoons, evidently."

He smiles again. I like his smile. It suits him.

"It's done," he says and pulls the pan from the heat. "I'll give it a few minutes, and then put it in the blast chiller." He turns to face me. "Would you like to taste it?"

"Now? When it's hot?"

"No. I've got some I made the day before yesterday."

"Oh. Okay."

He goes out into the main kitchen and returns a moment later, with a large container, which he sets down on the work surface beside me, pushing the pan of hot liquid to one side. Then he pulls out a spoon from a pot beside the hob – one of many tasting spoons, I suppose – and takes it over to the sink, running it under the tap for a few minutes.

Coming back over, he runs the spoon through the ice cream, creating a perfect tiny quenelle. I'm impressed and I look up at him as he holds the spoon toward me. I'm not sure whether to take the spoon, or lean forward and just eat the ice cream, but he solves that problem, by moving closer and directing the spoon at my lips. I open up and let him feed the spoon into my mouth, which I close and savour the intense coffee flavour, as he pulls the spoon back out again. His eyes are fixed on mine, and this close to him, I can see little flecks of amber in his deep brown irises, like fireflies, dancing in the dark. I'm captivated and only just remember to swallow.

"That's the best ice cream I've ever tasted," I manage to say, still staring at him.

"Gelato," he whispers.

"Tom-a-to, tomato," I reply, smiling, and he laughs. "Ali, you need to taste this," I say, turning, and it's only then that I realise she's not with me anymore.

"She's over with Jane," Ed says, nodding toward the main kitchen.

I expect to feel scared without her, or at least a little vulnerable and insecure, but I don't.

"Okay?" he asks gently, moving a little closer.

"Yes," I reply honestly. "I'm just fine."

"Where is the sister of my future sister-in-law?" Rob's voice echoes through the kitchen. "My God, that's complicated," he adds.

"Trouble's here," Ed says quietly, "and it seems he's looking for you."

"Me?" I look up at him, and he moves closer.

"Ah, there you are." Rob comes into Ed's area. "You're needed in the restaurant, Tess," he says.

"I am? Why?"

"Because there's a beautiful woman out there who wants to meet you," he replies, grinning.

"There is?"

"It's fine," Ed says, reassuringly. "My stupid brother's talking about Petra. She's his girlfriend, although heaven only knows what she sees in him."

"I have a great many hidden talents," Rob teases.

"I wish to God they were hidden," Ed replies, "then the rest of us wouldn't have to put up with them." I giggle at his comment and he looks down, his eyes widening, and I notice the tiny amber flecks seem to be just a little brighter.

"That's a nice sound," he says. "You should laugh more often."

I know I'm blushing, but I still can't help smiling at him. I may have only known him for a matter of minutes, but he makes me feel more at ease than anyone else here – except Ali, and I've known her all my life.

"Are you coming?" Rob asks.

"Um…"

"Do you want me to come with you?" Ed offers.

"You're busy."

"I can spare a few minutes."

I pause for a moment, and then nod my head.

"Okay," he says and quickly puts the ice cream back in the freezer, and the pan of warm coffee custard in the blast chiller. "C'mon then." He holds out his hand to me and I take it, noticing how big his hands seem compared to mine.

We all go back through the kitchen and, out of the corner of my eye, I see Sam and Ali watching us.

"Where are you going?" Sam asks.

"Just out front for a second," Ed replies. "Rob wants to introduce Tess to Petra. I'll be back before we open. Don't worry."

We go out through the kitchen doors and down the corridor, into the restaurant. It's busy out here, with everyone getting ready to open up in about fifteen minutes. Over by the bar, dressed in black trousers and a white blouse, is a very tall woman. She's got long black hair that falls in stunning curls, over her shoulders. Rob was quite right, she is very beautiful, and she greets me with a warm smile.

"You must be Tess," she says, stepping forward, and I notice her high heels. Without those, she wouldn't be quite so tall – probably around Ali's height, I suppose.

"Yes," I reply.

"This is Petra," Rob says, putting his arm around her and kissing her cheek. I get the feeling that the Moreno brothers are very protective of their women and I think that's probably quite a good trait to have. Even as I'm thinking that, I become aware that Ed's still holding my hand. I've grown so accustomed to his touch already, I hadn't noticed. I turn and see that he's not looking at his brother, or Petra, but he's staring at me.

"Okay?" he asks, and I nod.

"Yes, thank you."

He leans down a little. "Don't thank me," he whispers.

We turn our attention back to Petra and Rob, who are in each others arms.

"What do you do for a living?" Petra asks, managing to drag her eyes away from Rob and back to me.

"At the moment, nothing. I've got to find a job, and fairly quickly, or they'll be sending me home." 'Home'. *That's here now*, I remind myself and feel tears welling in my eyes.

I feel Ed squeeze my fingers and look back up at him again. His brows furrow and he moves closer, his body touching mine now, and a warm tingling sensation develops at the pit of my stomach. It's a nice feeling and I sigh into it.

"Well, what do you want to do?" Petra asks.

"I suppose I've always wanted to write," I explain. "My degree was in History and Comparative Literature——"

"It was in what?" Rob interrupts.

"It's two separate subjects," I tell him. "History, and then Comparative Literature, which is the connections between literary texts of different times, places, genres and traditions."

"And which did you prefer?" Ed asks, sounding interested.

"Comparative Literature," I answer. "Although in the final year, for our dissertation, we had to combine the two subjects, which was what I found most fascinating of all."

"So, does that mean you could write for a historical magazine?" Petra asks, taking me by surprise.

"Well, yes. I suppose I could."

"In that case, I might just have something for you," she replies, and moves a half step closer. Rob follows, keeping a firm hold of her. "I've got a friend," Petra continues. "Well, she's a former client, who I'm in touch with on Facebook, really, but you know how these things go. Anyway, she's giving up her job to have a baby. She writes for a historical magazine based in here Hartford."

"What kind of articles do they write?" I ask her. "I'm no journalist."

"I don't think you'd need to be," Petra replies. "I think the way it works is that people send in their stories about local historical items and families, and my friend researches them, and then writes them up. It's a monthly magazine and I think she had to write about two or three fairly substantial articles each month."

"So, there's going to be a lot of research, I guess."

"Yes. Does that worry you?"

"No. I love doing research."

Rob's shaking his head, like he doesn't understand. Maybe he doesn't, but I love losing myself in books, history, references, archives... it's my idea of heaven.

"I can send her a message and get the details, if you like?" Petra offers.

"Would you?"

"Of course. I'll send her a private message on Facebook, and let you know what she says."

"Thank you," I say, even though I'm blushing again. "That's very kind of you."

Rob checks his watch. "Sorry guys. Time to work," he says. "We'll have to catch up some more later," and, giving Petra another kiss, he moves toward the front of the restaurant, pulling his keys from his pocket.

"We'd better get back to the kitchen," Ed says to me.

"Okay." I turn to Petra. "Thank you again," I tell her.

"You're welcome, and I'll let you know," she replies, smiling.

Still holding Ed's hand, I follow him back towards the kitchen, but stop him before we go inside.

"I think I'll go back upstairs," I say.

"You can come in with me again, if you want," he offers. "Even when we're open and working, it's quieter in my area. Honestly."

So, he's noticed that the noise bothers me. "I know. And thank you. But you're going to be busy... and I'm still tired. I think I'll maybe check out American television for a while and then get an early night."

"I can promise you American television isn't anything to get excited about," he says. "But as long as you're sure?" I like that he doesn't push me, or hassle me.

"I'm sure. But thank you for the offer, and for earlier... and for..."

"For what?" he asks, moving closer again. I get that funny tingling feeling once more, and look up at him, which just seems to make it even more intense.

"For coming out here with me, so I wasn't on my own. I know you've got better things to do..."

"No. I don't have anything better to do than be with you," he replies. "And you never have to be on your own… unless you want to be." His voice pulses through me, his eyes connect with mine and that tingling feeling surges through my whole body. I have no idea what's going on, but whatever it is he's doing to me, I really like it.

I really like him too.

Ed

She looks at me like she wants to reply, and I hold my breath for a moment, but then she blushes and lowers her eyes.

"Thank you," she repeats. I really wish she'd stop saying that. I meant what I just said. Yeah, I'm busy, and I've gotta work, but that doesn't mean what I'm doing is 'better' than being with her. There really is nothing that's better than being with her. And she doesn't have to be alone. She can come be with me whenever she wants, for as long as she wants. I hate the idea of her being lonely. I know how it feels and I don't want that for her.

"You're welcome," I reply eventually, because it's easier than arguing about her need to thank me for every little thing I do.

She looks up again and smiles, and then goes along the corridor and through the door to Sam's apartment. I stare at it, even after it's closed behind her, even though I can hear the first of tonight's diners coming into the restaurant.

It was good having her in my little area of the kitchen tonight. She seemed genuinely interested in what I was doing, for one thing, but there's something about her that makes me wanna be with her, spend time with her, take hold of her and never let her go. I've never felt like that before – not once.

I'm not like my brothers when it comes to women. Take Rob; he's a womanizer, or at least he was before he got together with Petra. He used to pick up women in the restaurant, get their phone number and take them out to dinner, or for a drink and then to bed. He moved fast and left few casualties. He never saw them more than once, and that was how they liked it. They used him just as much as he used them – entirely for sex – and until he met Petra, he was quite happy with that. Now, he's a completely different guy, but I guess falling in love does that – especially when the woman you fall in love with has a four year old daughter. And then there's Sam. His tastes have always been a little 'different'. I'm not sure he knows that Rob and I are fully aware of that, even though Rob drops not very subtle hints every so often, just to wind Sam up. The thing is, we all lived together in the apartment above the restaurant, until Sam made the mistake of marrying Amber, so it was kinda hard to miss the ropes, the cuffs, the restraints and all the other equipment that went with his lifestyle. Still, he seemed happy enough… up to the point when Amber came into his life and seriously messed with his head, and he's been alone ever since – well, until Ali arrived and made everything better, for all of us.

As for me, I guess I'd probably be called more 'normal' – if there is such a thing. I've been with several women in the past, starting with Louise, who I dated right at the end of high school, when I was eighteen. I lost my virginity to her in the back of her car, although I was disappointed to discover I wasn't her first. I don't think I was even her second, or her third, for that matter. It didn't last, not surprisingly, and she soon moved on to her next conquest. Unlike my brothers, I don't jump straight into bed with the women I date. I usually go out with them for a while, get to know them, and then work up to sleeping with them… and that's when it all goes wrong. It's not because I do anything badly – well, none of them have complained about my technique, anyway – it's because they see us having sex as a 'step', a signal on my part that I'm willing to change, to become what they want… even though I thought I already was that, being as they'd been dating me for a while by that stage, and had made the choice to go to bed with me. The problem is always the same. They don't like my job, or my hours or my commitment to my family, my career and the business I own with Rob and Sam. All of that is my life; it's who I am and I need it, like I need to breathe, but none of them has ever understood that I love what I do; and I've never loved any of them enough to make any sacrifices for them. To be honest, I didn't love them at all. I liked them, obviously, but love never even came close to coming into it. Not once. I have issues with self-confidence though, so I've sometimes found it hard to know what to do, when they've started to make their demands that I should see less of my brothers, change my job, cut my hours, move somewhere else… At those times, I've turned to Sam for advice, and he's always done the same thing. He's asked me two questions, which were, 'can you picture your life without her', and 'what would you be willing to give up for her', and each time I've said 'Yes', and 'pretty much nothing', or words to that effect. That's how I've known I didn't love them, didn't need them, and probably didn't even want them that much, not in reality. It's also how I've known that they weren't right for me, or to be more precise, I probably wasn't right for them.

And, if I'm being honest, after ten years of that merry-go-round, I'd gotten kinda bored. Without actually being aware of making the conscious decision, I'd come to the conclusion that I didn't want another relationship like that… doomed to failure. I'd decided that I'd rather wait and find the right girl, than keep being with the wrong ones. And the result of that is that I've been on my own for over nine months. It's been lonely, but no less lonely than dating someone you know you're not meant to be with.

Being around Tess was different though. Not only did I want to be with her, but I wanted to stay with her, to protect her and keep her safe, and she looks like she needs protecting more than anyone I've ever met. When Rob came in and asked her to go into the restaurant with him, I could see the fear in her eyes and I didn't want her to go by herself. I wanted to go with her, to stop her feeling afraid, and when I offered to accompany her, the relief in her eyes was all the thanks I'll ever need. Holding her hand was second nature, and it felt really good. Keeping hold of it was all I wanted to do, and when she was talking about her degree, I could see the enthusiasm in her face for what *she* wanted to do. It reminded me of myself, and how I used to be, before my dad ground that out of me. That made me feel even more protective toward her. I don't want anyone to ever be able to take that passion from her, like he tried to take mine.

I stare at the space where she was standing a few minutes ago, and I can still smell her scent, and I'm struck by how much I miss her already, and by how much I like her. Actually, I think it may be more than 'like', which is odd, considering I've spent less than an hour in her company. Still, I guess when it's right, it's right, and when it comes to falling in love, time doesn't mean a damn thing.

The noise level picks up in the restaurant and I realize I've been staring into space for ages. I pull myself together and go back into the kitchen, where everyone's looking busy. Sam's standing at the preparation area on the far side, talking to Jane and doesn't appear to see me coming back in, so I go straight through to my section and start getting ready for service.

"Where have you been?"

His voice makes me jump and I spin around to see my big brother leaning against the open doorway into my area.

"I told you where I was going. I went out front with Tess."

His eyes narrow. "She's not the kind of girl you can mess around with, Ed," he says sharply.

I drop the metal bowl I'm holding and it clatters loudly onto the steel countertop. "Excuse me?"

"I'm just saying, Tess is different. Don't mess with her."

"Are you confusing me with Rob?" I ask him.

He chuckles and seems to loosen up a bit. "No. I know you're more responsible than he is – well, was – but that doesn't alter the fact that Tess is real fragile.

"I got that already, thanks. All by myself."

"Really?" He glares at me again. "You think you know how fragile she is after a few minutes with her. She's had a tough life." He pauses.

"In what way?" I turn to look at him, taking a step closer. I want to know. I want to understand her better.

He opens his mouth to speak, then closes it again and runs his fingers through his short hair. "It'd be better coming from Tess herself. She'll tell you if she wants to, when she's ready, and maybe that'll be a good way for you – and for all of us – to know that Tess really trusts you, because she doesn't talk about it much." He looks at me long and hard. "Are you interested in her?"

"Yes." I don't even hesitate before answering, and I keep my eyes fixed on his, just so he knows I'm being completely honest.

He nods his head slowly. "Okay. Remember what I've told you. I'm watching you, Ed. Fuck it up with her and you'll be dealing with me." From the tone of his voice, I know he's serious. He may be my brother, but he means it.

"You're worrying about nothing," I tell him. "I've got no intention of messing this up. None at all."

I can tell from the look on his face that he knows, I mean it too.

Friday nights have always been one of my favorite nights of the week. They're never usually as busy as Saturdays, and people have that 'end of the week' vibe about them, which means they're generally a lot happier than they are most other nights. I haven't seen much of Tess since Wednesday evening, but she's popped in and out occasionally when she's needed to ask Ali or Sam something, and she's smiled over at me. Pathetically, I've found myself anticipating those visits and looking forward to her smiles.

We've been open for about an hour and things are hotting up already in the main kitchen, and although it's still fairly quiet for me, I know it'll get crazy later, so I'm doing as much prep work as I can, which at the moment means I'm chopping hazelnuts.

"What are you doing?" I spin around the second I hear her voice and see Tess standing in the doorway.

"Hello. I didn't see you come in."

She smiles and I have to smile back. "I was bored upstairs," she replies, taking a step into my area.

"American television isn't cutting it then?" I ask, putting my knife down and going over to her.

"The programs themselves are okay," she explains, "but there are so many advert breaks, it's driving me insane."

"Don't you get those in the UK?"

"Oh, yes," she replies, smiling again. "But they're not as frequent, and of course, we have the BBC. There are no adverts at all on there."

"So you just get a whole program without interruptions?" She nods her head. "Sounds like heaven," I joke, and she chuckles.

"I wouldn't go that far, but it's better than having an ad break every ten minutes. And I watch a lot of things on catch-up, so I can fast-forward through the ads."

"You should get Sam to set up some of the box sets for you, then you wouldn't have to worry about ads either," I explain to her.

"Oh… I didn't realise he could do that. I'll ask him." She goes to turn away, but I reach out and take her hand.

"Do you have to go now?" I look down at her.

"Um…" She looks embarrassed.

"If all you're gonna do is go back upstairs and watch some mindless TV show, why don't you stay down here with me?"

"And do what?" She looks around.

"You could grate some chocolate for me, if you like?"

"Grate chocolate?"

"Yeah, for the Affogato."

"For the what?" She smiles again. She's got a really shy smile, but it lights up her whole face.

"Affogato. It's vanilla gelato, with hot, strong espresso poured over it, and then it's topped with chopped hazelnuts and grated chocolate. Because it can only be prepared at the last minute, the chocolate and the hazelnuts have to be ready in advance."

"Oh. I see." She looks at the board where I've been chopping the hazelnuts. "I'll help, if I can. Although I can't guarantee to be any good. I'm not like Ali."

"That's okay," I say, smiling down at her. "I'm not like Sam."

She giggles. "I don't think anyone's quite like Sam," she murmurs and we both laugh.

I grab her a dark blue apron from the shelf and motion for her to turn around, which she does. Then I unfold it and put it over her head, tying it up behind her. She unfurls her hair, then looks up at me again.

"I suppose I should put this up," she whispers, and without waiting for me to reply, she pulls a band from the pocket of her jeans and ties her hair up behind her head, leaving a few wispy strands hanging loose by her face. I'm so tempted to tuck them behind her ears, but I don't. "Is this okay?" she asks.

I want to say 'it's lovely', because it is, but I limit myself to, "It's fine."

"Okay. So what do you want me to do?"

I fetch the chocolate from the refrigerator and grab a microplane grater, and go back to her.

"If we wrap the chocolate in foil," I tell her, taking it out of the packaging and wrapping the foil around one end, "it stops it from melting so quickly."

"And it if melts?" she asks.

"Then you can put it in the deep freeze for a few minutes to chill off again."

She nods her head and watches me start to grate, before I hand it over to her.

"Okay?" I ask.

"I think I can manage that," she replies, looking up at me again.

"Mind your fingers," I warn her. "These graters are a lot sharper than anything you'll be used to at home."

"You're assuming I do a lot of grating, are you?" she says, as she starts to run the dark chocolate over the coarse grating edge.

"Well…"

She chuckles. "I might run to grating cheese, if absolutely necessary."

"When you've done that," I tell her, seeing how quickly she's working through the block of chocolate, "you can carry on with chopping the hazelnuts." That way, she'll stay a bit longer.

"Oh, okay." She's concentrating and doesn't look up. "What are you going to do?" she asks.

"I'm going to take advantage of having some help, and make the espresso syrup."

"Does that go with this dessert?" she asks.

"No. It goes with the panna cotta, which is on the specials menu."

"I see." She carries on with what she's doing and I glance over her shoulder, catching a glimpse of Sam, who's staring at me, a very slight smile on his lips. I guess that means I'm doing okay… so far.

Tess has just finished chopping the hazelnuts and I'm already into service, when Petra comes in.

"I can't stop," she says, a little breathlessly. "I meant to come and find you earlier, but I was a little late getting here."

"I didn't realize you were working tonight," I say, looking up from making gelato quenelles for the desserts on table fifteen.

"Yeah. Rob called me earlier and said it was going to be busy, and would I mind."

I notice the smile on her face and understand that she doesn't mind in the least. She wants to be with my brother just as much as he wants to be with her.

"What did you want me for?" I ask her.

"I didn't," she explains. "I wanted Tess."

Tess almost jumps out of her skin at the mention of her name, and I move a little closer to her, ignoring the melting gelato for a minute. "What's wrong?" I ask Petra.

"Nothing." She smiles and turns to Tess. "Do you remember I mentioned having a friend who was leaving the historical magazine?"

"Oh… yes." Tess seems very shy and hesitant again.

"Well, she finally came back to me just before I left the house to come here. I'm afraid she's one of those people who likes to organize everyone else, even though she's completely disorganized herself. So, she's already set you up with an interview." I notice Tess's shoulders tense. "I hope that's okay," Petra adds.

"Um… of course." Tess doesn't sound entirely convinced.

"When's it for?" I ask.

"Monday afternoon."

"Monday?" Tess's voice is now little more than a whisper.

"Yes. Is that too soon?" Petra asks.

"No… it's not that. It's just that… well, I know Ali and Sam are going to be out on Monday afternoon, so Ali won't be able to…" Tess leaves her sentence hanging.

"I'll take you," I offer straight away.

She looks up at me. I've moved a lot closer now and I can see the relief in her eyes again. "Are you sure?"

"Absolutely." I give her a smile, then turn to Petra. "What time Monday?" I ask her.

"Three-thirty, but it's only a couple of blocks from here, so you should be able to make it."

"It's fine," I say, before Tess starts to get doubtful, or worried that I won't have time to go with her.

"I've written the address down for you," Petra adds, handing Tess a piece of paper. I check it out over her shoulder and Petra's right; it won't take long to walk there. "And now I'd better get back to work," she says. "It's madness out there tonight."

"It's not a lot better in here." We all turn to see Sam standing in the doorway to my area, and I feel Tess tense beside me.

"I'm outta here," Petra says, ducking past him and back through the kitchen.

Behind Sam, I'm aware that Ali is approaching, maybe a little worried about what Sam's going to say or do. He looks at me and then over my shoulder.

"Your gelato's fucked," he says softly.

I turn and see that he's quite right. My perfectly formed quenelles are now liquid.

"I'm sorry," Tess says quietly and I hear the crack in her voice. "That's my fault."

"Hey, it's fine. It's not your fault, and it's just ice cream." I stand right beside her and I'm sure she moves closer, so we're almost touching. Ali's now standing next to Sam.

"It's not ice cream," he says, "it's gelato."

I look up at him and roll my eyes. "Do me a favor, Sam," I say quietly.

"Yeah, what's that?"

"Piss off back to your own kitchen."

He laughs really loudly, then gives me a knowing smile and, goes to say something, although Ali steps in front of him and moves him back into the main kitchen, whispering to him at the same time. I'm glad she did that because having Sam watch my every move around Tess is starting to annoy me… and I'm not that easily annoyed. I thought he'd accepted the fact that I like Tess, and that I'm not gonna hurt her. I guess not.

"Is he cross with me?" Tess asks, once they're out of earshot.

"No."

"Is he cross with you?"

"I have no idea. And I don't care much."

"So everything's okay?"

I look down at her. "Yeah. Everything's very okay."

Chapter Three

Tess

Friday evening was definitely the best so far.

Sam and Ali had made a point of telling me I could go down into the kitchens, or the restaurant whenever I wanted, but I didn't want to be in the way. However, by Friday, I'd already had enough of the television, and being as our books haven't arrived yet, and Sam's reading tastes aren't even remotely the same as mine, I was getting a bit bored. So, I decided to be brave and go downstairs to see Ed. He was really kind and gave me an apron, and some jobs to do that even I couldn't mess up, and when Petra came in and told me about the interview on Monday, he offered to take me, which was incredibly sweet of him, because there was no way I was going to be able to go on my own, and that's when Ali's arranged for her and Sam to visit the wedding venue.

I still find Sam a little intimidating, but somehow he's less so when Ed's around. Actually, I've noticed that everything seems better when Ed's around. I've also noticed that, when I'm with him, I smile a lot more, and I can almost forget how much I miss home, and that I'm not sure I'll ever fit in here... almost.

It's Sunday, which means the restaurant is closed. I've been looking forward to today, because Ali has assured me that everyone does their own thing, so I'll get to spend the day with her – well, and Sam obviously.

"What time are they getting here?" Ali asks as I sit down at the kitchen island unit where Sam's just dishing up breakfast.

"About twelve, I think," he replies.

"What's this?" I ask.

"Everyone's coming here for lunch," Ali explains.

I feel my heart sink. "Who's everyone?"

"Ed, Rob and Petra, and her daughter, April," Sam says, sitting down next to Ali.

She looks over at me. "I know I said it would be quiet, but Ed and Rob haven't really seen Sam for a while, and…"

"It's okay," I say, interrupting. "I do understand." I do. I really do. And I know all of them, except April of course, so it won't be too bad. And Ed will be here… "Who's cooking?" I ask, looking from Ali to Sam.

"Who do you think?" Sam replies, grinning.

"I'll help," Ali adds.

"Oh, will you?" He leans into her and kisses her neck. They're very intimate with each other and I keep my head down and eat my pancakes.

Not surprisingly, I'm the first to finish and I make my excuses and take my coffee along to my room, telling them I'm going to shower and get dressed. I hear Ali giggling as I close my bedroom door. I love that she's happy, and that they're so close, but sometimes I do feel awkward around them. Still, that's my problem, not theirs.

I take my time getting ready, not because I want to look especially nice, but because I want to give Sam and Ali some privacy – and because I don't want to get in their way. When I come out, they're both dressed and in the kitchen, and Sam's standing behind Ali, his hands on her waist. He's kissing her neck, and whispering something to her. They were like this in London, when they came back from Dorset, which I suppose means I should be getting used to it by now.

I sit down on the couch and pick up a magazine, flicking through the pages.

"Oh, hi," Sam calls. "We didn't hear you."

"It's fine." I get up again and go over to the entrance to the kitchen. "Can I help?"

"You can cut up the courgettes," Ali suggests, because she knows that while I'm not the best cook in the world, it's better to have something to do than to just sit and watch other people.

"You mean zucchini," Sam says, pulling her into his arms again.

"I mean courgettes," Ali counters, giggling once more. "Where Tess and I come from, that's what they're called."

She hands me huge courgettes, a chopping board and a knife.

"These are marrows," I say, looking up at her.

"They are a little large."

"What are you making?"

"Ratatouille, so it's fine. The size doesn't matter."

I nod. "You just want them sliced?"

"Yes, please." She goes back to chopping onions and I set about my task. I'm half way through the first one when the door to the apartment opens.

"I know I'm early, but I thought I'd come and help."

For some reason, Ed's voice soothes all the tension in my body and I turn and smile over at him as he walks across the living room. "Although I see you've got a great helper already." His eyes are fixed on mine and he returns my smile with one of his own.

"Yeah, we have," Sam replies. "But we can always use more."

Ed shrugs off his leather jacket and dumps it on the back of the couch, then turns round and, for the first time, I see him without his chef's whites. He's wearing pale blue jeans and a navy button down shirt and now I can see that, while he's not as tall as Sam – not quite anyway – he's just as muscular.

"Can you make the dessert?" Sam asks him and Ed rolls his eyes.

"Sure. What do you have in mind?"

"I was thinking of Amaretti peaches."

"Sounds good. There's plenty of vanilla gelato downstairs to have with them, if you like."

Sam smiles and pulls Ali into his arms again. "Perfect," he murmurs. "I've developed a taste for vanilla of late." Ali blushes, looking up at him, and Ed chokes. I've got no idea what that means, and I'm not sure I want to.

Sam releases Ali, going back over to the stove, and Ed strolls into the kitchen, and straight to the refrigerator, taking out ingredients and putting them down on the island unit.

"The reason he looks so at home," Sam explains, clearly noticing my expression, "is because he used to live here. So did Rob."

"Oh, I see."

"Before I married Amber, that is," Sam continues, glancing quickly at Ali. Her expression doesn't even change and I know she's accepted his past now. They've put it behind them, which is where the past should be.

"There was no way we were gonna live here with her," Ed adds.

"I wasn't sure *I* wanted to live here with her a lot of the time," Sam jokes and Ed laughs.

"Where do you live now?" I ask him.

"Rob and I have a place not far from here," he explains. "But Rob's pretty much moved in with Petra."

"So you're on your own?"

"Yeah." His eyes meet mine and for a moment, I sense he might be lonely. Not perhaps as lonely as I am, but his current situation isn't his choice, any more than mine is.

"If you can get the peaches ready to go in the oven." Sam breaks the moment and Ed looks away. "We can put them in while we're having the main course."

"Okay." Ed sets about halving the peaches and removing the stones, like he does it all the time – but then I suppose he probably does.

At almost exactly twelve o'clock, the door opens again and this time Rob and Petra come in, accompanied by the most beautiful little girl I've ever seen. She's like a miniature of her mother, dressed in a pretty pale pink dress, with her long black hair tied up in a loose pony tail.

With Rob's arrival, the noise level shoots up, as the three brothers fool around, and I can feel myself withdrawing.

"Everyone, this is April," Rob says, once his brothers have let him go. "April, this is Sam and Ali, and this is Tess, who's Ali's sister." She comes to each of us in turn and shakes our hands – without anyone prompting her to do so. She's so cute. "And this," he says finally, "is Ed." April turns to him, and then looks back to Rob.

"He's not uglier than you," she says.

Everyone laughs, including Ed, although April still looks confused.

"Care to explain?" Ed asks, looking at his twin.

"Well," Rob says, placing his hand protectively on April's head, "when April found out that I've got a twin, she assumed we had to look identical, but I explained that people can easily tell us apart because you're so much uglier than me."

Everyone laughs again, and Ed goes over to April and crouches down in front of her.

"Do you think we look the same?" he asks gently.

She looks at him closely, examining his face. Then she looks up at Rob, who's still standing right beside her, and studies him. "Rob's hair's shorter," she says, after some consideration, "but other than that, I think you look the same. But you're not the same really, because Rob lives with us, and you don't."

Ed laughs and takes one of her hands in his. "That's right," he says. "And I've heard from Rob that you like to cook. Is that true?"

April nods her head enthusiastically. "Yes, I do," she whispers, like it's a secret.

"What's your favourite dessert?" he asks her.

"Stawbie ice cream," she replies, clearly unable to say 'strawberry'.

Ed nods. "Ahh, I see. So, you're the one who taught Rob how to say 'stawbie' properly... I've been wondering about that, because he's been getting it wrong for years." April's looking at him, kind of in awe. "Well, one day soon," he continues, "your mommy's gonna bring you into the restaurant where we all work, and you're gonna spend some time in the kitchen with us, and I'll show you how to make a really special stawbie ice cream, and you can help me, if you like."

April looks at him, just for a moment longer, then turns to her mother. "Can I, Mommy?"

"Yes, baby girl. I'll fix it up with Ali," Petra replies, and April bounces with excitement, just as Rob picks her up and holds her in his arms.

"Okay," he says, looking at Ed. "Stop trying to steal my girl."

"As if I would." Ed gets to his feet and gives April a wink, which she tries to return, but ends up blinking at him. Everyone starts talking again and, before long, Rob sets April down on the floor once more. She looks over at me, then walks across and takes my hand.

"I've brought some jigsaws with me," she says quietly. "Would you like to help me with one?"

"Yes," I reply. "Yes, I would." I wonder for a moment, whether she could somehow sense how uncomfortable I felt around all the noise, or whether she felt equally ill at ease and wanted to escape too, and saw a kindred spirit in me. Whatever the reason, we settle down on the couch and I clear the books and candles from the coffee table, and we start doing the jigsaw together.

We're more than half way through the second jigsaw when Sam announces that lunch is ready and Petra comes over to take April to the table.

"Thanks for keeping her entertained," she says to me.

"I think it was the other way around," I reply and follow them over to the table, which is by the window.

April is sat at the head of the table, with me to her right and Rob to her left, opposite me. Ed is to my right, with Ali next to him, and Petra is beside Rob, with Sam opposite Ali. He's made roast lamb and as he carves, April taps Rob on the arm and beckons him to lean toward her. She whispers something in his ear and he shrugs his shoulders.

"I don't know," he replies. "Why don't you ask him?" April looks scared and stares at Rob for a moment. "I promise you, he won't bite," Rob adds.

April takes a deep breath. "Sam?" she asks and he stops carving and looks down the table at her.

"Yes?" He's deliberately kept his voice quiet.

"Are there chovies in the lamb?"

"Chovies?" Sam looks confused and I've got to admit, I don't know what she's talking about either.

"She means anchovies," Rob explains.

"Oh." Sam smiles. "No. There are no anchovies."

"Anchovies? In lamb?" I can't help but ask.

"Yes." Rob and Sam both reply at the same time and I feel myself blush, right at the moment that Ed moves closer.

"Sam comes up with these things every so often," he explains. "It sounds weird, but it works."

"I'll take your word for it." I turn to look at him and notice that those fireflies are dancing in his eyes again.

Once everything is dished up and the wine is poured, we all start to eat.

"I'm glad we're all together," Rob says all of a sudden.

"You are?" Sam looks along the table at him.

"Yeah. I've got an announcement to make." I notice the corners of Sam's lips curving upward. "I—I… well, I proposed to Petra earlier in the week…" He pauses for a moment. "And she accepted." He's grinning, and clutching Petra's hand, and she's smiling up at him.

"Crazy woman," Sam mutters, and everyone laughs.

"She's crazy about me, anyway."

"That just makes her certifiable," Sam replies, but then he gets up and walks down the table, and pats Rob on the back, before leaning over and kissing Petra on the cheek, congratulating them. I notice Rob looking at Ed and when I glance up at him, he's just smiling. It's like something passed between them in that moment, but I'm not quite sure what.

"We'll get married as soon as we can – probably sometime around Christmas," Rob explains.

Ed leans closer to me and whispers, "Petra's still married to April's father." I look up at him and he nods at April, and I understand why he didn't say that out loud. "Just on paper," he adds.

"Oh."

When I look up, my eyes meet Rob's and it seems like he's looking for my approval too, so I give him a smile. It's not for me to judge, or to even have an opinion. They love each other – what else matters?

"Yes," April chimes in out of nowhere. "Rob got Mommy a ring, and he got down on one knee and asked her to marry him, and then when she said yes, he gave me this." She reaches inside her dress and pulls out a beautiful silver or white gold necklace, in the shape of a heart, with a tiny diamond set in one side. "And he asked my… my…" She looks confused for a second, and turns to Rob.

"Permission," he offers.

"Yes. Permission. He asked my permission to marry Mommy." She holds the necklace out towards me. "He told me that I'm the diamond, and that the heart is his, and I'm in his heart, because he loves me, just like he loves Mommy… And when he and Mommy get married, he's gonna be my daddy." She beams a huge smile. The whole table has fallen silent, except for a slight sob from Petra. Rob moves closer and pulls her into a hug, although his eyes are glistening too, but everyone else is just staring.

For a moment, an awkward silence descends. It's like no-one knows what to say, or do.

"You're quite right," I say to her. "Rob is going to be your daddy. And do you know how lucky you are?" She looks at me a little quizzically. "Rob *chose* you to be his daughter," I explain to her. "And whatever happens, you must never forget how special that is, or how special you are, and how lucky you are to have him as your daddy."

"I won't. I promise." She says, seriously, and I take her hand and give it a squeeze, before I look back down the table again, to see that everyone is now staring at me. I hear a sniffle from beyond Ed, and Sam quickly gets to his feet and comes around to Ali to comfort her, while Ed himself leans a little closer to me.

"Did I say the wrong thing?" I whisper to him.

"No," he replies. "You said just about the best thing you could've done."

Ed

I wasn't kidding. That really was about the best thing anyone could have said at that point. None of us knew what to do, or say, but Tess just seemed to have the right words.

We've finished eating and Tess has gone back to doing the jigsaw with April, while Ali said she wanted to speak to Petra, so they've all gone to sit down on the couch. Rob and I are helping Sam to clear away, although I'm keeping half an eye on Tess. It's kinda hard not to notice how uncomfortable and insecure she is, and it's also comforting that she keeps looking over in my direction every so often too. I don't know why, but she does, and I like that.

"So, was that all true?" Sam says to Rob as he starts to stack the dishwasher.

"All what?" Rob's playing for time. You can always tell when he's doing that. His voice goes up a little.

"What April said about the proposal, and you being her dad." Sam stops what he's doing and stares at Rob, and I lean back against the countertop, waiting.

Rob looks at Sam, then over at me, and then shrugs. "Yeah, it was true," he mumbles. "Petra offered it, so I'm gonna adopt April, as soon as I can."

He's clearly expects a ribbing from Sam, and turns back to him in preparation.

But then Sam shocks both of us, by going over to Rob and hugging him. "She made a good choice. And that was a good thing you did, too," he remarks, "including April in your proposal like that."

"Well, I couldn't leave her out of it," Rob replies, as they separate.

"That thing with the necklace was a nice touch," I say, joining in.

He blushes, but doesn't answer me. I don't think he was expecting this reaction.

"While we're on the subject of getting married," Sam says, leaning back against the island unit, "I've got something I need to ask you... both of you."

"Okay." Rob looks at me and I shrug my shoulders. I've got no idea what's coming.

"Ali and I have decided we don't want a long engagement, so we're getting married at the end of June."

"The end of June?" I can't hide my surprise.

"Yeah, the last Saturday," Sam replies.

"She's not pregnant, is she?" Rob asks.

"No." Sam says, patiently. "We just want to be married, that's all. And… and I want both of you to stand up with me, and be my best men." He hesitates for a moment, but before we can respond, he continues, "I know you didn't approve of me marrying Amber, and weren't really involved in our wedding, but let's face it, we're a family, and I want you both with me this time. There's no way I can choose between you though, so I'll have to have two best men."

I'm not sure Sam's ever made such a long, sentimental speech in his life and, for a moment, we're both a little dumbfounded.

"We'd be honored," Rob says.

"Privileged," I add.

"Well, thank fuck for that." Sam grins, and carries on with stacking the dishes.

I glance over at Rob and he smiles at me. We both know that can't have been easy for Sam, and he's right, when he married Amber, the atmosphere between the three of us was so bad, there's no way he'd have asked us to be there for him, so this means a lot. It means we all know Ali's right. She's family too now.

"Speaking of family, your girlfriend really saved the day back there," Rob says, turning away to move the roasting pans over to the sink.

"Whose girlfriend?" I ask him.

"Yours." He turns back and looks at me.

"I don't have a girlfriend."

He smirks, his eyes catching mine. "Unless I'm very much mistaken, you will do soon," he says.

"Oh, will he now?" Sam pipes up from the other side of the kitchen and he turns to look at me. "Anything you wanna tell me?"

"No."

He gives me one of his hardest and most threatening stares and I meet it with my own. This is getting boring now.

"Give it a rest, Sam," I say eventually. "We're both over twenty-one, in case you haven't noticed."

"She's only just over twenty-one."

"Which makes her an adult, capable of making her own decisions, without your interference."

"Okay, guys," Rob interrupts, getting in our line of sight. "I'm sure Ed and Tess can work things out for themselves." He gives Sam a look, and then turns to me. "Either way, she definitely saved the day. So, tell her thanks from me."

"You could tell her yourself."

He shakes his head. "Well, I would, but I think she'd rather hear it from you."

Sam grunts and goes back to what he was doing, and I carry on polishing the wine glasses and putting them away.

We finish clearing up and go through to the living room. Tess and April are sitting on the floor, working on a new jigsaw on the coffee table, while Ali and Petra are on the couch, talking. Sam goes and sits beside Ali, while Rob pulls Petra to her feet, sits in her place and lowers her onto his lap.

"I have my best men sorted out," Sam says to Ali and she leans into him. He seems in better spirits now – probably because we're not talking about me and Tess.

"And I've got my bridesmaid now, as well as my maid of honor." She smiles across at Petra and then looks over at Tess.

"So we're all fixed?" Sam asks.

"Yes. I'll arrange a date with Tess and Petra for us all to go dress shopping."

"I'll ask Mom to have April," Petra suggests.

"Well, I was wondering if she'd like to be a flower girl," Ali replies.

"A flower girl?" April looks up. "What's a flower girl?"

"At our wedding," Ali explains to her, "you'd walk in ahead of everyone, scattering flowers on the ground."

April nods. "And I'd get a special dress?"

"Yes." Ali smiles.

"Okay then." We all laugh and for a while the conversation revolves around the wedding, until Sam offers to make coffee and, while he's gone, Petra asks Tess if she's prepared for her interview tomorrow.

"What interview?" Ali asks, before Tess can reply.

Tess explains about Petra arranging the interview at the magazine, and that she'd been planning on telling Ali about it this afternoon.

"How are you going to get there?" Ali asks.

"I'm gonna take her," I reply.

Ali looks at me and smiles, and seeing how insecure Tess looks, I'm really relieved she accepted my offer to take her. I don't like the idea of her being alone in the city.

Sam comes back in again, bringing the coffee, and sits back with Ali, pulling her into his arms. She looks up at him and he kisses her just briefly, and looks into her eyes for a moment. While Tess returns to the jigsaw, Rob turns to me and raises his eyebrows. It's unusual for us to see Sam being affectionate like this, and it's a different side to him, one we're not used to. He was never like this with Amber. With her he was always so tense, and while there is a tension between him and Ali, it's entirely sexual, like they can't wait for us all to leave, so they can jump on each other, or more precisely, so that Sam can jump on Ali, because whatever he might have said about liking vanilla – which I have to say surprised the hell out of me – Sam is still Sam. I wasn't entirely sure that Ali would fit in to Sam's lifestyle, and I'm still not, but I guess they've adapted to suit themselves, and I can see she likes whatever it is they've got together, so I'm really happy for them. Despite his attitude with me about Tess, I'm especially happy for Sam. He got it so wrong with Amber and it screwed him up for a long time, but he's over that now. He's a different guy – in some ways, anyway.

"Have you spoken to Mom and Dad about the wedding yet?" Rob asks Sam, breaking into my thoughts.

"No," Sam replies. "Have you?" He glares at Rob.

"No, but I'm not the one getting married in just a few weeks."

Sam smirks. "I guess not."

"When are you gonna talk to them?" Rob inquires and I wonder why he's pushing this.

"I don't know. Next weekend probably. Why?"

"Because I'd rather you didn't mention anything about Petra and me."

"Why?" Petra asks, twisting in Rob's lap and looking up at him.

Rob leans down. "Because Mom and Dad are kinda traditional. They'll expect to hear it from me."

Petra seems to pale, quite noticeably. "They're traditional?" she says. "Oh, they're gonna love me, aren't they? I've got a daughter already, and I'm still married to her father..." She says that last part in a whisper, presumably so April won't hear.

"I think they'll be more worried about me taking your name," Rob replies and a stony silence fills the room. We're all staring at him, except April, who's happily continuing with her jigsaw.

"You're gonna take Petra's name?" Sam's the one to speak first – unsurprisingly.

"Yeah." Rob turns to look at him, but I notice he's got a firm grip on Petra. "She's named after her father... Peter Miller."

"The photo-journalist?" Sam asks.

"Yes," Petra replies, her voice really quiet.

"I've seen some of his stuff," Sam continues. "It's really good."

"Well, he died about four and a half years ago," Rob continues, "and he and Petra were real close. If she takes my name, then his name dies. This way, it continues. I know it means a lot to her..." He falls silent.

"I think that's a lovely thing to do," Tess says.

"I doubt very much that Mom and Dad will agree with that sentiment," Sam replies, then turns to Rob again. "Good luck with telling them."

Rob smiles. "Well, I've got a plan to deal with that," he says. "I'm gonna charm them with April first."

I laugh, as does Sam. "You might be onto something," he jokes. "They're always moaning about none of us having given them grandchildren."

"That's what I thought," Rob says.

"Do you think they'll really object?" Petra asks. She sounds scared and Rob holds her closer, looking down into her face.

"I don't care if they do," he replies. "I'm marrying you, whatever they say."

"And, if they don't like it, that'll just be all three of us they're not talking to," Sam adds.

"Who did you marry that you weren't supposed to?" Tess asks, looking up at me.

"I didn't marry anyone," I explain. "I've never been married. I just went against Dad's wishes in the kitchen."

"Is that all?" She seems surprised.

"It was enough for Dad."

"Does your mum still speak to you?" she asks, moving a little closer.

"Not very often. That would mean her going against Dad and she won't do that. She's polite when she has to be, but that's about it."

She stares at me for a moment, her brow furrowed like she doesn't understand something and then she goes back to the jigsaw. I stare at her for a little longer, before becoming aware of Sam's eyes on mine again. This time, his expression is one of sympathy, rather than distrust over my feelings for Tess, and I know he's thinking about our dad, and nothing else.

April's brought some coloring books too, and when the jigsaws are all completed and packed away, she fetches her coloring books and lays one out, seemingly happy by herself. Tess takes the opportunity to come and sit on the couch, and luckily she chooses to sit beside me.

"What happened with your dad?" she asks quietly. Then she looks up at me. "I'm sorry," she adds. "It's probably none of my business."

"No, it's fine," I tell her. "We fell out over what he wanted me to do… well, to be. He wanted me to be like Sam and run the main kitchen."

"And you didn't want that?"

"No. I've hated every minute of the time Sam spent in England. I'm happiest in the pastry section. It's where I belong."

"But your dad couldn't see that?"

"Oh, I think he could see it. He just didn't like it."

"So what did he do?" she asks.

"He stopped talking to me. He stopped helping me; stopped teaching me. It was like I didn't exist."

"When was this?"

"It was during Rob's summer break in his first year at college... I guess I'd have been twenty at the time."

"And you haven't spoken since?"

"No. Sam and Rob have both tried to get Dad to see sense – while he was still talking to Sam, that is – but he won't. He regards what I did as a betrayal."

"Why?" she asks. "You're still cooking. You're still following in his footsteps."

"There's a difference," Sam's voice interrupts us and we both look over to him. "Dad regarded pastry work as kinda second rate. He wanted Ed to work in the main kitchen and eventually take over from him."

"But then what would you have done?" Tess asks him.

"I'd have worked under Ed," Sam admits and his eyes lock with mine. "You see, Ed's the better chef by a long way. Dad knew that. So did I."

I feel a lump rising in my throat. Sam's told me this in private many times, but he's never admitted it in front of anyone else, and especially not Rob.

"I—I can't run a kitchen like you can," I tell him.

"I think you just spent three weeks proving that you can," Sam replies, smiling.

"Well, I had to get Rob to step in, so no I didn't."

Rob turns to face me. "I wasn't running a single thing," he remarks. "I was just helping out and doing what you told me to do."

Tess leans into me just a little. "I think your brothers are trying to get you to accept that you're better than you think you are at what you do," she murmurs. "Maybe you should listen to them." She smiles at me, her eyes fixed on mine and for a moment, I'm kinda lost in them. "Parents can be selfish sometimes. They like to think that what they do is right," she whispers, "but sometimes it isn't, and their mistakes can cost their children dearly." I stare at her, but she looks away and I'm left wondering what the hell that meant.

Sam and Ali go to make more coffee, although I'm fairly sure they're just looking for an excuse to be alone together, because it seems to be taking a lot longer than necessary.

"How are you finding the city?" Rob asks Tess.

"I don't know," she replies. "I haven't really seen much of it yet. It seems just as noisy and busy as London." She looks a little depressed as she says that.

"You and Ali had a house by the sea, is that right?" I ask her.

"Yes." Her face lights up again.

"So you lived in London and rented out the house?"

"Yes. It was something our grandmother organized years ago."

That sounds a little odd, but I don't inquire. "The house and the London apartment belonged to our parents," Ali says, coming back into the room with Sam and the coffee. I notice the past tense and, putting that together with Tess's comments about their grandmother, I wonder if their parents are dead. It's not something Ali, or Sam have mentioned.

"What are you doing with them now?" Petra asks.

"We're selling them," Ali replies.

"Both of them?" I look at Tess as I ask the question.

"Yes." It's Ali who answers me. Tess is still looking away, but she turns back and the sadness I see in her eyes is heartbreaking. "We're cutting all ties," Ali continues, and now tears start to form in Tess's eyes. The sense that Tess isn't entirely comfortable with this decision is overwhelming and, as I look over at Ali, now sitting back down with Sam, cradled in his arms, and looking lovingly into his face, I wonder how she can be so blind to her sister's sadness.

Sure, she's decided to come here, and she's evidently decided to cut ties with home, but she seems far from happy about it. I wonder if she's unhappy enough to go back home again… and feel cold to my core at the thought.

When it's time to go, we're all gathered by the front door. Rob is holding April in his arms, although she's struggling to stay awake and, I've gotta say, she looks really cute.

"Will you be coming down to the kitchen tomorrow?" I ask Tess, pulling her to one side.

"No. I don't think so. I want to stay up here and get ready for my interview."

"Okay. Well, I'll call for you at three."

"I can come down…" She gazes up into my eyes again. She looks so doubtful, and so insecure, I just want to pull her into my arms and hold her.

"No, it's fine. I understand you want to stay up here until you're ready to go." She's gonna be nervous, I guess.

"Are you sure?"

"Of course I'm sure."

I've never been more sure of anything in my life.

Chapter Four

Tess

I still can't sleep properly, only tonight it's not thoughts of home that are keeping me awake. It's not even nerves about my interview tomorrow. It's the memory of how sad Ed looked when we were talking about his parents – or more specifically, his dad. It was such a short-sighted, selfish thing for his father to have done and I wonder whether he'd feel differently, if he knew how unhappy Ed was about his attitude. But then, like I said, sometimes parents can be the most selfish people…

"Hello?"

I'm sitting in my bedroom when I hear Ed's voice. I still can't get used to the fact that everyone has a key to this place and lets themselves in whenever they please, although to be fair, they don't do it all the time, just when they're expected.

I get up and go into the hallway and through to the living room, where Ed's waiting for me. He's wearing jeans and a dark grey shirt and he looks me up and down as I walk towards him.

"Does this look okay?" I ask him. I'm not sure what American people would expect to wear at an interview, so I've gone for a straight black skirt which ends just above my knees, and a pale grey short-sleeved blouse, and high-heeled black shoes. "I wasn't sure if this was too formal."

"It looks perfect to me," he replies and even from here, I can see those little fireflies in his eyes again. "We've got about a fifteen minute walk," he adds, "so we should probably go."

"Okay." I pick up my handbag and let him lead the way down the stairs, pulling the door closed and locking it behind us. Sam and Ali have already left for their appointment at the wedding venue, and I'm not sure which of us will be home first.

The walk doesn't take long, and Ed does his best to set my nerves at rest, telling me about some of the buildings we pass, and asking me questions about London and how different things are there, compared to here. He walks on the outside, nearest the traffic, the whole time and, when I flinch at a large truck passing, he takes my hand, and keeps hold of it until we reach the offices of Hartford Histories.

"This is it," he says, looking up at the building. It's seven floors high.

"All of this?" I can feel my breath catching in my throat.

"No." He smiles. "Just an office on the third floor. Do you want me to come up with you?"

I feel pathetic, but I can't help nodding my head, and he leads me through the door in the centre of the building and over to the lifts, pushing the button to go up.

"I'm sorry about this," I say in a whisper.

"Why? This is all new to you." He's very understanding. Having him here is probably even better than having Ali with me. She'd have tried to encourage me to do this by myself, telling me it would make me feel stronger. It wouldn't have done; it would just have terrified me more. It's like Ed seems to understand my boundaries, and accepts them without questioning me. I like that. It's a very comforting and comfortable feeling.

The lift opens and we exit onto a corridor. Ed looks both ways and leads me to the right, to the third door on the left, which is marked 'Hartford Histories', with the word 'Reception' underneath.

"I'd better let you do this bit by yourself," he whispers. "You'll be okay. Just be yourself and they'll love you." He stops speaking suddenly and I notice a tinge of red on his cheeks. "I'll wait for you in the lobby," he adds. "Good luck." He smiles, then turns and heads back towards the lifts, and I go in through the door.

There's no-one there, just a desk and a chair, and a lot of boxes, stacked up against the far wall. There are three doors off of the room, one to my right and two to my left, but they're all closed, although I'm fairly sure I can hear giggling coming from one of the rooms to my left.

I close the door behind me and stand for a minute, waiting. I check my watch. I'm exactly on time, but I don't know what to do now. Should I call out? Should I just stand here and wait? Should I leave? Should I go and get Ed?

I'm still contemplating my options, when the door to my right opens and a woman comes out. She's probably about twenty-five or six and has deep red hair, which is cut in a long bob style. Her skin is pure and pale and her eyes are the brightest green I've ever seen and, as she sees me, she smiles.

"I'm so sorry to have kept you waiting," she says, and she straightens her skirt a little. "You must be Tess... Bryan's ready for you now. Would you like to follow me?"

I nod my head and follow her back into the office. It's huge, with a large glass desk to the left and two cream coloured sofas to the right. The walls are decorated with photographs of historical Hartford – or at least that's what I assume they are. They look old, anyway. A man steps out from behind the desk and comes around to greet me, his hand extended. I'd say he's around thirty-five, with blond hair and blue eyes, probably around six feet tall. He's good looking, but he wears it with a certain arrogance that makes him less attractive.

"Tess Bishop," he says, like I don't even know my own name and he's telling me for the first time.

"Yes." I can't think what else to say, other than to agree with him, and I shake his hand to cover my embarrassment.

"I'm Bryan Oakley. I'm the editor of Hartford Histories."

"Oh. I see." He keeps hold of my hand and steers me toward the other end of the room.

"Let's sit more comfortably, shall we?" he suggests. "Zoe?" He turns to the red-headed woman. "Could you get us some coffee?"

"Certainly," she replies, her voice full of helpful acquiescence, although she's glaring at him now. She turns to me and smiles. "Is coffee okay for you?" she asks.

"Yes, thank you."

"Back in a minute," she says and leaves the room.

"Take a seat," Bryan offers, showing me to one of the couches. I perch at one end and fully expect him to sit opposite, but he doesn't. He sits right beside me, a little closer than feels comfortable, and I move as far away as I can, until I'm right against the arm.

"So, Tess," he says softly, "tell me about London."

"Um... what do you want to know?" It seems like such a broad question.

"You were at college there?"

"Well, university, yes. I was at St Mary's."

"Studying?" he asks.

"History and Comparative Literature."

His eyes widen, just a fraction. "Sounds ideal for us," he remarks, smiling. "And have you had any work experience?"

"Yes. I spent last summer working for an online genealogy company," I explain.

"And did you enjoy it?"

"I loved it." It's true. I did.

"What did you do there?"

"The company had a department that people could apply to for advice when they got stuck looking up their relatives. For a fee, we'd help them out, do more digging, carry out more extensive research and report back to them."

"I see." He smiles again. "So you're used to doing independent research?"

"Yes. I prefer working independently."

He looks at me.

"We're a small outfit, Tess," he points out. "There's quite a bit of teamwork involved too."

"Obviously," I add, just as Zoe comes back in with a tray of cups.

Bryan looks up at her. "I was just telling Tess here how we all have to get along," he says, smirking at her.

"We do," she smiles back at him and sits on the couch opposite.

"You'd be working mainly with Zoe to start with," Bryan says, taking a cup from the tray, while Zoe offers me another.

"Doing what?" I ask.

"It varies," Zoe replies. "We get people sending us personal histories, as well as ones that relate to the city. So, sometimes it can be that someone's cleared out their attic and discovered an old scrapbook, or newspaper and they send it to us, and we do some further research and see if there's anything worth writing up."

"I imagine sometimes there isn't."

"Sometimes," Bryan replies. "But mostly we can find something."

"And would I be researching, or writing?" I ask him, taking a sip of coffee. It's not very nice coffee, not compared to Sam's anyway, and I put the cup back down on the table.

"Initially," Bryan replies, "you'd probably be doing more research than anything, but eventually, once you'd learned the ropes and gotten used to how we Americans write and spell, I'd expect you to produce your own articles."

I feel a little disappointed. I like research, but I'm a lot happier writing. It's more absorbing. And I can't believe American spelling is that different from British…

"Okay," I reply, nodding my head.

Bryan looks me up and down. "I see no reason not to offer you the job right now," he says, all of a sudden.

"Really?" I know I sound shocked, but that's because I am.

"Yes. We haven't actually advertised the position yet, but I think you're just about perfect. You're exactly what I'm looking for," he continues.

"But I'm British. Don't I have to bring something to the table that you couldn't get from an American employee?" I ask him.

"Oh, don't worry about that," he says, smiling. "I'll deal with all the red tape and paperwork."

"Oh… okay."

"The position won't be available until the beginning of July," he adds. "Is that a problem?"

"No. I can stay for ninety days on my current visa before I have to worry, so that's fine."

"Good. Well, that gives me a few weeks to deal with your work permit." He looks at Zoe. "You can handle that, can't you?"

She nods and I get the feeling Bryan is someone who delegates. A lot.

He stands, letting me know that the interview is over. "Well," he says, guiding me back towards the door. "We'll be in touch about any personal details we need. Give Zoe your contact information and she'll liaise with you." He smiles. "And I'll see you at the beginning of July."

I offer my hand, because it seems polite. "Thank you," I say. He takes my hand, shakes and holds on to it again.

"It's entirely my pleasure," he says.

"How did it go?" Ed's waiting for me in the lobby, as promised.

I smile up at him. "I got the job."

"Really? Already?"

"Yes. The guy offered it to me there and then."

He takes my hand, just like he did before, and we head for the doors, going out and onto the pavement. "What about your work permit?" Ed asks as we start back to the restaurant.

"He said they'll deal with it."

He nods. "And you like the sound of working there?"

"Well, I think I'm going to be the office junior for a while, but it's my kind of thing. They do historical research and writing, just like Petra said. I'll be working with a woman called Zoe to start with, and she seemed really nice, so…" I leave the sentence hanging.

"Sounds great," Ed responds and pulls me just a little closer.

When we get back to the apartment, Sam and Ali have just returned themselves and are sitting on the couch, cuddled together. They look up as we enter and Ali immediately asks about my interview. I tell her the same thing I told Ed and she's overjoyed. I know she's been worried about what I was going to do for a living and this seems ideal.

"How did you guys get on?" I ask her, once she and Sam have finished congratulating me.

"We've booked it," Ali replies, beaming, as Ed and I sit down on the other part of the L-shaped sofa.

"What kind of place is it?" Ed asks.

"It's a clubhouse," Sam replies. "But there's a long, wide jetty leading into the lake, and we're gonna have the ceremony there, with all the chairs set out on the lawn that leads down to it, and then reception will be out there too, as well as in the clubhouse itself."

"Sounds lovely." I look at Ali and know it's exactly what she wanted.

"How dressed up are we expected to get?" Ed enquires.

"Ali wants to go all out," Sam replies.

"So, tuxes?"

"Hell, yeah." Sam laughs.

"I'll let you tell Rob." Ed joins in.

"What's so funny?" I ask them.

"Exactly. What's so funny?" Ali looks from Sam to Ed. "Rob's the one who gets dressed up each evening. Surely he'd be the last to object…"

"He's not a fan of suits," Ed replies. "Maybe because he gets dressed up all the time."

"Well, he's just gonna have to grin and bear it," Sam says definitively. "Because it's what Ali wants."

"You're making me sound like the bride from hell," Ali says, leaning into him.

"No, you're the bride from heaven." Sam bends his head and kisses her. "And Rob'll do as he's told."

Sam checks his watch and announces that they all need to get downstairs for the evening shift. Ed turns to me. "Are you gonna be okay up here?" he asks.

"Yes, I'll be fine. I'll make myself a sandwich, or something, and watch some TV."

Ed looks over at Sam. "It's okay if Tess watches some box sets isn't it?"

"Sure."

Sam switches on the TV and presses a few buttons on the remote until the screen displays a listing.

"Just flick through using the arrows until you find something you like, then press play," he explains, handing the device to me.

"Thank you."

They're about to all go downstairs, when I call Ed back. Sam and Ali hesitate, but Ed tells them to go ahead and they do, and then he comes back over to me.

"Is everything okay?" he asks, looking down at me.

"Yes. I just wanted to say thank you for taking me today."

He smiles. "You don't have to thank me. It was a pleasure."

"Well, you made me a lot less nervous."

"Good. I'm glad about that."

"I suppose you'd better go," I add, although I'd rather he could stay a bit longer. We don't know each other very well, but being with him makes everything here just a little more bearable.

"Yeah. I guess." He turns to leave, but then stops and faces me again. "I'd much rather stay up here with you, though," he whispers, and gives me another smile, before walking away.

I'm into my fifth episode of Friends, and have long since eaten the cheese and ham sandwich I made just after everyone went downstairs, when I hear footsteps coming up to the apartment. I press 'pause' on the remote and look over towards the door, to see who's coming in, feeling a little anxious.

"Hello?" Ed's voice soothes my nerves, even before he's entered the room.

"Hi," I reply. "What are you doing up here? Aren't you supposed to be working?"

"Yeah, but I thought I'd bring you something to eat. A sandwich didn't really sound very thrilling, or very filling."

He comes over and sits down beside me, placing a small cup of dark coffee and a plate of doughnut-looking things on the table in front of me.

"These are called Zeppole," he says, and his accent makes me smile. "What's funny?" he asks, looking down at me.

"Your accent."

"Which one? American, or Italian."

"Italian," I reply. "I'm getting used to the American one now."

"I'm getting kinda used to your English accent too," he replies. "It's tidy."

"Tidy? What does that mean?"

He smiles even wider. "It means you finish your words properly. I like that." He stares for a moment, focusing on my lips, I think, then he picks up the plate from the table, and offers it to me.

"Try one," he says.

"What are they called again?" I ask, taking one.

"Zeppole."

His accent makes me smile again. I can't help it. And I take a bite through the sugary, crusty outside, into the doughy centre. "They're delicious," I manage to say, when I've finished chewing. "And they're still warm."

"Yeah. They're best eaten fresh," he replies. "I've gotta get back." He stands up and looks down at me. "Enjoy."

"Thank you, Ed," I say, looking over at him as he's about to leave.

"Don't thank me," he replies, just like he always does. "I'm glad you like them."

"I do."

He smiles again, then turns and leaves and I pick up the plate, putting it onto my lap and switch the TV back on, wishing he'd been able to stay with me.

Ed

After the way a simple plate of Zeppole made her smile last night, I've decided to try that again, with something different. Actually, I'm not sure it was entirely the Zeppole. She seemed to find my accent just as amusing, which I thought was kinda cute. I guess we all get used to the way we talk, and she did say she was more accustomed to my American accent, it was just the Italian side she found different, which isn't that surprising, being as I don't think she's heard me say anything in Italian before.

I wait until about nine-thirty, when there's a lull in service and go out into the restaurant, and get Greg to make me a latte. After I'd taken up last night's double espresso, I figured it may have been a little late for Tess to be drinking something that strong, especially when I remembered her comment about the gelato. So, I've decided to go for something a bit less lethal.

"What are you up to?" Rob asks, coming over to me while I wait for Greg to steam the milk.

"Nothing."

"Right. So you've taken off your whites, you're in the restaurant, and you're ordering coffee, halfway through an evening service and I'm supposed to believe there's nothing going on."

I turn and look at him. "Okay. I'm taking this up to Tess."

"Because…"

"Because she gets lonely up there by herself."

He smiles. "I see."

Greg pushes the coffee across the bar toward me and I take it and leave Rob to his musings, going back into the kitchen and grabbing the plate of Bruttiboni on the way up to the apartment.

Just like I did yesterday, I call out as I open the door.

"Hello?"

"Oh God." Okay, so that wasn't the reply I was expecting.

I glance into the living room and immediately understand the reason for her response. Tess is lying on the couch wearing a pair of very short pajama bottoms and a skimpy t-shirt top. She jumps up quickly, but then sits again, realizing I guess that standing just reveals more of her than lying down did.

"I'm sorry," I say, trying to keep my eyes focused on her face, although I've already noticed her gorgeous long legs, slim waist and perfect breasts. It was hard to miss all of that, being as she was bouncing around, trying to decide whether to sit, stand or lie back down again. Or maybe run… being as I think she was contemplating that too.

"Um… it's okay. I wasn't expecting…" She's blushing, and she looks adorable.

"Clearly." I smile over at her, hoping to reassure her and she manages a smile back. "I brought you up another snack," I explain, moving into the room, and setting the plate and cup down on the table in front of her.

"No strong coffee tonight then?" she remarks, seeming to come out of her shell a little.

"No. I had a rethink on the coffee and decided to go for a latte instead."

She smiles up at me, then she turns her attention to the plate. "And what are these?"

I sit down on the end of the couch. "They're called Bruttiboni."

Her smile widens. "Say that again," she whispers.

"Bruttiboni." I oblige, putting as much 'Italian' into it as I can muster.

"You make them sound very romantic," she comments, and I laugh. "What did I say?" she asks.

"Well, their name in English is anything but romantic," I explain.

"Oh? What does it mean in English?"

"It means 'ugly but good'."

She looks at me for a moment, and then laughs. I've heard her laugh before, but not with quite so much gusto and, without warning, my whole body shudders. That is, without a doubt, the most beautiful sound I've ever heard in my life, and I resolve to make her laugh like that more often.

"Try one," I suggest and she picks one up and takes a bite.

"That's amazing," she says quietly. "It tastes of almonds."

"Well, that's because they're just basically almond flavored cookies, although they can be made with hazelnuts."

"Well, I like almonds." She takes another bite, and a sip of coffee. "And they go very well with the latte."

"Good." I stand up. "I'd better get back downstairs."

She looks up at me. "Thank you for this," she whispers, evidently shy again.

"You're welcome." I go over toward the door, but turn and face her again just before leaving. She's watching me, her eyes wide. "I apologize for scaring you… for coming up unannounced like that. If you'd prefer me not to, then you could always make your own coffee and I'm sure Sam's got cookies of some kind lying around."

She lowers her face and seems to be looking at the floor between us, and even in the dim light, I'd swear I can see the beginnings of tears glistening in her eyes. "D—don't you want to come up and see me?" she murmurs.

I cross the room and crouch down in front of her. "Yes. Yes, I do." She looks up again. I was right; there are tears brimming, waiting to fall. "I've been looking forward to this all day. But I don't want to do anything that makes you feel uncomfortable here. This is your home now and you should be able to lie around in your PJs, or wander around naked, if you want, without worrying about me coming and going."

She swallows and blinks, but the tears don't fall. "I'd hardly wander around naked," she whispers. "Sam lives here." She has a point. I hear her stutter out a long breath before she says, "I don't want you to stop coming up here." Her voice is so quiet, I can barely hear her.

"Did you say you don't want me to stop coming up here?" I ask, just to be sure I got that right.

She nods. "I like your visits."

"You do?" I move a little closer.

"Yes. So please don't stop." Her eyes lock with mine.

"I won't. I won't stop."

I want to cradle her beautiful face and lean in to kiss her. I want to hold her body next to mine and never let her go. But I don't. I feel a little more reassured that she's not about to get on the next flight back to London though, and I get to my feet again and smile down at her.

"I'll see you tomorrow then?" I say quietly.

She nods her head. "Same time, same place?"

"Different snack," I reply, and she chuckles.

As I close the door at the bottom of the stairs, I pause just for a moment. Yeah, I need to get back into the kitchen, but first I need a minute, just to reflect. She definitely said she liked me going up there, and she didn't want me to stop. But more than that, the look in her eyes was inviting. It was beguiling and entreating. I also noticed that she went from shy and embarrassed to familiar and at ease, even though she was still in her sexy pajamas. I like the fact that she felt relaxed with me – and she did, that much was obvious. There was also no trace of yesterday's sadness; I'd even go so far as to say she seemed happy to be with me, and that makes me feel about ten feet tall.

"Where the hell have you been?" Sam's voice cuts into thoughts.

"Upstairs." There's no point in trying to pretend otherwise; I'm standing right by the door to the apartment still.

"For any particular reason?" he asks.

"To check that Tess is okay and take her a coffee. Why?" I decide to challenge him.

"There's a perfectly good coffee machine in the kitchen up there," Sam replies.

"I know."

"But you wanted an excuse to see her?"

"Yes. Happy now?" I move past him, but he grabs my arm.

"I'm still watching," he says.

"There's nothing to watch," I tell him.

"Not yet, maybe."

I turn to face him. "Look, Sam… I don't know what you think I'm gonna do, but I'm not Rob, and I'm not you. I *never* mess around with women – even the ones I know are wrong for me. But I happen to think Tess is right for me, and I'm pretty damn sure I'm right for her, and I like her. I like her a lot. Which means there's no way I'm gonna do anything that hurts her. So, maybe you could just cut me some slack and let me work this out for myself, in my own way, which in my world means spending time with her, getting to know her, earning her trust and *not* jumping straight into bed with her."

He stares at me for a long moment and I wonder if he's gonna yell. But then, he steps back.

"Okay," he murmurs quietly. "I'm sorry."

I'm not sure Sam's ever apologized to me for anything and for a second or two, I'm dumbfounded.

"You don't have to apologize. You've just gotta trust me."

"I do," he says. "But I promised Ali I'd look out for Tess."

"And you are, but just take your foot off the gas a bit, can you? She's safe with me."

He smiles. "Yeah, I know she is." He turns and pushes open the door to the kitchen. "You've got a couple of orders waiting," he says.

"Be right there."

He gives me a smile, just as he disappears, and I stand for a moment longer, appreciating what he just said, and the fact that he might just be trusting me with Tess, and that I've admitted to him that I like her – a lot. What I didn't tell him was that I'm really falling for her and, after tonight, I've worked out that I'll do whatever it takes to keep her happy and safe, and to get her to make a home here... with me.

Chapter Five

Tess

Ed's evening visits have become a regular thing over the course of the week, and although I told him I liked his visits, over the last couple of days, I'd have to admit, I've come to depend on them. His company is the one thing that's keeping me sane, and keeping me here.

Last night, he brought me some Ricciarelli, which were a little like macaroons, only a lot better. I'm sure he's going to run out of things to bring me soon, but in the meantime, I'm enjoying the variety.

I've been spending my time doing some research into the history of Hartford, using a few websites and a couple of books I ordered online. I'm sure everyone else at the office will have some basic knowledge, and I don't want to appear ignorant on my first day. I've also been reading the online version of Hartford Histories, so I can get a feel for the kind of articles they write.

This afternoon, while I was making notes from the internet, I decided to check out the menu for the restaurant. I've never actually looked at it, but I'm intrigued as to how many more biscuits and cakes Ed's got at his disposal to bring up to me. I opened up the dessert menu section, and scrolled down, and even though I didn't know how to spell any of the items he's been bringing me, I could remember most of the names, and none of them were there, even as accompaniments, which was very confusing.

I wasn't sure he'd be coming up tonight. It's Saturday and I know they'll be busy downstairs, so I'm quite surprised when he appears at the top of the stairs as usual. I'm surprised, but I'm pleased.

"Hello," I say to him, getting my greeting in first for once. I suppose he'll realise I've been looking out for him, but I'm not sure I care.

"Hi," he replies, and smiles at me, coming over to the couch and sitting down, before placing the coffee and plate on the table in front of me.

"They look good," I say, looking at the rolled pastries – or at least I think they're pastries. They're filled with cream, anyway.

"You might have heard of these," he replies. "They're called Cannoli."

I shake my head. "No, I can't say I have. You have to remember, I'm not that well travelled. Not in my adult life, anyway."

"They're a bit richer than a lot of the other things I brought up for you so far, but I figured it's the weekend, so what the hell."

I pick up one of the Cannoli and am about to take a bite when I remember my research from this afternoon. "I meant to ask you," I say, hesitating for a moment. "I checked the menu and couldn't find any of these items. So, how is it that you have them lying around, ready to bring up here to me each evening?"

He lowers his eyes and I'd swear he's blushing.

"What's wrong?" I ask him, putting the Cannoli back on the plate for a moment. "Did I say something wrong?"

He turns back to me. "No. No, of course you didn't."

"Then…"

He takes my hand in his. "I don't have these things lying around," he admits. "I—I make them… just for you."

Now it's my turn to blush. "You do?"

"Yes." He nods his head.

"Why?"

He smiles broadly. "Because I like coming up here to see you. The ten minutes I get with you… they're the highlight of my day." His voice fades to a whisper and he lets go of my hand and goes to get up.

"Wait." I grab his hand and he stops and sits again.

"What's wrong?" he asks, his voice filled with concern.

"Nothing. I—I just wanted to say that you coming up here… it's the highlight of my day too."

"It is?" He's grinning and his eyes are positively alight with fireflies.

I nod my head and he leans a little closer and kisses me gently on my cheek.

"Would you like to do something with me tomorrow?" he asks.

"Like what?"

"There's an art gallery not far from here. The Wadsworth Atheneum. We could go there in the afternoon, if you like?"

"I'd love to," I reply. One of my greatest pleasures at home was to while away my spare time in art galleries and museums. "How did you know that's the kind of thing I'd like to do?" I ask him.

He shrugs. "I didn't. I just guessed."

"Then you guessed very well."

"I'll call for you at two?" he suggests, and I nod my head, unable to hide my enthusiasm. "I've gotta go," he adds and gets to his feet again.

"Thank you," I say, joining him and walking over to the door behind him.

"What for?"

"The Cannoli, the invitation… everything."

"Hey," he murmurs. "You don't have to thank me. I told you, you're the highlight of my day."

He gives me a last smile, leans down and kisses my cheek once more and then leaves.

And as I return to the couch, I can't stop smiling.

Today, as I was finishing getting dressed, I looked at my reflection in the mirror and, for the first time since I've been here, I felt like I looked happy. I also realised that a I'd taken a lot more care over my appearance than I have on any other day since my arrival. And I'd obviously done that without even thinking about it. Don't get me wrong, I haven't been wandering around with unwashed hair and dirty clothes, but apart from on the day of my interview, I've stuck to jeans and t-shirts, and I've left my hair long, and worn little or no make-up.

This morning, I pulled out one of my favourite dresses; a fairly short, pale yellow fitted sundress, with tiny blue flowers and matched it with a blue cardigan and blue sandals. It's the middle of May now and it's warm enough here to wear summer clothes. I put my hair up too, in a loose low bun, leaving a few strands hanging down the sides of my face.

When I go out into the living room and through to the kitchen for brunch, Sam and Ali are already there, and they both stop and stare at me, although Sam quickly goes back to making pancakes.

"You look lovely," Ali says.

"Thank you."

"Are you going out somewhere?" she asks, pouring coffee.

"Yes. Ed invited me to go to an art gallery with him. I can't remember what it's called now. The something Atheneum?"

"The Wadsworth Atheneum," Sam supplies, not turning around. "Is he coming to pick you up?"

"Yes." I sit down at the island unit and take a cup of coffee from Ali. "He's calling round at two."

Sam nods and flips the pancakes.

"You'll like that," Ali says. "You love art galleries."

"I know. It was Ed's idea," I tell her. "But he couldn't have chosen a better place."

"No he couldn't." She looks over at Sam and smiles and he smiles back. I don't know what that means, but I try to ignore their little signals.

"What time do you think you'll be back?" Sam asks.

"I don't know. Ed didn't say when the gallery closes."

"Well, I'm sure you'll have a lovely time," Ali says.

Once brunch is over, I go back to my room and put on just a little make-up. I don't normally wear much anyway, but for some reason I want to make an effort.

Ed arrives at exactly two o'clock, letting himself into the apartment as usual, and I go out and greet him.

"You look beautiful," he says and I feel myself blushing.

"Thank you," I murmur.

"Are you ready?" he asks, taking my hand.

"Yes." I look up into his eyes and he smiles.

"Okay."

"I'll see you later," I call out to Ali and Sam, who are sitting together on the couch, with Ali's laptop between them. They're looking at decorations for the wedding venue and I know they've both been dreading it: Sam because he doesn't want to do it, and Ali because she knows Sam doesn't want to do it.

"Have fun," Ali replies, looking up and giving me a smile.

"Behave yourselves," is Sam's response, although he's smiling too.

When we get out onto the street, Ed's still holding my hand and I turn to him. "Sam's very 'big brother' about everything, isn't he?" I remark.

He chuckles. "That's one way of putting it," he replies.

"He's protective," I add.

"Yeah. Sometimes that's a good thing, but he can take it too far. He's inclined to forget he's only a year older than Rob and me."

"Yes, but he's nine years older than me," I reply, and Ed looks down at me.

"Yeah. I sometimes forget how young you are." He grins. "Still look on the bright side, at least he's not your brother."

"He nearly is. I mean, he'll be my brother-in-law in just a few weeks."

"Yeah, I guess he will."

He stares at me as we walk, seemingly studying me.

"What's wrong?" I ask him after a while.

"Nothing," he says. "I'm sorry. I didn't mean to stare… it's just, you look so different."

"Oh." I feel a little crestfallen.

"In a good way," he whispers, leaning in to me. "I mean, there's nothing wrong with how you normally look, but I love your hair like that, and that dress is really…" He stops talking.

"Really what?" I suddenly feel nervous that I'm over-dressed.

He stops and turns me to face him. "Sorry," he whispers.

"Why? What have you done?"

"Nothing. But I was going to say that your dress is really sexy. Only that's not entirely appropriate."

"Isn't it?" The words have left my mouth before I can stop them and I notice his eyes widen and the fireflies spark to life again.

"Well, we're on our way to an art gallery," he says.

"Should I be wearing something else?" I ask him.

"No. Like I said before. You look beautiful." He pauses. "Beautiful... and sexy."

I glance up at him and his smile gives me a warm feeling deep inside. This is more than the tingling I felt the other day, and that I've grown accustomed to feeling whenever he's near me. There's something intensely sexual about this feeling, and much to my surprise, that thought doesn't bother me in the least.

"Let's take a look at the European Collection," Ed suggests once we're inside. He's still holding my hand and leads the way.

He's handed me the guide book and we make our way through the gallery, commenting on various landscapes, until we reach one called *The Shore at Trouville; Sunset Effect*, which was painted by Gustave Courbet. I stop and stare and, for a moment, I imagine myself back on the beach near Waterside.

"What's wrong?" Ed asks. He's standing right behind me, looking at the painting.

"It... it just reminds me of home," I say quietly, not wanting to disturb the other visitors. "Our house in Dorset had a private beach and although it's nothing like this, it just feels so real. I can almost imagine myself standing on the sand, sinking my toes in, with the water lapping up, over my feet." As I say the last few words, my voice cracks and I feel a tear fall onto my cheek.

"Hey." Ed turns me and pulls me into his arms, just as I start to cry.

"I'm sorry," I murmur into his chest.

"Shh." He puts his hand on my neck, stroking my cheek with his thumb. "It's okay."

I lean back a little, absolutely certain that my make-up's a mess. He looks down at me and I'm struck by the intensity of his eyes. "I don't even know why I'm crying," I tell him. "Not really."

"I do," he says softly, taking me over to a bank of chairs and sitting us both down, facing the Courbet. "You're feeling homesick."

He's holding my hand, and gives it a light squeeze as he speaks.

"Yes. Yes, I am."

"And that's just fine," he adds, reassuringly. "It's perfectly okay to feel homesick."

"It is?"

"Yes. I do understand, Tess." There's so much honesty in his eyes, and his voice, I can't doubt a word he says. "And I also know how hard you must find it to talk to Ali about how you feel, being as she's the one who brought you here, but you can talk to me anytime you need to. You know that, don't you?"

He really does understand. "Thank you," I whisper, gazing up at him.

"Don't thank me," he says.

"You always say that."

"Because I don't want your thanks," he replies.

"What do you want?"

He pauses for a moment. "Right now? I want to see you smile," he says.

And I do.

We don't get to see too many more paintings. The European Collection is quite substantial and, by the time I've recovered, it's nearly time for the gallery to close.

"We can come back another day," Ed says as we go out through the main entrance, into a sunny late afternoon. The sky is crystal clear and there's a light breeze, and as it's Sunday, there's less traffic. For the first time since I got here, I feel comfortable. "You're smiling." Ed's voice interrupts my thoughts and I turn to look at him.

"Yes."

"Unprompted," he adds, grinning at me.

"Yes. I was just thinking what a lovely evening it is."

He looks around. "Yeah. It is, isn't it?"

We walk down the steps and onto the sidewalk, turning toward the restaurant.

"Have dinner with me?" he says all of a sudden.

I look up at him. "Won't Ali and Sam be expecting us?"

"Yes." He smiles down at me. "But that's why cell phones were invented. We can call them and let them know what we're doing." He stops, waiting. "Say yes," he prompts.

"Okay." I can't stop my lips from twitching upward and he pulls his phone from his back pocket, taps on the screen a couple of times and holds it to his ear.

"Hey," he says by way of greeting. I imagine he's called Sam, rather than Ali. "I'm gonna take Tess out for dinner. I just thought I'd let you know." He pauses, listening. "Of course. See you later." He hangs up and puts the phone back in his pocket before turning to me and taking my hand again.

"Was he okay?" I ask. "I assume that was Sam?"

"Yeah. That was Sam, and he was fine." He leads us down the street.

"Where are we going?" I ask him.

"There's a place just down here that does the most amazing ribs…"

"Ribs?"

"Yeah. You like ribs, don't you?" he asks, doubtfully.

"Yes, I like ribs. I just didn't think you would."

"Why on earth not?" He turns to face me as we walk and I look up at him.

"Well, because you're a chef, in a fairly upmarket Italian restaurant. I suppose I just assumed…"

"What? That I wouldn't eat something like ribs?"

I nod my head, but don't look at him anymore, feeling embarrassed by my assumptions about him. We stop at a crossing and he turns to face me while we wait for the lights to change. Then he places his forefinger under my chin, raising my face to his, and I notice that his eyes are studying mine intently. "There's a lot we don't know about each other," he says quietly. "That's why I wanted to take you out… so we can make a start on finding out more."

I smile again. He has that effect on me, and, as we cross the road, he says, "And besides, this place serves really good ribs," and I laugh out loud.

We turn down a side road and arrive at the smokehouse, as Ed tells me it's called. He opens the door and ushers me inside, and once we're seated and have ordered our drinks, I take a look at the menu. It's really confusing and I glance up at him.

"Do you trust me?" he asks.

"Yes," I reply, without hesitating, and he smiles.

"Good." He calls the waiter over and places our order, although I've got no idea what I'm going to be eating and, in a strange way, I don't mind at all.

Ed

We talk for ages over dinner. We talk about art, books, movies, cooking, and food in general, and while I now know a lot more about her tastes, and I also know that we have quite a lot in common, I don't feel like I know her a great deal better than I did a couple of hours ago. I don't know what she's scared of, although I know she's scared of something, maybe lots of things. I don't know whether she's gonna leave, or stay, or why. I don't understand her, but I want to try. I really want to.

I pay the check and help her out of the booth, keeping hold of her hand and leading her out onto the street.

"Thank you for that," she says as we start walking slowly back to the restaurant. "I had a lovely time. And I'm glad you only ordered me the half rack of ribs. I'm so full." She pats her flat stomach and blows out her cheeks. Jeez, she's cute, and I have to smile at her – again.

"I didn't think you'd manage a whole one," I tell her.

"No way. I also didn't understand the idea of having macaroni cheese as a side dish. That seemed weird to me. Back home, that would be a main course."

I laugh, just as she drags me away from the roadside.

"Look," she says, marveling at something.

"What am I looking at?" I ask.

"It's a Subway."

She's pointing to the sandwich bar. "And?"

"We have those back home," she says, looking up at me.

I laugh again. "You're not in an alien land, Tess, just the United States."

She giggles. God, I love that sound. "In that case," she says, "why couldn't I understand the menu in the restaurant just now? I thought our two countries were supposed to share a common language."

"Really? Who told you that?"

She laughs again and we continue on our way. Tess spends most of the walk pointing out similarities between here and 'home', which I try not to let bother me. She doesn't see this as 'home' at all. I just hope she will – one day.

When we get back, I let us into the empty restaurant and she walks ahead of me through to the entrance to Sam's apartment, which I open with my own key.

"Do you all have keys to this place?" she asks as we walk up the stairs.

"Yes. Rob and I have never gotten around to giving ours back. It can come in useful – like when Sam takes off for England at a moment's notice." She turns to me and smiles as she opens the door to the apartment itself.

Sam and Ali are sitting in the corner of the couch together and they seem tense and on edge. I wonder if they've been waiting for us, although that doesn't really make sense. I did tell them we were going out and we're not late. It's not eight o'clock yet.

"Did you have a good time?" Ali asks, breaking the ice.

"I had a fabulous time," Tess replies and I feel relieved. She enjoyed it. That's good, because that's exactly what I wanted. "The gallery was amazing," she continues, sitting down at one end of the couch. "There was a picture by Gustave Courbet. It reminded me of home," she explains, "and I got a bit upset, but Ed was really kind to me, and we sat for a while and talked."

Sam looks at me over Ali's head and raises his eyebrows, but I don't react at all.

"And dinner was an education," Tess carries on. "I didn't understand word of the menu."

"Where on earth did you go?" Ali asks.

"Just to a smokehouse," Tess replies. "But I didn't have a clue what to order, so I left it all to Ed." Again, Sam glances at me, but this time, he just seems to smile. "I've never eaten so much in my life, but it was good."

I'm leaning against the wall near the door and, listening to Tess, seeing and hearing her enthusiasm, I can't help wondering if I can really be in love with her already.

She turns to look at me, a broad smile on her face and I know, without a doubt, that I can.

Because I am.

"It sounded like Tess had a great time yesterday." Sam's propped himself up against the countertop in my area of the kitchen, his arms folded across his chest.

"Yeah. She seems to have done."

He smiles. "It's okay. I'm not asking for details. And I'm not criticizing," he qualifies.

"Is there anything to criticize?" I ask.

"No."

"Good."

I expect him to leave, having said his piece, but he doesn't.

"I spoke to Mom and Dad yesterday afternoon," he says quietly, letting out a long sigh.

"Is that why you and Ali seemed so tense when Tess and I got back?" I ask, going over to stand a little closer to him.

"Yeah. Sorry about that."

"Can I assume it didn't go well?"

He shrugs. "I haven't spoken to them properly for years, not since my break up with Amber, so I think they were kinda surprised to hear from me in the first place."

"You told them about Ali?" I ask.

He looks at me. "Yeah."

"And?" He's not making this easy.

"Well, they're gonna come to the wedding."

"I sense a 'but'."

"I think they're only coming in the hope they can talk me out of it," he says.

"Why? Why on earth would they wanna do that?"

"When I told them I only met Ali in February, and only proposed to her a couple of weeks ago, they didn't seem too impressed."

"They assumed it was Amber happening all over again?" I ask.

"Yeah. That was what they implied."

"You put them straight?"

"Damn right I did. I won't have them – or anyone – making comparisons between Amber and Ali." He looks down at the floor. "They also didn't like the fact that she's English – or to be more precise, she's not either Italian, or American." He raises his head again. "So I guess you'd better be warned." A smile crosses his face and he pushes himself upright, before going back into the main kitchen.

For a moment, I stand, staring after him, and then I realize that he's just let me know he's fully accepted the idea of me and Tess being together – maybe even in the long term. Sam being against us wasn't going to stop me, but like I said, he's a kind of hero for me, so having him on my side means a lot, and he knows it.

Last night, after my conversation with Sam, I took Tess up some Bombolone, but tonight, I've gone all out and made Sfogliatella. They're real fiddly, but impressive and I hope she likes them. I think Sam and Ali must've talked and they've both decided to be on our side now, because Ali has said she'll cover for me for a while, so I can take a little longer with Tess, and I go up the stairs with the plate of pastries and a Latte, which Greg's just made.

As soon as I open the door, I know something's wrong. The living room is empty, although the lights are on, and I can hear a slight sobbing noise coming from Rob's old bedroom, which I know is where Tess is now sleeping. I dump the plate and cup on the coffee table, and go along the hallway, knocking on the closed bedroom door.

"Tess?" I call out. "Are you okay?" I know she's not, but I can't think what else to say.

I wait a minute and then she slowly opens the door. Once again, she's dressed in just her short pajamas, which is kinda distracting, but nowhere near as unsettling as the tears falling down her cheeks.

"What's wrong?" I ask her.

"I'm being pathetic," she whispers, sniffing and wiping her nose on a Kleenex she's got clutched in her hand.

"Are you feeling homesick again?" I ask.

"For once, no, I'm not."

I've got to admit, I'm relieved to hear that, but it doesn't resolve the immediate problem.

"Do you want me to get Ali?" Maybe she's got some kind of problem she doesn't want to talk to me – or any other guy – about.

"No," she replies.

"Then what's wrong? I just want to help, Tess."

"I know. But I'm being pathetic."

I smile, hopefully reassuringly. "I'm sure you're not. Tell me what the problem is."

"Come in here," she says and stands to one side.

I hesitate, just for a blink and then enter her bedroom, very aware of how I feel about her, and how little she's wearing, that she's very sexy and that there's a bed in this room. I don't need to worry though, because scattered across the mattress are several dresses, a few pairs of pants and some t-shirts and blouses. It looks like she's been clearing out her closet.

"I ordered these," she explains, picking up one of the dresses. It's really pretty and I have no doubt it'll look amazing on her.

"Right." I'm still not sure what the problem is.

"Only I forgot that the sizing is all different over here," she explains at last. "So none of it will fit."

"Too big, or too small?" I ask, because I have no idea how women's clothes work, either here, or in the UK.

"I'm a size ten at home, but over here, I think that makes me a size six."

"And you ordered everything in a size ten?"

"Yes." She puts the dress back down on the bed. "Which I think is a size fourteen back home… And now I don't know what to do with all this."

I go over to her and take her hands in mine. "You can return it," I say calmly, "and order the correct size."

"But what if the size six is wrong?" she asks. "I mean, I might need a size eight, or a size four. How do I know?"

I quickly check the label on the dress.

"This shop…" I tell her. "There's a branch in West Hartford."

"How far away is that?" she asks, sniffing again.

"About a fifteen minute drive," I explain.

"And can I get a bus there?"

"You can, but if you can wait a few days, I'll take you there on Sunday, and I'll help you out with the returns and then you can try on whatever you want to buy before you get it."

Her eyes light up and I feel my heart swell in my chest.

"You will? You'll take me?"

"Of course." I smile down at her.

"You'll go clothes shopping with me?"

I take a deep breath. "I will. If you'll do something for me."

"What?" she asks, although she sounds more inquisitive than fearful, which is good.

"Stop crying, and come out into the living room with me. I brought you something special tonight and I want you to try it."

She smiles and, before I realize what's going on, she leans up and kisses me very quickly on my right cheek. Almost immediately, she pulls back, blushing and I know her action was instinctive, impulsive, not calculated.

"Thank you," she whispers. "And don't tell me not to thank you this time."

"Okay." I take her hand, not mentioning the kiss, and lead her back into the living room, flicking off the bedroom light as we go. "Although you still don't have to thank me." The light giggle that I hear from behind me is more than enough reward.

"What are they called?" Tess asks, looking at the plate.

"Sfogliatella," I reply. "They're sometimes called 'lobster tails' in English, but I think that's just because they look like shells."

"And you made these?" She looks up at me.

"Yeah."

"Just for me?"

"Of course."

"They're beautiful."

"They're also edible." I smile at her and hand her the plate. "They're crumbly, so you're gonna get in a mess."

She takes a pastry and bites into it, and sure enough, the pastry crumbles, and crumbs drop down onto her top.

"That's amazing," she mumbles. "What's inside?"

"It's a mixture of semolina, ricotta, eggs, cinnamon and vanilla. They're a speciality of Naples, which is near to where our family comes from."

She looks over at me. "They're so delicate. Will you show me how they're made one day?"

"Of course."

"You love to cook, don't you?" she asks, wistfully.

"Yes. But there are a lot of other things I love too." I love her inquisitiveness, that fascinated look she gets when she tries something new. I love that she's so interested and keen to learn. I love her thoughtfulness, the way she has of looking at the world. Most of all though, I love her. I don't say any of that out loud, but I look into her eyes for a long moment and hope that maybe she understands.

"I know you're going to say I don't have to thank you," she adds, her soft voice making my skin tingle, "but thank you… for everything you do for me."

I lean over and very gently caress her cheek with the tips of my fingers. "Doing things for you – and with you – is one of the things I love most."

Apart from loving you.

On Sunday, I pick her up at eleven, and drive us out to West Hartford, parking in a lot not far from the shop she needs to visit.

When we get inside, we deal with the returns first, and then she sets about choosing some replacement items, letting me help pick them out. It feels like something a real couple would do, and that feels kinda special. Then she tries them all on to make sure the sizing is right, and with the things she's not sure about, she comes out to ask my opinion. Obviously, I think she'd look great in a sack, but where I can sense she's doubtful, I tell her not to get it, if she really doesn't like it.

Eventually, we finish up and she pays, and I'm just about to suggest lunch when she gets embarrassed, and I wonder if she doesn't want to spend any more time with me.

"What's wrong?" I ask her, standing by the entrance to the store we've just left.

She looks up and down the street. "I need to pick up something else," she says quietly, like it's a secret. My relief is palpable. It's not me then.

"Okay," I reply. "What do you need?"

She stops glancing around and looks at me, two patches of red appearing on her cheeks, just as she moves a little closer. "My period started yesterday," she explains. "It's the first one I've had since I got here, and I only brought over the few sanitary towels I had left at home. I could borrow some from Ali, but I'd rather just get my own." She stops talking and starts looking around again, while I marvel at her openness, and feel kinda pleased that she shared that with me, although I don't really know why I feel like that.

"So you need a pharmacy?" I ask.

"Yes, only I can't see one."

"That's because it's around the corner." I grab her bags, then take her hand and we start walking, going around the corner, where the pharmacy is the third shop along on the right.

"Thank you," she says, looking up at me.

"Do you want me to wait out here?" I ask her.

She blushes again. "Would you mind coming in with me?" she asks. "I'm worried that things will be different again."

I laugh. "And you think I'll know what to do about that?"

She giggles. "Well no, probably not, but hopefully we can work it out between us."

I smile and lead her into the store, loving the fact that she trusts me with this… and desperately trying not to read too much into it.

When we find the right section, Tess almost jumps for joy that the brand she uses 'at home' are also available here, and she picks up four packs. While I admit to knowing damn all about such things, that seems like a helluva lot to me.

"Do you need that many?" I ask her.

She chuckles. "Not right now, but it'll save me having to come back for the next few months."

I smile. "So how many do you actually need?" I ask.

She looks up at me. "Well, one pack should do it. My periods aren't that heavy."

I'm not sure I needed that piece of information, but I still like that she felt she could tell me. "Then just get one, or two, if you really feel the need."

"But I don't want to drag you back here next month," she explains.

"I wouldn't mind," I say, replacing a couple of packs on the shelf, and then leading her toward the cashier point. "But you won't need to. There's a perfectly good pharmacy between Rosa's and my apartment. It's less than five minutes' walk."

She flushes bright red. "I wish I'd known."

"Why?"

"Because then I wouldn't have troubled you with this."

"You haven't troubled me." She still looks doubtful. "You haven't troubled me at all. I love spending time with you."

Her eyes widen. "Me too," she whispers.

"Then have lunch with me?"

She doesn't hesitate, but nods her head, just as we get to the front of the short queue. And even as she pays for her items, she barely takes her eyes from mine for more than a couple of seconds.

Chapter Six

Tess

He took me shopping, as promised, and although I didn't expect to, we had a great time. He helped me deal with returning the clothes that were the wrong size, and then we went around the store together and picked out some new ones, and he waited patiently while I tried everything on, helping me make decisions when I wasn't completely sure about some of the new things we'd picked out. Then, he helped me buy sanitary towels, which was a little embarrassing, but also wasn't. He took everything in his stride, and his complete ease is one of the reasons I feel I can tell him anything – and I did, including the fact that my periods aren't very heavy. I have no idea why I blurted that out, but I did, and he didn't bat an eyelid. Of course, when he told me that I could've bought my sanitary towels just a short walk away from the restaurant, I felt a little mortified, but then he said the most perfect thing. He said that he loves spending time with me. I had to admit that I do too, because I do. The time I spend with him is when I'm happiest.

We went to lunch after that, to a seafood restaurant, where I managed to understand the menu, all by myself. I wanted to pay, to thank Ed for helping me, but he wouldn't hear of it. He said just being with me and seeing me smile was thanks enough, which I thought was very sweet of him.

Afterwards, we walked around the shops for a while, holding hands. He took me to a bookstore and I picked up a couple of fairly weighty novels, just to keep me occupied until our own books arrive from

England, which I'm hoping won't be too much longer, and then he took me back to the apartment and we had dinner together with Ali and Sam.

It was a fantastic day, and I've lived on his gentleness and his kind words ever since… but then I've had to, because I have't really had much time to be with him.

The following Sunday, he wasn't able to come out with me at all, because Ali, Petra, April and I went dress shopping. While I missed him, I have to admit, it was fun. Ali found her dress first time, which was incredible, as we both thought she'd find it much harder than that, especially after we'd looked on the Internet and seen what was available, but the dress she found is just perfect for her. April was easy too, but Petra and I were a little harder. Petra's very conscious of her size, although I don't know why, because I think she looks great. Ali wants us to wear the same thing, but it was hard finding something that suits us both, especially when I'm so much shorter. Still, we got there in the end, and left the store feeling happy with our purchases.

Since then, it's been a whirlwind of organising, with each Sunday being consumed by wedding plans, and very little time for Ed and I to enjoy ourselves. With Ali, I've looked at looked at flowers, table decorations, gifts, hair styles, buttonholes, and food. Sam decided he wanted nothing to do with the food – he wanted a day off. So, he's left all of that to Ali, and she roped me in to helping her. The only thing which Sam's taken complete control of is the honeymoon and neither Ali nor I have any idea what he's planned. He's being very mysterious about the whole thing. Not that we've really had time to wonder…

Ed's still come up to see me most evenings, but his visits have been fleeting, as Ali hasn't been able to cover for him. I still look forward to seeing him though and, judging from the look in his eyes, and his soft, tender smile, I think he does too.

I can't believe it's Ali's wedding day already. The last few weeks have flown by.

Sam spent last night with Ed at his and Rob's place, although Rob wasn't there, because they only have two bedrooms, so he stayed at

Petra's and brought her and April over here early this morning, before going on to meet up with Ed and Sam, and do whatever it is that grooms and their best men get up to on their wedding day. Since they arrived, it's been a whirl of hair, make-up, nails, champagne and giggles. There have been lots of giggles, thankfully, because that's helped to take my mind off the fact that Ali's moving on...

April looks beautiful in her flower-girl dress, which has a bodice made in the same deep plum colour as mine and Petra's dresses, but her skirt is white tulle and she loves spinning around in it and making it swirl – and making herself so giddy she falls over in fits of laughter.

We've all put our hair up, in roughly the same style, but April's wearing a plum coloured Alice band, just to hold hers in place and avoid using pins. And we're all wearing similar make-up and the same nail varnish. Ali's co-ordinated everything, right down to the last detail.

We're ready, with about twenty minutes to spare, and I have to say, although I obviously saw Ali try the dress on in the shop, she looks so much more beautiful today. She's wearing a very simple, but elegant gown, with a daring lace bodice, plunging neckline and capped sleeves, above an A-line tulle skirt. Sam is going to love it.

I think ideally, Ali would have wanted to have an open-topped car, but our hair would have been a complete mess by the time we arrived, so she settled for a nice black sedan, which is very comfortable.

She's not at all nervous, although she's clearly excited and I get the impression she can't wait to see Sam again, even though they've only been apart for one night. To be honest, I can't wait to see Ed either, and I think Petra feels the same way about Rob, so we're all just kind of impatient for the journey to be over.

When we arrive, the venue co-ordinator greets us and guides us all into the clubhouse, to a room that's been set aside for us. The ceremony is due to start in about ten minutes, and now, for the first time, Ali seems a little tense.

"Are you okay?" I ask her, keeping my voice quiet.

"Yes. It—It's just, I've got a favour to ask you."

"Then ask."

She looks around, then focuses on me again. "The thing is, you can't really say 'no', because I don't have a back-up."

"Okay... now I'm really intrigued."

She takes a step closer and, although we're both holding bouquets of cream and plum roses, she takes my hand in hers. "I want to ask you to give me away," she says, looking into my eyes.

"You do?" I'm dumbfounded and can't think what else to say.

"Yes. It means we walk up the aisle and onto the jetty together, and then when the celebrant asks who's giving me to Sam, you step forward and say 'I am'."

"And that's it?"

"Yes." She's looking at me so pleadingly, I can't say 'no'. I glance over at Petra, who's holding April's hand, and she gives me a nod, and a smile.

"Then I'd be honoured," I whisper, turning back to Ali.

"Thank you," she replies and, letting go of my hand, she hugs me, careful not to crush the flowers between us.

"Are we ready?" the co-ordinator asks, coming back into the room.

"As we'll ever be," Ali jokes, and gives me a wink.

We all walk out together and stand in front of double doors that face onto a lawn which slopes down to the lake, and the jetty, where I can see Sam standing, with Ed and Rob to his right. The people who've been sitting in the chairs facing the lake all stand and April is handed a little basket filled with cream coloured petals, and she walks out first, down an aisle between two sets of chairs, scattering the petals on the ground as she goes.

"It's taken me and my mom days to get her to do that right," Petra murmurs.

"Okay," the co-ordinator says. "Bridesmaid next."

Petra gives us both a smile and steps out into the sunshine, following her daughter down the aisle.

"Just you and me left," Ali whispers.

"Just you and me." *For the last time ever.*

The co-ordinator waits a few moments and then steps to one side and allows us both to move outside into the fresh air.

Arm in arm, we walk slowly between the chairs and a sea of unfamiliar faces turns to look at us — well at Ali, anyway. I notice that Sam has turned around too, and the look on his face, when he sees Ali, is pure love... well, maybe with a little bit of lust thrown in, judging from the way his eyes are raking up and down her body.

When we reach the front, he moves in closer and stands beside Ali, whispering something to her. I'm not sure what to do — whether I'm supposed to stay or move away, but Ali keeps hold of me and the celebrant gives me a nod, so I stay where I am and then he starts talking, beginning the ceremony. When it gets to the part where I have to give Ali away to Sam, she offers me her hand and I quickly realise what I'm supposed to do, and I pass it over to Sam's letting him take it from me and, in that moment, I know she's gone from me. Forever.

When the ceremony is over, everyone applauds, and Sam and Ali turn to face their guests before walking back down the aisle hand-in-hand, smiling at everyone, but mainly at each other. I follow, accompanied by Ed, who links his arm through mine and whispers, "Well done." I look up and see nothing but kindness in his eyes and have to blink back my tears. He pulls me a little closer as we continue our walk, followed by Rob, Petra and April.

We go back in through the double doors and along a short corridor, into a big hall, where we're offered champagne on silver trays. Ed takes two glasses, offering me one and I accept it gratefully, even though I don't usually drink very much.

"That was hard, wasn't it?" he asks.

"Harder than she'll ever know," I reply and take a large gulp of my drink.

We move further into the room to make way for the guests coming in behind us and, before long, the noise level shoots up. We're surrounded by uncles, aunts, cousins, second cousins... all of them Italian, all of them loud. And despite Ed's constant presence at my side, I've never felt so alone in my life.

Ed looks lovely in his tux and I'd really like to be able to tell him that, but this isn't the kind of place where I can speak to him, not in the way I want to. There's too much noise and too many people.

"Where are your parents?" I ask Ed, to make conversation. I have to lean in close to him to make myself heard above the noise.

"Over there." He points to a couple near the entrance, who are talking to an older man.

"Your dad's the man in the grey suit?" I ask, to make sure I've got the right person.

"Yeah. That's him."

I can't fail to notice the trace of bitterness in Ed's voice and I lean into him just a fraction closer, looking over at the couple. The man is probably an inch or so shorter than Ed, which means he's a good three inches shorter than Sam, and he's got pale grey hair. But as he's got his back to me, I have no idea what he looks like. Ed's mother, on the other hand, I can see, and she's exactly how I would have imagined her. She has dark hair, with maybe a little grey running through it; she's a bit overweight, but nothing to write home about, and has a round, jolly face.

Rob comes over. "Sorry," he says to Ed, raising his voice above the din. "We're needed."

"We are?"

"Yeah. Duty calls. I need your help getting the gifts Ali and Sam bought out of the car."

Ed turns to me. "I'll be back in a minute," he says. "Will you be okay?"

"I'll be fine. You go do your best man thing." I smile at him, trying to put a brave face on how despondent I feel. He smiles back and follows Rob across the crowded room, disappearing out of the main entrance.

He's only been gone a few minutes when someone jostles into me. I turn and see a man, probably around Ed's age, with dark hair and deep blue eyes looking down at me. He apologises, looking closely at me, like he's sizing me up, which makes me feel very uncomfortable.

"Don't worry," I say.

"And who might you be?" he asks.

"I'm Ali's sister."

"Ah. Well, I'm Fabio. I'm Sam's cousin." He offers his hand and I fumble with my bouquet and glass so that we can shake. "So, you're English," he says.

"Yes." I look up in the vague direction where I know Ali's standing and then turn back to Fabio. "I'm sorry, I think Ali needs me," I say to him.

"Okay. Well, I'll catch up with you later," he replies, as I walk away.

I head towards Ali, but once I know Fabio won't be able to see me anymore, I dart out of the door, leaving my bouquet and glass of champagne on a side table in the hallway.

Outside, the chairs from the ceremony have been removed, and several dining tables and chairs have been put out, together with a large, long serving table, and the caterers are currently loading it up with food for the buffet.

God, even out here there are too many people.

I dodge my way through them and head back out along the jetty.

At least here, I can be alone.

The lake is mirror smooth, the trees on the opposite shore reflected in its crystal surface, and I stand at the end of the jetty and and let the tears fall.

Ed

I honestly thought I was never gonna breathe again, when I saw Tess walking down the aisle with Ali. She looked simply beautiful in that wine colored dress and, although Ali was the center of everyone else's attention – quite rightly so – I couldn't take my eyes off of Tess.

She did amazingly well too. Sam told Rob and I this morning that Ali was going to ask Tess to give her away, and that she was going to do it at the very last minute, so Tess couldn't back out. I'm not sure that was the fairest thing for Ali to have done, but I didn't say anything: I guess it's her day. Even so, I could see from the look on Tess's face that she found that incredibly hard.

Rob hands me a bag out of the car and takes a box himself.

"What on earth is all this?" I ask him.

"How do I know? Ali just asked me to bring it in."

We head back towards the boathouse and in through the main entrance. "Where are we going?" I ask him.

"There's a room on the right," he says. "Ali told me to put everything in there."

He opens the door and we deposit the box and bag on a table, leaving and closing the door again.

"Is that it for now?" I ask him.

"I think so. I'm sure there'll be more to do later."

I can't complain. So far, our duties have been fairly non-existent. We worked late last night, as usual, and Sam came over to our place afterwards. I know he was reluctant to leave Ali, but he decided to go with tradition this time and spend the night away from his bride-to-be. He didn't do that when he married Amber, but then he didn't get much right with her. We didn't do anything special last night. We were both too tired, so we just fell into bed. Sam was clearly happy though, safe in the knowledge that the next time he goes to bed, he'll be married to the woman he loves.

Rob arrived unbelievably early, and in very good spirits. He'd already dropped Petra and April with Ali and Tess, and the three of us spent the morning together. We had brunch, which I cooked, because I wasn't gonna let Sam cook on his wedding day, then we showered and got dressed into our tuxes. We had to drive out here in two cars though. Rob's taking Petra and April home – probably fairly early, because April will need to get to bed. Sam and Ali are leaving on their honeymoon this evening, so they've got a cab booked for later on; and I'm taking Tess home with me. To be honest, I can't wait. The idea of having her alone, in my car, away from everyone else sounds like pure heaven to me.

Rob and I go back into the main hall, where everyone's still enjoying the champagne.

"I'm gonna find Tess," I tell him. "Let me know if you need me for anything."

"Okay." He pats me on the shoulder and disappears into the crowd, doubtless in the direction of Petra.

I go back across the room to where I left Tess; only she's not there. I stand and look around, but there's no sign of her. Behind me, Fabio's talking to a couple of our other cousins, Antonio and Carlo, and I pat him on the shoulder.

"There was a girl standing here, one of the bridesmaids," I start to say.

"Yeah," he replies. "Man, she's hot."

I glare at him. "What the hell did you do, Fabio?" He has a reputation that makes Rob look like a choirboy.

"Nothing, Ed. Honest." He holds his hands up. "I just asked who she was and introduced myself, that's all. She went over to talk to Ali."

"Okay."

I leave my cousins speculating about my interest in Tess and go over to where Ali and Sam are standing, roughly in the center of the room, surrounded by our family.

Moving in close beside her, I gently tap Ali on the shoulder and she turns to me.

"Where's Tess?" I ask her.

"I thought she was with you," she replies, looking around.

"No. I had to go outside with Rob. When I came back, she'd gone." She looks worried. "What's wrong?" Sam asks, moving closer.

"We can't find Tess."

He breaks away from the crowd, holding Ali's arm and moving us toward the side of the room. "What did you do?" he asks me.

"I didn't do a damn thing. Rob needed my help outside, so I went out there with him. I told Tess to wait for me, but when I came back, she wasn't there. Fabio said he spoke to her. "

"I'll kill him." Sam goes to move away, but I grab him.

"Calm down. He didn't do anything either. Well, he says he didn't. He says he just introduced himself, that's all."

"Well, she must be here somewhere," Ali reasons and we all move out toward the main entrance again. I get there first and, as I go down the first step, I look up and see her.

"There she is," I say, pointing along the jetty.

"I'd better go and see if she's okay," Ali says.

"Let me." I turn and look at them. "You both need to be here…"

Ali hesitates for a moment, then nods her head and I go down the steps, and walk quickly across the lawn and along the jetty, coming up behind Tess. Even as I approach her, I can tell she's crying and I walk right up behind her and, without saying a word, turn her around and pull her straight into my arms. She lets out a single sob and weeps into my chest. I can't stroke her hair, because it's pinned up, but I hold the back of her head against me and let her cry it out.

After a while, she leans back in my arms and looks up at me.

"I'm sorry," she murmurs.

"Don't be. It's fine. I understand."

"You do?" She looks puzzled.

"Yeah. You're happy for them, but you're worried about how their marriage changes your relationship with Ali."

She nods her head. "That makes me really selfish, doesn't it?"

"No. Not at all. You've relied on your sister all your life, and she's always been there."

"Yes," she whispers.

"I feel the same," I confess. "About Sam, obviously, not Ali."

She smiles. "You do?"

"Yeah. I depend on him too, and I'm really not looking forward to the next ten days, having to run the kitchens by myself."

"You'll be fine," she says, trying to sound reassuring.

"I was physically sick every day, the last time, when Sam took off to England to find Ali," I admit, acknowledging that for the first time to anyone.

"Really?" She's not judging, or being critical. She sounds more concerned than anything else.

"Yeah. He's looked out for me, ever since our dad decided I didn't exist any more. He's my hero, my rock, my guiding light. Not having him there is like losing a part of myself, and I can't imagine not having him in my life, right by my side to help me." I've never said that out loud before, but I think she needed to hear it; to understand she isn't alone. She really isn't.

"You're gonna miss him too, aren't you…?" she says softly, reaching up and touching my cheek with her fingertips.

"Well, yes and no."

"How do you mean?" she asks, looking puzzled.

"I mean that, yes I'm gonna miss him while they're on their honeymoon, but I know Sam's not gonna abandon me, any more than Ali's gonna abandon you. Them being married doesn't change how they feel about us."

"No, I suppose not." She sniffles and I sense there's something else behind her tears. I know what it is too.

"Are you still feeling homesick?" I ask her.

She nods again.

"Well, I guess that's fine too," I tell her and hold her close again, hiding my own fear that, now Ali's married, Tess might just change her mind about living here and decide to go back to England… back to the place she still calls 'home'.

Once she's calmed down, we make our way slowly back down the jetty. I keep hold of her hand the whole time. I'm not letting her go; not for anyone. The food is now being served and people are milling about the lawn and, as we move amongst them, I notice my parents talking to Sam and Ali. Tess squeezes my hand as we pass them; she's obviously noticed too.

"They're talking," she whispers.

"Looks that way." I can't think of anything else to say.

Rob and Petra come over, with April and I have to ask the question. "What happened with Mom and Dad?"

Rob shrugs. "I don't know, really," he replies. "Ali went and spoke to them, and the next thing I knew, Mom was leading Dad over to Sam and they were shaking hands."

I should've known Ali would find a way to bring them back together.

"Sam looks a little tense," Tess says. She's right. He does.

"Well, it's been a couple of years since they've spoken," I tell her. "I guess he's still wary of what might happen."

She smiles. "Ali won't let anything happen," she says quietly. Then she stands a little closer and looks right up at me. "Are you okay with it?" she asks.

"Okay with what?"

"Sam and your parents talking?"

"Of course." I can feel Rob looking at me and I glance over at him. He looks as concerned as Tess sounds. "It's fine," I say, loud enough for him to hear too. "I'm pleased for Sam, honestly I am. I know he'll still be there for me, even if Dad and I never work out our differences."

Tess points out our cousin Fabio, who's now talking to his dad, our uncle Giuseppe. "Who's that?" she asks.

"That's cousin Fabio," Rob explains, his lips twitching upwards.

"And what's so funny about cousin Fabio?" Petra asks, looking up at him.

"I can't tell you in front of April," Rob replies.

Petra's eyes widen. "You can't even hint?" she says.

Rob looks at me. "Well," I say, thinking it through. "Let's just say Fabio doesn't have a great reputation with women."

"He was the man who was talking to me before I went outside," Tess remarks quietly.

I turn to her. "He didn't do anything did he? Is that why you went out?"

"No. He just told me his name was Fabio and asked who I was. I went out because there were too many people." She lowers her voice to a whisper.

"Okay." I pull her closer and put my arm around her, just as Fabio looks over and gives me a sly wink. He really is an asshole.

Mom and Dad move away from Ali and Sam, and Tess looks up at me. "I'm just going to go and speak to Ali for a moment," she says.

"Okay. I'll be right here."

She walks away and I watch her. Once she gets to Ali, they speak for a few seconds and then move together, away from Sam, who comes over to us.

"Is she okay?" I ask Sam. "Did she say anything?"

"No. Just that she wanted to speak with Ali. What did she tell you?"

I'm not sure if I should tell him how she feels about Ali getting married, so I just say, "She's homesick."

"That's all?" He looks me in the eye.

I've never been great at lying to anyone, but especially not Sam.

"She's feeling insecure," I add. "Because Ali's married now." There, I said it.

"But surely she knows Ali will always be there for her. And so will I. And so will you." He smiles and pats me on the arm.

"I'll be here for her, as long as she is," I mutter, voicing my fear, somehow forgetting that Rob and Petra are still standing there, with April.

"What do you mean?" Rob asks, and I look up at him.

"Exactly what I say. I—I'm scared that now Ali's married, Tess will go home."

Sam moves slightly, so he's standing right in front of me. "I seriously doubt that," he says, looking me in the eye. "I don't think she could handle being on her own anywhere – not even in England. She needs Ali far too much for that."

I'd love to feel reassured by that. The thing is, I wish it was me she needed.

The afternoon speeds by. Thankfully, Ali and Sam decided against having speeches, but not long after the meal is over, I notice my mom going and talking to Petra. It seems like there's a brief moment of tentative introduction, but before long, they're deep in conversation, laughing and chatting for some time.

"Do they know each other?" Tess asks me, seeing the direction of my gaze.

"I don't think so. I guess my mom wanted to meet the woman who's finally tamed my brother."

Tess looks up at me and I see her face is filled with sympathy for my situation. It feels like my parents will talk to everyone and anyone, except for me.

After a while, Rob walks by and I take the chance and grab hold of him.

"I saw Mom talking to Petra a while ago," I say.

"Yeah. It turns out that Mom remembered Petra from years ago, when she and her husband – well, soon to be ex-husband – used to eat at Rosa's."

I nod my head. Our mom used to run the front of house, just like Rob does now, and it's typical of her to remember a face – even if it is from a long while back. "Did she remember Petra's ex?" I ask. I've given up referring to him as her husband.

"I don't think so." Rob looks relieved. "From what I can gather, it was Petra that Mom used to talk to."

"I see."

Tess grips my hand a little tighter as Rob walks away.

"Try not to take it too personally," she whispers.

"That's kinda hard," I reply, not bothering to disguise my sadness. I don't feel like I have to where Tess is concerned.

"I know."

I look down at her and she smiles at me. It makes me feel a little better, despite the lonely ache in my heart.

Before we know it, Ali and Sam are leaving for their honeymoon. Rob and Petra are going at the same time, to get April home for bed and we all say goodbye. Tess gives Ali a long hug and Ali reassures her that she'll be fine. Sam tells me to take care of her – which, of course, I tell him I will, and then they go and Tess moves back toward me, and into my arms. As the crowd starts to move away, I look over in the direction of my dad, hoping he'll maybe just give me a smile or a glance. He turns away from me, his expression blank and cold. Nothing changes – at least not for me, it seems.

"Do you wanna go?" I say to Tess, once everyone has drifted away.

"Shouldn't we stay until the end?" she asks.

"No. We can go now, if you want." I know she's uncomfortable, surrounded by my family.

"But what about everything here?"

"The boat club people look after it," I explain. "And Rob and Petra are coming by tomorrow morning to collect anything that might have been left behind. To be honest, from now on, it's only gonna get noisier, and rowdier."

"In that case, I'd definitely prefer to leave."

I smile down at her. "Me too."

Once we're on the road back home, she turns to me. "Do you know where they're going?" she asks, sounding tired.

"Sam and Ali? On their honeymoon?" I clarify.

"Yes."

Sam has kept this a secret from everyone but me and Rob. "Yeah, they're going to Positano."

There's a moment's silence and then I hear her sob and she bursts into noisy tears.

"Tess?" I glance over at her. She's dropped her head into her hands and is shaking with emotion. What the hell is wrong with her? Whatever it is, I can't let her cry like this for the whole journey. I check my mirrors and pull over to the side of the road, parking up alongside a large grassy field. It's twilight, but I can see her clearly, and she's distraught.

There's no traffic, so I get out and go around to her side, opening the door and crouching down beside her.

"Tess," I say, softly. "Tell me what's wrong?"

She looks up at me, her eyes filled with tears and sadness. "It's Positano," she murmurs.

"Yeah. What about it? It's where we're from."

"You are?"

"Well, not strictly speaking. The three of us were born here. But our parents are from there."

She nods and, for a moment, I think she's gonna be okay, but then she starts sobbing again.

"What's wrong, Tess?" She leans over into me and I pull her closer, holding onto her.

Again I wait, and again, she calms. "We—we went there," she murmurs through her tears, and I recall Ali telling us about a family holiday.

"Yeah, I remember. Ali said. Your parents took you, didn't they?"

She nods. "I was eight," she says. "It was the last family holiday we had." *Oh, shit.* I remember now, Ali got upset when she talked about it, and I've got a bad feeling about what's coming next. I hold her a little tighter, just in time to hear her whisper, "A month after we got home, they died."

"Oh, Tess." I lean over and kiss her cheek, tasting her salty tears. "I'm so sorry."

She looks at me and in the dim evening light, I'm struck by how lost and alone she looks. I can't handle that and, getting to my feet, I pull her up out of the car. This way, I can hold her a lot closer, and I do. "Do you wanna tell me about it?" I ask her.

"There was a fire," she says simply, looking up at me. "At our house." She swallows. "Ali wasn't there, but I was, and so were Mum and Dad. I don't really remember very much, except my dad coming into my bedroom and waking me up. There was smoke everywhere, and a noise like I'd never heard before… It was loud and scary. To me, it sounded as though the fire was a monster, eating through our house… our home." She shudders. "Dad picked me up in his arms," she continues softly, taking in a gulp of air. "And he carried me over to the window. Then he told me he loved me, and that I should tell Ali he loved her too, and that I shouldn't be scared. And then he lowered me out of the window." Her eyes are so wide now and I can tell she's reliving that moment. "There was a man below – a neighbor – and he caught me. But I didn't want to be with him. I wanted my dad." She starts to cry again, and I let her. Once she's calm, she continues, "My dad disappeared back inside the house and that's the last time I saw him…" Her voice fades.

So, this is what Sam was talking about. When he told me she was different, and fragile, this is why. Her need for her sister makes so much more sense now.

"I'm sorry, Tess," I whisper, my mouth close to her ear. "I understand now why you've always needed Ali so much."

She leans back and looks up at me. "Mum and Dad were found huddled together on their bed," she says, a little randomly. "Ali always told me that Dad already knew Mum was dead when he came to save me, and that he loved her so much he went back to her and simply lay down beside her and let death take him. He chose death with her, instead of life with us. And I can't forgive him for that," she weeps. "Ali… Ali created this kind of myth surrounding what he did, romanticizing the whole thing. But I never wanted him to be a romantic hero. I just wanted my dad back."

"Does Ali know that's how you feel?" I ask her.

She shakes her head vigorously. "No. And you can't tell her."

"I won't. It's okay. I promise I won't." I'm already aware of how much faith she's putting in me by telling me her story; there's no way I'm going to break her trust.

She nods her head. "Over the years, I've let Ali believe that I've gone along with her fantasy version of our dad, but really… honestly, I'm just so damn angry with him for leaving us. We were his children, and it was his job to protect us. That's what fathers do."

I can hear the emotion in her voice. She's torn between fear, anger and sadness. And she's not comfortable in any of those places.

"Try and remember the good times," I say quietly, brushing the backs of my fingers down her cheek. "That's what I do."

She looks up at me, then leans into my chest again and, although she's not crying anymore, I hold onto her until she lets out a long sigh and pulls back.

"Thank you," she murmurs.

I smile. "Well, you know my answer to that, don't you?" I reply.

"Hmm. Yes I do." She manages a slight smile and then something seems to catch her eye over my right shoulder. "What's that?" she says, pointing.

"What?" I turn to look.

"That. I saw something flickering in that field. Look, there's another one. And another."

"Oh. They're fireflies. You see them out here at this time of year."

"Fireflies?" She looks up at me.

"Yeah."

"They're… they're beautiful." I glance down at her and notice that she's not looking at the field, but at my eyes. "They remind me of you," she murmurs, and then bites her lip, like she didn't mean to say that out loud.

"How?" I ask, leaning closer to her.

She's silent for a minute, then she says, "You have speckles in your eyes, and I've always thought that they look like dancing fireflies."

God, I'm so in love with her.

"I think that's about the nicest thing anyone's ever said to me," I tell her, because I can't say that I'm in love with her at the side of the road, not when she's this upset.

She rests her head on my shoulder and I hold her while we watch the fireflies dance.

As the darkness descends, she shivers in the cool evening breeze.

"I suppose we ought to be heading home," she murmurs.

"Yeah. I guess." I wish we could stay here all night, but it's not practical, so I lower her back down into her seat and close the door again, going around to the driver's side and getting in.

"Thank you for this," she whispers, looking over at me.

"You're welcome." I start the engine and continue the drive home, aware of her sadness. "Tell me about your house by the sea," I say, wanting to cheer her up, and aware that she always sparks into life whenever she talks about it.

As usual, her voice goes up a notch and, even though I'm driving, and it's dark so I can't see her, I know she's smiling. "It's beautiful," she says. "It's right by the beach and even in the winter, when it's cold and isolated, and the wind's coming right in off the Channel, there's no place quite like it."

"It belonged to your parents?" I ask her.

"Yes. They bought it years ago and renovated it. We used to go there for weekends and some of the school holidays. It's filled with happy memories."

"And Positano?" I remember Ali saying how much she loved the place, but that doesn't mean Tess feels the same, although I hope she does.

"I loved Positano too," she replies, a little more wistfully. "Obviously, there's the memory of it being our last holiday together, but nothing can detract from the beauty of it. I know Ali's going to love having her honeymoon there. It's such a special place, maybe more so for her than for me. She remembers the holiday better than I do."

"Have you noticed all the pictures at the restaurant?" I ask her.

I'm aware of her turning to face me. "Not really. What about them?"

"They're all of Positano."

"Oh. I noticed the one on the back wall, but I haven't paid much attention to the rest."

We get back to the restaurant and I park up outside. It's legal at this time of night, so I don't have to worry about it. Getting out, I go around to Tess's side and help her out, then hold her hand and lead her across the sidewalk and into the restaurant, before flicking on the lights.

"Look," I say, guiding her over to the left hand wall. "They're all Positano."

"Oh yes. So they are," she whispers, looking at all the photographs. "Did you ask Ali to do that for you?"

"No, she chose to do it. She commissioned a photographer and got him to find out where our parents were born and he went and took photographs of their houses." I point them out to her. "She made this place like a piece of home for us."

I look down and notice that she's crying quietly to herself.

"Is it too much for you?" I ask her, pulling her into my arms and holding her.

"No. I think it's a lovely thing for her to have done. And the photographs are beautiful."

She leans back a little, but I keep my arms around her. "Don't," I whisper. "Don't move away. I like holding you."

"I like you holding me too," she murmurs, looking up into my eyes.

"I—I know you've always relied on Ali, and she'll still be there for you, but I want you to let me protect you, Tess. I want to keep you safe."

"I think I want that too." She leans forward again, and rests her head against my chest.

"Are you gonna be okay here by yourself?" I ask.

"I'll be fine," she mumbles into me.

"You're sure?"

She nods and, although I'm not convinced, I help her up the stairs and into the apartment and, despite the fact that I'd really like to stay, with great reluctance, we say goodnight.

Chapter Seven

Tess

I've hardly slept at all and, as I climb out of bed at around ten-thirty and wander around the apartment, I'm struck by how quiet it is, and how alone I feel. I may have felt like a gooseberry for at least some of the time when Sam and Ali were here, but I think I'd rather feel like that than face the next ten days by myself. I make a coffee and take it back to my room, sitting down on the bed to drink it. I reason that, if I stay in here, I can somehow convince myself that I'm not alone; that Sam and Ali are downstairs in the restaurant, or still in bed, and that I'll be seeing them later. If I go and sit in the living room, I'll have to face the emptiness of the flat, and I'm not ready for that.

I reach out for my laptop, deciding to keep busy, when I hear the door to the apartment open. Who on earth can that be? My palms are instantly sweating and my mouth's gone dry.

"Who's there?" I call from the assumed safety of my room.

"It's me, Ed." Just the sound of his voice makes me feel better and I go out into the hallway. He's standing, wearing jeans and a dark grey t-shirt, looking around and, when he sees me, a smile appears on his face and his eyes sparkle. "Hello," he says. "I just came round to check that you're okay. I hope you don't mind me letting myself in."

"No. Of course I don't mind." I'm not going to tell him how frightened I just was. He'll think I'm completely illogical. There are only five people with a key to this place, if I include Ali and myself, and none of them would do me any harm.

His eyes move slowly down my body and I remember that I'm still wearing my pyjamas, but he's seen me like this before, so what does it matter?

"I wondered if you'd like to come out with me today?" he says, still smiling.

"I'd love to." I don't even hesitate. The thought of spending the day here by myself wasn't inspiring me, but a day spent with Ed is just what I need.

"Okay. Why don't you go shower and I'll make us some coffee?"

I know I made a cup earlier, which is still sitting in my bedroom, but who cares? It's just a cup of coffee.

"Twenty minutes okay?" he asks.

"That's fine."

I dart into the bathroom, and have one of the quickest showers of my life, before wrapping myself up in a towel and dashing back to my room to dry my hair. Today is even warmer than yesterday was, so I decide to wear cut-off denim shorts and a white vest, with an oversized check shirt on top to protect me from the sun, because I burn way too easily.

Once I'm ready, I go out through the living room, where Ed's sitting on the couch, with two cups of steaming coffee on the table in front of him. He looks up at me.

"Wow," he says, then stops. "I mean… you look lovely."

"Thank you." I can feel myself blushing.

I sit beside him and take the cup he offers.

"I'm glad you're here," I tell him honestly, after a few moments, "but wouldn't you rather be spending the day with Rob, or your family?" Aside from his parents, a lot of his family travelled here for the wedding, and I know they're staying locally.

"No," he replies simply. "I'd rather be with you."

"Thank you," I murmur, and then, before he can tell me not to, I add, "Where are we going?"

"I thought I'd take you to Talcott Mountain State Park."

"What's there?"

"It's a country park. There are walks and a tower, which we can climb if you want to. The views are pretty spectacular."

"How far away is this place?" I ask him. I imagine to get 'spectacular views' of anything other than buildings, we're going to have to travel some distance from the city.

"I guess it'll take us about thirty minutes or so to get there," he replies.

"Is that all?"

"Yeah." He smiles. "You'd be amazed how quickly you get into the countryside from here."

"I like the idea of spending time in the countryside," I say quietly.

He leans into me a little and murmurs, "Somehow I thought you might."

He's absolutely right. He pulls up into a parking space just over half an hour after we left the city, and then climbs out and comes around to open my door. "I like your car," I tell him as he opens the boot of his dark blue Nissan saloon.

"You do?"

"Yes. It's normal."

He laughs. "Do you mean 'boring'?"

I look up at him. "No. I mean it's just like the cars back home. It's kind of comforting to be driven in something that doesn't resemble a truck."

Again, he chuckles. "In that case, I'm glad I bought it."

He reaches into the boot and pulls out a wicker picnic hamper.

"You brought a picnic?"

"Of course." He smiles down at me. "We're having a day out."

He closes the boot again and takes my hand, leading me out of the parking area and down a pathway. We're surrounded by trees and, for a moment, I'm able to forget that I'm in a different country, and just soak up the sun-dappled, leafy fresh air.

After about ten minutes, we reach a clearing, where a few picnic tables have been set out.

"Let's eat first," Ed says, picking out a table beneath the wide branches of a tree, slightly set apart from the others. "And then I'll take you up the tower."

"Okay."

I sit, and watch while he unpacks the picnic.

"What on earth have you brought?" I ask him, looking at all the boxes and packages he's laying out before me.

"Just some cold meats, olives, cheeses, figs, a spinach tart and some bread."

"Just?" I look up at him, and he smiles. "And I suppose you're going to tell me you prepared all of this before coming over this morning?"

"Yeah." He suddenly sounds doubtful, but finishes unpacking and deposits the hamper on the ground beside us, taking a seat next to me.

"What time did you get up?" I ask him.

He turns to look at me. "Early," he replies.

I lean into him and, after just a second's hesitation, I rest my head on his shoulder. "Well, it looks lovely. Thank you."

"You're welcome," he murmurs.

The hamper also contained fresh lemonade, crockery, cutlery and glasses, and I feel like royalty as he serves me a slice of tart.

"What's it like, being a twin?" I ask him, once we've started to eat. The food is delicious, but I want to find out more about him, not just talk about what he does all the time.

"It has its ups and downs," he says, looking out across the clearing. "People expect Rob and I to be the same, all the time. And we're not."

"I'd noticed," I reply and he turns to look at me, smiling.

"Good," he says. "Even so, I know he'll always be there for me, despite the fact that he's settled down with Petra." He pauses for a moment. "She's good for him. He was always a bit wild, especially when it came to women."

"I sort of gathered that from Ali," I tell him.

He smirks. "Yeah. But he's very different now."

I nod. "Are you closer to Rob than you are to Sam?" I ask him.

"No. I don't think so. Rob and I might be twins, but Sam's always been the one to stand up for me, especially with our dad." He takes a slice of salami and puts it into his mouth, chewing and clearly thinking. "They argued so much, when I first decided I wanted to go into pastry cooking, even though it was pointless. Sam tried so hard to get Dad to see that all I was doing was following my heart."

"I can't imagine Sam liked losing the argument… or any argument, come to that."

He smiles. "No. Sam's never been great at that."

"Has he always been as bossy as he is now?"

He shakes his head. "No. He used to be a lot worse."

"Worse?" I can't hide my surprise. "What on earth was he like before?"

"When he was with Amber, he was hell to be around," he says quietly. "He was always on edge, always yelling at everyone." He pauses. "He's so different since he got together with Ali. He's so much calmer."

"He wasn't always like that with her though, was he?"

He shakes his head and looks down at his plate. "No. To start off with he was a complete idiot. He liked her right from the beginning… I think he might even have loved her… He just didn't want to admit it."

"Is that why he was so mean to her?"

"Yeah. He didn't know what else to do."

"Well, I'm glad he worked it out," I say quietly.

"So am I."

"Although I still think he's really bossy in the kitchen," I add.

Ed smiles again. "Well, a leopard can't completely change its spots," he says. "Sam will always strive for perfection in the kitchen. And on the day you heard him yelling, a couple of people were being particularly dense. I think even I'd have yelled at them for doing what they were doing – and I rarely yell at anyone." He turns to look at me.

"I'm glad to hear that. I'm not great with people who raise their voices."

"I noticed," he replies. And as I look into his eyes, I notice the fireflies are dancing again, and I have to smile.

When we've eaten all we can, we pack up the hamper and, with Ed holding my hand, we walk it back to the car, depositing it in the boot, before setting off on the trail that leads to the Heublein Tower, as he's informed me it's called.

All the way there, he keeps hold of me, pointing out some rabbits and deer in the woodland as we pass, his voice a whisper against my ear, so as not to disturb the animals, I suppose. His breath against my skin sends a tingle down my spine and I shudder into him.

"You okay?" he murmurs.

I nod. "I'm fine."

He gazes down at me, like he doesn't quite understand, and we move on.

The climb up the steps is exhausting, but I have to say, it's worth it. Ed was right. The view is spectacular.

"That's Mount Monadnock," he says, pointing to a distant summit. "I guess it's around eighty or so miles away, in New Hampshire."

"In a different state?" I turn to look at him and he nods, and then moves me around so we're looking in a different direction.

"Do you see that strip of blue on the horizon?" he asks, standing behind me and pointing, his body pressed against mine. I follow the line of his arm, although I'm constantly aware of him being so close.

"Yes," I manage to say.

"That's the Long Island Sound."

"And I assume the city we can see is Hartford?"

"Yeah."

"It seems so far away."

"Even though it isn't." He smiles down at me.

"Thank you for bringing me here," I say, gazing into his eyes. "It's beautiful."

Ed

I've seen the view from up here before. But even if I hadn't, I'd still have to acknowledge that, the most beautiful thing I can see right now, is Tess.

"I know I said this earlier," I tell her, realizing that I have to let her know something of how I feel, "but you really do look lovely."

She'd been looking directly at me, but her eyes drop, like she's embarrassed, although she murmurs, "Thank you," very quietly.

"Do you want to go down?" I ask her. We've been up here some time, and I'd like to take her for another walk before we head home.

"Okay."

She lets me take her hand and I lead her down the stairs, which are much easier going down than up. We take the trail back to the car and it's only then that I notice how tired she is.

"I was gonna suggest we take another walk," I confess, "but I can see you're already exhausted."

She leans back against the car and I stand in front of her, her hands in mine. "I—I didn't sleep very well," she says, looking at my chest rather than my face.

"You didn't?" I let go of one of her hands and place my finger beneath her chin, raising her face to mine. "Why didn't you say?"

"Because I wasn't tired before. It's just kind of… hit me."

I sigh softly. "I was gonna ask you to come out to dinner with me tonight, but I'm not sure you could stay awake."

She smiles, just lightly. "I don't think I could."

I move a little closer, taking care not to let our bodies touch, because I got really hard being that close to her when we were standing at the top of the tower, and my erection isn't going anywhere, anytime soon. "Why don't I take us back to the apartment, and I'll cook dinner? And while I do that, you can sleep."

Her eyes widen slightly. "Oh. I couldn't do that. It would be so rude."

I can't help but chuckle. "No, it wouldn't. You're tired."

She looks up at me. "You wouldn't mind?" she asks, tentatively.

"Of course not."

"Okay."

I open the car door and help her into her seat and then go around to my side and get in beside her. Just before we start off, I turn to face her.

"Thank you for today," I say.

"Why are you thanking me?" she asks. "You did all this."

"Thank you for spending time with me," I clarify.

"I enjoyed it," she says. "And thank you for inviting me. I had a lovely time, and I really enjoyed the scenery, and the view from the tower."

"Did it help you to feel just a little more at home?" I ask, slightly fearful of her answer.

She hesitates, clearly thinking. "A little," she replies, although I wonder if she's just being kind... just being Tess.

When we get back, I let us into the apartment and take her upstairs, telling her to go lie down, and making sure she's comfortable, before I go down into the restaurant kitchen and find what I need to make us dinner. I've worked out on the way home that, if I make us roast lamb with Italian beans, that will give her at least two hours to sleep, because it takes that long to cook.

Once everything is in the oven, I lie out on Sam's couch and switch on the TV. There's not much to watch, but I leave it on for background noise and, with my hands behind my head, I think back over the weekend... about holding Tess down by the lake at the wedding; about her revelations over her parents, and Ali's insistence that their father was a romantic hero, which clearly doesn't sit well with Tess. I think about holding her last night, by the roadside, and watching the fireflies together. That was real special, but it wasn't as special as that moment when I told her I wanted to keep her safe, and she told me she wanted that too. I thought my heart was gonna burst when she said that.

I also can't help thinking about how good she looked when I arrived this morning, with her hair dishevelled, and her short pajamas showing off her gorgeous legs. That said, when she came back fully clothed a little while later, she looked just as good. Of course, her legs were still gorgeous, but that oversized shirt made her look so cute I just wanted to hug her. I could have done – it's not like I haven't before – but I've always had a reason, like the fact that she's been crying. This time it would have been just because I wanted to, and despite everything she said to me last night about wanting me to keep her safe, I wasn't sure she was ready for that, and the last thing I wanted to do was to scare her off, when I had a whole day out planned for us.

We've had a good day, too. She seemed to enjoy it. No. She did enjoy it. She said so, and from the look in her eyes, I know she meant it.

About ten minutes before the lamb's ready, I go along the hallway to Tess's room. She's left the door slightly open and I give it a gentle push, and stand on the threshold, holding my breath. She's lying on the bed, curled up on her side, fast asleep and, to be honest, I'd be quite happy to just stand here and watch her… for maybe the rest of my life. But as much as I'd like to do that, I'd rather sit and talk to her, spend time with her, look into her eyes and hold her hand.

I go over and stand beside her. "Tess," I whisper softly. She doesn't move, and I crouch down beside her, moving a stray strand of hair from her face. "Tess," I murmur again, gently brushing my fingertip against her cheek. She flicks her hand up, and makes a cute snuffling sound, and then opens her eyes.

"Oh," she says, her voice all sleepy. "Sorry."

"Don't be. I just came to let you know that dinner's nearly ready."

"Oh, okay. Thank you."

"You really don't need to thank me for this."

"But you made dinner.," she says, and sits up on the side of the bed. I move back, making space for her to stand, without feeling crowded.

"Yeah. I do that quite a lot." I smile at her. She looks up at me, kinda shy, and I take her hand and lead her into the living room. "Sit down. I'll dish up and bring it through."

"Shall we sit at the table?" she asks.

"We can, if you want. Or we can eat here."

"I think I'd prefer here." She sits down on the couch.

"You're still tired, aren't you?" I ask her, going through to the kitchen.

"Yes," she calls. "I haven't slept that well since I got here, to be honest. I…" She falls silent.

"What?" I come back into the room, and stand behind her, leaning over the couch. "What's wrong?"

She looks up at me. "Oh, I don't know. I suppose it's just a strange bed, strange room… you know." She turns away and I know she's not telling me everything.

After we've finished eating the lamb and beans, which I served in shallow bowls to make it easier to eat, I clear away and stack the dishwasher, and then make coffee and go and sit back with Tess on the couch.

"Do you want to talk about it?" I ask her.

"About what?" She turns to look at me.

"About whatever it is that keeps you awake at night."

Her eyes drop to her hands, which are clasped in her lap. "I explained. It's just because I'm in a strange place."

I move a little closer. "You've been here for weeks now, Tess," I say, softly. "Surely, you're getting used to it by now."

"You'd think I would be, wouldn't you?" she mumbles. "But I guess the nightmares don't help…" And again, she falls silent, like she said more than she meant to. She keeps doing that. I'd like to think it's because she's relaxed enough around me to be herself, but I'm not sure. It could just be the tiredness.

I edge closer still, so we're almost touching. "Tell me about them," I urge her. "It might help."

She looks up at me. "They're always the same," she whispers. "I dream about the fire…"

I reach out for her and pull her into my arms, just as she starts to cry.

"I'm sorry," I murmur. "I shouldn't have asked."

"No," she manages to say, through her sobs. "You're right. It does help to talk. It makes me remember that it's in the past. It's not real... well, not anymore, anyway."

"Then talk to me, anytime you want to." She leans back a little and looks up into my eyes. "Would you like me to stay?" I ask her.

Her eyes widen. "Stay?" She sounds uncertain.

"Yeah. You're sleeping in Rob's old bedroom, but mine's vacant. I can stay in there, if you want... if it'll help you to sleep better."

"You want to stay?" she asks.

"If it helps you, yes. I won't do anything. I won't touch you."

"You won't?" She sounds disappointed, which is a surprise, but it makes me hope she might return at least some of my feelings.

"I won't do anything you don't want me to." I clarify and pull her back into my arms again. "But I have to tell you... I want you, Tess. I really do."

"You do?" She sounds surprised now.

"Of course I do." I take a breath and steel myself to ask my next question. "I was wondering...?"

"Wondering what?"

"Whether you'd be my girlfriend?" I ask, holding my breath.

She leans back again, looking up once more. "Your girlfriend?"

"Yes." Her gaze is intense. "Like I said last night, I want to be with you, to protect you and keep you safe. I want us to be together."

"Boyfriend and girlfriend?" She whispers the words, like they're alien to her.

"Yes."

She rests her head on my chest again. "I like the sound of that," she whispers softly and I feel like my heart just burst with happiness.

"Would it be okay if I kissed you?" I ask her.

She leans back and nods her head, and I place a finger beneath her chin, raising her face to mine and brushing my lips across hers, so, so gently. She sighs and lets out a gentle moan and I caress her lips with my tongue. Her moan becomes louder and she opens up to me, her tongue meeting mine as I pull her closer, her breasts crushed against my chest. I feel her hands come around behind my neck, her fingers knotting into my hair and she holds me close and steady while our lips and tongues explore. I keep my movements limited, careful to avoid letting her feel my erection, which is painfully hard against my zipper. I know I can't take things too fast with her, but I don't want to anyway. I want to savor every movement, every sound, every second of my time with her. I just have to keep telling myself that's because I'm in love with her, and not because I'm still scared she's gonna leave at any minute…

Eventually, we break the kiss, although I'm not sure either of us really broke away first. It was just a kind of mutual ceasing.

"Did you like that?" I ask her, because there's still a hint of doubt, or maybe confusion in her eyes.

"Yes," she whispers. "Yes, I did."

I smile, and she brings her hands down, letting them rest on my biceps, which feels good. "Would you like to do it again?" I suggest.

"Yes, please," she replies, and I lean in and kiss her a second time, taking her just a little harder this time, my tongue delving deeper, discovering more… like that she makes a soft, whimpering sound when she gets aroused. It's cute.

"Please don't ever doubt that I want you," I tell her, the moment we lean back. "Because nothing could be further from the truth. I want you so much, I'm struggling to think straight, or even breathe right now."

Her eyes lock with mine, and I see a flare of desire come from somewhere deep inside her. She wants me too. I know she does. I also know, without having to ask the question, that she's a virgin, and despite the look I just saw, she's not ready for that to change yet. So, we're gonna take this real slow…

"Please stay," she whispers.

"I will." I let my forehead rest against hers. "I'll stay in my old room." She nods and smiles her gratitude, and I know I was right.

We're taking it slow.

I slept really well, got up early, had a shower and, with a towel wrapped around my hips, snuck into Sam's room and borrowed some clothes. Tess and I may have moved forward last night, but I really don't think it would help for her to find me wandering around the apartment in nothing but a towel – especially not as I've been bone hard since we kissed last night, and I don't think that's gonna change in the near future.

Once I'm dressed, I go into the kitchen and put the coffee on, and am just thinking about what to make for breakfast, when Tess appears, wearing nothing but a towel herself, tucked just above her breasts. She sees me, blushes to the roots of her hair and, giving out a yelp of surprise, bolts back into her bedroom. I have to smile, because she looked so damn funny. But she also looked really sexy and I busy myself whisking eggs to take my mind off how much my dick hurts right now.

"I'm sorry." I flip around when I hear her voice.

"Why are you sorry?" I ask her.

"I didn't realize you'd be out here," she explains. "I'm starting work today." Of course. I'd forgotten that. "And I left my blouse hanging up in the laundry room."

She's wearing a t-shirt over the top of a smart knee-length skirt, which we bought when we went shopping together the other week.

"You didn't have to run away," I tell her, going over and standing in front of her. "You looked really nice in just a towel."

She blushes again. "Are these Sam's clothes?" she asks, touching the t-shirt I'm wearing, and clearly trying to deflect my attention.

"Yeah. I'll go home and change before I start work."

"I see." She looks me up and down. "I think I prefer your clothes," she whispers, and smiles. "I'd better grab my blouse."

"Okay. I'll get breakfast ready."

And I'd better hurry if she's gonna eat before getting off to work. How the hell did I forget that? I guess I've been too wrapped up in the wedding… and Tess.

She comes back out a few minutes later, with the blouse on, looking even smarter than she did before. "That looks lovely," I tell her.

"Thank you."

"Sit down and I'll dish up the breakfast. It's nearly ready." She checks her watch. "You've got time," I reassure her.

"Okay."

Once I've served the food, I sit beside her. "How did you sleep?" I ask her.

She turns, a forkful of eggs poised, ready to eat. "So much better," she replies.

"No nightmares?"

She looks down at her plate. "I still had the nightmare," she admits, "but I got back off to sleep more easily than normal, knowing you were just across the hallway."

I put my fork down and turn to her, twisting her seat, so she's facing me. Then I take her fork and put it down too. "You should've woken me," I tell her.

"There wasn't anything you could've done," she replies.

"Oh? I could've reassured you that it was a nightmare; I could've made you a hot chocolate, sat and talked with you, if you'd wanted. I could've held you until you went back to sleep."

"You'd have done that?"

"Yes. I'd do all of that, and more, to make you feel safe and happy, Tess."

She reaches out and touches my cheek with her fingertips. "Thank you," she whispers.

"Don't thank me. Just wake me up next time." We go back to eating. "Speaking of next times," I say, between mouthfuls, "do you want me to stay again tonight?"

"Yes," she replies immediately. "Why?" The question is an afterthought, like she really doesn't understand why I might have doubted it.

I smile over at her. "Because I'll pick up a few things when I go home," I explain. "Just some clothes and a toothbrush. It'll save me time."

"And you'll stay?" she asks, like she's scared I'll change my mind. As if that's gonna happen.

"I'll stay for as long as you want me to." Forever wouldn't be long enough for me.

She nods her head, smiles, says, "Okay," and checks her watch again. "Oh God. I'd better be going."

"I'll walk with you," I suggest.

"It's out of your way," she replies.

"So? I don't have to be at work for an hour and a half. I can walk you to your office, go home, change, pack a bag and still be back here in time."

She gazes into my eyes. "Are you sure?"

"Absolutely. It's your first day. You don't wanna go by yourself."

"No," she says, wistfully. "No, I don't.

Once I've dropped her off and kissed her goodbye – which was the highlight of the day, so far – I walk back to my own apartment. On the way, I can't help but wonder how well Tess would sleep if I could hold her and keep her safe, all night long.

Chapter Eight

Tess

Zoe shows me to my desk, which is in the same office as hers, and then gives me a quick tour of the premises, consisting of the outer reception area, Bryan's office, the room I share with Zoe and another room, which is where we find three girls, Brittany, Mel and Taylor. Their jobs appear to be to keep an eye on the reception – although they seem particularly poor at doing that, in my experience – general typing, and handling the initial email and telephone enquiries… as well as gossiping with each other, from what I can gather. Zoe doesn't seem to think too highly of any of them, and tells them off for having their door closed, pointing out that they can't hear anyone coming in. Judging from the looks they all exchange, it seems the feeling of dislike is mutual. There's an odd atmosphere to this place, one I'm not entirely comfortable with and I'd really like to just get on with my job.

As we go through into our own office, Zoe tells me that there is actually a receptionist as well, but she hasn't been well for the last couple of months. Bryan wanted to replace her, but Zoe persuaded him that she and the other girls could cover the work.

"It's just a shame the others don't bother," she adds wistfully, leaving the door open, so we can see the outer room.

Zoe sets me to work on a new project which revolves around a newspaper clipping a woman has sent in. She found it in a box of photographs in her mother's attic, and it concerns a civil war hero. My job, to start with, is to look into the newspaper report, which is about his death, and which seems to be shrouded in some mystery.

To start with, I find it hard to concentrate. It's not made easy by the constant interruptions – usually from Bryan, who buzzes through fairly regularly, demanding to see Zoe in his room, or else from people arriving in the outer office for various reasons, from those making enquiries, to delivery men. And then there's Brittany, Mel and Taylor, who seem to feel the need to ask questions, roughly every ten minutes. Obviously, none of them want to talk to me, and I'm now no longer surprised that they needed to employ someone to help Zoe. In fact, I'm amazed she gets anything done at all.

The other reason I'm finding things difficult though is that I'm struggling to forget Ed's kisses. Every time I get settled, the memory of his lips on mine comes flooding back. I had no idea it would feel like that, and I keep wondering how he'd have reacted if he'd realised I'd never been kissed before. I wonder if that would have freaked him out and sent him running for the hills. I hope not, for so many reasons. Partly because I slept so much better just knowing he was there, even if I did still have a nightmare. But also because I really did like how it felt to be kissed by him, and held by him. And I liked his words, and the way they made me feel. But best of all, I liked the fact that he asked me to be his girlfriend. He's gorgeous, handsome, kind, thoughtful, and considerate... and he wants *me* to be his girlfriend. That thought still makes me quizzical, but it also makes me smile.

Over the course of the morning, it's become clear that there's something going on between Bryan and Zoe. He's popped into our office twice, as well as calling her over to his several times and, when he suggested lunch to her and she said she was going to take me somewhere, as it was my first day, he scowled and sulked, but accepted her decision, and then said we could take an extra half hour, if we wanted. I guess office romances happen, but I don't think the situation is helped by the fact that Brittany seems to like Bryan too. She positively dotes on his every word and that probably accounts for at least some of the awkward atmosphere in here.

At lunchtime, Zoe asks what I want to do, but obviously, I have no idea.

"I don't know the area," I admit. "I only know one restaurant."

"Why don't we go there then?" she suggests.

"Will we have time?" I ask her.

"Where is it?"

I explain and she says it won't be a problem, and besides, Bryan has said we can take some extra time. She gives me a smile and a wink and, picking up our handbags, we set off.

I don't know why I'd forgotten, but I had. Today is Jasmine's first day back at work and, although she was at the wedding, with her husband Cole and their two children, we barely spoke. So when Zoe and I arrive, Zoe asks for a table for two and Jasmine simply takes us to the back of the restaurant and sits us down, offering us menus and asking what we'd like to drink. We both ask for mineral water, because we've got to work, and she tells us that our waitress will be Abi. I've never met her either, so although I live here, I feel like a stranger.

We order our food and, once Abi – who's very nice – has gone into the kitchen, Zoe takes a sip of water and leans forward.

"How's your first morning been?" she asks me.

"It's been great," I lie. It hasn't been bad, but I feel like I don't know what I'm doing, and the office politics is something I hadn't anticipated.

"How are you getting on the with case I gave you?" We've hardly spoken since she handed me the file this morning.

"Okay," I reply. "I'm not sure I'm going about it the right way, but…"

"Well, Bryan's going out later this afternoon, so we should get some peace and quiet, and I'll be able to sit down with you and go through things."

"Great," I say, feeling relieved. "That'd be a huge help."

"Tess?" I hear Rob's voice and twist in my seat. He's just appeared from the corridor that leads to the kitchen, his office, and the apartment. "What are you doing here?"

"Um… having lunch." He comes over and stands at the table, between us. "This is my colleague, Zoe."

"Hi," he says, offering his hand, which she shakes. "Why didn't you let us know you were coming in?" he asks, turning back to me.

"Because I didn't know I was. Zoe invited me to lunch and asked where I wanted to go… and I only know Rosa's."

"Best place in town," he jokes. "So, Ed doesn't know you're here?"

I shake my head. "No."

"Let me get him."

I grab his arm. "He'll be busy," I say.

"Yeah. But he'll also kill me if he finds out you were here, and he missed you – *and* I knew about it."

I let him go and he disappears again.

"Who was that?" Zoe asks.

"He's one of the owners," I reply, uncertain as to exactly how to explain who Rob is. I suppose I could just say that he's my boyfriend's brother, but then he's also my sister's brother-in-law, which feels complicated. Too complicated to explain over lunch on my first day at work, anyway.

"Tess?" Ed's voice is soothing and I turn again and drink him in. He's wearing his whites, looks glorious, and comes straight over, taking my hand and pulling me to my feet and into his arms, ignoring Zoe and every other customer in the restaurant. "What are you doing here?" he asks.

"Are you and Rob programmed to ask the same questions?" I enquire, smiling up at him.

"No." He smiles back. "I guess he just asked you the same thing?"

I nod. "So I'll tell you what I told him." I turn and introduce Zoe, with whom he shakes hands, before focusing on me gain. "Zoe offered to take me to lunch, and asked where I wanted to go, and I said Rosa's was the only restaurant I knew in town."

"You should've called me," he says, looking down at me. "You could've ordered in advance. I'd have had your food ready for you."

"Speaking of food… if you're out here, who's cooking?"

"Rob's covering for me," he explains.

"So we have to eat Rob's food?" I tease.

"The guy can cook," Ed says, "but I'll get back and see to your lunch myself. As it's you."

He hugs me again, just briefly, then leaves, but stops abruptly and comes back. "I'll come see you before you go," he murmurs, and this time, he really does walk away.

"Um…" Zoe says as I sit back down again. "Now I really need an explanation. So, the first guy was one of the owners. This second guy looked almost identical – so identical they could be twins – and he seems to know you pretty well. And judging from the way he was looking at you, I think he'd like to know you even better." She smirks.

I blush. "Okay," I say. "I guess I'm busted."

"You sure are," she replies. "And now you're gonna dish the dirt on the two hot guys you seem to have hanging on your every word."

"They're not," I stammer.

"Well one of them is."

I look down at my fingers, which I've got clasped around my glass in front of me. "The guy you saw first is Rob," I explain. "And the second guy is Ed. They're twins."

"Yeah. I kinda worked that out for myself. And they own this place?" She looks around.

"With their older brother, Sam, yes."

"Is he gonna come out and hug you too in a minute?"

"No. He's in Italy at the moment, with my sister… on their honeymoon."

She stares at me for a moment. "Oh. So that's the connection. You're kind of related to these two guys by marriage?"

"Yes and no."

"Are you trying to confuse me even more?" she asks, smiling.

"Not intentionally." I twist the glass in my hands. "That's not the whole connection. Ed's also my boyfriend," I say quietly, marvelling at how good that sounds.

"Good for you, girl," she says. "He's gorgeous."

I look up at her. She's smiling a kind, friendly smile. "I know," I reply.

"And you're beautiful," she adds. "So you can stop looking embarrassed, because I think you're perfect for each other."

I can feel myself blushing even more, and I have no idea how to reply to her, so I don't.

"What about the other guy… the first one who came out here?"

"Rob? He runs the front of house normally, although he's also working in the kitchen while Sam's on honeymoon, which means his fiancée, Petra will be coming in to help out for the next ten days." This was all arranged before the wedding, with the agreement of Petra's mum, who has to babysit April. I did say that I would be happy to watch her in the evenings, but Petra wants to stick to their routine, which is fair enough.

"So, when you said you knew of this restaurant, what you actually meant was, you're pretty much related to the owners."

"Well, I suppose so, yes. And I live in the apartment upstairs," I add.

She laughs. "I'm not complaining," she says. "It's really nice in here… but I think I'm gonna have to get you to come out with me. You need to see some more of the town, broaden your horizons beyond your own front yard."

Just the thought of going anywhere without Ed fills me with dread, but I'm saved the necessity of having to reply by Rob bringing out our lunches.

Once we've finished, Rob comes over and takes our plates away, offering us dessert and coffee, both of which we decline. I ask him for the bill, determined not to let Zoe pay for a meal that was essentially my idea, and he shakes his head smiling.

"Get real, Tess," he smirks, and wanders off into the kitchen.

A few moments later, Ed comes back out. The restaurant's quieter now and he pulls up a chair and sits down beside us. "Are you going back to work now?" he asks.

"We'd better. We've already been out for over an hour."

"Okay." He smiles. "I'll see you tonight." He reaches over and takes my hand in his. "Was lunch okay?" he asks.

"Lunch was lovely. But Rob won't give me the bill… I mean check."

He laughs. "Damn right he won't." He stands and pushes the chair back under the table, looking at Zoe now. "It was nice to meet you," he says.

"Likewise," she replies and we both get up too. "I'll wait outside for you," she murmurs to me, giving us as much privacy as the restaurant affords.

"Come with me," Ed whispers once Zoe has gone out the front and, taking my hand again, he pulls me back down the corridor and into the office, which is empty.

"I can't be long," I exclaim as he shuts the door behind us.

"You can be long enough for a kiss," he replies, and covers my mouth with his, pulling me close in his arms and holding me. His tongue parts my lips and I respond in kind as we delve and discover each other. His deep groan tingles across my skin and I moan back my reply, feeling his hands roaming up and down my back.

He pulls away eventually and looks down at me. "Thank you," he murmurs.

"What for?"

"For coming in here; for choosing to be here, rather than anywhere else."

"Of course I was going to choose to be here," I reply, feeling self-conscious.

"Yeah, I know. You don't know any other restaurants." He stops for a moment. "Wait a second. You do know another restaurant. You know the smokehouse."

I pull back from him and open the door just a fraction, getting ready to go. "I know. But you're not at the smokehouse." And with that, I make my escape.

The afternoon hasn't gone a lot better than the morning, as it turns out. Bryan's meeting was cancelled and Zoe spent the last hour of the day in his office, which meant she didn't have time to go through anything with me. When it was time to finish, Zoe still hadn't come out, and I wasn't sure what to do, so I went and knocked on Bryan's door. He called out that I could enter, but when I did, the atmosphere was almost visible. Zoe managed a smile and came out into our office to see what I'd done during the day. She seemed pleased with my efforts and then told me that she and Bryan would be late in tomorrow morning. She offered no explanation and I didn't ask for one. When we went back out into the reception area, I noticed Bryan's office door was closed again and Zoe stood and stared at it for a moment, before coming to her senses and saying goodbye to me.

Riding down in the lift, I can't help wondering if every day is going to be like that. I hope not. I hate awkward atmospheres and strained silences and those two things exist in abundance throughout the office.

The doors open and I step out, and I have to smile. Standing, leaning against the wall opposite the lifts, is Ed. He smiles too and pushes himself upright, walking over to me.

"Hi," he murmurs softly, taking my hand in his.

"Hello." I look up at him as he leads us out onto the street. "Um… what are you doing here?" I ask him. I hadn't expected to see him really this evening – not until he finishes work later on.

"I'm between services," he explains, "so I thought I'd come and meet you."

My smile broadens. "That's really sweet of you."

"How was your first day?" he asks, letting go of my hand and putting his arm around me as we walk.

"To be honest, I'm not sure…" I take the fifteen minutes of our walk back to the restaurant to fill him in on my day – or at least my perceptions of it.

"Sounds like a lot of office politics to me," he says when I've finished.

"Yes. Well, except for Bryan and Zoe. I think they're together."

"Which will be fine as long as they stay together," he remarks.

I hadn't thought about that, but when Ed says it, the consequences of them splitting up are obvious. Bryan's in charge, so if they can't work together, Zoe would be the one to leave, and although I've only known her for a day, I'm not sure I like the thought of working there without her.

When we get back to the restaurant, he lets us in. Petra and Rob are getting ready for the evening service and we say hello to them as we pass through, before going straight upstairs.

"I made you some bolognese sauce," Ed explains when we get into the apartment. "It's simmering on the stove, so all you've gotta do is cook some pasta."

I drop my handbag on the floor, turn to him, reach up and pull him down to kiss him. Our tongues clash and, within an instant, we're both breathless. He takes a pace closer, and so do I, and I hear his deep groan shudder through my body. I've got no idea what's happening to me, or why every kiss seems to be more intense than the last, but I don't want it to stop.

He pulls back eventually and looks down at me. "Is that just for the bolognese?" he asks, smiling.

"It's for being you."

"I guess I'll keep being me then," he replies.

"Please do." He holds my head against his chest and strokes my hair for a while.

"I've been thinking," he murmurs.

"And?"

"And I don't have your cell number."

"My mobile number?" I clarify.

"Yeah."

"Why do you need it? I'm only upstairs."

"Not all day, you're not. You're at your office. I realised after you left this afternoon that I had no way of contacting you, other than to look up your office number and call that."

"Why did you need to contact me?" I ask.

"I wanted to thank you for what you said… about the fact that you chose to come here for lunch because I'm here. That… well, that meant a lot, Tess."

I pull back from him and pick up my handbag, reaching inside for my phone. "What's your number?" I ask him and he reels it off. I add him to my very short contacts list, then type out a message to him. His phone beeps and he pulls it out of his back pocket, looking down at the screen.

I know what he'll be reading and I blush…

— This is my number. I don't know it yet, so keep it safe. Like me. T x

He looks up, his eyes gazing deep into mine for a moment, before he types something into his phone and I feel my own vibrate in my hand, and check the screen. He's sent me a reply.

— I'll always keep you safe. E xx

Even before I can look up, his arms come around me and he holds me close.

And even though I have tears in my eyes, it feels good to be held.

— Have you eaten yet?' E xx

It's nearly eight o'clock and I know Ed must be busy, but this is the third message he's sent me since going downstairs to get ready for the evening service. We both realised before he went down that, because Sam and Ali aren't here, he won't be able to come up and see me. I know he's sending messages to make sure I'm not lonely. I also know I could go down and see him, but he's busy, and having to run the kitchen means he's also very stressed. I don't want to make things worse for him, so I think it's best if I stay up here. Besides, all our things arrived from the UK a couple of days before the wedding, so I've got books to read. Lots of books…

— Yes. Your bolognese is delicious. Thank you. T xx

— It's my mom's recipe, and probably her mom's before that. Don't thank me ;). What are you doing? E xx

— Of course I'm going to thank you. You made me dinner… and lunch for that matter. I'm reading, and drinking coffee, and missing you. T xx

I hold my breath as I press 'send', hoping I don't sound too clingy.

— It's my pleasure to cook for you. Hope it's a good book. I miss you too. E xx

— It's a very good book. It's about Catherine of Aragon. I've had it for ages and not read it yet. T xx

— Sounds interesting. If you're so engrossed, do you still have time to miss me? E xx

— Yes. T xx

The phone goes quiet for a while and I settle down onto the couch and get back to reading, although my mind keeps wandering to Ed's kisses, and the way it feels to be in his arms. It's too distracting and, after a while, I put the book down on the coffee table and close my eyes...

Something tickles my cheek and I flick it away with the back of my hand, returning to my dream... *I'm back down by the lake where Ali and Sam got married, only this time, it's just me and Ed. We're having a picnic on a blanket, and as the sun sets, he takes me in his arms...* This time the tickling is against my lips and I open my eyes to find Ed leaning over me.

"Hello," I whisper.

"Hi."

"Did you just kiss me?" I ask him.

"Yeah. Is that okay?"

"Yes. I just wasn't sure if it was real, or part of my dream."

"You were dreaming?" He kneels down on the floor beside me.

"Yes." I wish I hadn't mentioned it now.

"Was I in the dream?" he asks. I nod my head. "Was it a nice dream?" I nod again and he smiles, and stares at me for a moment.

"What time is it?" I ask, because I don't really want to tell him about my dream – not yet, anyway.

"It's just after eleven-thirty."

"Oh, God. I've been asleep for hours."

"Yeah. I thought you might have nodded off when you didn't reply to my text message."

"You sent me another text message?"

"Yeah... I got busy with an order, but I replied eventually."

"And I didn't get back to you." I feel awful.

"Hey... don't worry about it. I knew you were tired." He gets to his feet and goes into the kitchen. "I'm just gonna have a glass of wine. Do you want anything?" he calls.

"Not wine, no."

"Coffee?" he offers.

"Not at this time of night, no thanks."

"How about I make you a hot chocolate?" he suggests.

"Oh. Yes please." I can't help smiling and he grins across at me.

"Okay. One hot chocolate coming up." I take advantage of his absence to check my phone. There are actually two messages from him. One's timed at eight-forty, and the other at nine-twenty. The first message reads:

— *Well, you won't have to miss me much longer. I'll give you a hug when I get upstairs. E xx*

The second…

— *I guess either that book is more interesting than me, or you've fallen asleep. If it's the book, I guess I'll get over it. If you've fallen asleep, please dream of me. E xx*

I feel a lump rising in my throat, but swallow it down and quickly type out a reply:

— *I did. T xx*

And I press send.

Ed's phone beeps very quietly, but he's busy at the stove and I can't see him from where I am without changing position, so I wait… and wait.

Eventually, he comes over, a glass of red wine in one hand, and a large mug of hot chocolate in the other. It's topped with whipped cream, with chocolate flakes and mini marshmallows on top.

"That's a serious hot chocolate," I say as he puts it down on the table in front of me, together with his wine.

"Was it a serious dream?" he asks, sitting down beside me.

"Not serious, no."

"Okay. But I was in it?"

"Yes."

"Did I have a starring role, or was I just an extra?"

I chuckle. "You had the starring role," I reply.

He leans back and looks down at me. "Good," he whispers, then he pulls back and hands me my hot chocolate. "I guess you'd better drink this," he says, "before it gets cold." He doesn't move away, but sits us both back into the couch with our drinks, his arm tucked around me.

I take a sip and taste the rich chocolatey, creamy drink he's made for me. "Wow. That really is a serious hot chocolate," I say and he smirks. "What?" I ask him.

"You have no idea how much I want to lick your lips right now," he says.

"You… you want to lick my lips." I do so myself and he closes his eyes just for a second, letting out a very slight groan. "Oh. I see… because they're covered in cream." I lick them again to make sure I'm clean.

"Not entirely, no." He leans closer. "I'd wanna lick them anyway – even without the cream."

I can't help the tiny gasp that escapes my lips and he gazes into my eyes for a full minute before pulling away and taking a sip of his wine. God, I wish he'd kiss me.

"Did you manage to pick up some clothes earlier?" I ask him, to take my mind off the way my thoughts are turning.

"Yeah. I put them in my old room before I came and picked you up from work," he explains.

"And how's it been today?" I ask, remembering what he told me about the last time Sam went away.

"Okay," he replies.

"You were… alright?" I ask, and he turns to look at me, seemingly confused. "You said you weren't well when Sam went away last time," I explain, although I don't want to focus too much on it, if he doesn't want to. And I wonder if I should have kept quiet.

"Oh, I see what you mean," he says. "No, I was fine today, thanks."

"That's good."

"Yeah. I thought I'd be sick with fear again, but all I thought about, while I was doing the prep and getting everything organised, was you and how your day was going. And then you came in at lunchtime, and although I'd had a few nervous moments right after we opened, just seeing you made everything better." He smiles. "And then I saw you again this afternoon…" He stops and looks at me. "It's having you in my life that makes the difference, Tess," he says slowly.

"I'm sure you could talk to Rob about it," I suggest, feeling embarrassed. "You must've spoken to him before, when Sam came to England to find Ali."

He shakes his head. "No. I kept it to myself. Rob was distracted by Petra at the time."

"He'd have made time for you." Surely he must know that.

"Yeah, I'm sure he would. But I didn't wanna talk about it. I was ashamed at not being able to cope and I didn't want him to know. We spent our whole childhoods sharing everything. And I didn't wanna share that… I'd probably have told Sam, if he'd been here…" He leaves the sentence unfinished, because obviously Sam wasn't here, and that was the problem in the first place.

"Did your whole family used to live here?" I ask him, picking up on the fact the he and Rob shared so much, and trying to change the subject, for his benefit, more than mine.

"Yep. Mom and Dad had the room that's now Sam and Ali's; Sam had the room that you're in and Rob and I shared. Like I said, being twins, sharing was kinda expected."

"It must've been a tight squeeze," I say.

He chuckles. "Let's just say it was real hard to keep anything secret."

"That must make you value your space."

"I guess… Mom and Dad retired about five or six years ago and moved to Florida and, for a few months, Sam, Rob and I lived here together. Obviously we moved the rooms around, and we had more space, but then Rob and I decided to get our own place."

"Because of Sam's first wife?" I ask, remembering his conversation with Sam about this.

"Yeah. Sam was about to marry Amber," he explains simply. "Rob and I didn't really like her. Actually Rob hated her, but then…" He stops talking suddenly and looks away.

"What's wrong?" I ask him.

"It's nothing." He turns back to face me, but I can tell something's troubling him.

"It's not nothing, Ed."

He smiles. "No, it's not. It's just something Rob and I don't talk about."

"Oh. I'm sorry, I didn't mean to pry…"

He reaches over and touches my cheek with his fingertips. "You're not prying."

"You don't have to tell me," I say quietly.

"Yeah, I do. I don't want there to be any secrets between us." He sighs. "The thing is, if I tell you, you have to promise not to say anything to anyone else – especially not to Ali, because Rob would be real mad if Sam ever found out."

"Okay."

He takes a deep breath, and another sip of wine, then looks at me. "About a week before Sam and Amber got married, Amber went over to our apartment – the one Rob and I had just bought – and she came onto him."

"She... she what?"

"She offered to have sex with him – quite blatantly."

I have a feeling my mouth is open and I know I'm staring at him. He's still looking at me, and I've got to find a response of some kind. "What happened?" I ask eventually.

"Nothing. Rob threw her out, and when I got home, he told me about it, and then the following weekend, we came over here and tried to talk Sam out of getting married. Rob and he almost got into a fight about it, but Rob was adamant about not telling him."

"Why? Surely if he'd realised what she was like…"

"He needed to find that out for himself," Ed explains. "Sam isn't the kind of guy you can just talk into or out of something. He's way too stubborn for that."

"And you've never told him since?"

"God no. He'd be so offended to think his ex-wife had done that."

"Did she ever try anything with you?" I ask him, almost fearful of the answer.

He smiles. "No. Rob's reputation went before him. I guess Amber thought he wouldn't be able to resist, but even Rob has his limits."

I take a long drink of my hot chocolate and think over what he's just told me. That would be like me trying something with Sam, or Ali with Ed. I can't imagine either of us ever doing anything like that. Ever.

"Do you like Ali?" I ask him, although I'm not entirely sure where the question came from.

"Of course. She makes Sam happy – she's part of the family now, like the sister we never had."

That lump is back in my throat, but I don't want him to see how upset I am, because then I'd have to explain it.

"It's late," I say instead. "I'd better go to bed."

"Yeah. You've got work tomorrow." He puts down his empty wine glass and helps me to my feet.

"Shouldn't we clear up?" I ask.

"It's fine. I'll do it in the morning." He flicks off the lights.

"Thank you for the spectacular hot chocolate," I say as he leads me down the hallway to my bedroom.

"You're welcome," he replies.

I open the door to my room and turn back to face him. "Goodnight," I murmur.

"Goodnight, Tess." His voice is quiet, his eyes still fixed on mine. I go to pull my hand away, but he holds on fast, moving closer, and leaning down to kiss me, his lips soft and gentle against mine. Our tongues meet and he pushes me back gently against the door frame, and I'm sure I can feel something hard pressing into my hip... Before I have time to process that thought, he pulls back and gazes down at me, his fingers caressing my cheek.

"I want you so much," he whispers, his voice filled with emotion, and I gulp down my own. "But I'll wait," he adds quickly. "I'll wait as long as you need me to... until you're ready. I—I just want you to know though... I'm falling for you, Tess."

Before I can reply, he lets me go and turns around, opening his bedroom door and going inside, then closing it quietly behind him.

Inside my own room, I sit on the edge of the bed, thinking over what he just said. He's falling for me... Well, that's good, because I'm pretty sure I'm falling for him too. And he wants me. I have no idea what that entails. But I know that the ache deep inside me means something, and that only Ed can make it go away. So, I guess that probably means I want him too. He said he'll wait until I'm ready, but how will I know when that is? Will there be a sign? Or will I have to work it out? I wish I knew the answers...

I slowly get undressed, put on my pyjamas and climb into bed, settling into the soft pillows.

My dreams are strange and short-lived, and I wake between each of them, feeling distressed and uncertain. I keep imagining Ed and I together, but then we're apart, and he's with with Ali and Sam, and Rob, Petra and April, telling me they're a family now, and I'm excluded, on the outside. It's disturbing, upsetting and, on a couple of occasions, when I wake up, I'm already crying, wondering if I'm really as alone as I feel.

My alarm goes off at six-thirty, but I feel as though I've hardly slept. Well, I suppose I haven't, or at least I haven't very much, in between all those dreams. I put on my robe and go through to the bathroom, showering quickly, then coming back to my room, drying my hair and getting dressed.

When I go out into the living room, Ed's in the kitchen, preparing breakfast.

"Good morning," I say.

"Hi," he replies. "Did you sleep okay?"

"Yes, thanks," I lie, because I don't want to explain my dreams, not while he's pre-occupied with cooking.

He looks at me for a moment, then turns away, whisking something in a bowl. He's making scrambled eggs, which he serves up, together with toast and coffee and we eat in an uncomfortable silence. Even if I wanted to explain my dreams, I'm not sure I could now. There's something very different about him this morning. I just don't know what it is.

"Is everything okay?" I ask him as I finish my meal.

"Yeah. Everything's fine," he replies, although it clearly isn't and I wonder if he's regretting what he said last night, whether it was a heat of the moment thing that he didn't mean to say. And whether I really am on the outside…

"I'd better get ready for work."

He starts to clear the plates. "I'll walk you," he says.

"It's fine. You don't have to."

He turns to look at me. "I want to."

I shrug. "Okay."

What happened to us?

Was there even an 'us'? Or was that just a dream too?

It's only when I get into the office that I remember Zoe told me that she and Bryan would be in late this morning. She didn't say how late though and, after the first fifteen minutes, I realise the consequences of this. I'm having to field all the queries from Brittany, Mel and Taylor, who seem incapable of dealing with anything by themselves. By ten-thirty, I'm stressed and fed up, and in need of coffee. I'm in the outer office, doing some photocopying, when the door opens and Zoe walks in, followed by Bryan. Neither of them speaks, and they both head into their separate offices. Zoe leaves our door open, but Bryan slams his shut.

I finish what I'm doing and go back into the office I share with Zoe, sitting down at my desk.

"Is everything okay?" I ask her.

"Yeah," she replies, forcing a smile. "We had a meeting this morning. It didn't go quite to plan."

"Oh. I see."

"I'll get the coffee, shall I?" The false cheerfulness in her voice lets me know she's not telling me the truth, but I don't know her well enough to ask anything more.

And besides, I've got problems of my own. I'm still trying to work out why Ed was so different this morning; why he barely said two words to me; why he didn't kiss me goodbye when he dropped me off, and what I've done wrong.

Ed

I'm standing in the kitchen of Sam's apartment, whipping some cream and staring into space. I've had a bitch of an evening. Actually, I've had a bitch of a day, if I'm being honest. Literally everything I've done all day has gone wrong. I know why. I've spent the whole day wondering whether I went too far with Tess last night. Was it too much to tell her I want her, and that I'm falling for her? And how would she react if she knew that was a lie? I'm not falling for her at all… I'm completely in love with her.

I walked her to work, and I picked her up this evening, but our conversations have been stilted and fairly monosyllabic and, compared to previous days we've spent together, I feel like we've taken such a backward step. It's all my fault, I just need to work out what to say to her to make it right again.

I spoon the cream over the top of her hot chocolate and take it through to the living room, putting it down on the table in front of her, and placing my wine beside it. If only finding words was as easy as whipping cream…

"Ed?" she says, as I sit.

"Yeah?" I turn to look at her, the sadness in her eyes catching me unawares.

"Can I ask you something?"

"Sure."

"What did I do wrong?" she asks. "I mean… why was everything so different this morning? And this afternoon? Didn't you mean the things you said to me last night?" Her voice cracks and I move closer to her and pull her into my arms, and then take the plunge and lift her onto my lap, holding her close to me.

"Oh, Tess," I whisper. "I'm so sorry."

She struggles against me.

"Where are you going?" I say, keeping hold of her and looking down into her face.

"You don't want me," she says, an edge of defiance in her voice.

"I *do* want you. I want you so much I ache." She stops and looks up at me. "That's what I'm saying sorry for. I'm sorry for making you feel like that. I'm sorry you felt you'd done something wrong. I'm sorry I made things seem different between us."

"I don't understand," she says, leaning into me.

"I didn't sleep very well," I tell her, starting my explanation. "Because I was worrying."

"Why?" She sounds wary again.

"Because of what I'd said to you."

"So you didn't mean it?"

"Yeah, I did. But I don't want you to feel obligated to me, in any way. This is your home now, Tess, not mine, and I don't want you to feel awkward here."

"I don't. Well, I didn't." She takes a breath. "I—I feel the same way as you do," she whispers, and for a moment, I can't do a damned thing, except stare at her. She stares back and eventually the uncertainty in her eyes brings me back to my senses.

"You want me?" I ask, just to be sure. She nods her head. "And you're falling for me?" She nods again.

"Yes I am," she says, making certain I've understood, I guess.

Cupping her face with my hands, I lean in and kiss her deeply, pouring everything I've got into the connection, letting her feel my love, even though it's still silent.

I break the kiss, but only because I have to, and hold her in my arms. She leans back and looks up at me, smiling and kinda satisfied.

"Why did you lie to me, Tess?" I ask her, fearful of spoiling the moment, even though I have to know the answer to my question.

She sits up abruptly. "I didn't lie to you," she says, going defensive on me.

"Yeah, you did. This morning… I asked you if you'd slept well last night, and you said you had. That was a lie, wasn't it?"

"How do you know?" she asks, confirming my fears.

"I just do. Now, why did you lie to me?"

She looks down at her hands, clenching her fists nervously and, using my free hand, I clasp them, holding them tight. She gazes up at me again. "I had some horrible dreams," she explains. "They kept me awake, but because you were different this morning, I didn't feel like I could tell you."

"Then I'm sorry for that too. I really don't like the idea that I made you feel too uncomfortable to speak to me."

"It doesn't matter."

"Yeah, it does. Do you wanna tell me about them now?"

She stares at me for a moment, then looks over my shoulder, avoiding eye contact. "You were with your family," she says quietly. "With Sam and Rob, and Ali, and Petra and April."

"And where were you?" I ask her.

"I was on the outside. You wouldn't let me in."

"*I* wouldn't?"

"Well, none of you would."

Even though she's not looking at me, her eyes are glistening with unshed tears and I pull her close into my arms, holding her against me.

"It was just a dream, babe," I murmur. "You're never gonna be on the outside. I'll never let that happen." I pull back just a little and brush my lips gently over hers. I so want to tell her I'm in love with her and, as I break the kiss, I open my mouth to utter the words I hope will give her the reassurance she craves.

"I—"

"Ed," she interrupts.

"Um… yeah?"

"Why did you just call me 'babe'?" she asks and I have to smile, even though my moment to say 'I love you' for the first time has just been stolen, albeit by a really cute question.

"It's a term of affection, endearment. Kinda like 'darling' or 'honey'… but maybe a little more American than you're used to."

She chuckles and buries her head on my chest. "I'm not used to anything," she says, and I decide to take the chance and bring up the other thing that was plaguing me during the night, and most of today…

"Tess," I say, leaning back and placing my finger under her chin, raising her face to mine. "I get that you're inexperienced, and we don't have to do anything you don't want to—"

"How do you know that?" she interrupts again, blushing bright red.

"That you're inexperienced? It's kinda obvious." Her blush deepens, if that were possible, and within the blink of an eye, she's broken free of me, scrambled off of my lap and bolted down the hallway. I don't hesitate, and jump up off the couch, running after her, and reaching her door just as she's about to close it. "Hey," I say, putting my hand up against it to stop her. "What's wrong?"

I push the door open and that's when I see the tears falling down her cheeks.

"Tess. Don't cry. Please." I step into her room and pull her into my arms again. "Tell me why you ran, and why you're crying."

She shakes her head, but doesn't try and pull away from me, which is a blessed relief.

"Is it because you're embarrassed?" I guess. She shrugs, so I suppose that could be part of it. "There's nothing wrong with being a virgin," I point out and she leans back at last, looking up at me. "I like the fact that, when the time comes, I'll be your first," I tell her, with total honesty. I'd like to add that I want to be her 'only' too, but now probably isn't the time for that.

"It's more than that," she says.

"More than what?"

Her eyes drop to my chest and she focuses them there. "You say my inexperience is obvious, but I—I'm more than just inexperienced," she whispers. "You're the first man who's ever kissed me. No-one has ever touched me… I've never done anything… anything at all."

I stare at her for a moment, and I guess it's maybe a moment too long, because she pulls away from me again.

"Whoa… stop. Where are you going now?"

She doesn't look up, but just murmurs, "It's fine Ed. You don't have to be with me."

"Yeah, I do." She looks up, her eyes almost overflowing with tears. "I really do. I want you, Tess. I want you so much."

"Then why did you hesitate?" she asks, quite reasonably.

"I don't know. I guess I was trying to work out how on earth someone who looks as good as you do has never been kissed."

She looks down once more and when she replies, I have to step closer to hear her. "I suppose with everything that's happened in my life, I've just kind of hidden myself away. I've never wanted to be with anyone… until now." She raises her eyes to mine as she says those last two words and I close the gap between us and take her in my arms again.

"We can take it slow," I whisper. "There's no rush to do anything. We'll go at your pace, and I won't do anything you don't want me to."

She keeps her eyes fixed on mine. "That's lovely," she says, "and I am grateful, but the thing is, I don't know what I want you to do. I've got no idea what's involved."

"None at all?" I can't hide my surprise and she leans back in my arms, although I don't think she's trying to get away this time.

"Well, I understand what goes where," she clarifies quietly. "Ali explained that to me when my periods started. But that was really just a glorified biology lesson. I—I've got no idea about anything else you might want to do." She pauses for a moment and places her hands on my biceps, letting them rest there. "I get the impression from some of the things Ali's said since she got together with Sam, and from a few things I've overheard between them, that they do quite a lot… but I'm not sure what, or whether I want to do any of that."

I have to smile at her. She's so damn adorable. "It's okay," I say, pulling her real close to me. "Just because Sam and Ali might do certain things together, in certain ways, that doesn't mean we have to."

"So you and I… we'd just make love?" she says, with breathtaking candor.

"Well, no. At least, I hope not. There are all kinds of things we can do that lead up to making love, and there are lots of ways of making love. We can do them all. We can do whatever we want – in our own way. And I can show you how good it can be. You mustn't worry about what other people do, or think. What we do, and how we do it is entirely up to us; it's for us to know and experience together."

She smiles, sweetly and rests her head against my chest. "I feel so safe with you," she murmurs.

"Good. I like that." I stroke her hair gently. "I want you to understand you can talk to me about anything, Tess. Anything at all. I'm here for you."

"I know." She looks up at me. "I know that."

"And one day soon, when you're ready, I will make love to you."

"How will I know I'm ready?" she asks, enquiringly.

"I'll know. Trust me, babe."

She smiles, like she's relieved, and whispers, "I do."

Her scream wakes me, and I'm out of bed in an instant, bolting across the hallway and through her bedroom door, without bothering to knock. She's crying softly now, muttering incoherently between sobs and I know that she's still asleep, her mind somewhere else… somewhere terrifying.

"Tess," I whisper. She weeps a little louder. "Tess," I say again, adding a little volume to my voice. She shakes her head violently from side to side, thrashing in the bed, and I kneel up beside her and grab her shoulders, saying her name once more, and this time her eyes open.

"Ed?" She seems confused and stares at my bare chest for a moment, before moving her eyes up to my face.

"Yes, babe. You were dreaming." I let her go, feeling the need to make it clear that I'm not kneeling half-naked on her bed, for any reason other than to help her.

"Yes," she murmurs and sinks back onto the pillows. "It was awful."

I sit down right beside her, on the edge of the bed. "Do you want to talk about it?"

"Not really," she replies. "It wasn't that different to the normal dream. Just the fire, the noise, feeling alone."

I reach over and touch her arm. "You're not alone," I tell her and she manages a smile.

"Do you want anything?" I ask her. "A drink of water? A glass of milk?"

She shakes her head. "No. I'll be fine."

"Sure?"

"Yes. You need to get some sleep," she adds. "I know how hard it is to deal with broken nights."

"Don't worry about that," I reply. "If there's something you need, then tell me."

She looks up at me. "Could I have a hug?" she asks, and I smile.

"Of course you can."

I'm not sure whether she wants me to lie down with her, but she answers the question by sitting up and holding out her arms to me, and I pull her close, holding her tense body against my chest and stroking her hair until I feel her relax a little.

"Better?" I ask, leaning back and looking down at her.

"Yes, much," she says, yawning.

I smile. "Try and get back to sleep. And dream of happy things this time." I wonder if I should give her some ideas to help her along, and I get to my feet and pull the covers up, then lean over and kiss her forehead. "Dream of the beach by your house," I tell her.

She looks up at me, her hair fanned across the pillow. "I was going to try and dream of you," she replies and I feel my heart swell. "Like I did the other evening. You and I on a picnic together."

"Okay. You and I, on a picnic together, on your beach," I suggest, and kiss her again, this time on the lips, just briefly. "Sounds perfect."

"Hmm," she murmurs all sleepy now. "It does."

I go over to the door and watch her for a few minutes, until I hear her breathing change, and then I go back to my own room, leaving both of our doors open, so I can hear her next time, before she starts to scream. I'd rather lose hours of sleep than have her go through that again.

Chapter Nine

Tess

After Ed hugged me and I went back to sleep, I managed to get through to just before six-fifteen before I woke up again. That was nearly four straight hours of sleep, which is almost unheard of for me.

I have to admit, there was part of me that wanted to ask him to stay with me last night, and not just for the reassurance of his presence. It was hard not to notice how good he looked in just a pair of shorts, and I enjoyed being hugged by him like that, but more than anything I felt grateful to him for caring so much. And he did care; that much was obvious.

I thanked him this morning over breakfast, and of course, he told me not to. He also explained that he'd left our doors open so he could hear me if I needed him, which I thought was very sweet of him. Just knowing he's there, that I can go to him, and talk to him is such a weight off my mind.

Today has been another weird one. Bryan spent most of it shut away in his office, shunning everyone, including Zoe, who seemed equally withdrawn. I wondered if they'd had an argument, and contemplated asking her, but decided against getting involved. It's awkward. I took lunch in with me today, which Ed made for me, and discovered that Zoe had done the same thing, so we sat together and talked. She told me she's actually from Chicago and moved here about three years ago after she broke up with her fiancé. She wanted a change of scene, and found it here. She explains that she's an only child and misses her parents, but travels back home to see them whenever she can. I picked up on the fact that she still thinks of Chicago as home, which gave me some reassurance about my own homesickness. After three years, she's still not completely settled, but she's getting on with life. And if she can do it, I guess I can too. I can at least try.

I've almost finished the research on the file she gave me on Monday, and at the end of the day, I let her know I should have it completed tomorrow. She seems pleased and I leave, going down in the lift, to find Ed waiting for me in the lobby.

He pushes himself off the wall, comes over and takes me in his arms, kissing me.

"What was that for?" I ask him, when he breaks the kiss and leans back.

"I've missed you today," he says.

"Hmm. I've missed you too." I look up at him as he takes my hand and leads me out onto the street.

"I've made you some dinner," he explains as we walk back to the restaurant.

"I can cook, you know."

"Yeah. But you've been working all day."

"As have you."

"Well, I finished about two hours ago. I've gotta do something to fill in the time. And I like that something to revolve around you." He looks down at me and squeezes my hand.

"I wish we could eat together."

He stares at me.

"We could, I guess," he replies. "I usually grab something just before we open, but there's no reason why I can't have dinner before I go downstairs, as long as you don't mind eating really early."

I shake my head. "No. I don't mind."

He smiles. "Okay then. I'll eat with you."

"And what are we having?" I ask, grinning up at him.

"Tonight, we're gonna be having Beef Braciole."

"And what's that when it's at home?"

His smile broadens. "It's thin slices of beef wrapped around prosciutto, cheese, herbs, beans and garlic, cooked really slowly in a rich tomato sauce."

"Sounds delicious."

"I left it cooking, thinking you'd just help yourself later, but it won't hurt to eat it when we get back."

"Good." I hesitate for a moment. "And you'll be up later?"

"Of course."

Over the next few nights, we let ourselves get into a really comfortable routine. Ed makes something amazing for dinner, comes and picks me up from work and we eat together – albeit slightly rushed – then he goes down to the kitchen and I settle down to read, or watch a movie, quite often falling asleep by the time he gets back upstairs again. He then makes me a hot chocolate and we sit for a while, holding each other, kissing, talking, discussing our days, before going to bed.

I've woken up every night, having the same nightmare as usual. Ed's come in and sat with me for a while each time, giving me hugs, drying my tears, and reassuring me that everything is okay, before going back to bed. I feel guilty for disturbing his sleep, but he says he doesn't mind.

Saturday is quite hard for me, because Ed has to work, and I don't. So I spend the day cleaning the flat, changing the sheets, doing the laundry and keeping busy. Ed sends me regular texts to make sure I'm okay, and spends his break with me, sitting on the couch, kissing. By the time he's ready to go downstairs again, I'm fairly sure I'm ready for more than kissing, and I think he is too and we're both reluctant to part. Because we've been sidetracked, we've forgotten to eat, and although I tell him I'll get something for myself, he says he'll deal with it and, about an hour later, he runs up the stairs, carrying a tray.

"What's that?" I ask him.

"Your dinner."

"You made me dinner?"

"Of course. I told you I'd deal with it." He smiles at me, putting the tray down on the table. "This is one of Sam's new specialities. It's salmon with a black garlic, liquorice and herb crust."

"Liquorice?" I query.

"Sounds weird, but it works," he reassures me. "I can't stop." He stares at me for a moment. "But I wish I could." He leans down and gives me a very quick, very intense kiss and then disappears again.

When I've finished eating, I send him a text.

— *You were right, the liquorice works. Thank you for dinner. T xx*

— *It's not me who's right, it's Sam. And you're welcome. Anytime. I miss you, babe. E xx*

— *I miss you too. T xx*

— *I'll be back soon. E xx*

— *Can't wait. T xx*

I switch on the TV and select a movie to watch, deciding that *Mission Impossible* should keep me entertained, and if Ed isn't back by the end of it, I can just move onto the second one.

"Wake up, sleepyhead," he whispers, his breath brushing across my cheek.

I open my eyes and smile. "Sorry. I keep falling asleep."

"It's okay," he replies. "It means you can stay up a bit later with me."

He's already made my hot chocolate and it's on the table, next to his glass of wine. He sits beside me and pulls me into his arms, placing his finger beneath my chin and raising my face to his.

"I missed you so much today," he murmurs as he presses his lips to mine, and our tongues meet. I reach up holding his head still and close, kissing him back as I feel his hand move beneath my t-shirt, his fingers caressing my skin. I suck in a breath and shift closer, letting him know I like what he's doing, and his hand moves higher until he's touching my breast through the thin lace of my bra. His fingers tweak my nipple, just once and I feel a tingling between my legs that makes me squirm in my seat and breathe more heavily into him, moaning out my pleasure. As I move closer, I feel a dampness between my legs. Actually, it's not a dampness at all... I'm soaking. What on earth is going on?

I pull back from him. "What's wrong?" he asks. "Do you want me to stop?"

"Um… I don't know."

"Then tell me what's wrong," he suggests. "Let me see if I can help."

I hesitate for a moment, and then look up at him. "I don't know how to tell you."

"Just tell me. You know you can say anything to me."

He's right. I can. "I—I feel like I'm wet," I mutter.

"Right." He takes it in his stride, like he's expecting me to say more. "Well… is that normal?"

He smiles, leans down and kisses me gently. "Yeah, babe. That's normal."

"When I say 'wet', I mean *really* wet. It's not just my knickers that are wet, I think my jeans must be too."

"That's okay," he says.

"It is?"

"Yeah. In fact, it's more than okay." He smiles.

"Why am I so wet?" I ask him, still feeling confused.

"Because you're aroused."

"Oh." Now I'm blushing, as well as feeling confused.

"And please don't be embarrassed. You weren't a moment ago when you asked the question."

"Yeah, because I didn't know why then. Now I do…"

"And? I think it's great that you're enjoying what we're doing, and that you're wet for me."

"I think 'soaking' would be a better word." I reply, tying to make light of things.

He chuckles. "Soaking is even better," he murmurs.

I look up at him again. "I am enjoying what we're doing," I confirm, smiling again. "And that's definitely why I'm wet?"

"Yeah. You're wet because you're turned on. If we were gonna make love, you'd need to be lubricated. It's just your body getting ready for that. It's kinda like me getting hard."

"Hard?"

"Yeah. Getting an erection."

"Oh." I keep my eyes fixed on his. "Are you hard now?" I ask, because I want to know whether it's just me who was finding our kissing exciting.

"As nails," he replies, grinning again.

"Oh," I whisper.

"That doesn't mean we have to do anything," he adds quickly.

"But what happens if we don't do anything?"

"Well, I don't stay hard forever," he says, leaning down and kissing me. "Although sometimes it feels like it, when I'm around you."

I giggle, and try not to blush this time. "So it just goes away?"

"Eventually, yeah. I'll probably have to wait a while… and I'll have to be in a different room to you… or maybe a different state."

I laugh. "So this is totally normal?"

"Completely." He moves closer. "So, you definitely liked what we were doing?"

I nod my head.

"Good," he replies. "Maybe tomorrow we'll do it again."

"Tomorrow? Why not now?"

He laughs. "Because it's late."

"And neither of us has to work tomorrow," I reason.

He chuckles. "No, we don't, but I forgot to tell you, Rob's invited us over to Petra's place tomorrow."

"He has?"

"Yeah. They're having a barbecue."

"Just them?" I hope there won't be a crowd of people; I'd hate that.

"Just them, and Petra's mom, and her boyfriend," he says. "I wouldn't have agreed if there were going to be lots of people there. I know you wouldn't like that.

I nod. "Thank you."

"Don't thank me," he says, kissing me gently. "But, I'm afraid we need to get to bed, although we'll get some time to ourselves tomorrow, I'm sure."

"I really hope so," I murmur, as he helps me to my feet.

"You liked it that much?" he whispers.

"Yes, I did."

So far this morning, Ed and I have done nothing but kiss… well, we've both managed to shower and get dressed – separately – but other than that and eating breakfast, all we've done is kiss.

We're lying down, side by side on the couch, our arms around each other, and his legs wrapped around mine, so I'm cocooned in him.

"You can touch me, you know," I say to him, almost out of frustration that he's keeping his hands to himself today.

"I know," he smiles. "But if we start down that route now, I doubt we'll get to Petra's anytime this year."

I smirk. "Personally, I always thought barbecues were overrated."

He laughs. "Yeah. Me too." He checks his watch. "But unfortunately, it's time to get ready to leave."

I pout and he kisses my bottom lip, biting it gently, which causes a distinct tingling between my legs.

"Do you have any idea how sexy you are?" he asks.

"I'm not even remotely sexy," I tell him as he gets up and pulls me to my feet.

"Um… yeah, you are." He stands back a little. "What's more, I can prove it."

"You can? How?"

He stares at me for a moment. "Don't be scared," he whispers. "Give me your hand."

"What am I going to be scared of?" I ask.

"You might not be," he replies. "I'm just warning you." He takes my offered right hand in his and lowers it to the front of his jeans, placing it there, so I can feel his erection through the denim. Then he pulls his own hand away, giving me the choice whether to remove my own hand, or leave it where he put it. I choose the latter and run my fingers gently along his length. He sighs.

"It's big," I say without thinking.

He smirks, and says, "Why, thanks," with a nonchalant air.

"No, I mean… well, it's very long. And it seems quite thick. Not that I've got anything to base that assumption on, of course. Is it uncomfortable, having it squished up in your jeans?" I ask him.

"Yeah. Right now it is," he says, smiling at me.

"You don't look unduly upset by that," I remark.

"That's because you're touching me," he replies.

"And that feels good?"

"That feels great," he says, and as I rub my hand back along him, his erection twitches and I jump, pulling my hand away.

"What did I do?" I ask.

"You didn't do anything," he replies, chuckling. "That just happens."

"So, I didn't hurt you?"

"No, babe. You didn't hurt me." He leans down and kisses me. "But if we're gonna get out of here anytime today, we'd better stop this and get ready."

"I am ready… apart from finding my shoes, which I think are in my room."

"Yeah. I need to change my shirt," he says.

"You do? What's wrong with wearing a t-shirt?"

"It's not long enough," he replies, going toward his bedroom. I follow, feeling confused.

"I don't understand."

He leaves the door open and I stand, watching as he pulls his t-shirt over his head. I've seen him topless a few times now, but that's always been at night, when he comes into my room to help me through my nightmares. I've obviously been aware of how muscular he is, but this is the first time I've seen him in broad daylight, and I can't help but admire him. His chest and stomach are solid muscle, all rippling and firm, covered with just a dappling of dark hair. His shoulders are broad, his arms strong and toned. I'm staring – I can't help it.

"You're gonna be with me," he explains, going to his bag in the corner of the room and pulling out a white shirt. "I need to wear something longer, and on the outside of my jeans, to hide the fact that I've got an erection."

"Oh." I can feel myself blushing again and become even more aware that I'm visually feasting on him. "Sorry… I'll let you get on."

He comes over quickly and grabs my hand. "Don't go," he says. "I like having you here. I like you watching me. Especially as it turns you on." He shrugs the shirt on and stands in front of me buttoning it up.

"How can you tell?" I'm not denying it, but I'm intrigued as to how he knows.

"Because you were biting your bottom lip, and there was something in your eyes… in the way you were looking at me."

"Oh… I'm that transparent, am I?"

"Yeah, but who cares?" he laughs.

The barbecue is fun. Petra's mum is called Thea and her boyfriend is David. He seems like a really nice man and they're obviously very happy together. They laugh and smile a lot, and hold hands all the time, and David's really good with April too.

I've spent a lot of the day talking with Petra about all kinds of things, from Rob, to Ali and Sam, the restaurant, her work, my work, London, and Greece. I've also been playing with April… and watching Ed, who's been cooking with Rob and David. There's something about barbecues that makes men want to cook, even if they normally don't, although I think Ed and Rob would have cooked anyway.

Watching Ed has reminded me of how great the last few days have been with him, how close we've become and how happy I am, which in turn makes me recall that everything could soon come crashing down around us. Sam and Ali are coming back on Tuesday and, although I know Rob and Ed are looking forward to it, I'm dreading it. That sounds odd, I know, because you'd expect me to be thrilled that my sister's coming back, and I am. But I'm also scared, because I've got a horrible feeling that they'll want Ed to move out again and, if I'm being honest, that's the last thing I want. I've got used to having him around. I might still have my nightmares, but I sleep better with him near to me, that's for sure. It's more than that though. He's become my first best friend over the last few days. I know I can tell him anything and everything. We laugh a lot, we talk a lot and he's never phased or bothered by anything I tell him, no matter how bizarre. He lets me ask him really random questions; he lets me rant about work; he lets me share my hopes, my dreams and my nightmares. He holds me when I'm scared, dries my tears when I'm sad, and laughs with me when I'm happy. He's become my world, and I don't want him to go.

Because I'm in love with him.

We've had such a good time with Rob and Petra and their family that we don't get in until nearly midnight.

"It's late," Ed says quietly, letting us into the flat.

"Yes, it is."

"It's much later than I thought it would be."

"I've had a lovely day though," I tell him.

"Good," he says. "I'm glad you enjoyed it… But I guess we should probably go to bed."

I feel a little deflated at that thought, but I can't deny he's right. We've both got to work tomorrow. "Yes, I suppose so."

He leans down and kisses me gently, then pulls back, before leading me down the hallway to my room.

"Don't you want to kiss a bit more?" I ask him.

He smiles and moves me backwards, until I'm up against the wall beside my door. "Oh God, yeah," he says. "I wanna kiss you a lot more." He runs his fingertips down my cheek and I sigh into him. "But if we start something, I'm not sure I'm gonna be able to stop."

"Oh."

"And we're both tired," he adds.

I nod.

"So, we'd better say goodnight… for tonight."

"Okay." I'm reluctant and so is he, and he kisses me once more.

"God, I wanna stay with you," he murmurs.

I rest my forehead against his. "I wish you would," I whisper.

"I wanna hold you while you sleep, and be the first thing you see when you wake up," he continues.

"Hmm."

He pulls away, putting a little distance between us.

"See you in the morning, Tess," he says softly, and turns towards his own room. As he gets to the door, he looks back. "Please don't just stand there looking like that," he murmurs.

"Like what?"

He sighs. "Like you want me to hold you while you sleep, and be the first thing you see when you wake up."

"Even if I do?" His eyes close for a moment. "I mean... would it hurt?" I ask him, and he opens his eyes again and, even in the dim light out here, I'd swear they've darkened.

"No," he replies. "But I think I'd find it real hard not to make love to you, and I don't want our first time – your first time – to be rushed because we're thinking about getting up tomorrow. I wanna take my time with you."

"Oh." I stare at him for a moment. "That sounds perfect."

"Then we'll say goodnight... And we'll miss each other," he adds, and my heart swells with love for him.

Saying goodbye to Ed when he drops me at work on a cloudless Monday morning is nearly as hard as it was to let him go last night.

"I'll pick you up this afternoon," he says, leaning down and kissing me gently.

"I'm counting the hours already."

"I'm sure you'll have a good day in between," he replies.

I roll my eyes. "Somehow I doubt that."

"Well, try and enjoy the work, if nothing else."

I've told him over the course of the week how much I despise the office politics and bitchiness at work, and having such a lovely weekend with him and his family has made me realise how little I enjoy my job.

Luckily, everyone seems in a slightly better mood today. Bryan's actually smiling and whatever differences he had with Zoe last week seem to have been overcome – so maybe they had a good weekend too. Zoe and I are busy. I've finished the research on the project she gave me and she's given me another one to work on, while she writes up my notes. This seems a little odd to me, because she has to keep asking me questions, and I'm sure it would be easier if I could write my own articles, but I suppose I have to learn their ways, and prove myself first...

Just after lunch, which I have with Zoe again, I get an email on my phone, which stops me in my tracks. It's from Miles Kingston, our solicitor in London. He's getting in touch with me because he knows Ali's on her honeymoon, but he's got some urgent matters that need to be dealt with. I guess he doesn't realise that she's coming back tomorrow… Our flat in London has been sold to a cash buyer, and the money came through last week. He needs to know what we want to have done with our shares of the proceeds. But, more importantly, he wants to know what we want to do about Waterside. The house has had several viewings, but no offers. The market in that area is fairly flat, he assures me, and he's suggesting that we reduce the price. I have no idea what to do and I don't feel like these are decisions I can make by myself.

"What's wrong?" Zoe asks, looking at me from her side of the room.

"Nothing… Well, it's just a message from our London solicitor – lawyer, I suppose you'd say."

"Is there something the matter?"

"Yes, and no."

"You look worried."

"That's because I am. I don't know what to do."

She gets up and comes over. "Can I help?" she asks.

"No, not really. But thanks for offering." I pause for a moment. "Is it okay if I take a break? I just need to call Ed."

"Of course. You didn't really take a lunch hour today."

I smile at her and get up, going out of the office and down in the lift, then outside onto the street, before calling Ed.

"Tess?" He answers on the first ring. "What's wrong?"

"How do you know anything's wrong?"

"Because it's two-thirty in the afternoon and you never call during the day. So, tell me what's wrong."

I explain to him about the message, and even as I'm speaking, I can feel the panic rising inside me.

"Calm down," he says, as I finish talking.

"But I don't know what to do."

"Let me get this straight… your share in the London apartment is three quarters of a million?" he clarifies.

"Yes."

"Wow." I can hear him smiling.

"I know. I mean, Ali and I have both got around seven hundred thousand in the bank, from our parents' estate and from selling granny's house when she died, although Ali might have a little less now, because of having to re-vamp her business in the UK, and I think she paid for some of the wedding, but…"

"Jeez, Tess."

"What?"

"So, when you get this money, you'll have over a million pounds in the bank?"

"Yes, I guess so. I hadn't thought about that."

"You hadn't?"

I shake my head. "No. It's just money." He chuckles.

"So, I'll be dating a millionaire?" he adds.

"I suppose so… Does that bother you?"

"Not in the slightest," he says.

"In which case, can we get to the problem at hand?"

"Which is?"

"What to do about Waterside. The guy made it sound urgent. And it must be. It's seven-thirty in the evening in London. Why is he contacting me now, if it isn't urgent?"

"Maybe he just likes working late," Ed suggests. "And urgent or not, I'm sure it can wait until tomorrow. Twenty-four hours' delay can't hurt."

I smile. He's right. "I'm panicking over nothing, aren't I?"

"Yeah, but don't worry about it." I can hear his smile. "Hold on a second… Jane, don't let that go yet, I need to check it, and the pork isn't ready."

"I'm sorry," I say quickly. "I'd forgotten you'd still be working."

"Don't be sorry. It's fine."

"I'll let you go," I reply.

"I'll never go," he says.

"You know what I mean," I tell him. "I'll see you later?"

"Of course." He pauses. "And don't worry."

He sits next to me at the island unit in Sam's kitchen, a plate of pasta in front of each of us.

"I really am sorry I interrupted you today," I say, not daring to look at him.

"Hey, I told you, you don't have to be sorry."

I put my fork down, not having tasted a thing, and turn to him. "I wish I was stronger," I murmur, speaking my thoughts. "I wish I could just make decisions, and get on with things."

"I guess it's understandable though, after what happened to your parents," he says, turning to me.

"It is?"

"Yeah. You were only eight when they died. Your whole life was turned upside down and you lost the people who everyone naturally turns to in times of indecision or need. Instead you had to turn to your grandmother and to Ali and I guess you've just gotten used to that, rather than naturally growing away from it, like most kids do with their parents."

"Ali's just always been there," I tell him, trying to make sense of it. "She's always done everything."

He stares at me for a moment. "Can I ask you something?"

"Of course."

"If you're so close to her, why don't you tell her how you really feel about your father? You know, that you don't have those same feelings of hero worship that she does, and that you're angry with him for leaving you?"

"I couldn't do that to her," I reply simply. "I'd hate to hurt her like that."

"But wouldn't it be better to be honest?" he asks. "Rather than hiding how you really feel?"

"No. Not in this case. Whatever Ali might think and say about the story protecting me, she's the one who needs to believe our father was a hero. She needs that romantic fiction about him to be true, and I can't take that away from her. She's done so much for me, I have to let her have that."

He moves closer and pulls me into a hug. "That's very brave of you," he whispers in my ear, "and very kind."

"I don't know about that," I reply softly. "But I'll never tell her, even if I do wish I could be stronger, more independent, in other ways."

"You don't have to be," he says, leaning back and gazing into my eyes. "I'll always be by your side to help you whenever you need me."

"Ed, I'm trying to be independent here, not replace one decision-maker with another." That feels unnecessarily harsh, even as I'm saying it, and I want to take the words back. "I'm sorry," I say quickly. "I didn't mean that."

"It's okay," he says calmly. "I get what you're saying, but please understand, I'm not suggesting that I want to make your decisions, or take away your independence. I'll never stand in front of you, Tess, other than to protect you. I'll never stop you from doing anything. I think you need to learn to make your own way, and take your own chances, and make your own mistakes. But I'll be beside you for as long as you need me, every single step of the way, to help you and support you."

"That's the most beautiful thing anyone's ever said to me," I murmur, a tear falling onto my cheek. "Thank you."

He wipes away the tear with his thumb, and kisses me, and then we eat, holding hands.

After he's finished work, Ed comes up and sits down beside me on the couch. He doesn't bother to make a hot chocolate, or pour himself a glass of wine. Instead, he just sits and puts an arm around me, pulling me close.

"Are you okay?" I ask him.

"Yeah. Busy shift," he replies.

"You look tired."

"I feel whacked."

"Maybe we should go to bed," I tell him.

"In a while. I just wanna hold you."

I nestle into him, enjoying the warmth and security of his arms, clasped tight around me.

I wake with a start, and look around the room. I'm in my bedroom, the curtains are closed but I can see it's morning, and I'm lying beneath the duvet, fully clothed. How did I get here? And why didn't I get undressed?

I get up, feeling woolly headed and go to the bathroom, taking my clothes off and getting into the shower. I have to admit, I feel better afterwards and, when I come out, I wrap myself in a towel and go back to my room, where I quickly braid my damp hair, and put on some work clothes.

Out in the kitchen, Ed's sitting at the island unit, drinking coffee. He looks up as I approach.

"Good morning," he smiles. "Did you sleep okay?"

"Um… yes. Although I have no idea how I got to bed."

"I carried you there," he explains. "You fell asleep on me."

"I did? Oh. I'm sorry."

"Don't be," he says. "It was lovely holding you while you slept."

"You didn't undress me though?" I sit beside him and look up into his eyes.

"No," he says, turning to face me properly. "I'm not that strong willed. And besides, I didn't want you to wake up while I was in the process of taking your clothes off, and have you wonder what I was doing."

"Thank you," I murmur.

"For what?"

"For being a gentleman."

"I'm not that much of a gentleman," he says, smiling. "And anyway, I want our first time to be special."

"So do I." I look down at the space between us. "Even if I don't have much of a clue what will be involved."

He reaches out and places a finger under my chin, raising my face so I'm looking at him again. "I do. I know exactly what I wanna do with you," he replies quietly.

I smile at him. "I can't believe how little I know," I comment, feeling inadequate.

He chuckles. "I think it's kinda cute," he says, and gets up, going over to the cooker to start making the breakfast. "So, how old were you when Ali explained to you about sex?" he asks.

"My periods started when I was twelve. I was at home with granny and I went and told her, and she just said it was part of growing up, and it would happen every month, but she didn't explain what it was about. Then Ali came back at the weekend…"

"She didn't live with you then?" he asks.

"No. She'd moved to London by then and was at cookery school." He nods. "So, she came back and, I imagine granny spoke to her about it, and she came up to my room and sat on my bed and told me a bit more detail about how babies are made – or how to avoid them being made, to be more precise." I clasp my hands together and look down at them. "She explained that when a man and woman love each other, they have sex, and she told me what that involved." I look up at him.

He's staring at me. "She said it had to be about love?" He seems surprised.

"Yes. Why? Doesn't it?"

He puts down the knife he's holding. "No. Not always."

I feel a cold chill run down my spine and the panic starts to build inside me. "Oh. I'm sorry… I thought…"

"You thought what?" he asks, coming around to my side of the island to stand right beside me.

I can feel myself blushing and wish I could run and hide somewhere. I've obviously completely misunderstood the situation between the two of us. I thought this was about love; he thinks it's about sex. The problem is, I'm not sure I can do one without the other. But it feels like it's a little late in the day to be working that out. "Nothing. It doesn't matter," I bluster.

"Yes it does," he reiterates, stepping closer. "Tell me what you were thinking."

"Nothing."

"Tess, you always tell me everything. You rarely even bother to filter, so tell me."

I look up at him. "It's just I've always thought that love had to be a part of it. That's probably a bit naive of me." I try to sound as nonchalant as I can, although I'm feeling desolate inside.

He smiles. "No, it isn't," he says. "It's not naive at all."

I swallow hard before asking my next question. "Have you loved all the women you've had sex with?"

"What makes you think I've had sex with that many women?" he asks.

"Well, you're a lot older than me, for a start. And you seem… experienced."

He smiles again. "Not that experienced," he replies.

"You're more experienced than me," I point out, but then most people are, so that's not saying much.

"Yeah. But I'm probably not as experienced as a lot of guys my age… certainly not as experienced as my brothers."

"How old are you?" I ask him. How can I not know that?

"I'm twenty-nine."

"And how many women have you had sex with?"

He thinks for a moment and I feel my palms start to sweat. What would be an acceptable number, I wonder. More than five? Less than fifty? I don't know… "Nine," he says, eventually, and I surprise myself by feeling completely okay with that.

"And did you love them?"

He shakes his head slowly. "No," he says, simply

"None of them? Not one?"

"Not one." He moves closer. "They didn't love me either. Love really doesn't have to be a part of it, Tess. A lot of the time, it's just about being attracted to to the other person."

"Oh. I see." I didn't know it was possible to feel so dejected.

"Tess?" His voice is soft, but strong at the same time and I look up into his eyes. "I may have had sex before," he admits. "But I've never been in love… until now."

"You… you're in love?"

"Yes. Completely. With you."

The smile that forms on my lips is entirely involuntary and I move from dejection to joy in an instant. "You're in love with me?"

"Yes. I think I started to fall in love with you when you first walked into the kitchen, that day you arrived with Ali. It kinda built from there, and I knew for sure after we went to the gallery together. I knew I wanted to be with you, to protect you, to take care of you, and to see things the way you do. You've got a beautiful way of looking at the world, Tess."

"Really? I don't think I do. The world scares the hell out of me most of the time."

He laughs. "Well, maybe that's what I love about you – the fact that it scares you, but you face it anyway. That and your honesty. I love the way you talk to me. I feel like we can tell each other anything, and everything."

"I feel like that too." I smile up at him, and he closes the final gap between us. "And that being the case, I have to tell you, that I'm in love with you too."

He stills. "You are?"

"Yes." I nod my head, just to be sure he's understood. "Yes, I am. I don't think I worked it out quite as quickly as you did. I think it came on more gradually for me, but I do love you, Ed… so very much."

He leans down and very gently places his lips against mine.

"You do realise, don't you," he says, standing up again, "that just because a man and woman love each other, doesn't mean they *have* to have sex."

There's a glint in his eyes and I think he's teasing me, so I go along with it. "They don't?"

"No. Not if they don't want to."

"And if they do want to?"

He leans down again, his lips barely an inch from mine. "Then I imagine it's the most magical thing in the world."

Ed

"What kind of time do you call this?" Sam turns to face me as I walk into the kitchen, holding Tess's hand. He stills and looks at our joined hands, then back to my face. Despite his stare, I don't let go of her. I'm in love with her. I'm never letting go of her again.

"Around five-thirty?" I say, smiling, and his lips twitch, just slightly. I know they've only just got back, but Tess still had to work today, so I was always gonna walk down to her office to collect her, even if doing so meant I wouldn't be here for when Sam and Ali got back.

"It's good to see you." Ali steps forward and gives Tess a hug first, before turning to me. "You've both been okay?" she asks.

"We've been fine," Tess replies, although I notice she's a little stiff, a little quiet. She's been fine all day; in fact, walking her to work this morning, she was about as carefree as I've ever seen her. But then finding out that your love is reciprocated can do that to a person. I should know. I feel exactly the same, and I've kind of floated through my day.

Rob steps in front of Sam, who's still looking at me. "Seems like Italy agreed with you," he says, slapping him lightly on the arm.

"Yeah," Sam says, smiling properly now. "It was spectacular. I'd forgotten how beautiful Positano can be."

Ali turns to face him, her hand resting on her hip. "Even though I incorporated so much of it into your restaurant?" she says.

"There's not a lot of Positano in the kitchen," Sam replies, going over to her and pulling her into his arms. They both look relaxed, and happy, and very much in love.

"You're not as tanned as I thought you'd be," Rob says to Sam.

"It's hard to catch a tan in hotel suite," Sam replies, his eyes twinkling. Ali blushes, just slightly, but nestles into Sam's arms.

"You did go out occasionally, right?" Rob asks.

"Once in a while, yeah," Sam replies.

"But you just said how beautiful Positano was," Rob queries.

Sam grins. "The view I had was fucking spectacular." Ali slaps him playfully on the chest, although I don't think she really minds.

Tess stays beside me, quiet and shy throughout their conversation and seems really withdrawn.

"You okay?" I whisper to her.

She doesn't reply, but looks up at me and nods her head, just once. I'm not convinced, but I doubt she'll tell me what's wrong in front of everyone. When I turn back to face the others, I notice that both Sam and Ali are looking at us now and Tess takes a half step back. I get the feeling that, if I wasn't holding her hand, she'd run.

"I—I need the bathroom," she says quietly. "I'm gonna go on upstairs."

"Okay," I reply. I'm not buying her excuse, but I can't argue with her. She pulls her hand from mine and, without looking back, or saying a word to anyone, she leaves the room. Silence descends until her footsteps have faded, we've heard the door to the apartment open and close, and can be sure that she's upstairs.

"Is she okay?" Sam asks, taking a step toward me.

Ali puts a hand on his arm, presumably to calm him.

"She's been fine, until just now," I reply. I don't tell them that she was the happiest I've ever seen her this morning. Or why.

"Has something happened?" Ali asks, more calmly than her husband.

"Nothing that I'm aware of. Apart from her getting an email from your lawyer in London," I explain, because it's a good enough reason for Tess to be acting weird in front of them. At least it's enough to hopefully throw them off the scent until I can speak to her and find out what's really wrong.

"Saying what?" Ali asks. "Do you know?"

"Yeah. It was something to do with the money from the sale of your London apartment, and what you want to do with it, and whether or not you want to reduce the price of the house in Dorset."

"How did she react to getting that?" Ali inquires, still holding on to Sam, and nestling into his arms once more.

"She went into a kind of tailspin," I explain. "But she was okay once we talked it through."

"Has she been sleeping alright, do you know?" Ali looks at me.

"She didn't the first night," I reply. "So… so I moved in upstairs."

No-one says anything, but Sam raises an eyebrow.

"Before you say anything, I'm sleeping in my old room. Tess is sleeping in hers. Nothing's happened. I haven't done anything I shouldn't have."

"I'm sure you haven't," Ali says thoughtfully. "But something's obviously making her unhappy." She turns to Sam. "I'll go and speak with her."

"I'll come with you," he replies. "I'm sure these two can manage one last night without me."

"We'd expected to," Rob puts in, before I can say anything.

"I've been eating with Tess before the evening session," I say, before they leave the kitchen, "but I thought the three of you might like to eat alone tonight."

"That's fine," Sam says. "I'll cook something for us."

I'd assumed I was doing Tess a favor, giving her a chance to catch up with Ali, but now I'm not so sure, and I wish I'd decided to cook and eat with them. Still, it's too late now and Ali is her sister, so she'll be fine.

"Stop worrying about her." Rob comes over and puts his hand on my shoulder. We're only about an hour or two into service and I can't focus on anything.

"Am I that obvious?"

"Yeah." He smiles. "She's with Ali. She'll be okay." He looks into my eyes. "And you'll see her in a couple of hours." As he turns to leave again, he stops. "I told you, didn't I?"

"You told me what?"

"That when you fell in love, you'd fall harder than any of us."

I shake my head and smile, but I'm not about to disagree with him. I can't stop thinking about her, or worrying about her, or dreaming about her, even when I'm not asleep.

"Ed?" Sam's voice drags me back to reality, with a bump.

"Yeah? What's wrong? Is Tess okay?" She's my first thought, but then she always is.

He doesn't reply, but looks at me for a moment, before turning away. "Listen up," he calls out, loud enough for everyone to hear. "Rob's in charge for ten minutes." He looks toward Rob. "Don't break my kitchen," he growls, but his lips are twitching upward, and then he comes over to me. "We need to talk… in the office."

"We do?"

"Yeah. Come with me."

He doesn't wait for me to reply, or argue with him, but walks away, out of the kitchen and across the corridor. I follow and we go into the office together, and I close the door behind me.

"What's wrong?" I ask him. "This has to be about Tess, so tell me."

He stares at me for a moment. "I was gonna ask you the same question."

"How do you mean?"

"I was gonna ask you what's wrong with her."

"Nothing was wrong with her. Like I said earlier, she's been fine until today."

"So, what was different about today?" he asks.

"I don't know." I reply. "Maybe something happened at work." Although that doesn't make much sense to me. I'm sure she'd have told me on the walk home. She usually does, when something's not right.

He shakes his head. "Ali already asked her that and she said work was okay." He looks at me inquiringly. "She doesn't seem overly happy in her job," he remarks.

"She's not, but she's trying to make the best of it."

"Ali's sent an email to the lawyer," he clarifies, "just telling him to wait until she and Tess have had time to discuss what they wanna do about the house and the money. But even after that, Tess was really on edge, and now she's gone for a bath."

"Maybe she's just tired."

He stares at me again. "You definitely haven't done anything?" he asks.

"We've kissed, nothing more." That's not strictly true, but we haven't done anything she didn't want, and I'm not telling him about my relationship with Tess. That's between the two of us.

"And she was okay about that?"

"Of course she was damned well okay with it, Sam." I raise my voice.

He holds up his hands. "Okay. I'm sorry." He looks perplexed. "I just don't understand why she's being so aloof."

I lean back against the wall. "I'll talk to her after work," I say, calming down.

"You think she'll tell you, if she won't tell Ali?"

"Yeah. I do."

His eyes bore into mine, but I don't flinch.

"Okay," he says eventually. "We'll stay up and we can all talk after you've finished."

I want to tell him not to. I want to tell him that it'd be better if I can speak to Tess by myself. But I don't for one second think that either he or Ali are going to let that happen, not when they're clearly so worried about her. I guess that whatever's wrong, she's just gonna have to tell me in front of them…

We finish up at about eleven-fifteen, and start cleaning down the kitchen.

"Go," Rob says, coming over to me.

I don't need to ask what he means. "You sure?"

"Yeah. You need to work this out with Tess – and get Sam off your back."

I give him the best smile I can manage, take off my white jacket, dumping it on the countertop, and head up the stairs to Sam and Ali's apartment. Just before I go through the upper door, I take a deep breath, and hope that whatever's wrong with Tess, isn't going to backfire on our relationship.

Inside, the three of them are sitting on the couch. Ali and Sam are cuddled together at one end, and Tess is sitting awkwardly at the other. The TV is on, but I get the feeling none of them is really watching. Tess looks up when she sees me and gives me a smile that renews my hope.

Without a second's hesitation, I go over to her, sit down right beside her and take her hand in mine, turning my back on Sam and Ali, and focusing on her.

"Something's wrong," I say, not beating around the bush.

She looks up at me, her eyes filling with tears, and gives me a single nod of her head.

"Tell me." I keep my voice soft, giving her as much reassurance as I can. She hesitates, staring into my eyes. "Do you want to talk to me alone?" I offer, even though I know I'm probably gonna have to fight Sam to get him out of here.

She shakes her head. "No," she whispers. "It's fine." She shifts in her seat, so she can see Sam and Ali, and I sit back, getting out of the way and letting her. "I'm sorry," she says, just about loud enough for them to hear. Sam turns off the TV. "I know I've been a bit distant since you got back, but I needed some time to think…" She hesitates. "And I didn't want to have this conversation without Ed." I squeeze her hand and she manages a slight smile.

"Tell us what's wrong," Ali says, leaning forward, even though Sam's still holding her.

Tess blushes slightly, and looks at me again. "I—I want Ed to stay," she says, blurting out the words, and I have to smile. I can't help it. "Obviously this is your home, and I'd understand if you asked him to go, but I really don't want him to." She stops talking abruptly and stares down at our clasped hands.

"Is that why you've been so quiet?" Ali asks, and Tess nods her head silently.

"You thought we'd insist Ed went home?" Sam clarifies, and again Tess gives a single nod. "We'd never do anything that made you unhappy," he adds, is voice about as gentle as I've ever heard it. "If you want him here, then he can stay… for as long as you both want."

She looks up now, and I pull her into my arms.

"I wish you'd said something earlier," I say quietly. "I could have put your mind at rest."

"How?" she asks. "We had to wait for Sam and Ali to come back."

I shake my head. "No, we didn't. I could've told you what their answer would be. And, in any case, nothing – not even Sam – could make me leave you, not if you needed me." I kiss her gently. "I told you, for as long as you need me, I'll be right here."

She smiles, despite the tears that are almost overflowing from her eyes, and it's the kind of smile that could light up Vegas, or melt the polar ice cap. She puts her arms around me. "I think I've always needed you," she whispers, "even before I met you."

I hold her for a while, before we sit back and realize Sam and Ali are still in the room, looking at us, smiling.

"Do you think you can bear to be apart for a few minutes, while I show you the things I bought in Positano?" Ali asks, getting up and holding out a hand to Tess.

She glances at me and I nod my encouragement. "I guess so," she says and gets up off the couch, going through to Sam and Ali's bedroom.

"Well, who'd have thought," Sam says, once the bedroom door closes behind them.

"Who'd have thought what?" I look over at him. He's still smiling.

"Who'd have thought you could make her smile like that," he says, and then his eyes narrow just slightly. "Are you sure you haven't done anything more than kiss her?"

"Positive."

He leans back into the couch, his eyes still fixed on me. "But you wanna do more?"

"Yes. And so does she. We've talked it through, Sam."

"You need to take care of her, Ed," he says, and for split second, I see red.

"What the fuck do you think I'm doing? I couldn't take any more care of her if she was made of cut glass."

Sam gets up and comes over, sitting down beside me. "Calm down," he says, because I almost never lose my temper and hardly ever swear, so he knows he got to me. "I'm sorry," he adds. "I get it. You're in love with her."

"Yeah. I am. And she's in love with me."

He smiles. "That's great," he says. "Just… try and remember how young she is."

"I know." He's trying my patience – again.

Sam takes a breath and looks at the coffee table. "Have you ever… um… have you ever been with a virgin before?" he asks.

Part of me wants to laugh at the fact that Sam Moreno, of all people, is embarrassed talking about sex, but I don't.

"No, I haven't," I reply. "And before you say anything else, I'm pretty damn sure that neither you or Rob have either."

He smirks. "I can't speak for Rob," he says, "but I haven't."

"Look," I say, and he turns to face me again, "I know you mean well, but I don't need your advice – or anyone else's. I know what's involved, and I know Tess. I know about her past; I know how young, how vulnerable, and how inexperienced she is. We talk a lot, Sam, and she's shared everything with me – and I mean *everything*. I'm not an idiot."

"I know," he murmurs.

"And I get that you're looking out for her, because you promised Ali you would, but – if it's all the same to you – can you just leave me to get on with this now. I love her. I won't hurt her, and I won't let anyone else hurt her either."

He looks closely at me, then nudges into me with his shoulder.

"She's good for you," he says quietly. "She's making you stand up for yourself for the first time since Dad dragged you down."

"Yeah, because I wanna stand up for her."

"I know. It's just good to see you being a bit more assertive for once."

I get to my feet and look down at him. "Yeah, so watch your back in the kitchen." I tell him, jokingly.

"I always have, when it comes to you," he replies, seriously and looks up, giving me the most sincere smile I think I've ever seen on his face, before getting up and offering me his hand. I take it and he pulls me into a hug, whispering in my ear, "Mind you, fuck it up with Tess, and there won't be anywhere you can hide from me."

I guess some things never change…

Chapter Ten

Tess

Over two weeks have gone by since Ali and Sam got back.

The restaurant is as frantic as ever, although Ed usually manages to find the time to come up and see me during the evening service. He sometimes brings me a treat, but not always. It depends on how busy he's been. I don't mind. I just like seeing him. We snatch a few minutes to talk, and kiss.

We have breakfast together every day, and he still walks me to work each morning, and picks me up in the afternoons, and we have our evening meal together, with Sam and Ali, who've taken to joining us upstairs to eat. Sometimes, Rob and Petra come too, if she's working, although on the days when she isn't, Rob goes back to her place and eats early with them. I gather that this wasn't how things used to be done, and that the three brothers would usually just eat whenever they could, but judging from how much they seem to enjoy our meals together, I think they all prefer the new system. It's always a rushed, noisy meal, after which they dash downstairs to open up the restaurant, leaving me to clear up. I don't mind that though, because it gives me something to do.

I have to admit that, while it's nice having everyone together, and I love to see how much Ed enjoys being surrounded by his family, I miss the quiet times he and I shared on our own.

Work has become quite difficult for me over the last few days. Zoe and Bryan have been arguing a lot, and each day is filled with them shouting at each other behind Bryan's closed office door. Brittany seems to do nothing but spread rumours and gossip, and the atmosphere, which I always found a little hard to take, feels positively toxic to me.

I talk it through with Ed each evening on the way home from work, and he tells me to try and block it out, and – being as there's nothing I can do about Bryan and Zoe's relationship – he's suggested taking my headphones into work, so I can listen to music, rather than listening to the arguments. If it carries on for much longer, I might try that.

It's Friday today, and while I've come to hate Saturdays, because I get so lonely in the apartment on my own, I do look forward to Sundays, and Ed's said we'll try and do something by ourselves, being as the last few weeks have been spent doing 'family' things. We had the barbecue with Petra and Rob, then Sam and Ali came back and Sam wanted to have a family get-together at the apartment the following Sunday, and last weekend was Petra's birthday and we all went out for dinner together.

Ali and I arranged to have lunch together today, which was nice. We went to a sandwich bar that Sam recommended and had a long chat for the first time since she got back from her honeymoon. She's been working with Sam in the kitchen, fairly non-stop, and with me being out all day, we don't really see much of each other. She asked about my work, but I didn't tell her how awful I'm finding it at the moment. She'd only worry, or tell me to leave and find something else and, while that's tempting, I do enjoy the actual work, and I like Zoe, even if the atmosphere surrounding her and Bryan is becoming intolerable.

I'm careful to just take an hour, and no more, fearful of incurring Bryan's wrath, which it seems is easily done these days, and Ali and I part a short distance from my office, as she returns to the restaurant and I go into the lobby and get into the lift.

When I go into the outer office, Bryan's door is closed, but I can hear voices coming from the other side. There seem to be two women in there, as well as Bryan himself, and I wonder whether he's got a meeting that no-one told me about. It doesn't matter to me. I'm busy researching two separate cases at the moment, one of which is proving a bit tricky. I've kind of decided to put it to one side until after the weekend, and hope that a new week will give me some fresh insight… or that Zoe will have time to help me.

I've left the door to our office open, and I'm right in the middle of copying out some notes when the door to Bryan's office slams open.

"You fucking bastard." Zoe's voice is loud and tearful.

"Zoe, don't be like that." Bryan follows her out, but she turns on him.

"Don't even speak to me, you asshole." She gulps back her tears and opens the outer door, running through it into the corridor outside.

I get to my feet and go out. Bryan looks at me, shrugs his shoulders and goes back into his office. I catch a glimpse of Brittany, just before he closes the door again, and I go out into the corridor, which is empty. I imagine Zoe will be in the ladies' toilets, so I head straight there, and find her sitting on the floor, in the corner of the room. As I open the door, she looks up and starts.

"Shit. For a moment, I thought you were him," she says, sobbing into a handful of tissue.

"No. He went back into his office," I reply, going over and sitting down beside her.

"Well, what a surprise. And I'm sure Brittany will be very accommodating." She gulps back a sob and wipes her nose, before turning to me, her eyes red and puffy. "He's a cheating asshole, Tess," she mutters.

"Cheating?"

She gives me a vague smile. "Surely you noticed?"

"Noticed what?" I decide to play dumb.

"Bryan and me."

"Oh. That." Playing dumb never did work very well for me.

"Yeah. That. We've been together for over a year," she says quietly, sniffling every so often.

"That long?" I'm really just making conversation here. I have no idea how long I thought they'd been together.

"Yeah." She looks at me. "Do you remember your second day here?"

I think back. "You mean the day you came in late?"

"Yeah. That was because I thought I was pregnant."

"Oh my God." I'm not making conversation anymore.

"I made an appointment to see my doctor and asked Bryan to go with me." She reaches out and I take her hand. "I was terrified, Tess."

"I can imagine."

"He wasn't happy about it, but he agreed to go with me."

"And are you? Pregnant, I mean?"

"No." She smiles, just slightly. "No, thank God. But then he got real mad at me for wasting half the morning, and we had a huge row on the way back to the office."

"I noticed."

She shrugs. "Even so, I thought we were over it… until last week."

"What happened last week?" I ask her.

"Well, I didn't know, until today, but he just started picking holes in my work, and getting really moody with me at home."

"You live together?"

"Yeah. Well, I live at his place," she replies, and starts crying again. "Oh God," she mumbles.

"What's happened?"

"I went into his office this morning to ask him a question, and caught him kissing Brittany."

"He was kissing her?"

"Well, it was a little more than just kissing. She was lying on his desk, and he was leaning over kissing her, with his hand inside her panties."

"Oh…" I don't know what else to say.

"I have to leave," she says, struggling to her feet and going over to the mirror.

"But where will you go?" I get up and join her.

"Home, I guess."

"Home… You mean, Chicago?"

"Yeah. I can't stay here any longer. I've got nowhere to live and no job, thanks to him."

"He fired you?" I ask, incredulous.

"No. I quit. I can't be around him. Even though he said he wanted me to stay."

"He wanted to try again?"

"No. Not with the relationship. He made it very clear that's over and told me I'd have to move out of his apartment. But he wanted me to keep working here."

"Seriously? I can't believe he'd think that was okay."

"There are a lot of things you'd probably find hard to believe about Bryan," she says, straightening her hair. She turns to me. "I'm sorry to leave you in the lurch," she adds, "but I've gotta go."

"Right now?"

"Yeah, right now."

She squares her shoulders, dumps the handful of tissue in the waste basket and, taking a deep breath, goes out into the corridor.

I give her about five minutes, and then follow, by which time she's pretty much cleared her desk.

"Stay in touch, won't you?" she says to me, putting a couple of books into the box in front of her.

"Of course. Will you be okay?"

"I'll be fine. I've already called my mom. She's gonna meet me at the airport. I'll head back to Bryan's place now and pack my things and then I'm catching the six-thirty flight out of Bradley, so I'll be home by about nine, tucked up in my own room." She sighs. "Give me a couple of days, and I'll get myself a new job and hopefully be able to look back on this as just another bad experience to add to the long list." She smiles.

"I'll miss you," I mutter.

She comes around the desk and pulls me into a hug. "I'll miss you too." She leans back, holding my shoulders. "Don't take any bullshit from him," she says. "Keep your head down, do the work, and ignore Bryan… and Brittany. I'm sure she'll try and run the place. Don't let her intimidate you." She hugs me one last time, then grabs the box from her desk and, without looking back, heads out of the door.

A little later, Bryan's door opens and Brittany comes out, straightening her clothes and looking flushed, and misty-eyed. She peers through my open door and gives me a knowing smile, like the cat that got the cream.

When Ed comes to collect me, I tell him everything that's happened.

"Do you want to stay on there?" he asks.

"What choice do I have?" I ask him. "I'm not a US citizen. Changing jobs isn't easy for me."

He stops dead and pulls me into his arms. "I don't like the idea of you being so unhappy."

I look up at him. "I'm not unhappy. I like the work."

"Okay. I don't like the idea of you being so lonely," he says, hitting the nail on the head.

I rest my head on his chest. "I've got you," I murmur. "And Ali, and Sam." I don't mention that the fact that I barely see any of them is becoming harder to take.

He holds me tight.

"We'll work it out, babe," he whispers. "I promise."

Oh God… How I wish I could believe him.

Ed

Sometimes I really feel like the world is conspiring against me and Tess. Or at least my brothers are, anyway. For the last few weekends, our Sundays have been taken up with family things and I'd really hoped to be able to spend the one that's just gone with Tess… just the two of us. Especially after she had such an awful time at the end of last week, with Zoe leaving. However, Sam and Rob had other ideas and, unbeknownst to me, they'd planned a picnic, which they announced late on Saturday evening.

I told them Tess and I had plans, but they wouldn't take no for an answer, and told me they were doing it to cheer her up, because they'd noticed how down she'd been. Part of me wanted to tell them that she and I needed the time alone, but at the same time, I was grateful to them for making the effort, and it was a good day. Tess enjoyed it too. We went for a walk by ourselves during the afternoon and she reassured me that she's okay with continuing to work at the magazine. For myself, I'd rather she didn't – especially now I know what a philandering asshole her boss is – but she has to make her own decisions. I'd told her I'd stand beside her, not in front of her, so that's what I'm gonna do.

As this week has progressed though, I've noticed that she's become quieter and more insular. I asked her about it tonight on the way back from her office and she told me she's just lonely. Evidently this Brittany girl, who's now sleeping with the boss, is in cahoots with the other girls in the office, and they're all lording it over Tess, which leaves her very much on the outside. The only upside is that, with Zoe's departure, Tess is now writing as well as researching, so she's at least being kept busy, and brings files home with her most evenings. While I don't really like her working so hard, I know she doesn't enjoy sitting upstairs by herself doing nothing. At least this way, she's occupied, and she's doing something she loves. I'd just like to see her smile a little more.

We're fully booked tonight, as usual, which is good, because it makes the service go quicker, and I'm just prepping the espresso syrup, when Sam comes over to my section. Ali's talking to Jane, at the other end of the kitchen, but Sam comes right into my area and stands beside me, leaning back against the countertop, his arms folded across his chest.

"I don't think I ever told you how grateful I am to you for stepping in and taking over for me... twice," he says, looking right at me.

"Yeah. I think you did," I tell him, continuing to stir the syrup.

"Well, Ali and I have been talking it through, and we think you should have the evening off."

I stop stirring and stare at him. "I'm sorry? Did you say 'the evening off'?"

He smiles. "Yeah."

"And how is that gonna work? You know you hate working the pastry section."

"Damn right I do. But Ali doesn't. She's said she'll cover for you."

"For the whole shift?"

"Yeah." He smiles.

I look over at her, but she's deep in conversation.

"Is this about me, or Tess?" I ask him.

"Both," Sam replies. "You'd have to be blind not to see how lonely she is. And it doesn't matter how many family outings we arrange, it's you she wants to be with."

"You noticed then," I reply, smiling up at him.

"Yeah. Of course."

"And Ali's sure she can handle all this?"

"She wouldn't have offered if she wasn't. And I'll help out, if she gets stuck," Sam adds. "Now go, before I change my mind."

I'm not about to turn him down; and not because I need a night off, but because the thought of a whole evening spent with Tess is like a dream come true.

"Is this why we didn't have dinner together earlier?" I ask him, as I start to unbutton my whites.

"Yeah."

"So when you told us that there was too much to do down here..."

"That was pretty much bullshit," he finishes my sentence for me. "I thought you could cook something, just for the two of you. Ali and I will grab something later, during service."

I shrug off my white jacket, trying hard to disguise my haste. "Thanks for this, Sam."

"Anytime," he says. "I really am grateful to you for stepping in for me."

"That's what brothers are for," I reply, going out into the kitchen.

"Yeah... that and being a royal pain in the ass, if Rob's anything to go by," Sam says, following me.

I glance over at Ali as I walk through and she gives me a smile, but I don't hang around to talk. I've got places to be...

The door to the apartment is open, but I close it behind me, and look around. There's no sign of Tess anywhere.

"Tess?" I call out.

"Yes?" She's in her bedroom and I wander along the hallway to her door, which is slightly ajar.

"Can I come in?" I ask.

"Um… yes."

I note the hesitation and push the door open slowly. She's sitting on the bed, braiding her slightly wet hair, wearing a towel, wrapped around her, and nothing else. She must've just had a shower, and just thinking about that, and the fact that she's so nearly naked has me instantly hard, although for once I don't care, and I wander over and stand in front of her. She looks up.

"What are you doing up here?" she asks.

"I've got the evening off," I explain, grinning. "And, although I could paint the town red, or watch the latest Yankees game, or even catch up on some sleep, there's nowhere else in the world I'd rather be than with you."

"The whole evening?" she whispers, like she only heard the first part of what I said, and doesn't quite believe me.

"Yeah."

"And you wanna be with me?" She did hear me then.

"Of course." I smile down at her.

"More than you want to watch the Yankees. Whoever they are."

"You don't know who the Yankees are?" I sit down beside her and lean into her with my shoulder. "How is that even possible?" She shrugs and I put my arm around her, feeling her naked skin beneath mine, which just makes me even harder. "They're the best baseball team in the world," I tell her.

"You like baseball?" she looks up at me.

"Not especially. But I like the Yankees. I'm more of a football fan, but it's not football season at the moment."

She nods her head. "And what's your favorite football team?" she asks.

"The Giants."

"The what?"

"The Giants," I repeat.

"I've never heard of them either," she says, snuggling into me a little. God, that feels good… and distracting. "Would I have heard of any of their players? I know David Beckham came to the US to play once he'd finished his career in Europe."

"David Beckham?" I lean back, holding onto her and looking into her eyes. "You're talking about soccer."

She shakes her head. "I'm talking about football."

I chuckle. "Okay. I'm gonna have to give you that one, being as I think the game was pretty much invented in England."

"I believe it was," she replies, nodding her head.

"And David Beckham played for LA Galaxy," I tell her, just to let her know I follow soccer, as well as football – and baseball.

She looks up at me, her eyes fixed on mine. "Why are we wasting our precious evening together talking about football, and David Beckham?"

"I have absolutely no idea." I lean down and kiss her gently, managing to pull back before I get carried away with the thought that she's only wearing a towel. "Shall I go and make us something to eat?" I suggest.

"Um... okay." She seems doubtful and I wonder if that's because she wants the same thing as me. I wonder if she wants to skip dinner, and just go to bed... "I was wondering what to have," she adds, breaking into my wayward thoughts. "I felt like a salad, but wasn't feeling very inventive."

I rest my forehead against hers and smile. "I'm sure I can come up with something."

"And I'll get dressed," she whispers.

"Well, only if you feel you must." I run my fingertips down her cheek and get to my feet, tearing myself away from her while I still can. As I walk around the bed and out the door, I can feel her watching me... It's a good feeling.

I rummage around in Sam's refrigerator and find what I'm looking for, piling the ingredients on the island unit, before crouching down and pulling out a large bowl from the lower cabinet.

"What are we having?" Tess's voice makes me jump, and I stand, and nearly choke. She's wearing a t-shirt. Just a t-shirt. It's quite long, finishing just below her ass... and although she may be wearing panties, I'd swear to God, she's not wearing a bra.

"Um… salad."

She casts her eye over the ingredients before her. "It looks like it'll be a far more exciting salad than I would have made," she says. I can't stop staring at her. "Are you okay?" she asks, once the silence has stretched almost to the point of being ludicrous

"Yeah. Sorry." I put the bowl down on the island unit. "Can I ask you a question?"

"Yes."

"Are you wearing anything under that t-shirt?"

"Yes."

I nod. "Okay." I guess I got that wrong then.

"I'm wearing knickers, but no bra," she clarifies with her usual openness, which still sometimes takes me surprise. "Is that a problem?" she asks.

"What?"

"Me not wearing a bra?" She's looking me right in the eyes.

"Hell, no."

She sits up on one of the stools opposite me. "Why did you ask me that? Are you saying you'd rather I didn't have anything on under the t-shirt? Or you'd rather I did?" she asks.

I stare at her, and then move slowly around the island unit. "I'm saying that whatever you wear is just fine… but I'm also saying that, maybe later, I'd like to take that t-shirt off, along with whatever else you're wearing underneath."

She gasps and blushes, but then smiles the sexiest damn smile I've ever seen.

I retreat to my own side of the unit before I'm tempted to blow dinner altogether, rip her clothes off, and take her virginity on Sam's butcher's block. Judging from the sparkle in her eyes, though, I don't think she'd mind one bit if I did.

I make us a quick fig, prosciutto and goat's cheese salad, which takes about ten minutes to prepare – thank God. And then we sit together at the island unit. I thought it was hard standing opposite her and cooking, but sitting beside her, looking at her crazily sexy legs, knowing she's only wearing two items of clothing, and watching her eat is about as tempting as it gets.

"This tastes amazing," she says, after the first mouthful.

"Thanks." I take a bite myself and lean toward her. "I'll bet you taste better though," I whisper.

She gasps again and looks up at me. "Taste?" she queries.

"Yeah. Taste. I wanna taste you."

"Where?" she asks.

I put down my fork and turn to her, twisting her stool so she's facing me. She always tells me what she's thinking, sometimes with disarming honesty, so I'm gonna do the same, and hope I don't scare her off. "I want to lick your clitoris," I say, holding her gaze. She bites her bottom lip. "I want to dip my tongue into your vagina and discover how sweet you are."

"Oh, God," she murmurs.

"I want to swallow down your juices, and lick them from my lips."

"Yes… yes, please, Ed."

Her whispered entreaty is more than I can take and I grab her hand and pull her to her feet.

"Come with me," I mutter and lead her through the apartment, back to her room, and straight over to the bed. "You want me to taste you?" I ask her, and she nods quickly, her enthusiasm obvious and so damn cute.

I lean down and kiss her, and then lower her onto the bed, on her back, and slowly move down her body, lifting the t-shirt just a little when I get to the hem. She's wearing white lace panties which take my breath away for an instant. But I quickly recover and pull them down, dropping them on the floor behind me, and revealing the most perfect pussy I've ever seen. She's got a neat triangle of dark blonde hair, which is already glistening, and her lips are swollen in anticipation. I settle between her parted legs and look up at her. She's watching, her eyes wide with wonder, as I lean forward and blow gently across her pubic mound.

"Oh, yes…" she hisses and, when I look up again, her head's rocked back into the mattress. I haven't touched her yet, and she's already responding like that?

Using my fingers, I gently part her swollen lips, and delicately run the tip of my tongue over her clit. She bucks into me.

"Yes! Oh, yes," she calls out.

"Hush, babe," I whisper, as I lick her again, and this time let my tongue linger longer, flicking it across her several times, before delving lower and dipping into her vagina. She's really wet, and tastes so sweet, I take my time, enjoying her, as she writhes and moans beneath me. Moving closer still, I lick her clit once, twice more and, without warning, she explodes in a violent orgasm, her hand holding the back of my head in place as she rides out her pleasure, calling my name, in a breathless frenzy. Her climax seems to go on forever, but eventually, she calms and her breathing returns to something like normality, and I look up at her. I can't see her face, so I crawl up her body. She's lying flat, her head tilted back, but she opens her eyes and looks directly at me as I raise myself above her.

"You okay?" I ask her.

"Um… yes." She smiles. "I had no idea."

"About what?"

"That it would feel like that."

"That's only the beginning, babe. It gets better."

Her eyes widen. "Better than that?"

I nod my head, and very slowly lick my lips. She sucks in a breath, watching my tongue. "Yeah, better than that. Although I don't think there's anything in this world that tastes better than you do."

"What do I taste of?" she asks.

"Wanna find out?"

"How?" She looks down, clearly trying to work out how that's gonna be possible.

I rest on my elbows, my mouth maybe an inch from hers, and then I kiss her. She's tentative to start with, but then her tongue clashes with mine and she heats it up, her hands coming around behind my back, her nails digging into me. She raises her hips off the mattress and I grind mine into her, letting her feel my erection again. She moans and sighs, and her breathing alters, becoming still more ragged, before I eventually break the kiss.

"I taste sweet," she says, smiling.

"Yeah. You do." I have to smile back. She does that to me. I raise myself up again. "I guess we'd better have dinner now."

"Are you kidding?" she asks, clearly surprised.

"No."

"But I thought…" She looks so disappointed, I have to chuckle.

"I wanna do all that again," I tell her. "Then, if you're okay with it, I'd really like to make love to you. And if you're not too sore, I think I'll probably wanna make love to you a second time, which means we're gonna need some energy. And that means food."

"Right now though?" I laugh this time.

"Yeah, right now. My erection isn't going anywhere, and neither is your soaking pussy… trust me." She stares at me, but doesn't blush this time. "We can go and eat dinner, and then come back to bed…"

"And we can't make love, and then go and eat dinner, and then come back to bed again… or even better, make love, and then eat dinner in bed?"

"God, you're impatient. Honestly, give a girl an orgasm and she wants the world," I joke.

"No. She just wants you," she whispers.

"She's already got me." She smiles and I stare down at her. I'd wanted to take a break to give myself a chance to calm down, but it looks like that's not gonna happen, so I guess I'd better hope I can keep going long enough to satisfy her. "Okay. We'll do it your way."

Her smile broadens and I know I'm gonna find it real hard to ever say 'no' to her. I kneel up and pull her with me, so she's sitting, then slowly pull the t-shirt over her head and throw it onto the floor.

"Christ," I whisper.

"What?"

"You're perfect." I lower her back onto the mattress and lean down again, capturing first one nipple and then the other gently between my teeth. She gasps out her pleasure, her legs parting a little further, as if by instinct. Her breasts are small and firm, like the rest of her, and her nipples harden like pebbles as I suck them.

"I need you," I murmur.

"I need you too."

I don't say anything else, but stand up and, without taking my eyes from her, pull my t-shirt over my head, then undo my jeans and pull them down, together with my trunks, and kick off my shoes. I'm standing naked before her and she looks me up and down, her eyes wide, her bottom lip caught between her teeth.

"You're the perfect one," she says simply, and I rest my knee on the edge of the mattress, just as a thought occurs to me.

"I'll be one minute," I say quickly and run out of the room, across the corridor and into my bedroom, grabbing what I need from my bag, and heading straight back.

"Where did you go?" she asks, leaning up on her elbows and looking at me.

I hold up the carton of condoms, showing them to her, before throwing them onto the bed. "I figured we might need these?" She blushes and nods her head.

"You brought them with you?" she asks, sounding doubtful for the first time. I sit down beside her, resting my hand on her leg.

"No. I went out and bought them a couple of days ago. I've got some at my place, but when I packed my bag, I didn't know if we'd get to this stage while I was still staying here, so I didn't bring them. That seemed unbelievably presumptuous."

I look down at her and she's smiling again. "Thank you," she says.

"What on earth are you thanking me for now?"

"For being a gentleman… yet again."

I smile. "Let's see if you're still calling me a gentleman in an hour…"

"An hour?" She's shocked. "This takes an hour?"

"Why? Are you having second thoughts about stopping for dinner first?" I tease.

"No," she giggles. "But… does it really take an hour?" Her voice has dropped to an incredulous whisper.

"Minimum," I reply, but then I realize I'd better manage her expectations and move up her body, so I'm right above her, our lips almost touching. "Although it's been a while," I add, "so it might be a bit quicker, just this once."

She gazes into my eyes. "It's been a while?" she queries.

"Yeah. Over a year now," I tell her, working it out in my head.

"Why?" she asks, just because she's interested.

I think back to how lonely I was before she came here, and I lean down and kiss her. "I think I was waiting for you," I whisper.

"You didn't know I existed."

"Yeah I did. I knew you had to be out there somewhere."

She raises her head off the bed and kisses me, really gently. My cock's pressing into her hip, and I know I need to be inside her. Now.

I break the kiss and lean back, parting her legs with mine, getting them as wide as I can.

She looks up at me. "Is this going to hurt?" she asks. She's not doubtful, or even fearful. She's just inquisitive.

"Yeah," I tell her honestly. "Yeah. It probably is."

"But it will fit?"

I look at how tiny she is and palm my cock, realizing how much I'm gonna stretch her.

"It'll fit," I reassure her. "You've just gotta relax. And trust me."

She puts her hands on my biceps and lets them rest there. "I do," she says.

I lean over and grab the pack of condoms, opening it and pulling one out.

"How many of those do you get in a pack?" she asks.

"Twelve."

She smiles. "Will that be enough?" she asks, jokingly.

I lean over her, lowering myself down so our lips are almost touching again. "For tonight? Yeah." She gasps. "Just kidding," I say quickly, and she sighs. "This pack might last us a couple of days, maybe three – tops."

She slaps my arm playfully. "Stop fooling around."

"I wasn't. Not that time."

Her eyes widen and she coughs. "Oh."

"Yeah. Oh." I kneel up again, rip open the foil pack and very slowly roll the condom down the length of my shaft. She watches, fascinated, her eyes fixed on my cock, until I lower myself down over her body again, and then she looks deep into my eyes. "I will do everything I can not to hurt you," I say quietly.

"I know," she whispers.

I balance on one arm and rub the head of my cock along her soaking folds, finding her entrance easily. She gasps at the contact and I still, waiting. Then I push inside her very gently and she sucks in a deep breath.

"Relax, babe," I murmur, leaning down and kissing her. "Just relax."

She takes another breath and I edge a little further inside her, and a little further… and then she lets out a cry, clutching at my shoulders, and I stop. After a minute, maybe more, she opens her eyes. *Jesus.* I never knew… I never knew making love could mean so much, and my breath catches in my throat.

"It's okay," she says.

"Sure?"

She nods and raises her hips just slightly, wanting more, I guess.

"I've got this," I tell her and she relaxes and lets me take over, inching slowly inside her until she's taken my whole length. "We're one," I whisper, and I lean down and kiss her, just as I pull back and start moving, building a slow, steady rhythm.

"I think we always were," she whispers in my ear, when I eventually break the kiss.

I lean back up again, because I want to watch her, and see her skin flush, her nipples harden, her breasts heaving. She stares up at me, her hands moving up and down my arms.

"I love you," she mouths.

"I love you too."

She parts her legs a little wider, and then brings them up around my hips, clasping me in place.

"You're mine," she says.

"I always was."

I increase the pace and she rocks her head back, sighing into me.

"That's good," she murmurs.

"Yeah. It is."

I hope to God she's close, because I know I am.

I swivel my hips into her and she gasps, and then – once more without warning – she explodes, gripping my cock with her tight walls, and convulsing into an almighty, screaming orgasm.

"I'm g—gonna come," I stutter out, and with one last thrust, I let go deep inside her, howling out her name as my body spasms through the best orgasm of my life.

It takes a while for either of us to be able to speak properly, but by the time we can, I've rolled us over onto our sides, facing each other.

"Are you okay?" I ask her, stroking her hair.

"Yes. I'm more than okay," she replies, smiling. "You were quite right."

"What about?"

"When you said it got better," she says. "I didn't think it could be possible, but…"

I smirk. "It's possible."

She nods her head and snuggles into me, her head resting against my chest.

"You were right about something else too," she adds.

"What was that?"

"I need food."

I brought dinner through into her bedroom, and we ate in bed, and then made love again, for a lot longer that time, and then Tess fell asleep on me. I guess I must've fallen asleep too, because the next thing I know, it's daylight.

I check my watch to find it's just after seven am.

"Tess?" I whisper.

"Hmm?"

"It's seven in the morning."

"It is?" She's awake in an instant. "I haven't slept that well, or for that long, in years."

I smile at her. "Good. Maybe I should make love to you every night."

"And sleep with me?" she suggests.

"Yeah, and sleep with you." I lean down and kiss her. "But now, you need a shower, or you're gonna be late for work."

"You could always come and help me… if you washed my back, I'm sure it'd save time," she teases.

I don't need to be asked twice, and offering her my hand, I get out of bed and pull her with me. She puts on her robe, but I don't have mine, so I grab my trunks and pull them on, hoping we don't bump into Ali because I've got a hard-on already and, picking up a condom from the carton on the nightstand, I lead her along the hallway to the bathroom. Tess brushes her teeth, and then drops her robe to the floor and climbs into the shower. Jeez, she's hot. I follow her and we stand together under the cascading water.

"You want me to wash your back?" I ask her.

"Not especially." She smiles up at me.

"Then what am I doing here?" It's my turn to tease.

"I'm sure you'll think of something."

"Damn right I will." I lean down and kiss her, and walk her back until she hits the tiled wall. "Ready?" I ask.

"For what?"

"For what we came in here for…" I hold up the foil packet that I've got hidden behind my back.

She nods quickly, grinning, and I unwrap the condom and roll it over my cock, then I lift her left leg, holding it high over my bent right arm, exposing her. She locks eyes with mine as I enter her, giving her my whole length in one go.

"Oh, yes," she hisses between her teeth. "God, that's good."

"Want more?" I ask her.

"More?"

I nod. She bites her bottom lip and then nods back at me.

"Okay. Put your arms around my shoulders and don't let go." She does as I say, and still connected to her, I lean down just slightly, lifting her right leg over my bent left arm, so she's suspended, her legs wide apart, supported by my arms, my cock embedded deep inside her.

"Oh, God… that's so deep," she groans.

"Now. You have to move, babe. Use your arms to support you."

She starts to grind up and down on my cock, taking me deeper with every stroke, and grunting out her pleasure, her moans getting louder with each movement. I'm pretty sure Ali and Sam will be able to hear her, but I don't care. She feels too good, and she's enjoying this way too much to stop her.

I'm just starting to think that I can't take much more of this, when I feel her muscles start to tighten around me, her head rocks back, and she lets out a loud scream of utter joy. I tense inside her, right before I explode, and capture her mouth, trying to stifle her cries, even though there's no way Sam and Ali can't have heard that much noise.

She calms slowly and, as I break the kiss, she looks up at me.

"Thank you," she murmurs.

"What for?"

"That. It felt amazing."

"You felt amazing."

She doesn't mention the amount of noise she just made, so neither do I. I know she's gonna be mortified when she works it out, and all I can hope is that Sam and Ali were otherwise occupied themselves and won't bring it up.

We finish in the shower, get dried and dressed real fast, and Tess braids her hair because it's quicker than drying it. Then, hand-in-hand, we go out into the living room and through to the kitchen. There's no sign of Ali, but Sam's in the kitchen, making coffee. He's just wearing shorts, so I'm hoping he and Ali may have been busy until a few minutes ago and Tess's noise might have gone unnoticed.

"Good morning," Sam says once he notices us.

"Hi," Tess replies, and I notice how cheerful she sounds, which makes me feel really good about myself, and about us. I guess she's used to seeing Sam without a top on, though, because she doesn't bat an eyelid at seeing him like that.

"Sleep okay?" he asks.

"Yes, thanks." While she's quite upbeat, she's also completely calm and normal, and nothing like the wild woman I just held in my arms in the shower.

Sam turns and looks at me. "And you?" he asks.

"Fine thanks."

He smiles and, just before he turns back to the coffee, he gives me a noticeable wink. *Jerk*.

I don't even have time to react, or to say anything, before Tess has pulled her hand from mine and fled through the living room, down the corridor and slammed the bedroom door behind her.

"Way to go, Sam," I murmur, following her at a slower pace. "Thanks for that."

"Sorry," he calls out.

I open the door to Tess's room, closing it again behind me. She's lying on the unmade, dishevelled bed, where me made love last night – twice – her head buried in the comforter, her shoulders shaking, crying loud sobs. I go straight over to her and lie beside her, pulling her into my arms. She's reluctant, but I'm not giving in and eventually, she lets me hold her.

"It's okay," I say softly.

"But he knows," she replies between sobs.

"Yes."

"How? I mean, how does he know?"

I hesitate, but decide she probably needs to know the truth. "I imagine he heard us."

"You mean, he heard *me*, don't you? You weren't that noisy."

"Well, you weren't that noisy either," I try to reassure her, "but this is a small apartment."

"So Ali knows too?" She stares up at me.

"I imagine so, yes."

"Oh God." She buries her head again.

"Why is this a problem?" I ask her. "Are you ashamed of what we've done?"

"No." Her answer is immediate and she sits, looking at me. "Never."

"Then don't worry about it."

"But she's my sister," she says, her bottom lip quivering again. "And he's… Sam."

I smile. "Yeah. He is." I pull her close again. "And you've heard them from time to time, haven't you?"

She nods her head. "Yes, sometimes."

"And that's how it works when couples live together like we are now. You just have to kind of accept that you're gonna hear things. Christ, if I told you about some of the things I've heard coming from Rob's room over the years…" I leave the sentence hanging. To be honest, I haven't heard that much from Rob's room, because in general, he didn't used to bring his dates back to our place, but went to theirs instead. But, I figure Tess might feel better to know that this is quite normal – because it is.

"And they'll understand?"

"They'll understand," I reassure her. And I'll talk to them to make damn sure they don't bring it up again, or embarrass her about it. I look into her eyes. "We're allowed to make love, and to sleep together, and to be happy with each other. Sam and Ali, or anyone else, knowing about that doesn't change a damn thing. It doesn't change the fact that I want you, or that I need you, or that I love you, more than anything in the world. Nothing – absolutely *nothing* – will ever change that."

Chapter Eleven

Tess

Ed's words have echoed around my head for the last few days, just as I'm pretty sure my screams have echoed around Sam and Ali's heads too.

Fortunately, by the time Ed and I came back out of the bedroom, Sam had disappeared and Ed made us a quick breakfast and then walked me to work as usual. That evening, he picked me up, took me back to the apartment and we had dinner together – with Sam and Ali. I half expected it to be really awkward. But it wasn't. Ed was right. If anything, they seemed even more relaxed than normal, and they were certainly a lot more affectionate with each other. Apart from our evening meals, I rarely see Ali and Sam. When they're not working, they're in their bedroom – and, to be fair to me, Ed's right... they're not exactly quiet themselves. If anything, since Ed and I got together, they've become noisier, which Ed explained was because they know about us now, and feel freer to be themselves. Knowing that has made me less embarrassed in front of them – well, kind of.

Ed and I have made love, and he's slept with me, every single night since our first, and it seems to get better and better each time. Sex is nothing like I expected – although I'm not entirely sure what I expected. He's gentle and caring, and he's fun. He puts me first and makes me feel good about what we're doing, and about myself. My room, and especially my bed, have become a kind of bubble for the two of us – the perfect place where we can be ourselves and lock out the rest of the world. It would be even better if we could spend a little more time together – other than when we're asleep. I worked it out the other day; if we go to sleep at twelve-thirty and wake up at seven, we get about three to three and a half hours together – and awake – each day. The problem is, he doesn't finish work some nights until gone twelve-thirty, and if I'm not up by seven, I struggle to get into work by eight-thirty, so that equation doesn't always work out. As such, we've both started to cherish every moment we get together, and treasure everything we do, because it's all so good.

If I could just feel the same way about the rest of my life, things would be perfect. But at the moment, I just can't. I really hate work; the atmosphere has become even more poisonous since Zoe left, and the bitchiness is really starting to get me down. I don't know whether Brittany sees me as a threat, but I'm not. I couldn't be less interested in Bryan if I tried, but that doesn't stop her making snide remarks and rude comments about me whenever she gets the chance. I haven't told Ed or Ali about that, because I'm fairly sure they'd just tell me to leave – or to stand up for myself – and I don't think I can do either. The first is impractical, and the second is beyond my capabilities.

Despite my hatred of work, my least favourite day of the week is still Saturday. Everyone else works both shifts, and I spend a lot of time by myself upstairs. Because I'm not working, I take care of the chores. It not only keeps me distracted, it helps to pass the time, and although Ed usually manages to come upstairs for an hour or so, we don't get a lot of time to ourselves.

Today, I've finished the laundry and tidied the apartment, and am just finishing cleaning the kitchen, when Ali appears. I check my watch.

"I had no idea it was three o'clock already."

She smiles. "That's because you've been busy." She looks around the apartment. "It's so tidy."

"It won't last," I tell her. "Not once Ed and Sam come up here."

"No." She laughs. "I guess we'd better make the most of it."

"Aren't they coming up?"

"Not yet. They're having a discussion with Rob."

"Oh." Ed didn't mention this.

"Don't look so worried," she says, coming over to me. "It wasn't planned. Rob's been working on their figures for the last quarter and wanted to go through everything with them."

"I see."

"Ed said to tell you he'll be up later. I'm gonna cook us something to eat before tonight's service." She comes around the island unit and opens the fridge. "Although personally, I'm so hot, I'd like a salad."

"Then make a salad. I won't complain." I smile over at her.

She closes the fridge door and sits at the island unit. "I don't need to think about that yet," she says. "Come and sit with me for a while." I join her and she turns to face me. "Is everything okay?" she asks, barely giving me time to get comfortable.

"What with?"

"You and Ed."

"Yes."

"You're happy with him?" she asks.

"Yes, of course I am. He loves me and I love him."

She looks at me, studying my face. "Then why don't you seem very happy?" She moves a little closer. "Is there anything he's doing – or not doing – that you're not okay with? Because if there is, you need to tell him, not suffer in silence. Ed will understand, Tess. He's a good guy."

"I know. I know he's a good guy. I've always been able to talk to him, even before we started seeing each other."

"Then what's wrong?"

"It's work, really." I have to tell her something and this is easier than telling her that I'm still feeling homesick. I can't tell her that; she'd only blame herself. "I hate my job and the people who work there, and now Zoe's left, it's even worse."

"You like what you're doing though, right?"

I nod my head. "Yes. Most of the time."

"I'm sorry," she whispers, and I notice she's got tears in her eyes too. "I had no idea you were so unhappy."

"I'm not, at least I'm not when I'm with Ed."

She looks up. "But you're not with him very much?" she queries, and I nod my head. "Is what you've got with him enough to keep you here?" she asks, sounding fearful.

"We cut our ties with home." I avoid answering her directly, because I don't know the answer myself yet. Most of the time I think it is – when he and I are together, anyway. "We sold the flat, and the house will sell eventually," I add.

"Speaking of which, do you want to reduce the price?" she asks me. "We never did go back to Miles about that, or the money..."

"I suppose so. It's not like we really need the cash, is it?"

"Not really. I'll contact Miles and tell him to deal with it." She swallows hard. "I wish you'd told me how bad it was at work," she says.

"It's fine, Ali," I reassure her. "I'll sort it out in the end, I'm sure."

"You can talk to me, you know," she reiterates.

"I know." *Except I can't. Not really, because I can't tell you that I still miss home so much it hurts. And I can't tell Ed that either...*

Ali makes us both a coffee and we move into the living room and sit on the couch.

"Now the wedding's out of the way," I say, trying to steer the conversation away from me, "are you going to look into starting your business over here?"

Ali looks at me and bites her bottom lip, seemingly a little shy.

"Is it more complicated than you thought it would be?" I ask her.

"No," she replies. "It's not that." She puts her cup down on the table and twists in her seat to face me. "Sam and I have decided to shelve the idea for now."

"You have?" I'm surprised. "That's a shame. You were really good at what you did, Ali. I think this place proves that."

"Thanks," she says, blushing slightly. "The thing is... we want to try for a baby."

For a moment, I'm stunned, but I recover quickly. "You do? But you've only just got married. Surely you want to wait a while and spend some time together first." I know I would.

"I'm nearly thirty, Tess."

"And?"

"And Sam wants to have at least two children – maybe more."

"How many do you want?" I ask her.

"Two… minimum. After that, we'll see. But I want them fairly close together. Not with a big age-gap like us. And I'd like to have them while Sam and I are both young enough to enjoy them."

"You're not old, Ali," I reason.

"I know…" She looks away for a moment, and then returns her gaze to me. "I never thought Sam would want kids at all," she admits. "But we talked about it before the wedding, because… well, because I think it's the kind of thing everyone should discuss before they get married, and we agreed we both wanted kids at some point, and then he brought the subject up again while we were on our honeymoon, and he asked me if there was any reason why 'some point' can't be now." She's smiling and looks so contented with life, I can't help but feel happy for her. "I've already stopped taking the pill," she confides, her eyes alight.

"So you're really going to do this?"

She nods enthusiastically. "Yep."

"And I'll be an aunty?"

"You will." She smiles at me. "Best aunty in the world."

I lean over and give her a hug. "I'm really happy for you both," I tell her.

"We haven't got there yet," she replies.

"You will," I say, leaning back. "This is Sam we're talking about."
She looks at me for a moment and we both burst into fits of giggles.

Ed did make it up to the apartment during the afternoon break, together with Sam and Rob. Petra joined us just in time for dinner, being as Thea and David had taken April out for pizza, with his grandchildren, and we all sat around the table together and ate the delicious couscous salad, with olives, asparagus and grana padano, that Ali made. We didn't get much time to talk, but Ed held me in his arms for most of the time he was up here and we kissed a few times. To be honest, just being in the same room as him is enough sometimes. Today was one of those times. Knowing that Ali's really settled here and that she and Sam are going to start a family of their own just made me feel even more on the outside. I didn't say that, of course, but that doesn't mean I didn't feel it.

Once everyone's gone back downstairs, I settle down with the TV remote and find a movie. Tonight, I know I'm not up to watching anything romantic, or that might make me cry, so I start watching the first part of *Lord of the Rings*, knowing it's long, and that there's nothing in it to remind me of my own problems. I'm not being hunted by Ringwraiths, after all.

"Hey." The voice whispers across my skin and I open my eyes and find Ed looking down at me. "Do you have any idea how beautiful you are," he murmurs and leans down to pick me up, holding me in his arms.

I'm not really awake, but I manage to clasp my arms around his neck and hold onto him as he walks to my bedroom.

"The TV?" I murmur into him.

"It's okay," he says quietly. "I already turned it off."

"And the lights?" He's not switching them off.

"Sam and Ali are still downstairs. I finished before them and came to check on you."

"And found me sleeping?"

"Yeah… my very own sleeping beauty."

He sets me down gently on the bed, and reaches around behind me to unzip my dress.

"You're gonna have to stand," he says and I do, holding onto him, while he undresses me, removing my underwear.

"I appear to be naked," I say, teasing him.

"I noticed." He leans down and kisses me. "You appear to be awake too."

"Are you complaining?"

"Certainly not."

He pulls back the duvet and I sit on the edge of the bed and watch him undress. He's already taken off his chef's whites and quickly pulls his t-shirt over his head, dropping it to the floor, before lowering his jeans and shorts and kicking off his shoes. As he stands again, I come face to face with his erection and, dragging my eyes away from it, I look up into his face.

"May I?" I ask.

"May you what?"

"Touch."

He smiles. "Of course you may." He takes a step closer and I reach out and take hold of him, wrapping my fingers around his thick shaft. He feels hard, but velvety soft at the same time and he sucks in a breath as I touch him, lettings his head roll back.

"Is that okay?" I ask, stilling.

"It's perfect," he replies, looking down at me.

"I'm sorry, but I don't have a clue what I'm supposed to do."

He smiles again and places his hand over mine, and then starts moving it up and down his length. "Just stroke it, babe," he says and, as I increase the pace, he lets out a soft groan. My fingers barely fit around him and I bring up my other hand to encase him properly. "Oh Jeez," he mutters, putting his hands behind his head and closing his eyes. There's a drip of clear liquid on the end of him, and just before it falls, I lean forward and gently lick it away with my tongue. It's kind of salty and I like it. "Christ, Tess," he says, his voice deep and almost pained.

"What?" I stop what I'm doing, release him and lean back, looking up at him. "I'm sorry."

He drops to his knees before me and clasps my face in his hands. "Why the hell are you apologising?" he asks.

"I assumed I did something wrong?"

He smirks. "No, babe," he says quietly, moving closer and kissing me. "You did everything perfectly."

"Oh. So it's okay for me to lick it?"

"It's more than okay."

"And what about taking it in my mouth?" Because I have to admit, I was tempted just then.

"That's very much okay too," he says, grinning. "As long as it's what you wanna do."

I nod my head. "Maybe not tonight, being as it's so late, but I'd like to, yes."

"Okay. We'll save that for another day. When we've got more time."

I nod my head "Good. I'd like to take my time and enjoy you."

He stands and places his hands under my arms, lifting me back onto the bed and laying me down. "I wanna enjoy you too," he whispers. "Right now." He reaches over to the bedside cabinet, opens the drawer, rips into the packet he's just pulled out, and rolls the condom over his erection.

"You'll have to show me how to do that," I say to him.

"Gladly," he replies. "Just not right now... okay?" He's impatient tonight and that thought makes me giggle. As he crawls up my body, I part my legs, letting him settle between them. He puts his hand around his erection and guides it into place and then pushes inside me. The stretch is still hard to handle to start with and I gasp in a breath. He stills and lets me get used to the feeling, the sensation of being so full, before he starts to move, very slowly in and out of me, taking me deeper and deeper with every stroke. I don't know quite what he does, or how he does it, but whenever we make love, there's a spot inside me that he seems to touch and it sets my whole body on fire.

"Lift your legs," he says and I do, looking up into his eyes as he leans up a little and takes hold of them, putting them over his shoulders, so I'm bent back on myself. He stills. "This is gonna be deep," he says and I nod, just before he plunges into me.

"Oh God," I cry and clamp my hand across my mouth.

He stops, and looks down at me. "Too much?" he asks and I shake my head.

"No."

"More?"

"Yes. More."

He smiles and starts to move again, his hands up by my head, supporting his weight as he moves in and out of me again, hitting that sweet spot every time.

"Please, Ed..." I whimper. "Please." I can't speak any more. I'm gone... I throw my head back and let out a scream of pleasure, feeling wave after wave pulse through me, as he thrusts hard into me twice more and then stills, his body convulsing deep into me as he calls out my name.

It takes me a minute or two to come back to reality and I open my eyes and stare up at his beautiful face.

"I don't think either of us was particularly quiet that time," I murmur and he smirks.

"Nope. But then I'm not sure I care." He lowers my legs then moves himself down gently and rolls us both onto our sides, so we're still joined, and we're facing each other. "You were spectacular," he murmurs, kissing me softly.

"I think that was mostly you." I kiss him back. "And I don't think we need to worry about being noisy – at least not for the time being."

He tilts his head to one side, looking puzzled. "Why not?"

"I don't suppose for one minute that Sam has mentioned this, but Ali spoke to me earlier and… well, evidently they're trying for a baby."

"They are?" He smiles as he speaks.

I nod. "Yes."

"I wasn't sure Sam wanted kids," he adds, like an afterthought.

"No. Neither was Ali, evidently, but they talked it through before the wedding…"

"They did?"

"Yes."

"How sensible," he smirks.

"Eminently," I agree, and he hugs me.

"And they decided to start a family straight after their wedding?" He's as surprised as I was.

"No, not at the time. They decided to have kids, but didn't put a timeframe on it, and then Sam made the suggestion while they were on their honeymoon."

He raises his eyebrows. "Sam?"

"That's what Ali told me, yes."

"Well, I'll be…"

"Anyway, it got me thinking…" I start to say.

"What about?" He looks a little confused and I smile at him.

"Not about having kids, if that's why you're looking so terrified," I tease.

"I'm not terrified," he says quietly. "Not about that, anyway. I know you weren't thinking about having kids."

"You do?"

"Yeah. Of course I do."

"How?" I ask, feeling a little frightened myself now.

"Well, it's not because we've only been together for a short while, or because we're not married, or even because you're still quite young… It's because having kids would be a dumb thing to do, and you know it, considering you don't feel all that settled here."

He knows? "H—How did you know?" I ask him, tears pricking my eyes.

"Because I know you. Because you're not happy," he replies.

"I am with you," I say quickly. "I honestly am."

"I know." He strokes my hair and kisses me. "I know you are. But you're not happy the rest of the time, are you?" I shake my head, because I can't speak, and we just lie together, looking at each other for a while, both knowing that, with that short exchange of sentences, that started with a silly joke, our relationship has changed, just slightly, and not for the better.

"So what were you thinking?" Ed asks eventually. "About Sam and Ali?" He clarifies, because he knows I'm distracted enough to have forgotten.

"Oh… I just figured they might want some privacy," I explain. "I wondered if maybe we should try and spend some more time away from the apartment on Sundays, to give them a chance to be alone and…"

"Make babies?" he says, smiling. And I feel relieved that the realisation that I'm not settled here doesn't seem to have affected him too much. He's still got a sense of humour, anyway.

"Yes."

"I admire your generosity, but to be honest, I seriously doubt Sam would be held back by us being here."

"Even so…"

He caresses my hair gently. "This is as much about you feeling embarrassed as it is about giving them space, isn't it?"

"Yes, I suppose so."

He nods. "Then that's fine." A shadow crosses his face, just for a moment.

"What's wrong?" I ask him.

"Nothing... It's just that, if we're not here, how are we supposed to find time for ourselves?"

I hadn't thought about that and, for a moment, I wonder about the wisdom of my idea, but then I have a brainwave. "You've got an apartment, haven't you?"

"Yeah." A slow smile forms on his face.

"So we could spend our Sundays there, couldn't we?"

A smile spreads across his face. "We could move in there as far as I'm concerned." Even as he says the words, I feel myself shiver. "Rob lives at Petra's place now," he continues, oblivious to my discomfort. "And it would mean we'd have our privacy and so would Sam and Ali. And maybe having a place of our own would help you to feel more settled, make you feel more at home... What do you think?" He gazes at me, and then stops sharply. "What's wrong?"

"Um..."

"Tess, you're shaking. Tell me what's wrong?"

"I'm not ready," I whisper.

"To move in with me?"

I nod. "I'm sorry. So many things have changed in my life over the last few weeks. I just feel like I need to stay with Ali, for a little bit longer."

"It's okay."

I shuffle up the bed so I can face him better, even though it means disconnecting us. "Then why does it feel like it isn't?"

He takes a deep breath. "Do you feel safe with me?" he asks bluntly.

"Yes. I've never felt safer with anyone else."

He sighs, but doesn't say anything.

"I do feel safe with you. And I know you'll take care of me. And I know it didn't help that I just admitted to feeling unsettled here... but that has nothing to do with you." I move closer, so our bodies are completely fused. "I can't lie to you, Ed. This doesn't feel like home yet. But I'm sure it will. I just need to give it more time. Please try and be patient and don't give up on me."

"Hey, who said anything about giving up?" he says softly. "If you need more time, I'm okay with that. We don't have to move in to my place if you're not ready. We don't have to do a damn thing, if you're not ready." He leans down and brushes his lips across mine. "I'm okay with whatever makes you happy. I love you, Tess."

"I love you too. So much, Ed. I honestly do."

We kiss for a few minutes, and then he gets up and goes to the bathroom, before returning and switching off the bedside lamps, plunging us into darkness.

"There's something else I forgot to tell you," I murmur as he settles back into bed and puts his arms around me again.

"More bombshells?" he asks.

"Not really. Ali and I decided to reduce the price of the house, that's all. She told the lawyer we'd talk about it, but we hadn't had time to discuss it properly until today. The thing is, we don't really need the money, and there's no point it just sitting there waiting for a buyer."

"Makes sense, I guess," he replies. "I meant to ask," he adds, "while we're on the subject of your properties, what did you decide to do with the money from the sale of your apartment in London? Am I officially dating a millionaire now?" Even in the moonlight, I can see his wide smile.

"Yes, you are," I tell him. "I decided to have the money transferred into my account at home." He tenses at once, and his smile disappears.

Ed

"Home?" I query.

"Well, you know what I mean," she says quickly, like she's trying to make amends; like she knows her saying that will have hurt me.

I don't know why it hurts, but it does. I mean, she just admitted that she's not feeling all that settled here, and that she still feels the need to live with Ali, rather than me, so why the hell am I feeling hurt by the fact that she had her money moved to the UK, and that she still sees that as home? This has certainly been a night for revelations – none of them good.

She sighs and looks up into my eyes and, even in the moonlight, I can see her own hurt.

"Do you wanna go back there?" Even as I say the words, I'm not sure I want to know the answer, but I feel I have to ask. I have to know.

"Like I said just now," she replies, after a moment's pause, "I'll get used to it here in time."

She hasn't answered my question, and now I'm not sure what's worse; knowing she wants to go back, or knowing that the person who can usually tell me everything, can't tell me she wants to go back. Because those are the two realities I've just realized I'm facing.

I hold her close and pull her head down, so it's resting on my chest. This way, she can't see my face, which is a good thing, because I'm struggling to hold it together at the moment. She sounds so sad, so desolate. And being here is what does that to her. Being with me might make her feel good, but I belong in a place she sees as alien, a place she's struggling to fit in to.

"I love you," I hear her whisper, and she pulls back, looking up at me again. "I really do, Ed."

"I know. I love you too." I gaze into her eyes. *I just wish you could accept that I'm your safe place; that you don't need 'home', or Ali, or anyone else anymore, because you've got me. I'm your home. And you've got all of me. Always.*

"Where's the door?"

I wake with a start.

"I can't get out! Daddy... where are you?"

Tess is tossing and turning on the bed beside me, sweat pouring off of her, strands of her hair stuck to her face. She's had nightmares before, but nothing like this. Normally, she just screams or murmurs something incoherent and wakes up, crying. She never speaks.

"Tess?" I raise myself up on one elbow and gently shake her with the other hand.

"Please... please, Daddy." Shit... this isn't good. "There's too much smoke. Daddy... the fire. It's so hot... It's coming for me..." The panic in her voice is heartbreaking.

"Tess. Open your eyes. You're having a nightmare. Look at me, babe."

"I can't find you..." She tosses her head from side to side. "Daddy!" she screams.

"Tess." I raise my voice and her eyes snap wide open. She focuses on me and then bursts into tears. "Hey, babe." I hold her close. "It's okay."

"He never finds me in my dreams," she says softly, sobbing into me. "It's like he doesn't care enough to even bother."

"But he did find you, Tess. In real life, he did save you."

"And then he went back..."

I can't answer that. I don't understand his reasoning any more than she does.

"I know."

"He left me," she whimpers.

"Not because he wanted to." I hope I'm right in that. "And you're safe now. I'll never leave you."

"Promise?" There's a hint of desperation in her voice.

"I promise."

"No matter what?"

"No matter what."

I open the door to my apartment and stand to one side to let Tess in.

"Jeez, it's warm in here," I mutter, as I follow her.

"I suppose that's the problem with the place being closed up during the week," Tess replies, helping me open the windows.

"Yeah."

We've been coming here on Sundays for over a month now, and while we've had plenty of sex at Sam's apartment, we both need the release of being able to be ourselves here. The thing is, the last week has seen temperatures soar, and the apartment feels like an oven.

She comes over to me, walking slowly and not taking her eyes from mine. "We could always take our clothes off," she whispers, a slow smile spreading across her lips.

"And take a cool shower?" I suggest.

"Hmm… sounds lovely." She takes my hand and leads me into the bathroom, where we start undressing real slowly, before ripping each other's clothes off and kissing passionately.

"I want you. Now," I murmur into her as I bite her bottom lip.

"Then take me," she replies and, bending to grab a condom from my jeans pocket, I roll it over my dick and, without a moment's pause, I lift her into my arms and impale her onto my erect cock.

She squeals, then groans, and then shudders, clinging onto my shoulders, as I walk us into the shower.

"Turn on the water, babe," I say to her and she does. It gushes out cold and she screams as it hits the back of her neck.

"God, that's freezing," she yelps.

I turn us and, supporting her with one arm, I adjust the setting just slightly, so the water heats up a little, but not too much. The last thing either of us needs is a hot shower. Once the temperature's right, I settle her back against the cool tiles and start to move inside her, taking her long and slow, but going deeper with every thrust. She clings to me, and after just a few minutes, she comes apart, screaming my name and begging for more.

"You want more?"

"Yes," she nods, breathless. "Yes."

I look into her eyes and see my own desire reflected back at me, then lift her off of my straining cock.

"Oh," she murmurs her disappointment.

"Turn around," I whisper.

"Turn around?"

I nod and she does as I've asked.

"Place your hands on the tiles," I instruct and she does, as I pull her ass toward me, bending her slightly, and placing the tip of my cock at her soaked entrance. "Still want more?" I ask her.

"Yes." She nods.

I slam my cock hard into her and she screams her pleasure, coming hard after just a few strokes of my dick. I have no idea how she does that, but I love the fact that she does, and I continue to plough into her, taking her harder and harder as she rides out her orgasm.

"More?" I ask, as she starts to calm.

"Yes," she breathes. "Yes, please."

I think for a moment, and then pull out of her once more. "I wish you'd stop doing that," she says.

"Trust me… with what I've got in mind, there's no way we're gonna be able to get into position if I stay inside you."

She turns to me and places her hand on my chest, standing beneath the cascading water. "What have you got in mind?" she asks.

"That would be telling." I lean down and kiss her, and then drop to my knees. "Move your legs apart," I whisper and she does. I bend forward and gently part her lips, and lick her clit, brushing the tip of my tongue across it.

"Oh… that feels so good," she mutters, her hand clamping onto the back of my head.

"Yeah… but that's not what I had in mind," I tell her. "That was just a perfect distraction." I lean back and, grabbing her hips, I pull her down, straight onto my cock. Her legs are either side of mine, and she wraps them around me, our bodies joined.

She stutters out a groan and kisses me, her tongue clashing with mine as she starts to move, riding my cock hard.

"Take me, babe," I murmur into her. "Take me hard."

Her breasts are crushed against me as she grinds harder, taking me deeper, and her breathing becomes more labored. She's close, but so am I.

"Come for me, Tess. Now. I need you."

Her eyes pop open and she comes apart, just as I let go and bury my head in her shoulder, holding her close, while I cry out her name.

"Can I ask you something?" Tess asks. We got out of the shower eventually, but didn't bother with clothes and have been lying on my bed ever since, naked in each other's arms.

"Of course you can." I turn toward her, holding her closer. "What's wrong?" Since our conversation that night, we've not really discussed how she feels about living in Hartford, and every time she starts talking to me, I wonder what she's gonna say. That means I'm living on the edge all the time, but I keep hoping that, one day, she'll tell me she's feeling better about things. Of course, I also live in fear that she could tell me she feels worse. The thing is, I think I'd know if she did, and so far, she seems to just be happy for things to continue as they are. And if Tess is happy, then I'm happy…

"Nothing," she replies and I try to disguise my sigh of relief. "I just wanted to ask if you'll do something for me."

"I'll do anything for you. You know that."

She smiles. "You might change your mind in a minute."

"I doubt that."

She runs her finger down my cheek, then my neck and onto my chest, where she stops, looking suddenly shy.

"What's wrong, Tess?"

"I think I want to go on the pill," she whispers.

"The birth control pill?" I clarify.

She nods her head. "Only I don't know how to go about it. Not over here, anyway."

I smile at her. "And you think I do?"

"Well, I'm assuming you'll have more idea about how the health system works than I do."

"Fair point." I lean back a little, so I can look at her properly. "You really wanna do this?"

"Yes. I want to feel you properly," she replies. "All of you." She swallows and before I can say anything, continues, "I realize you'll have experienced it before…"

"Experienced what before?" I interrupt.

"Sex without a condom." I love that she's so open, even if she is completely wrong.

"No." I shake my head. "No, I haven't. I'm a firm believer in safe sex."

"So if I went on the pill, would you still use one?" she asks, and I have to chuckle.

"No, babe. It's different for us. I love you. I wanna feel all of you too." She smiles. "So, you'll help me?"

"Of course." I've got no idea how, but it can't be that hard. "We'll go on the internet together and find a doctor."

"And will you come with me?" she asks.

"You don't want Ali?"

She shakes her head and moves closer again. "No. This is between us."

And for the first time in quite a long time, I feel like I've taken just a very small step away from the edge.

"That was complicated," Tess says, as we leave the doctor's office.

"It wasn't that complicated, babe. You did understand it all, didn't you?"

"Yes, I think so. I just didn't realize I'd have so many options as to when to start taking it. Or that I'd have to pay so much to see the doctor, or for the prescription."

"Welcome to America, sweetheart. So, which one are you going to go for? In terms of when you start it, I mean." I ask her, taking her hand and starting down the sidewalk.

"I think I'll just go with starting it today," she says.

"That makes sense. You only had your period a couple of weeks ago, so you'd have to wait for the next one to start," I point out, recalling those four days and how Tess wasn't kidding when she said her periods were light. I'd hardly have known she was having one, except for the fact that she wore panties in bed, and we didn't have sex. And I wasn't complaining about that either. We hugged, we kissed, we talked, we slept in each other's arms. It was good. "And as for starting it on a specific day, like a Sunday… well, what's wrong with a Wednesday?" I add.

"Precisely." She looks up at me. "So, we just have to wait seven days…" Her eyes sparkle.

"We don't really have to 'wait' at all," I tell her. "We just have to keep using condoms for seven days."

"So, next Wednesday, we're good to go?"

I nod my head. "Yeah."

Wednesday can't come soon enough for either of us, but now it's here, and we both wake early.

"I know I should probably say 'good morning'…" Tess says wistfully.

"But you'd rather I just made love to you?" I suggest.

She nods her head, smiling, and I roll her onto her back.

"God, it's good not to have to think about a condom," I tell her, settling between her parted legs.

She stares up at me and, for some reason, it feels just like the first time, all over again, and I lean down and kiss her tenderly.

"It'll be okay," I whisper.

"I love you," she says.

"I love you." I place my cock at her entrance and push inside her, feeling her soft, wet walls surrounding me for the first time.

"Oh… God," she mumbles, her eyes closing and her head rocking back. "I didn't know… I didn't know…"

I still. "You didn't know what, babe?"

"That it would feel so much better," she says, opening her eyes, which are filled with tears, and staring up at me. "It feels so perfect… so beautiful."

"That's because you're perfect, and you're beautiful."

I start to move, really slowly, savoring the feeling of her tight muscles around me, as she brings her legs up, clasping me tightly to her. I feel a very slight rippling sensation inside her, just before she explodes around me, her nails digging into my back as she comes hard.

She calms slowly and I change position, just slightly, raising her legs onto my shoulders so I can take her even deeper.

"That's so good," she mutters, through gritted teeth, and I start to move a little faster. "Oh, yes," she whispers. "Take me, Ed… please."

I give her everything I've got and, within moments, she comes again, yelling my name, and I plunge deep inside her, truly filling her for the first time, crying out my pleasure.

Once we're both breathing properly, I focus on Tess. She's smiling and looking flushed. "I'm fairly sure Sam and Ali will have heard that," she whispers.

"Who cares?" I reply. "You felt amazing."

"So did you." She leans up and kisses me, her hands holding my face. For a brief moment, it's perfect.

Then Tess gets up and goes for her shower, and once I'm left alone, I wonder whether it'll always be like this, or whether the need to be at 'home' will prove too much for her. And whether I won't be enough to keep her here.

When I get back from taking Tess to work, Sam's already downstairs in the kitchen and he looks up as I go in.

"Can we talk?" he asks, sounding serious.

"Yeah. Should I be worried?"

"No." He follows me down to my section of the room.

"What's up?" I ask him, leaning back against the countertop.

He sighs. "Don't take this the wrong way," he begins, propping himself up against the door frame, "but you have remembered that you've got your own apartment, haven't you?"

I stare at him for a moment. "Um… yeah. But you said it was okay if I stayed here."

"I know. And it is. It's just... Ali and I were wondering if you guys would like some more privacy." He smirks.

I have to smile. "I'm guessing you heard us this morning?"

"We hear you every fucking morning," he replies. "This morning was just louder than the average."

"Sorry."

"Hey. Don't be sorry. We're not exactly quiet ourselves."

"We had noticed," I reply.

He looks at me, unabashed and shrugs. "It's just that Ali and I were saying you two might find it easier if you had some more space, a place of your own... and you've already got one."

"I know," I tell him. "We spend our Sundays there already."

"You do?" he asks.

"Yeah. Ali told Tess that you guys are trying to start a family, so we figured we'd give you some peace and quiet."

He nods his head. "I didn't realize."

"No. You've been too busy with Ali."

He smirks again. "Yeah. I guess so." He smiles, clearly remembering something. "So, if you're spending your Sundays at your place, why don't you just move in there? You're living together now... what difference would it make?"

"A lot... to Tess, evidently," I reply. "I've already suggested it to her."

"And she said 'no'?" I nod my head. "Did she give you a reason?" he asks.

"Yeah. She said she still needs Ali, and she wants to take it slow."

He pauses, goes to speak and then stops.

"What, Sam?" I ask.

"It's just... Well, you're not exactly taking it slow, are you?"

"She meant in terms of us, not in terms of what we do. Moving in with me is a commitment too far for her. That would mean she's accepting staying here on a more permanent basis, and she's not ready for that yet."

"She said that?"

"Pretty much, yeah."

He moves across and stands in front of me. "Are you okay?" he asks.

"Not really. When we talked about moving in together, she admitted that she doesn't feel settled here. She says she loves me, but… well, if I'm being honest, I'm convinced that one day I'm gonna wake up and find she's gone back to the UK. She still calls it home. All the time. I know she's lonely too… She's not happy here, Sam."

"She's happy with you though, right?"

"Yeah. She says she is, but…"

"Then give it time," he says softly. "She's taken a huge step."

"I know. And I am giving her time. I'm not pressuring her to do anything."

He takes a step back, but keeps his eyes fixed on mine, before turning away and heading for the door. "She'd never just leave, you know," he says, flipping around to face me again. "She wouldn't just go like that. She wouldn't do that to Ali."

My heart sinks to my shoes. "That's great," I reply. "But I'd feel a whole lot better if it was me keeping her here, not her sister."

He bites his lip, like he regrets what he just said, and then he moves closer to me again and does something he rarely does with me – he pulls me into a hug, and I'm reminded why I've always needed him so much. "I'm sorry," he murmurs. "I wish I could make it right for you. But I'm here if you wanna talk, okay?"

I nod my head, because I can't speak at the moment. I wish he could make it right too. All my life, Sam's been the one to make everything right for me, but this is beyond even his capabilities.

He pulls back and looks down at me, then without saying another word, he turns and walks away.

I pick Tess up from work and she seems to have had a reasonable day, made better I think by the fact that Bryan's been out for most of it. Evidently that's meant that Brittany has taken charge, but Tess says she's just ignored her and gotten on with her work. It sounds horrendous to me, but she insists she really enjoys the actual work.

The evening shift isn't too bad and I make it upstairs before eleven-thirty, taking Tess straight to her bedroom. She starts to undress before

I've even closed the door and, by the time I turn around, she's already topless, her bra and t-shirt lying on the floor.

"Are you trying to tell me something?" I ask, going over to her.

"Yes. I want you."

I can't help but smile. "Well, that's nice to know."

She reaches for me, but I take a step back.

"What's wrong?" she asks.

"Nothing." *Apart from the fact that I don't know whether I'm enough for you.*

"Then why did you move away?"

I reach out and take her hands in mine. "Because I want to try something with you."

She smiles. "You do?"

"Yeah."

"What?" she asks.

"A different way of pleasuring each other," I start to explain.

"You mean you don't want to make love again – even though it was so perfect this morning?"

"We can do that later," I tell her.

"Later?" she whispers.

"Yeah. I wanna try something we haven't done before… although you mentioned it once, a while ago."

She thinks for a moment. "Are you suggesting I take you in my mouth?" she asks.

"Yeah." I smile down at her. "*While* I lick you."

"At the same time?" Her eyes widen.

"Yes." I nod my head and and move closer again, so we're almost touching. "Now," I say, lowering my voice, "the only question is, do you wanna go on top, or underneath?"

She stares into my eyes. "I don't know," she replies eventually. "Which do I want?"

I laugh. "I don't know, babe."

"Well, you decide for me."

"As it's your first time, I'd say you probably wanna go on top," I suggest, because in fairness, I think she's gonna find that easier.

She nods her head in avid agreement. "Okay," she says.

I quickly undress, while she removes her skirt.

"You need to take your panties off," I tell her.

She turns to face me. "Why do you call knickers panties?" she asks.

"Because they are," I reply, grabbing her and pulling her closer. "And right now, you shouldn't be wearing any."

I kneel down in front of her and pull hers down.

"The word 'panties' makes me cringe," she whispers as I expose her pussy.

"Okay… we'll call them knickers, if it makes you feel better," I say, looking up at her, and she smiles at me. I toss them to one side and get up again, taking her hand and pulling her over to the bed.

"So you're going underneath?" she says. She's not nervous, she's excited. I like that.

"Yeah."

I lie down on the bed, on my back, my erection stiff and upright, and without even realizing it, Tess licks her lips and then captures her bottom lip between her teeth, her eyes fixed on my cock.

"Come over here," I say, and she kneels on the bed.

"What do I do?" she asks.

"Turn around, so you're facing away from me, and then straddle me and put your ass over my face."

"Seriously?" The smile on her face makes me want to laugh.

"Yes, seriously." I smirk.

"That's very intimate," she says, even as she's carrying out my instructions.

"No more intimate than when I lick you while you're lying on your back," I tell her.

"I guess not," I hear her say, as she sidles up my body and I get a perfect view of her beautiful ass. She comes to rest right above my face, her legs spread wide, her pussy glistening and exposed to my tongue and I have to lean up and lick along her soft, tender fold. I hear her suck in a sharp breath and instinctively, she wiggles down onto me and I lick her a little harder.

"W—what should… Oh God… Ed… um… what should I—I do now." She's struggling to speak and starts grinding her pussy onto me, and I have to lean my head back to speak.

"Well, that's up to you, babe," I murmur, licking my lips and tasting her sweetness. "You don't have to do anything, but if you want to, you can suck my cock."

"How?" she asks.

"Just take it in your mouth and do whatever you like with it." I have no idea how to tell her what to do when it comes to this, so I decide to leave her to it, on the basis that anything will be great. I'm about to move back into position when I have a thought. "Only keep your teeth out of the way... okay?"

She laughs. "I think I'd worked that out for myself," she replies and I feel her moving slightly, leaning forward. For a moment, nothing happens and then I feel her hand come around the base of my shaft, and then her lips surround the head, and she starts to move lower, taking me. Oh God, that's good. She starts to move, going a little deeper each time and I realize she didn't need any instructions; she's a natural.

I part her ass cheeks with my hands, taking in the sight of her wet pussy, and then I lick her again, tasting her, before I also start to finger her, gently teasing her opening with just the tip of my forefinger, then plunging it inside, and then teasing again. My attentions make her move a little faster and I feel her breathing change, her hands pumping my shaft as she gets closer. I can feel the tip of my cock hitting the back of her throat and I'm so tempted to come, but I'm not going to. I want to make love to her, and besides, I'm not sure how she'd feel about me filling her mouth... that can wait until another time. I suck her clit, then flick my tongue across it a couple more times, and she explodes, squealing and moaning, sucking my cock so damn hard, it's all I can do not to climax, but I hang on, until she's calm, and I slowly pull my finger from her. She takes a moment to release my aching dick, and falls sideways onto the bed, lying on her side.

"That was incredible," she murmurs. "Just incredible."

"It's not over yet," I tell her, sitting up on the bed. "Come here."

"Where?"

"Here." I lean over and lift her onto me, lowering her over my erection as she puts her arms around my neck and sighs.

"That feels so good," she whispers.

"Yeah, it does."

I'm buried deep inside her now and she looks right into my eyes, just as she starts to move, riding my cock, alternating between grinding her hips down onto me and pounding me really hard. The sensations are something else and I know I won't last for long.

"You'd better be close, babe," I mutter, holding her hips and pulling her onto me.

"Yes…" she groans. "Yes… now." And with that, she comes spectacularly, throwing her head back and screaming my name.

It's too much. I hold her steady, impaled on me and fill her with everything I've got.

She collapses into me and we fall back onto the bed, Tess lying on top of me, her breasts crushed against my chest.

"I liked that," she says after a while, her voice little more than a whisper.

"Which bit?" I ask, just to clarify.

"All of it." She leans up, with some effort, resting on her elbows, and looks down at me. "I like having you in my mouth."

I smile up at her. "Well that's good, because I like being in your mouth. And I've gotta say, you're very good at that."

"Is it very different if you go on top?" she asks, tilting her head to one side.

"No, not really. But I have more control. You don't get to dictate the pace quite so much. And if you're not ready for that, then that's fine."

"And can I do that without you doing anything to me?" she adds.

"Yes. But you don't have to, not if you don't want to."

She smiles. "Oh, I want to," she says, sweetly and I feel my cock twitch. She tilts her head again and I know she's trying to work out how to ask a question. I wait and give her time. "You gave me an orgasm," she says slowly, "while we were doing that… but you didn't have one until we were making love. Is there a reason for that?"

I put my arms around her and hold her close. "Yeah. I wasn't sure how you'd feel about me coming in your mouth," I explain. "Not everyone likes it."

"They don't?"

"No."

"How will I know if I like it?" she asks.

"I guess we'll have to try it and see," I suggest.

She leans down, resting her head on my chest. "Well, I'm kind of tired right now, so maybe we can do that in the morning?"

I laugh. "We can do that any damn time you like, babe."

We tried it in the morning, after we'd showered. Tess wanted to do the same thing again, but with me on top this time, and she wanted me to come in her mouth. It turned out she liked it. Actually, she liked it a lot, and over the last few weeks, I honestly believe that the physical side of our relationship has gotten even better. It's beyond anything I could ever have imagined, and whenever we're together, I know without a doubt that there will never be any other woman for me. Tess is it, as far as I'm concerned. She tells me she feels the same, that she loves me and that she needs me, all the time.

Even so, every day, when I wake up, I turn over, just to check she's still there. So far, she has been, thank God. But that won't stop me from checking… or from worrying that one day, I'm gonna wake up to find the other side of the bed is empty.

Chapter Twelve

Tess

I've had such a special summer with Ed.

We've spent a lot of it at his apartment – well most Sundays, anyway. And since I went on the pill back in August, we've had some magical afternoons there together. Our habit now is to have breakfast with Sam and Ali, and then leave for the apartment, and when we get there, we immediately take our clothes off. That's mainly because the place is so hot and stuffy, but it's a good excuse to be naked with him. And I really do like being naked with him…

We've spent a few Sundays with the family as well. We've gone on picnics and had more barbecues at Petra and Rob's place, with her mum and David. I am finding those gatherings a little easier, now that I know everyone better. It's not that I don't still find them noisy, but I think everyone has accepted that I'd rather just be quiet and play with April, or sit with Ed, and they don't hassle me to do anything else. We're all getting used to each other.

I've also started writing a novel, which I work on during the evenings. It gives me something to do, and I've set it in England – specifically in London and Dorset – so I can escape to my favourite places, at least in my imagination. Ed knows all about this and, to start off with, while he was supportive of my writing, he was quiet about my choice of setting. I don't blame him for that. It must be hard for him that I'm struggling so much to accept Hartford as my home. Now though, he seems to have accepted my choice – at least as far as the novel is concerned – and a small part of our Sundays are spent with him reading over what I've written during that week. He tells me my descriptions are very vivid and he can easily picture the places I'm describing, even though he's never been to any of them, so I guess that's a good thing.

Work is still pretty dreadful. Bryan and Brittany still seem to be together, although they don't spend as much time in each other's company as he did with Zoe, not that Brittany seems to notice, or care that much. As far as she's concerned, she got what she wanted: the boss.

The magazine is celebrating its tenth anniversary, and there's going to be a big party at the office. When I first heard about this, I tried desperately to get out of it, but Bryan came and saw me and tasked me with organising it. Initially, I was dreading it, but it's actually been okay. It's set for the first Friday in October and I've organised the caterers, and the drinks – both of which Rob helped me to source. I've sent out the invitations, which Ali helped me with, and I've arranged the decorations for the office. I managed that by myself, and Bryan seems pleased with what I've done so far.

This last week, leading up to the party, has been particularly hard, because not only do we have the last minute planning to deal with, but we've also got the magazine to complete in time for the print deadline. It's meant I've had to work late, so Ed hasn't been able to pick me up, because he's needed to be in the kitchen by the time I've finished. I've only had to work an extra hour or so each night, so I've still been able to walk back to the apartment by myself, but I've missed having him there to greet me in the lobby.

On the way to work this morning, Ed told me that he's missed our afternoon walks too.

"I know how you feel," I reply. "But the party's tonight and, once that's over, things will go back to normal. You can pick me up from work in the afternoons, we can eat together again, and I can get back to writing my book, and waiting up for you." I reach up and kiss him.

"I'm sorry," he says. "I'm being selfish."

"No, you're not."

"I keep forgetting how much time you spend on your own. I've only had to spend a week by myself – and then not all the time – and I've hated it."

I lean into him. "I don't mind, Ed. Honestly."

"What time's this party going to finish?" he asks.

"Around eight."

"Oh, so it's not really late then."

"No, but it does start at five, pretty much the moment we close the office for the day… and I'm going to be on 'duty' for the whole three hours. I'm dreading it."

"You'll be fine," he says, leaning down and kissing my forehead. "And when it's done, call a cab to take you home. Don't hail one off the street. Call one."

"Who do I call?" I've never done this before.

"We've got a company we use when customers are a little over the driving limit," he suggests, and looks them up on his phone, giving me their number. "Tell them to put it on our account," he adds.

"Are you sure?" I ask.

"I'm damn sure. You're not walking, or hailing at cab in the dark."

"Okay."

We stop outside the office and he looks down at me. "Try and enjoy the party," he says softly, leaning down and kissing me gently.

"I doubt that very much," I reply, returning his kiss, which he deepens.

"God, I can't wait for Sunday," he remarks, grinning.

"How about…" I hesitate to voice the thought that's just crossed my mind.

"How about what?" he asks, moving closer, his feet either side of mine.

"How about if we spend Saturday night at your place too?" I whisper.

He stills, staring down at me. "Did I just hear you right?" he asks. "Did you just suggest spending the weekend at my place?"

"Not the whole weekend," I clarify quickly. "Just Saturday night. I don't want to spend the whole of Saturday there by myself."

He nods his head. "That's okay. I'll take whatever I can get," he says, his eyes sparkling with love. "Thank you, babe."

"Why are you thanking me?"

"Because it means a lot to me that you're starting to see this as your home."

I lean back and look at him. Is that what this means? I'm not so sure and I guess that must show in my eyes, because I notice the fireflies suddenly stop dancing in his as they dull into a frown.

"I'm reading too much into it, aren't I?" he asks, his voice betraying his sadness.

"Let's just see how the weekend goes, shall we?"

He nods his head and kisses me tenderly.

There's half an hour to go, and rather than quietening down, the party just seems to be getting louder and louder. Certainly most of the attendees are getting drunker and drunker.

I noticed earlier that Bryan and Brittany didn't seem to be getting along too well, so I'm not sure what's going on there. I also saw Taylor disappearing into the men's room with one of the guests, who was in the process of undoing his trousers before the door had even closed. They came back out roughly twenty minutes later, looking a little dishevelled and went in opposite directions.

I've already got my mobile phone in my hand, ready to call the taxi company to book my cab home, when Bryan comes up to me. Surprisingly, he's not as drunk as most of the people here, or if he is, he's better at hiding it.

"You've done a really good job of organising this," he says to me, coming and standing beside me.

"Thank you," I reply, politely. "I was just going to call myself a cab to go home."

He stares at me. "Can you hang on until everyone's left?" he asks. "I've been meaning to talk to you for a while now about taking over Zoe's role officially." He never did bother to replace her and slowly but surely, I've just taken on her workload. "I think it's about time I rewarded you for all your hard work," he adds.

"Oh. Okay. I guess I can hang on for a while."

"Hopefully this crowd will fall out the door soon," he murmurs, moving away, but turning and walking backwards. "And then we can get together and talk."

I nod my head as he drifts back into the throng of people.

It's just after eight-fifteen by the time Bryan ushers the last of the revellers out of the door.

"At last," he says triumphantly. "I thought they'd never go."

"I'd better just send my boyfriend a message," I tell him as he leads me into his office. "He's expecting me back."

"Leave that for now," he insists. "I won't keep you long. And I can always drop you home, rather than you waiting for a cab. It'll save time." He moves behind his desk and I take the chair opposite, grateful for the chance to sit down.

"Do you need me to sign a new contract?" I ask him. I'm aware that my status here is dependent upon my employment, and I'm not sure how things work.

"No. That won't be necessary," he replies. He fumbles in his top drawer and eventually pulls out a box. I recognise the packaging… It's a box of condoms.

"Um… what are those for?" I ask, as he walks around to my side of the desk and stands in front of me.

"What do you think?" he says, taking my phone from my hand and putting it down on his desk.

"Well, you're not doing anything that involves using them… not with me."

He smiles. "Yeah… I am," he says, placing his feet outside of mine, and leaning over. "It's late," he whispers. "All the other offices will be closed, so don't bother to scream, because no-one's gonna hear you."

Oh shit…

"Just let me go," I beg him, looking up into his face. "I won't tell anyone about this. I promise. I won't even come back here, ever again."

He chuckles, standing upright again, but doesn't say anything and just undoes the button and zip on his trousers before pushing them down, followed by his boxers. He's hard and I look up at him again, and see he's smiling. It's a cruel, heartless smile.

"Open your mouth," he says.

I shake my head. I'm not even going to speak – because it means opening my mouth.

"Okay. Have it your own way," he replies, and for a split second, I think he might give up and let me go, but then he moves closer and grabs the back of my neck, pulling me forward so his penis touches my face. "I said, open your fucking mouth," he repeats, using his other hand to pull on my lower jaw. I struggle against him, pushing on his thighs, but he's stronger and the grip he has on my neck is starting to hurt. He gives up with my jaw and pinches my nose instead, blocking my airway, so after a short while I have to open my mouth to breathe, and he takes his chance, shoving himself inside. I gag against him as he pushes deeper and deeper, but he's nowhere near as big as Ed, thank God and he stops once he's pushed his entire length into my mouth, his pubic hair tickling my nose. "Now, suck it hard, bitch," he says, triumphantly, and uses the hand that's holding my neck to pull me onto him, while his hips thrust back and forth. I choke and gag, with every movement, my eyes watering, but that just seems to arouse him more. "Look at me," he urges, his voice desperate. I shake my head and he stills, then slaps my cheek hard enough to hurt. "I said, look at me," he repeats, and I raise my eyes to his. "That's better," he says and starts to move again. "Fuck, you're good," he murmurs, and then he starts to groan loudly, before pulling out of me, breathless, and letting me go. He takes a step back and I grab my chance and get up, going to run, but he pulls me back, then pushes me down onto the floor beside his desk. I try to scrabble away from him, but he kneels down, holding me firmly in place, his legs between mine, pushing my skirt up around my hips. "Nice panties," he says, rubbing his hand over the lace panel at the front of my knickers. I can feel bile rising up in my stomach and I want to retch.

"Leave me alone," I cry, trying to push my legs back together again, but he's in the way, and I can't. "Please, just leave me alone."

"You nearly sucked men off back then, so you know you don't mean that," he smirks, putting his fingers inside the top of my knickers and pulling hard, so they tear through the seam. I'm exposed to him. "Beautiful," he murmurs. "Fucking beautiful."

I bring my hands down to cover myself, but he grabs them, pushing them up above my head and holding them there with one of his, while his other hand moves back down between my legs again, parting my lips. He inserts two fingers inside me, roughly.

"Let's get you nice and wet, shall we?" he says, like I'm supposed to be aroused by him.

I shake my head, but he starts to move his fingers in and out of me really hard and fast, ignoring my falling tears.

"Please don't do this," I plead. "Please stop."

"No," he replies simply, panting hard, building the pumping motion, adding a third finger I think and increasing the speed. It hurts. I'm so dry, I feel like he's chafing me, cutting me, and I want to scream, but I'm scared of what he'll do if I make too much noise.

He lets go of my hands for a moment and changes position slightly, and I take the chance to slap his hand away from me.

"Don't!" he shouts, bringing his free hand down across my cheek in a hard slap, much harder than his earlier one.

I cry out in pain, clasping my hands to my stinging cheek.

"Don't fight me," he adds. "It'll only hurt you more."

My tears are falling freely now, but he's unmoved and turns, looking around.

"Shit," he says suddenly. "The fucking condoms are on my desk."

They're out of reach. To get to them, he's going to have to stand up. And that means I'll have a chance to run. I stare at him.

"Don't get any ideas," he warns.

I try to keep my expression placid as he pulls his fingers from me, then stands, and hauls me to my feet, keeping a firm grip on my wrist. Damn. My chance is lost.

He pulls me with him to the desk, and sweeping the few things on its surface to one side, he pushes me over, bending me so I'm face down, my face hard against the green leather inlay.

"It's better this way, anyway," he says, pressing his hand against my head and leaning over me, "you've got a perfect fucking ass." He chuckles, leaning back, releasing my head and running his hand roughly over my bottom, before slapping me hard. "Or should that be a perfect ass for fucking." He laughs more loudly, and I hear the sound of the box being opened, and the tearing of the foil wrapper that I'm so familiar with. *Oh God… Ed. Forgive me…*

I shake my head. I don't have time to think about Ed. If I'm going to stop Bryan, I've got to do something. Now. He moves in behind me and I feel his erection pressing against me.

"Spread your legs," he says.

I remain still.

"Spread your fucking legs," he repeats and puts his feet between mine, forcing my legs apart.

I'm wearing heels for once, because of the party, and as I feel the tip of his arousal start to enter me, I strike out backwards, my heel making contact with his shin.

"You fucking bitch!" he screams and steps back, hopping on one leg.

I don't wait, I don't look back.

I stand up, and I run, pulling my skirt down as I go.

I don't even break my stride as I grab my handbag from the desk outside, and I keep running, dodging past the lifts and making for the stairs. I can't afford to wait for the lift, or risk getting caught by Bryan in one of them. I take the stairs at a run, and find myself on the street, in a drizzle.

And it's then that I realise my coat and my phone are still upstairs.

I can't go back though. I can't even wait here, just in case he comes out.

I can't do anything, but run.

I've got no idea how long I've been running for, or even where I am. I've stuck to busy roads, where there are people around and the streets are well-lit and, every so often, I've checked behind me to make sure Bryan isn't following.

I need to be safe.

The apartment and the restaurant won't be safe; not any more. He's got that address. He could easily find me there and get someone to let him upstairs on the pretext of returning my phone and coat to me. I can't go back there. I couldn't anyway. How will I ever face Ed again? He'll be so disappointed in me… I shake my head again. I can think about that later. For now, I need to find somewhere safe. Somewhere that feels like home.

Home…

I need to be at home. I'll be safe there.

A cab drives past me, followed by another and I turn, raising my hand as a third comes into view. The driver pulls over and I climb in the back.

"Can you take me to the airport, please?"

"Which airport?" he asks, turning in his seat.

"I don't know," I reply. "I need to get a flight to London."

He whistles. "That would be Logan," he says. "It's gonna cost you, lady."

"I don't care."

"Well, I do. Can you afford it?" He looks me up at down. I don't blame him. I'm wet, my blouse is torn, my hair's a mess, I'm not wearing a coat, despite the weather, and I've been crying. Unbeknownst to him, I'm also not wearing any knickers – they're on the floor in Bryan's office.

I fumble in my handbag and find my bank card, handing it to him. "There's over a million pounds in that account," I tell him. "Do you take cards?"

"Yeah." His eyes are wide open now.

"Okay. Then charge me however much you like… just take me to the airport. Please."

He slowly and gingerly hands me back the card. "I'll charge you when we get there," he replies. "Are you okay?"

"I'm fine," I answer, fresh tears falling now. "I just need to get home."

"Home being London?"

"Yes." It's close enough.

"Okay, lady. I'll get you to Logan."

"Thank you."

He pulls away from the kerb and I glance up at the tall buildings, the lights haloed in the rain-streaked glass of the taxi that's taking me on the first leg of my journey home. Ali and Ed will be angry with me. Everyone else probably will be too, when they find out.

At least this way, I don't have to face them, or tell them what's happened.

I can go home and hide. And pretend everything's okay.

Even though it's never going to be okay again.

Ed

I've spent the whole day thinking about the weekend. Well, Saturday night and Sunday, anyway. It's not a whole weekend, but it's a start. Everyone has to make a start. That's what I've been telling myself, ever since I left Tess at her office this morning. I know I made too much of it, suggesting that her agreeing to spend Saturday night at my place was some kind of acceptance of living here permanently and seeing this as her home, but during the course of today, I've worked out that, even if it isn't that, even if it isn't everything I want it to be, it is at least a start.

"You're a lot more cheerful tonight," Sam says, coming over to me near the end of the service.

"Yeah." I move closer to him so I can lower my voice. "Tess suggested spending tomorrow night at my place."

"She suggested it?" he queries.

"Yeah. It was entirely her idea." I can't help smiling.

"That's a step forward."

"I know."

"Keep being patient with her," he says, patting me on the shoulder before he walks away.

I know I'm gonna be finishing late tomorrow night; it's Saturday, we always finish late. But I'm gonna take her back to my place and make love to her, no matter how late it is. And as far as I'm concerned, we're not getting up at all on Sunday.

"I wonder how Tess's party went?" Ali says as Sam switches off the lights.

"I don't know. I half expected her to stick her head around the door and let us know," I reply. "But I guess she was tired."

"It's been a tough week for her," Ali adds.

"Yeah. Still, she can have a nice relaxing weekend," Sam puts in, grinning and giving me a nudge.

We go upstairs together and, as Ali's first, she opens the door.

"Tess?" she calls out. The apartment is in darkness.

"Shh," Sam says. "She's probably gone to bed."

"She wouldn't go to bed," I reply quickly, speaking normally, pushing him out of the way and going down the hallway to her bedroom. "She wouldn't do that. She always stays up, even if she falls asleep on the couch."

"She's exhausted," he calls after me, still talking in loud whispers.

I push open the bedroom door, to find the room in darkness. Even in the moonlight, I can see the bed is empty and still made.

"She's not here," I call out and go back along the hallway.

Sam flicks on the lights. The apartment is eerily quiet.

"Where the fuck is she?" I say, moving into the living room. Sam stares at me, but that's probably because I just swore. "She's meant to be here."

"Stop panicking," he says, coming to join me and putting his hands on my shoulders. "I'm sure there's a perfectly reasonable explanation."

"I'll call her mobile," Ali suggests and I want to kick myself for not thinking of that first. Ali pulls her phone from her pocket, presses on the screen a few times and holds it to her ear. "It rang five times and went to voicemail," she says.

"Do you think the party might have gone on later than planned?" Sam suggests, looking from Ali, to me.

"It was meant to finish over four hours ago." I check my watch. It's gone midnight.

"Okay," he says. "Come with me."

"Where are we going?"

"To her office." He turns to Ali. "Keep dialing her number. If she picks up, call me."

Ali nods, her face pale, and Sam kisses her quickly.

Sam and I run down the stairs. "Are we driving, or running?" I ask him.

"Which is quicker?"

"By the time we get into the parking garage and get your car out, at this time of night… running."

He takes a breath and shrugs his shoulders. "Running it is then."

It takes us just over five minutes to run to Tess's office. The building is still open and I remember that she's on the third floor. The elevator arrives immediately and we get inside, both breathing hard.

"She'll be okay," Sam pants.

I just look at him, then watch the numbers light up above the door, impatient to get to her, to make sure she's okay.

When the doors eventually open, we go along the corridor until we find the offices of the magazine, but there are no lights on. We try the handle, but it's locked. Sam knocks, but no-one comes and there's no sound from inside.

He looks at me.

"Might she have gone out for a drink after the party? Does she know anyone else who works here?" he asks.

"Not anymore. Zoe was her only friend here and she left a few months ago now. And if she was gonna do that, I think Tess would have sent me a text."

"Does she live here still? This Zoe?" he asks, ignoring the second part of my comment.

"No. She moved back home to Chicago."

He nods. "There's nothing more we can do here," he says quietly. "We'd better get back to the apartment and see how Ali's getting along."

I don't really know what to say to him, so I just follow as he leads the way back. We run again, because it seems like the right thing to do, even though I don't think either of us knows why.

Back in the apartment, Ali is perched on the edge of the sofa and, as we enter, she jumps to her feet.

"Oh, it's you," she mutters. "I thought…"

"No, it's just us," Sam replies, going over to her. "I take it you still can't get through?"

"No. It goes straight to voicemail now, so I guess either she's turned it off, or her battery's died."

"I'm gonna call Rob," Sam says, pulling his phone from his back pocket and connecting the call. It takes a moment or two. "Hi," he says abruptly. "Yeah. I know it's late. Listen, did you see Tess this evening?" he asks, and waits for a moment, watching Ali closely as she paces the floor. "I don't know. I guess any time after eight-thirty? She'd have come in through the restaurant." He waits again. "Sure?" He sighs. "No… well, it's just she's not here." There's another pause. "We already tried that and the office is closed up." He pushes his fingers back through his hair and looks up at the ceiling while he listens. "No, I don't think there is, but thanks. I'll keep you posted." He hangs up and looks down at Ali. "Nothing," he says. "Rob didn't see her all evening. I guess I could try the other wait staff…" he suggests.

I flop down on the end of the couch, my head resting in my hands, so I don't have to watch any more of this. They haven't worked it out yet, but I've just realized where Tess is, and I feel cold and empty.

"What did you do?" Ali asks, her voice loud enough to break into my misery.

I raise my head again and find she's standing in front of me, glaring down.

"Me?"

"Yes. You. What have you done to her?"

"Ali…" Sam puts his hand on her shoulder, but she shrugs him off. "Ali, don't do this," he perseveres.

"He must've done something," she continues.

"Why?" I get to my feet and stare down at her "Why must I?"

Sam moves fractionally, so he's right beside Ali.

"Because she was fine… and now we can't find her."

"Ali," Sam puts in, "you need to calm down, baby."

She glares at him. "Calm down? Don't you understand, Sam? She's my little sister, and she's all alone in Hartford."

"No she's not." Even to me, my voice sounds harsh.

Ali turns and stares at me. "What do you mean?"

"She's not in Hartford. Haven't you worked it out yet?" She doesn't reply. She's still staring at me with her mouth slightly open. "It's blindingly obvious where she's gone, Ali. She's gone home… to England."

"She wouldn't do that. Not without saying goodbye to me."

"Don't you believe it," I say. "There's a lot you don't know about Tess." I bite my tongue, remembering I told her I wouldn't betray her secret. I can't break that promise, even though she's broken me.

"What are you talking about?"

"Nothing. It doesn't matter now. What matters is that she's gone."

"Yes. But why? What did you do to her?"

"I didn't do anything she didn't want me to," I yell. "She's left because she never wanted to come here in the first place, and you're the one who made her do that."

"Jesus, Ed." Sam steps forward. "I know you're hurting, but…"

"But what?" I turn to him. "But what, Sam?"

"Take it out on me, not Ali," he whispers. "I'm the one who made her come here."

I stare at him for a long moment, wishing I could punch him. I can't. I'm just not that kind of person, and I turn way from them both, fighting the tears that are threatening to fall.

"You told me earlier she was gonna come and stay at your place," Sam says quietly, and I feel his hand on my shoulder.

"Yeah. She was." I don't turn around. I can't face either of them. "But maybe I read too much into that."

"What do you mean?"

"I told her I thought her staying the night meant she was starting to see this as home, but I was wrong. She looked completely terrified when

I said that. I guess she didn't want the same things as me, after all. She must've worked out she didn't wanna be with me as much as I wanted to be with her, and I guess she couldn't handle it and made a run for home." I swallow hard, but a lone tear falls down my cheek. "I always… I always knew this would happen one day. She was just biding her time."

"Oh, I'm sorry, Ed… I didn't realize this was all about you," Ali says sarcastically.

"Ali, don't," Sam replies.

"Don't what? He can wallow in self pity after we've found her. Until then, Tess is the only thing that matters."

I turn to face her, no longer worried about them seeing my tears.

Sam sees my face and takes a step toward me, but I hold up my hand to stop him.

"You're damn right, Tess is the only thing that matters." I raise my voice again. "As far as I'm concerned it's always been about her. Always."

"And? What are you going to do about it?" Ali challenges me. "Are you going to sit and wallow, or go after her?"

"Why? Why would I do that? Tess doesn't want this life, Ali. She never did. And no matter how much I want her, I can't make her want to be here. I don't have that kind of power… and I'm not sure I want it. Not if being here makes her unhappy."

Ali steps forward now, and she keeps coming, so she's right in my face.

"Good God," she says. "You really aren't worthy of her."

"Ali!" Sam's voice cuts through everything.

She turns to him. "Remember?" she says. "Do you remember what I told you about our father? About what Tess was looking for in a man?" She turns back to me and glares at me with something approaching hatred, and I keep my eyes fixed on hers. For a brief moment, I'm tempted to tell Ali the truth about Tess's feelings towards their father and her own myth surrounding him, but I promised I wouldn't. And, in any case, why would I? Telling Ali the truth won't bring Tess back. It won't do anything other than make Ali see me in a different, maybe slightly kinder, light… and I couldn't give a damn what she thinks about me.

"In case you're wondering," she says at last, a lot more calmly, "Tess has always worshipped our father. She's always worshipped the fact that he put his love for our mother first, to the point where he chose to lie down and die with her. *That's* what she was looking for in a man… someone who'd always put her first." She pauses and takes a breath. "And she got *you*."

I don't answer her. I can't betray Tess's trust.

"That's too much, Ali," Sam says quietly, turning to her.

"It's not enough," she replies. "You once told me that Ed was the best of all of you, Sam, but he's not. He's nothing like the man you are." She falls into him and starts crying, just briefly, before she pulls back and turns to me again. She goes to speak, but I hold up my hand to stop her. I need to calm the situation before she says anything else.

"Ali," I whisper. "I know you don't think much of me, and that's your right, I guess. But I won't do anything that makes your sister unhappy. And being here was making her unhappy. Anyone could see that. I obviously wasn't enough for her, for whatever reason… And if there's one thing I learnt from *my* dad, it's that you sometimes have to love someone enough to let them do what they want, rather than making them unhappy by trying to make them do what you want."

She stares at me again, her eyes widening slightly. "Nice words, Ed," she says. "But being as you're clearly not going to go after, then I will. Only don't be surprised if she doesn't want to know you when she comes back here."

"She won't be coming back, Ali. She didn't want this life in the first place. You forced this on her, and now she's made the decision to do what *she* wanted. And I won't stop her. Because I love her."

She turns away from me, like she didn't even hear me. "Sam? Will you help me?" she asks, sounding doubtful.

"Help you with what?" He's looking shocked and confused.

"I need to get to London. Now."

"Um…"

"Fine. I'll work it out myself," Ali says, trying to dodge past him. He grabs her and holds on.

"Stop this," he commands. I've never heard him speak like that outside of the kitchen. "Just stop. Right now." Ali stares up at him. "I'll go to London," he says, more quietly. "You're too distressed."

"No." Ali pulls away from him. "This is one time in your life I don't need you to be in charge, Sam. I just need you to help me get on a goddamn flight."

He pulls her into his arms. "I love you, Ali," he whispers. "And I'll help you. You know I'll help you." She nods her head. "Only will you please calm down?"

"I'll calm down when I've found Tess and I know she's okay."

He takes her over to the couch and they sit as he pulls his laptop out from the shelf underneath the coffee table. I stand, aloof and alone, and watch as he books her on the next flight, which leaves at eight-thirty tomorrow morning. Once that's done, he tells her to go to bed, to get a couple of hours' sleep, and helps her to their bedroom.

I take advantage of their absence and leave.

I've got no idea how long I've spent wandering the streets, or where I've been, or where I'm going. Everything's a blur, except for my thoughts. I know with absolute certainty that I love Tess, and nothing's ever gonna change that. I know she said she loved me, but it seems that her love wasn't strong enough, for whatever reason, to keep her here. Maybe Ali's right. Maybe I wasn't the right man for her. I just wish she'd told me what she was gonna do. I wouldn't have tried to talk her out of it; not if she really wanted to go. I'd never try and force her to do anything. Ever.

I thought she understood that…

Chapter Thirteen

Tess

The cab driver turned out to be really kind. He didn't charge me more than the going fare, even though I'd told him how much money I've got. He also didn't talk too much on the journey. He did ask if I wanted him to call anyone, or if I needed any help. I declined both offers, but thanked him and tried really hard not to cry in front of him.

I managed to get one of the last seats on the last flight of the day to London, which was a good thing, as otherwise I'd have had to wait until the morning for the next one. I felt grateful that I've made a point of carrying my passport around in my handbag with me ever since I've been here. I don't know why I've done that – I suppose I just thought it might be useful to be able to prove I'm British. It's ridiculous, I know, but I'm glad I did it now.

I didn't have long to wait before boarding, and the fact that I had no luggage whatsoever helped in terms of speeding things up. In the few minutes that I had to spare, I did manage to find a store at the airport that sold basic clothing, and I bought a t-shirt and some knickers, which I changed into in the ladies' toilets. I also had a quick wash and tried to freshen up. It didn't work. I still feel grubby.

The flight was uneventful and I landed at Heathrow at nine o'clock this morning, and hired a car.

As far as I'm concerned, there's no point in heading towards London – there's nothing there for me anymore, so I'm driving to Dorset. At least the house is still ours and I can stay there while I work out what the hell I'm going to do.

I drive like I'm on auto-pilot, but then I feel like I'm on auto-pilot. Nothing's really registering with me at all… not the scenery, the traffic, the directions. Thank God for SatNav.

I arrive just after lunch, although I don't remember the last time I ate anything and, weirdly, I'm not hungry. Letting myself into the house, it feels a little musty and it's odd, seeing our London furniture set up here, but I flop down on the couch, let my head rock back, and close my eyes.

I wake with a start. It's dusk outside and the setting sun casts long shadows into the living room. I shudder, feeling scared, and jump up straight away, turning on the light, and then wincing against its brightness.

It feels cold in here now and the open fireplace beckons, but there's no way I'm lighting a fire. It's something Ali would have done, if she were here. Ali… Oh God… and Ed. I suppose I should let them know where I am. I pick my bag up off the floor, where I dropped it on my arrival, and delve inside. Oh hell… My phone. I don't have it. Bryan took it from me and put it on his desk, and I didn't pick it up. We don't have a landline here and the nearest public phone box is miles away. In any case, I can't call America from a phone box. Can I?

I sit back down, shivering. I need to speak to Ed. I need to tell him I didn't leave because of him. I'm not sure I can tell him the real reason, but I'd hate for him to blame himself.

I shiver again and glance out of the window. The wind's picking up and coming off the sea. I go through to the kitchen and turn on the heating. It'll take a while, but eventually it will warm the house up. I turn and look at the table and chairs. They're new – well, they're new to me, anyway. Ali and Sam must have bought them when they were renovating the house.

Suddenly the whole situation feels overwhelming and I crumple to the floor, tears streaming down my cheeks, as I sob and sob, crying Ed's name. He's not here, and the chances are he'll never be here. And I certainly can't go back there. I can't. Ever.

Whatever we had; however perfect it so nearly was for that brief moment, it's over.

Ed

The sun is coming up by the time I get back to the apartment, although I have no idea what the time is. I let myself in and find the place is deserted. The door to Sam and Ali's room is slightly open but they're not there and I guess he must've taken her to the airport to catch her flight.

I go along the hallway and into my own room, grab some clothes and head for the bathroom, where I shower quickly. If I don't hang around for too long, I can pack up my things and get out of here before Sam comes back.

I dress in the bathroom and then go to Tess's room to grab the stuff I've left in there. It's hard being in here when she isn't. There are so many reminders of her, especially considering that she took nothing with her. That's kinda odd. Everything is still here, exactly as she left it yesterday morning. Her hairbrush is still on the bed, her hand cream is still on the dresser – and she didn't put the lid back on properly – her perfume bottle is standing beside it. She's taken absolutely nothing... Man, she *really* didn't wanna be here anymore.

I shake my head and start collecting my things, just as I hear the door to the apartment open and close again.

"Ed?" Sam's voice rings out.

I could ignore him, I guess, but if I do, how am I gonna get out of here?

"Yeah. What?" I call and continue with what I was doing, pulling my t-shirts from Tess's drawers and putting them on the bed.

"What the fuck is going on?" Sam asks. I turn to find him standing in the doorway, leaning on the frame and blocking my exit.

"I'm packing. What does it look like?"

"I don't mean that. I mean, what's going on with Tess, and why didn't you wanna go with Ali?"

"I explained that already."

"You love her, don't you?" he asks, like he didn't hear me.

"You know I do."

He takes a step forward. "Then why the fuck are you wallowing in self pity? Why aren't you on a goddamn plane going after her and trying to bring her back?"

He's getting madder by the moment… but so am I.

"I told you. I already explained this to your wife. Tess doesn't want to be here, so the last thing I'm gonna do is try and bring her back. I love her too much for that… And I'm not wallowing."

"Looks that way to me," he replies.

I drop the t-shirt I'm holding and stride over, squaring up to him. "I've known all along that she'd go back to England," I tell him, raising my voice, "for the very simple reason that she never wanted to be here in the first place. Ali's decision forced that on Tess, and she came here because she loves Ali. But that doesn't mean she was happy about it, or that she ever felt like she belonged here." I take a breath, but don't give him time to say anything. "I thought she loved me enough to stay. Evidently I was wrong. And it really hurts that she didn't even say goodbye to me… I thought I meant more to her than that. Even so, none of that gives me the right to go after her and try to change her mind. She's an adult, Sam. Maybe it's about time Ali treated her like one."

He stares at me, then sighs. "I get all that," he says. "I even agree with some of it." He steps around me and sits down on Tess's bed, looking up at me. "The thing is, hasn't it dawned on you that Tess must've had a reason for going so suddenly, and not taking anything with her? Hasn't it occurred to you that something bad must've happened, if she didn't even feel like she could come back here and talk to either you or Ali before she left?" He runs his fingers through his hair. "I've been telling you all along… Tess and Ali are close; they're real close. I thought you knew about Tess's past, but it seems to me you don't know anything at all."

"Yes I do!" I yell. "I know a damn sight more than you."

"Oh, really?"

"Yeah. Really. I know about her parents, and the fire. I know how scared she gets. I know about her nightmares. I've held her through them, listened while she describes them, and tried to get her to see that I can keep her safe. Christ, I know her better than she knows herself. I know what she likes and what she doesn't; I know what every look and sound means – even the ones she makes in her sleep, when she's building up to screaming. I know what her tears taste like…" I pause for a moment. "I know that Tess has been deceiving Ali all along," I say more quietly.

"How?" he asks, sitting forward.

"I can't tell you."

"You fucking well can."

My shoulders drop. "Only if you promise not to tell Ali. The only person who can tell Ali about this is Tess. You have to respect that, or I'm not telling you a damn thing, even if you beat it out of me."

He waits for a minute and then nods his head.

"Tess never believed in their father as a romantic hero," I tell him. "Tess has been mad at him since she was eight years old. She's angry with him for leaving them, for not putting them first. As far as she's concerned, Ali's story of the romantic hero is just bullshit. She lets Ali believe it because she knows it helps Ali, but she's never thought of their father that way herself." I let out a long breath and stare at Sam. I can see he's surprised and it takes him a moment to compose himself.

"Okay," he says calmly. "If that's the case… if you know her so intimately, then surely, you'd know that, if she was feeling homesick, or just had a problem, she'd come to you, like she has with her nightmares, and with everything else, evidently." He gets to his feet and comes over, standing right in front of me. "I think you should maybe be a little bit scared."

"What of? You?" There's nothing he can do that would make me feel any worse than I already do.

"No. You never have to be scared of me. But I think you should be real scared of whatever it is that made Tess run."

"Scared?" I whisper the word.

"Yeah." He looks down at me and we stare at each other. And suddenly I realize that she wouldn't have run without talking it through with me. Of course she wouldn't. No matter how bad she felt, she'd never have run out on me, not without an explanation; she'd have discussed it first, openly and honestly, just like she has with everything else. She's always done that, right from the beginning, and I can't see why she wouldn't have done now… unless it was something so bad, she felt she couldn't. *Oh shit…*

"Can you take me to the airport?" I ask him.

"Sure." He nods his head, smiling.

"I'm gonna finish packing these things and take them with me."

"Okay." He walks out of the room. "I'll check the flights," he calls over his shoulder.

It doesn't take me more than ten minutes to throw my clothes into the bag, add my wash gear and join Sam in the living room.

"Don't rush," he says quietly. "The next flight isn't until six-fifty this evening."

"What time will that land?" I ask him, sitting beside him on the couch.

"Five tomorrow morning, local time."

I nod. "And I'll need to rent a car when I get there?"

"Yeah, and then head for Dorset. I'll give you the address."

"Okay."

"And in the meantime…" He checks his watch. "We've got a restaurant to run."

"You're kidding, right?" He expects me to work?

"No, I'm not kidding.. You need to do something to take your mind off of Tess."

He's probably right. I'm gonna drive myself insane just sitting here waiting for my flight.

"Okay. Will you get an update from Ali before I leave?" I ask him.

"No. She'll be taking off any time now." He checks his watch and nods his head. "She'll land at around seven-thirty tonight, their time, which is two thirty this afternoon, here."

"And how long does it take to drive to their house?"

"She's gotta clear the airport first, and then it's about a three hour drive."

"So it's gonna be around midnight their time, by the time she gets there?"

"Around that, yeah. That's when she's gonna call me, as soon as she's made sure Tess is okay. We decided she wouldn't call any earlier… She said she just wants to focus on getting there," he says. "And by that time, we'll have already left for the airport." He thinks for a moment. "Actually, thinking about the timings, I'll probably have to get Rob to take you and get Petra to cover the front of house," he adds. "And I'll run the kitchen."

"By yourself?"

"I'll manage until Rob gets back."

I'm not gonna argue with him. "Okay." I get to my feet. "I'm gonna make some coffee." I need to do something. "Do you want one?"

"Yeah, okay… I will in a minute, and I'll call Rob while you're making it and update him, and check that Petra can work tonight, but in the meantime, can you just sit down again?"

"Why?"

"Do as I ask, Ed?" I sit and he takes a breath. "Ali told me to tell you she feels really bad for saying all those things about you before she left."

I don't reply. If I'm being honest, I'm not sure how to. There's a part of me that feels she was out of line, but there's also a part of me that feels I deserved everything she said… and more.

"She worries about Tess," he adds. "Sometimes I think she worries too much. And maybe you're right… maybe Ali does need to treat Tess more like an adult and less like a child. I know she's scared right now, so when you get to England, can you go easy on her? She really does feel bad about what she said."

"Of course I'll go easy on her," I reply. "What did you think I was gonna do?"

He shrugs. "I don't know." He looks at me, long and hard. "I guess if the shoe had been on the other foot, I'd have been pretty mad at having all those things said to me," he says.

"Yeah, well… I'm not you."

"No." He pauses. "Like I told Ali, you're better than me, Ed."

"Is that why I was sitting here, wallowing?"

"You weren't wallowing, you were hurting. I just said that to get you to wake up and see the bigger picture."

"I should've seen it for myself. I should've known that Tess is way too nice to just leave."

He shakes his head. "It's not because she's too nice," he says calmly. "She wouldn't just leave, because she loves you. Stop being so down on yourself, Ed. Stop thinking you're not enough for her. You are."

I stare at him. "I'm not enough to keep her here, Sam."

"Yeah, you are."

"In that case, why is she three thousand miles away?"

He looks at me for a moment. "I don't know. But I think you're gonna find out she's got a damn good reason – a hell of a lot better reason than you not being enough, anyway."

I'd like to feel comforted by that, but I just feel cold at the thought that something's happened to Tess, something's scared her into running for home, and I wasn't there.

Chapter Fourteen

Tess

I managed to move back to the sofa, where I curled up and eventually fell asleep, pulling the patchwork quilt over my legs.

I wake with a start as the front door opens.

"Go away… Don't touch me! Get away from me!" I scream and jump to my feet, running through to the kitchen and up the stairs, into the back bedroom that's always been mine, where I slam the door and lean back against it, breathing hard.

The room's in darkness, but I daren't move away from the door to switch on the light, just in case whoever it is can get in.

I hear footsteps running up the stairs. They're light, like a woman or a child. Not those of a man.

"Tess?" The voice comes from the other side of the door.

"Ali?"

"Yes. Open the door."

"Are you alone?"

"Yes."

I turn and open the door just a fraction. The hallway is lit. Ali must have turned on the lights and she's standing right by the door, wearing jeans and a t-shirt, and looking exhausted.

"Ali?"

"Yes." She takes a step forward and I open the door fully and fall into her arms, just as I start sobbing again. "Oh God," she says quietly, holding me up. "What's happened?"

I shake my head, because I don't want to talk about it, and just cry into her.

"Come on," she whispers and slowly guides me back into my room, sitting me down on the edge of the bed and turning to switch on the bedside lamp. A soft glow fills the room and I glance around properly. This is the furniture from my room in the apartment in London. It fits well in here, although why that thought is even occurring to me right now, I have no idea. I suppose it's just that I'm trying to avoid thinking about the obvious...

Ali comes and sits beside me, really close, leaning into me.

"Tell me what's wrong," she urges. "Why did you run away?"

I turn and look at her. "I'm sorry," I say simply.

"You don't have to be sorry. Just tell me what happened. We've been worried sick."

"We?"

"Yes. Me and Sam... and Ed."

I notice the hesitation. "Is he here?"

"No."

"He didn't come with you?"

"No."

"Why not?"

"Because he's hurt. He's upset," she explains. "So was I. I wasn't very nice to him."

"You weren't?" Ali's normally nice to everyone, so that tells me how worried she must've been.

"No. I thought he should come after you himself, but he thinks you didn't love him enough to want to be with him. He thinks you wanted to be here more than you wanted him and he loves you too much to try and make you go back." She pauses. "I think that was the gist of what he said, anyway."

"He said that?"

"Yes."

"I've really hurt him, haven't I?" I start to cry again.

"I'm sure it's nothing he won't forgive you for… if you want his forgiveness, and if you still want him. But he's as confused as I am, Tess. Why did you run?"

"I had to."

"Why?" she urges.

"Because of what he did."

"Who? Ed?"

I shake my head.

"Did someone else do something to you?" she asks, her voice a mere whisper.

I nod my head this time.

"Who, Tess?"

"Bryan." I can barely hear myself.

"Your boss?" Ali clarifies and I nod again. She reaches over and takes my hand in both of hers. She's cold and I cover her hands with my free one to warm her up. "What did he do?" she asks softly.

I look up into her eyes. She looks scared.

"He… he…" I stop for a moment. "He hurt me."

"Oh God." She pulls one of her hands from mine and covers her mouth. After a moment, she lets it drop away again. "Can you tell me what he did?" she says calmly.

I spot a thread of cotton on the floor and stare at it while I rock back and forth, and recount what Bryan did, pausing frequently to cry.

"He didn't rape you, did he?" she asks, as I'm trying to describe his final act.

"No. I felt him… He was about to, but I kicked him. And then I ran. I didn't look back."

"Why didn't you call?" she asks.

"Because I'd left my phone behind. I only had my bag."

"Then why didn't you come back to the apartment?"

I turn to her. "I was scared he'd follow me. He had the address on file. I thought he might come round and persuade one of you to let him in."

"Not if you'd told us what he'd done, Tess. Ed, Sam and Rob wouldn't have let him within a mile of you."

"Yes, but then I'd have had to tell you, and I couldn't face that. I couldn't face any of you."

"Why? Why, Tess?" I can hear the tears in her voice.

"Because of what he'd done. I knew how angry you'd be."

"Me?" She lets go of my hand and pulls me into a hug. "I'm not angry with you, Tess. I think you're so brave. So bloody brave. You should've come back us. We'd have helped you."

"How was I supposed to face Ed?" I ask her, pulling back and looking into her eyes. "He's the only man I've ever been with."

"I know," she says.

"Well, he's not going to want me now, is he? Bryan's ruined everything."

"How?" she asks.

"Because… well, I'm not sure I can ever face being intimate with anyone… ever again. I love Ed and he said he loved me. But why would he want a future with someone who's too afraid to be touched?"

"Love is about a lot more than sex," she says, shaking her head. "And besides, you might feel like that now, but for all you know, it could pass and, whatever happens, Ed's a good guy. He'll help you. You can work it out together."

"You're assuming he can forgive me."

"What for? Don't you dare start thinking this is your fault…" Her voice hardens.

"I should've known better than to go into his office."

"Stop. Stop right there. You were doing your job, and you're entitled to do that without being assaulted… molested." Her voice cracks.

"I ran away, without even saying goodbye," I wail. "He'll never forgive me for that."

"Yes, he will. He would have done anyway, but once he knows the reason…"

I stare at her. "We can't tell him."

"Yes we can. I'll help you, if you need me to, but he's entitled to know. He's especially entitled to know that you didn't leave because of him."

She's right. "Oh, God…"

She holds onto me and I cling to her, weeping.

After a while – I don't know how long – Ali pulls away and leans back. "Why don't I go and make us a cup of tea?" she suggests.

"It must be past midnight," I point out.

"Even so…" She takes my hand and gets to her feet, pulling me with her. "I'm thirsty. I'll go and put the kettle on. You go to the bathroom and freshen up a little, and I'll see you downstairs. We'll just drink our tea and then I'll bring my bag in and we can go to bed. Tomorrow, it won't seem so bad… I promise."

She leads me toward the bathroom and, as she goes down the stairs, I really wish I could believe her.

Ed

I land at five in the morning. London is gray, overcast and miserable… kinda like my mood really.

Rob took me to Logan yesterday afternoon, just like Sam suggested. It meant everyone had to move their schedules around. Petra had to arrange for her mom to sit with April and Rob had to re-arrange a late afternoon meeting, but no-one minded once Sam had explained the situation. Rob and I didn't talk much on the way to the airport. I wasn't in the mood for conversation and, because we're twins, I think he worked that out without me needing to explain it to him. When we said goodbye, he wished me luck and gave me a hug… which isn't something he'd normally do. I kinda appreciated it though.

It takes me a while to get through immigration and then I hire a car and it's only when I'm sitting in the driver's seat of the Mercedes that I realize I ought to check my messages and turn my phone back on.

It beeps immediately and I see I've got a message from Sam, which is timed at seven-thirty EST, last night.

— *Ed, when you pick this up, call me. Doesn't matter what the time is. Call me. S*

His tone has me worried and I connect a call to him straight away, checking the clock on the car's dashboard. It's eight in the morning here, so it'll be three am at home. I hope he meant the bit about it not mattering what time it is…

"Ed?" he answers on the second ring, sounding groggy.

"Yeah. What's wrong? Has something happened?"

There's a pause. "Ali called yesterday evening, just after you'd taken off," he explains. "She told me that something bad happened to Tess."

"What? What happened?" I'm going frantic now and I start the engine of the car.

"I don't know. Ali wouldn't tell me over the phone and she said that you had to know about it first. But she was crying…" I hear him let out a breath. "It's gotta be bad, man. She said Tess doesn't want you to know." There's another pause. "Ali was worried that you weren't gonna go over there still and she was calling to tell me to get you on the next flight. I told her you were already on your way and you should be there by lunchtime today."

"I will be. I'm already in the rental car."

"Okay. I'll let you go. Take care… and stay in touch."

"I will."

I disconnect the call, select 'drive' and pull out of the parking bay, driving slowly around the parking lot and typing the zip code of Tess and Ali's house into the SatNav at the same time. As soon as it's registered and started giving me directions, I floor the gas.

I'm really pleased that Sam warned me before I left home yesterday that I should trust the SatNav and ignore my instincts, or I'd never have found this place. But now I have, I've gotta say, I can completely see why Tess loves it so much. It's breathtakingly beautiful and it's so right for her.

I leave my bag in the car, together with my jacket and run up the pathway, knocking on the front door.

Ali answers and sighs, smiling. She seems relieved to see me. Despite what Sam said, I wasn't expecting that. She was madder than hell at me the last time we saw each other and I still kinda expected to see her anger. But there's none of it. Instead, she looks tired and upset.

"Hi," I say.

"Come in." She stands to one side and lets me into a large living room.

"Where's Tess?" I ask, because that's all I care about right now.

"She's upstairs," Ali replies.

"Can I see her?"

Ali nods and leads me through the room and down a few steps into a really great kitchen, and then up some narrow stairs to a landing, with four rooms leading off of it. We go to the one at the back of the house, which is closed.

"This is her room," she whispers, and knocks. "Tess?" she says, raising her voice. "You've got a visitor."

"Who is it?" I hear her voice, from the other side of the door, although she sounds wary. Actually, she sounds terrified.

"It's me." I step forward, closer to the door and speak loud enough for her to hear me. "Can I come in?"

"No."

I look at Ali. "Tess. Ed just wants to talk," she says.

"I can't," she replies and I can hear her crying.

"It's okay," I say quickly. "You don't have to. I'll go back downstairs."

I move away from the door. "We'll be in the kitchen," Ali adds and joins me at the head of the stairs. "Sorry," she whispers.

"Don't worry." I let her go down the stairs in front of me and then join her in the kitchen, where we sit at the antique table, facing each other.

"Can I get you a coffee?" she offers.

"Okay, thanks."

She gets up again and busies herself preparing coffee for both of us.

"Can you tell me what's happened?" I ask her, once she's sat back down again.

"I'm not sure if I should," she replies, twisting her cup in her hands.

"Well, someone's gonna have to. I'm going crazy here."

She looks up at me. "Okay," she says eventually. "I'll tell you. But please remember it's not her fault."

I feel a cold shiver run through me. "Go on…" I urge her.

"After the party at Tess's office, her boss asked Tess to go into his room. He was talking about promoting her, or something…"

"And?"

"And… he… God, I don't know how to say this."

"Well, try… please, Ali."

She swallows hard. "He attacked her."

I get to my feet, pushing the chair over. Ali stands too and walks around the table, putting her hands on my arms. "Please, Ed. Think about every single thing you do and say, from now on," she says quietly.

"I am." I breathe deeply. "Tell me what he did."

"He forced her to perform… oral sex on him." She pauses and swallows hard, while my heart breaks. "He tore her clothes and he… he put his fingers inside her." I hold up my hands for her to stop and she does, and I turn away.

"Did he rape her?" I ask, fearing the worst.

"No. She says he didn't. She says he tried, but she kicked him and she managed to run away."

I turn back to face her. "And why didn't she come to us… to you, or to me?"

"She thought we'd be angry with her," she says, her voice breaking and tears filling her eyes. "And she didn't think you'd want her anymore. She still doesn't."

"What?" I cover my face with my hands to hide the tears that are forming in my eyes.

"She said she's not sure she ever wants to be intimate with anyone ever again." I hear her let out a sob and lower my hands, pulling her into my arms, comforting her. "She… she said Bryan's ruined everything for both of you," she mumbles into my chest, "and she doesn't think you'll ever forgive her."

"What for?" I lean back and look at her. "What for, Ali?"

"For running…"

"And?" There's more, I know there is.

"She feels responsible."

"For what he did?"

She nods. I hold her for a moment longer, then let her go. "I told her she's not to blame," she adds.

"Of course she isn't."

She stares at me for a moment.

"How do you feel?" she asks, softly.

"Devastated… Angry."

"With her?"

"Christ, no. With him."

"Does it change how you feel about her?" she asks.

"No. I love her, no matter what."

"Maybe you should go and tell her that."

"Do you think she'll let me in?"

"The door's not locked." She leans back on the countertop. "Just be gentle with her. She's really fragile."

"She always was." I look over at her.

"I'm sorry," she whispers.

"What for?"

"For what I said before I left. I was upset about Tess. I didn't mean all of that."

"It doesn't matter, Ali. None of that matters."

"Even so, I'm sorry." She needs me to forgive her.

"Please, don't worry about it. It's fine."

She smiles. "I'd better call Sam," she says.

"For Christ's sake, don't tell him about this," I say quickly.

"Why not?" She looks up at me, confused.

"Because Sam will go and find Bryan and beat the shit out of him… or worse. And if Rob finds out, he'll help."

"You think?"

"No. I know. Besides, Tess might not want them to know."

She nods slowly. "No. I suppose not." She sits down again. "I'll just call and tell him you're here and you're dealing with things, and leave it at that."

"Okay."

"You don't want to beat the shit out of Bryan yourself?" she asks.

"Yeah. Of course I do. I wanna rip his fucking head off with my bare hands. But that's not gonna help Tess, is it?"

She stares at me for a moment, then closes her eyes and shakes her head.

I stand outside Tess's door, wondering whether to knock or go straight in. If I knock, she'll probably just tell me to go away again, so I take a breath and open the door. She's lying curled up on the bed, her back to me and, as I go in, she turns, her eyes opening wide.

"I thought…"

"You thought I was Ali? Or you thought I'd gone?"

She shrugs. "Both, I suppose."

I close the door behind me and notice that her eyes dart toward it.

"Do you want the door left open?" I ask her.

She nods her head. "Is that okay?"

"Of course." I open it again, leaving it ajar. "If it makes you more comfortable, it's fine." I move further into the room. "Can I come sit with you?"

She hesitates and then nods her head again, and I go over and sit on the edge of the bed beside her.

"I'm so sorry, Tess." It's all I can think of saying.

"Why are you sorry?" she asks.

"Because I wasn't there to protect you. I said I'd protect you and I didn't."

"You weren't to know," she murmurs.

She looks kinda helpless. "Can I hold you?" I ask her, moving a little closer.

She stares at me, her eyes boring into mine, and then says, "Why?"

"Because I want you to know that I may have let you down, I may not have been there to protect you, but I'm here for you now, and I'm not going anywhere. Nothing's changed, babe." Her eyes widen again.

Tears start falling onto her cheeks as she silently raises her arms up to me.

I lean down and pull her up onto my lap, holding her close to me, while she sobs and sobs. I stroke her hair, but don't say a word, because I don't have any. Nothing that I can say is adequate for how she's feeling right now. Eventually though she starts to calm and leans back in my arms, looking up at me.

"Can you tell me about it?" I ask her.

She swallows. "Didn't Ali tell you? I assumed from what you were saying that she had…"

"Yeah, she did. But I want to hear it from you."

And, very slowly, she repeats what Bryan did to her. She finds it really hard explaining how he made her take him in her mouth and I have to fight down my anger when she describes his brutality. Then she struggles over telling me what he did with his fingers, and how that felt… how much it hurt her, physically as well as emotionally. She takes her time over the part where he bent her over his desk, and the feeling as he was about to enter her, as well as her fear of what might happen when he did. She's kinda triumphant in telling me how she kicked him, but that's real short-lived, her triumph replaced by terror as she made her escape. I can only imagine how scared she must've been. Actually, I can't even do that. I've never been in that kind of situation and I probably never will be. When she reaches the end of her story, I hold her really tight and look down into her eyes. "Is that everything?" I ask her. "He didn't do anything else to you?" She stares at me. "He didn't rape you?"

"No. I explained. He tried to, but I got away." She hesitates. "Why? Would it make a difference?"

I tighten my grip on her. "No. It makes no difference at all to how I feel about you. I love you, no matter what."

"Then why…?"

"I just needed to know the worst, babe, that's all."

After a couple of hours upstairs with Tess, during which I explain my initial reaction to her leaving and how I came to eventually work out that something must've happened to her – with Sam's help – I manage to persuade her to come down with me and we discover that Ali's cooking us dinner. She explains that she went out shopping while we were talking. She got Sam to email her our mom's bolognese recipe and we sit together in the kitchen and eat it, along with a really good Chianti for Ali and me, and bottled water for Tess. While she was out, she also picked up a couple of outfits for Tess – just jeans and sweaters – because she has nothing here, other than what she was wearing when she left the US.

Afterwards, we sit and watch a movie together, with Tess lying in my arms on the couch, although I don't think any of us is really interested. It's just something to do to avoid us having to speak to each other. At about eleven, Tess asks if it's okay if she goes to bed.

"Of course," Ali replies and gets up herself, clearing away our coffee cups from earlier and going out into the kitchen.

"How do you feel about me sleeping with you?" I ask Tess. "I know there's another bedroom here, and I can use that, if you prefer."

"Do you want to sleep with me?" Her voice is so quiet, even in the silence of the room, I struggle to hear her.

"Yes. I'd really like to hold you."

"Just hold me?" she asks, sounding nervous.

"Yeah. Just hold you. We don't have to do anything you don't want to, Tess. We can leave the door open, if you prefer. I just wanna be there for you. I wanna try and make you feel safe, if I can."

She nods her head. "I'd like to be held by you," she says quietly, and I get up, pulling her with me and, saying goodnight to Ali, we head upstairs together.

I go to the bathroom and, when I come back into Tess's room, she's already in bed, wearing pajamas, borrowed from Ali, I guess. I don't comment, but grab a pair of shorts from my bag and go back to the bathroom to change into them. I don't want to make her feel uncomfortable by being naked in front of her, even to get changed.

It doesn't take either of us along to fall asleep. We're both physically and mentally drained, but I don't let go of her, which is how I'm aware of her thrashing in her sleep.

"Don't!" she mutters. "Stop! No!"

I'm wide awake in an instant.

"Hey… Tess." I kneel up beside her, holding her shoulders gently. "Hey, babe. Wake up."

"Don't touch me!"

"Tess."

"Please… please don't!" She starts to cry and struggles against me, but I hold on.

"Tess." I call her name a little louder and her eyes dart open. She lashes out against me, hitting me hard in the chest and pushing me back.

"Don't!" she screams. "Don't touch me!"

"Tess. It's me. Ed."

She calms in an instant and starts to sob loudly. "I'm sorry. I'm so sorry."

I pull her into my arms and hold her. "It's okay. You were having a nightmare."

"He… he had me on his desk," she mumbles into me and I try real hard not to let my muscles stiffen. I can't react to what she's saying. "He was trying to force himself inside me," she continues. "And he was slapping me again."

"Again?"

She looks up at me. "Didn't I tell you that?"

"No."

"Oh… he hit me."

"He hit you…" I repeat her words.

"Yes. Twice around the face and once on my… behind." She tenses. "It hurt."

"No-one is ever gonna hurt you again, Tess. I won't let them."

"Promise?"

"I promise."

"No matter what?"

"No matter what."

She nestles into me and I move us back down the bed again. It takes her a while to get back to sleep, but I don't let go of her. Not once.

When we get downstairs this morning, Ali's already sitting at the kitchen table, a cup of coffee in her hands. She gets up and makes us both one, and then we all sit together.

"Shall I make us breakfast?" I offer.

"I think we should talk first," Ali says.

"What about?" Tess looks at her, fear written all over her face and I move closer, taking her hands in mine.

"I know you don't want to hear this," Ali begins, "but we've got to face facts."

"What facts?"

"Bryan sexually assaulted you," Ali says blankly. "He tried to rape you."

Tess flinches into me but doesn't say a word. "Where are you going with this, Ali?" I ask her.

"We can't just sit here and do nothing," she replies, still looking at Tess. "That's not who we are, is it?"

Tess stares at her. "I can't," she whispers.

"Can't what?" I don't understand what they're talking about.

"I think we should go back to the US," Ali says, putting it in words of one syllable for me.

"You want Tess to go back to America?"

"Yes." Ali nods. "Don't you get it?"

"Clearly not. How's that gonna help her?"

Tess leans into me. "I think what Ali's trying to say is that I should go to the police... but I can't."

"And if he does it to someone else?" Ali says, still staring at her.

I feel Tess slump into me and I know she's beaten.

"Is there no way she can do that from here?" I ask, even though I'm already fairly sure there isn't.

"No. I asked Sam last night."

"I thought we agreed..." I start to say, but she holds her hand up.

"I didn't tell him what had happened. I just said that if someone had done something illegal and Tess needed to get the police involved in America, how would she go about it… Sam spoke to your cousin… Antonio, is it?" I nod my head. "And he said she really needs to go back to the US to file a charge there."

"And then what?" Tess asks, her voice incredibly small and hollow.

"And then I imagine you'll have to stay in America until he goes to trial," I tell her.

"I can't." She shakes her head fiercely. "I can't."

"No-one can make you do this," Ali says, softening her own voice again. "But I don't think you'll be able to live with yourself, if you know he's still out there and could do it to another girl."

Tess lifts her head and looks at Ali, then turns to me. "How long would I have to stay?" she asks.

I shrug. "I've got no idea. A couple of months… maybe more."

"And would I have to find a job?"

"No," Ali says. "Sam checked that with Antonio. Obviously, if you want something to do, you can help out in the restaurant, but there's no pressure."

Tess stares at her, as though she's questioning that statement. I've got to admit, I am. The pressure on her is enormous.

"Okay," she says, meekly. "I'll do it. I'll go."

I expect to feel pleased that she'll go home – well, my home. But I don't. I feel her sadness. It's overwhelming.

"Can we just spend one more day here?" she asks, pleading.

Ali smiles at her, and replies, "Of course we can."

We spend the day doing the things Tess wants to do. We walk on the beach – twice. The first time all three of us go together, and the second time, it's just me and Tess. The beach itself is really small and private and Ali explains on our first visit that it's only for the people who live in the houses down their lane. I like the seclusion and, looking at Tess, I get the feeling she does too. It's really cold and windy, but it feels good to spend that time with her. We don't talk much, but she holds onto me the whole time. It's a special moment, and a special memory.

We go out for dinner together, to a pub in a nearby village, which is nice and then afterwards, we go home and go to bed early, because we've got to drive back to London to catch our late afternoon flights back to Logan.

Tess is in bed before me again and as I climb in beside her, I pull her into my arms. She comes willingly and snuggles down beside me.

"Can I ask you something?" I say, feeling unsure of myself, but needing to ask the question.

"Yes." She twists and looks up at me.

"Do you still love me?"

She leans back a little. "Yes," she says simply. "Yes, I do."

"I'm sensing a but…" I say, fearing the worst.

She hesitates. "I— I feel like everything's different now," she replies eventually. "We had such a perfect, fun, happy time before… and I think we were honestly getting somewhere. I'm not sure we'll ever get that back."

"I don't care," I tell her. "What we had before is in the past. I love you, and we can make a different future…"

"Can we? Even though you belong in a place I now hate and fear?"

I can't answer her and, after a moment, she rests her head on my chest again. It's only when I feel the wetness spreading that I realize she's crying. I don't say a word. I just hold her until her breathing changes and I know she's asleep.

I've gotta admit, I feel more depressed than I think I ever have in my life. She's right: *everything's* changed between us. And that's not because of Bryan attacking her. Well, not from my point of view, anyway; it's because I've seen her here… I've seen her where she belongs and I know now that what we had back home was a dream, a fantasy… a memory. And everything I just said to her about making a different future, is just me wishing and hoping, because we don't have a future.

Sure, she's coming back to Hartford with me tomorrow, but that's temporary. She's coming back to talk to the cops, and to get justice… and if it wasn't for that, I don't think there's anything on this earth that could persuade her to get on board a transatlantic flight again. She doesn't belong in America and, while having her there might make me feel better, I know it's not the right place for her. It never will be.

She never belonged with me. She belongs here in this beautiful house by the sea, and I belong in Hartford with my brothers, and as much as I know it's gonna break me, I've decided that, when the time comes for her to come back here again, I'm not gonna stop her.

I owe her that.

Chapter Fifteen

Tess

Ed and I sit in the back of Sam's car and I lean against him. I feel like I've been leaning on him for hours… maybe days. Maybe even forever.

"You're not gonna tell me?" Sam says to Ali for about the tenth time, changing lanes on the motorway… or freeway, or whatever they call it over here. I've forgotten now.

"When we get home," she replies patiently. "None of us wants to say this more than once, and we think you and Rob both need to know."

We discussed this on the flight. I wasn't sure I wanted anyone else to know, but I can't expect Ali to keep it a secret from Sam, and she and Ed both pointed out that the police getting involved is going to mean that it'll come out eventually. Besides, as we all agreed eventually, if we don't tell Sam and Rob, it's going to lead to some really awkward silences and difficult conversations.

"You okay?" Ed whispers, leaning down.

I nod my head, but don't reply and let my eyes close.

It's only when we park up beneath the hotel that I realise it's late in the afternoon.

"What about the restaurant?" I say Ed, looking up at him.

"Sam closed it for the day," he replies. "Don't you remember? He explained that when he picked us up at the airport."

I nod, vaguely recalling Ali questioning why Sam was there and not someone else.

"Oh, yes."

He puts his arm around me as we walk to the lifts. "Don't worry about anything," he says. The lift doors open and we step inside, Ed and Sam carrying the bags between them, and the doors close again. No-one says a word, although Sam looks like he swallowed a wasp and can't wait to spit it out.

The hotel lobby is busy and Ed pulls me closer as we walk through, and out onto the street. The noise out here seems even louder than usual and I flinch.

"It's okay," he says calmly, moving me so I'm nearer the buildings and he's closer to the road.

Sam and Ali are walking a few paces ahead of us, but they stop and Sam turns around. "Give me your bag," he says to Ed, putting Ali's over his shoulder, and Ed does, and then he leans down and lifts me into his arms.

"What are you doing? Everyone's looking…" I try to wriggle free.

"I don't care if they're looking," he says. "I want you to feel safe; and there's nowhere safer."

I stop struggling and look up into his face. "Thank you."

He swallows hard. "Don't… please don't thank me," he whispers, and I rest my head on his chest.

Ali unlocks the restaurant, using Sam's keys and we go inside, although Ed keeps hold of me, but we've barely had a moment to breathe before Rob appears from the office.

"You're back," he says.

"Yeah," Sam replies, and we move towards the rear of the restaurant.

Rob looks at me, then at Ed, but doesn't say a word and an awkward silence descends.

"I—I suppose I'd better explain," Ali says.

"Can I go upstairs?" I murmur. "I can't be here."

"Of course," Ali replies and they make enough space for Ed to carry me down the corridor.

"It's open," Sam says as we pass them by.

Ed carries me easily up the stairs and through the door at the top.

"Sorry," I murmur as he deposits me on the couch.

"What for?" He kneels down on the floor beside me.

"I couldn't face being there when Ali told them. I couldn't face seeing their reactions."

He brushes a couple of loose strands of hair off my face. "It's okay," he says softly. "Everything's gonna be okay."

He's just getting up, when we hear footsteps running up the stairs and I turn to see Ali fall through the door, followed by Sam.

"What's wrong?" he says, pulling her back. "Tell me."

"I can't," she cries, tears falling down her cheeks. "I can't tell you."

Sam looks from Ali to me. "Is this about Tess, or you?" he asks, clearly concerned.

"It's about Tess, of course."

"What's wrong, Ali?" I ask her, sitting up on the sofa and turning to face her properly.

She looks over at me, her shoulders dropping. "I can't tell them," she says. "I'm sorry… I can't."

"I'll do it," Ed says, and goes to walk away, then stops and leans over me. "How much detail do you want them to know?" he asks.

I shrug. "I guess they'll find it all out eventually…"

He nods. "Okay. I'll tell them everything, shall I?" He cups my face in his hand. "I won't be long. You stay up here with Ali."

Sam's looking very confused as Ed goes over to him and leads him back downstairs again, despite his reluctance to leave Ali.

Once they've gone, I take a deep breath and let my breathing return to normal. Ali closes the door and comes over.

"Shall I make coffee?" she asks.

"Okay." Frankly, I couldn't care less, but I guess she wants something to do. "What happened?" I ask her.

"When?"

"Downstairs."

"Oh… I thought I could tell them, just like I told Ed," she says softly, coming over and sitting beside me, "but I couldn't. I don't know why… it just all seems so much more real back here than it did at Waterside."

I want to scream at her that she should try being in my shoes, but I don't. I lean into her and we sit in silence for a while, before she goes and puts the coffee on.

I don't know how long Ed is downstairs for, but eventually he comes back alone.

"Where's Sam?" Ali asks.

"He and Rob are downstairs still," he explains. "They didn't want to crowd Tess. They're gonna come up in a little while."

Ali nods her head and moves down the couch a little to make room for Ed to sit, which he does, right beside me. He puts his arm around me.

"How was it?" Ali asks him.

"Horrendous," he says simply, resting his head on mine.

"You told them everything?" I ask him, looking up at him.

"Yes." He kisses my forehead very gently. "They know everything I do."

"That's everything." Tears prick my eyes, but I have to ask, my voice barely a whisper, "Do they blame me?"

He sits forward, holding me at arm's length so he can look at me. "No," he says sharply. "No-one blames you. Don't ever think that. This is *not* your fault, Tess."

I lean into him again and let him hold me as I cry, vaguely aware of Ali getting up and then hearing her footsteps on the stairs.

We're alone. It's just me and Ed.

"I'm sorry you had to do that," I murmur into him.

"Hey. Don't be sorry for anything. It's okay."

"How am I going to face them?"

"By remembering that it's not your fault… and that they care about you. We all just want you to feel safe here. Or at least as safe as you can feel."

"That's not going to be easy."

"I know," he says. "I'll be here for you. I'm not going anywhere."

I put my arms around his waist and hang on.

It's the smell of food that wakes me.

"What's that?" I murmur.

"Sam's cooking," Ed replies, leaning down and kissing my cheek.

"How long was I asleep?"

"A couple of hours."

"Sorry. I'm sure you must have better things to do than sit with me while I'm sleeping."

"I think I told you once, I don't have anything better to do than be with you. And I love holding you while you sleep. So don't apologise. For anything."

I stare at him for a moment, wanting desperately to thank him, but knowing he'll just tell me not to, and that I'll probably cry again. He manages a slight smile, which I think is his way of saying he knows how I feel. I can't smile back, but I nod my head, and then sit up a little. Sam and Rob are in the kitchen, working together on whatever's cooking. Ali's curled up in the corner of the couch.

"Are you okay?" I ask her.

"I'm fine," she replies, smiling. "Just tired."

I look up at Ed. "You must be tired too."

"Don't worry about me," he says.

Rob comes out of the kitchen. "Can I get anyone a drink?" he offers and looks over at me. He gives me the sweetest smile and my eyes fill with tears.

"I think Tess would probably like some water," Ed says on my behalf, looking down and waiting for my nod of approval. "And I'll have a beer, thanks."

"White wine for me, please," Ali replies, smiling up at him.

"Coming right up." Rob returns to the kitchen and a few minutes later, comes back with drinks, and Sam, and they both sit down. Sam settles beside Ali and holds her in his arms, and we all sit and stare into space for a while until I can't bare it any longer.

"I thought the whole point of telling Sam and Rob was to avoid awkward silences?"

Ed's arms come tight around me as Sam looks over. "I owe you an apology," he says.

"What on earth for?" I don't know what he's talking about.

"Well, I owe you and Ali an apology."

"That still doesn't explain what for," I reply.

"When I convinced Ali to talk you into coming over here, I promised her I'd keep you safe. I promised her I'd look after you and that I'd never let anyone hurt you. I let you down, Tess… I let you both down. And I'm sorry."

"This isn't your fault," Ed says quietly, because he knows I can't speak. "I feel the same way. I promised to keep Tess safe too, and I didn't. I couldn't. I failed her more than anyone—"

"No you didn't," I interrupt.

"Yeah, I did, babe. But the thing is, none of that helps. We've gotta keep ourselves focused on the person who's really responsible, which is Bryan."

"He's right," Rob adds. "Bryan is the only person to blame in this."

"And besides," Ed continues, "I don't want to get hung up on how I feel, or what any of us did wrong, or how we could have done things differently. Because none of that's gonna help Tess, and she's the only thing that matters."

Ali leans forward, focusing on Ed. "I take back all the bad things I said about you," she murmurs through building tears. "Sam was completely right."

We all look at the two of them, but it seems like they're not going to explain and eventually Rob turns to me. "I think you're very brave to come back here," he says quietly.

"I'm not feeling very brave at the moment," I point out. "I'm dreading tomorrow."

"We talked about that while you were asleep," Ed says softly. "Petra's gonna come in and cover for Rob, so he'll be in the kitchen, which means Ali and I can both come with you," Ed says softly. "I won't leave your side. Not for a second."

The police station is noisy. There's a man sitting in a chair, waiting to see someone I suppose, but he keeps shouting something incoherent.

Ed pulls me away from him, putting himself between us, but the noise levels are still much greater than anything I'm used to.

Ed explains why we're here, and the officer behind the desk looks at me sympathetically, and shows us into a quieter room, with a table in the middle. There are only two chairs, one on either side, but he returns a few moments later with two more, and we sit down and wait.

The door opens suddenly and a tall, muscular, blond man walks in. I'm instantly reminded of Bryan, and I start to shake.

"Tess?" Ed says quietly. "It's okay. This guy's a cop. He's not gonna hurt you."

The man stops and seems to sum up the situation in the blink of an eye. "I'm sorry." His voice is deceptively quiet and I feel a little easier. He looks from Ed to Ali, and then lets his eyes settle on me. "The desk sergeant said you wanted to report an assault?"

"A sexual assault…" Ed clarifies, and the policeman nods his head in understanding.

"Oh. I see." He sits down opposite me. "Would you prefer me to get a female officer to take your statement?" he asks. "There isn't one available right now, but you can wait… or come back."

"No," I say quickly. "I just want to get this over and done with." I look up at him. "I'm sorry, that was rude," I add.

"Hey, don't worry about that," he says, smiling. He's got a kind smile and I notice he's wearing a wedding ring. For some stupid reason, it makes me feel a little bit more at ease.

He opens a file, with some blank lined pages inside and says, "Okay, I'm Detective Brandon Daniels. Why don't you start off by giving me your name…"

I suppose it probably takes around an hour for me to tell him everything. He's very kind and sympathetic, and lets me go at my pace, taking breaks whenever I need to, and he doesn't bat an eyelid when Ed holds me while I cry. When I've finished giving my statement, he goes back through it all carefully, asking the occasional question.

"We're going to have to speak to Mr Oakley," he says, his mouth set in a thin line.

"You may wanna talk to some of his former female employees as well," Ed suggests, leaning forward a little.

"Why's that?" Detective Daniels looks up at Ed.

"Because he was definitely sleeping with one of them, and they broke up. She went back to Chicago after that. We know she wasn't the only one…"

The detective nods his head. "Okay," he says. "I'll keep that in mind."

He tells us he'll be in touch as soon as he's got any news and reminds me not to leave the country, and then tells us we can go.

Ed hails a cab to take us back to the apartment and, for the first time ever, I'm relieved to be back here in the peace and quiet of the living room. I'd quite like to shut myself away in here and never leave again… except I wouldn't, because I'd really like to get on the next flight back to England, and then drive down to Dorset, and go to Waterside, and just sit on the beach and feel the wind in my hair and the sun on my face, and pretend this didn't happen… except it did.

"You okay?" Ed's voice brings me back to reality.

I nod my head.

"Ali's fixing us some lunch," he explains. We've been out longer than any of us expected and I guess they must be hungry. I'm not. I don't really notice hunger any more, or thirst. I just eat and drink when someone puts something in front of me, but none of it really tastes of anything.

"Do you need to get back to work?" I ask him.

"No. I can stay here with you all day. Everything's covered downstairs, remember? Petra's working front of house and Rob's in the kitchen."

"And tonight?" I don't want to be on my own, but I'm worried about saying that to him. I know he needs to work…

"Ali's gonna cover for me, Rob's gonna float between the kitchen and the front of house and Petra's coming in too."

"Does she know?" I ask. "About me? About what happened?"

"Yeah. Rob told her last night when he got home. He had to, babe."

"I know." I nestle into him. "No-one else though. I don't want anyone else knowing."

"I understand. It's okay."

For the next three days, they manage to make it that Ed is with me most of the time, and if he can't be, then Ali is. Having Ed step out of the kitchen is evidently quite hard. A lot of the recipes he uses are in his head, so he's spent some of his time writing them down, so that Ali and Rob know what they're doing when he's not there. They've popped up every so often to ask questions, which is how I know how tough they're finding it. Petra's been amazing too, and seems to have put her whole life on hold to come in and help out. I haven't actually seen her, because I haven't ventured downstairs, or out of the apartment at all, but I've asked Ed to pass on my thanks to her. He told me she said she feels guilty for suggesting I take the job at the magazine in the first place, and Ed reassures me he's told her not to. This isn't her fault.

Four days after I went to the police, during the afternoon break, I'm sitting upstairs with Ed. Sam and Ali are with us, but Rob and Petra have gone home to spend some time with April. There's a knock on the restaurant door, and Sam goes down to see who it is, returning a few minutes later, with Detective Daniels.

"I'm sorry to intrude," he says, looking around at all of us.

"Take a seat," Sam offers.

"No, thanks," he replies. "I won't be long. I just came to let Miss Bishop know that we've spoken to Mr Oakley. He's not denying that anything happened, but he's saying you were willing. He says you consented to everything he did and then got cold feet because your boyfriend might find out, and changed your mind about going further…"

"I—I didn't. That's… that's not what happened." Panic swells inside me, like a raging tide and I turn to Ed. "I swear I'd never…"

"Tess. Calm down," Ed says, soothingly. "I know that's not how it was. We all do. It's okay."

"But he's lying."

"Guys like him usually do," Detective Daniels points out. "He had a look about him," he adds. "It's a look I've seen before. One that says he thinks I can't touch him, because I can't prove anything."

"And is he right?" Sam asks, sitting forward.

Detective Daniels looks at Sam. "I hope not." He turns back to me, softening his voice. "I've spoken to two other women who worked for him in the past," he explains. "They've both alleged that he did similar things to them too."

"Then he can't keep denying it, surely?" Ali says.

"Well, he can, because we've got no physical evidence," the detective says. "But the weight of all of that testimony is going to count against him."

"So I'll have to testify?" I ask, staring at him.

"Yes. I'm afraid so."

"But if you've got these two other women, surely they can say what he did to them. Why do you need me?"

"Because what he did to them wasn't as bad as what he did to you," he explains. "Their testimony is only going to show that he's that way inclined. You're the crucial witness in this. Without you, we don't stand a chance…"

"And that means I have to stay here?"

He nods. "Yes. You do."

"Even if I don't want to?"

I feel Ed tense and pull away from me a little.

"Well, I guess you could drop the charges and go home," the detective says, "but then this would all have been for nothing, and none of you would get justice… and he'd be free to keep doing this to other young women."

"I see." I sigh. "I suppose I'll have to stay then."

Detective Daniels smiles. "You're doing the right thing. We'll stay in touch and you'll hear from the DA when a court date has been set… but don't hold your breath."

He turns to go. "I'll show you out," Ed offers and gets up.

"I can find my own way."

"No, really. I'll need to lock the door again."

Ed accompanies him down the stairs but, even once the front door closes, he doesn't come back, and I know I've hurt him… again.

"What were you doing downstairs?" I ask Ed when he finally comes back, after about an hour.

"Oh, nothing much." He sits beside me and puts his arm around me. Sam and Ali both get up and go into the kitchen.

"I'm sorry," I whisper. "I'm sorry I can't want to be here."

He pulls me closer. "It's okay."

"No it isn't. I can tell from your voice that it isn't."

Neither of us says anything else. He can't deny the truth of what I'm saying and I can't keep apologising, or explaining.

The truth is, what I'd really like is for him to come to England and make a home with me there, but I know that can't happen. He's told me before how much his brothers mean to him and I know it's too much to ask for him to give them up, which is why I've never asked him, and I never will. I have nothing back home; no family, no work, no ties, no man I love, but I'd still rather be there than here. At the same time, I know Ed can't leave here. His whole life is in Hartford… his business, his family, his friends, his career, his past… his life. I know how much he relies on his brothers, especially Sam, and he'd be giving up all of that for an unknown, and possibly barren future with a woman who can't commit to anything right now, except a need to be somewhere else.

He spends the evening with me, while Ali covers the kitchen for him, and we go to bed early. We've slept together every night since he arrived at Waterside, and although he holds me, we haven't been intimate. Sometimes, I think I want to, but then the memories of Bryan creep in, and I can't. I wonder whether it will always be like that, or whether maybe the court case might help me forget.

I still have nightmares pretty much every night, and Ed helps me through those, just like he always has. The broken sleep is starting to tell on both of us, but unlike him, I don't have to try and work through my tiredness. I just have to try and forget.

I really don't think my life is ever going to be happy again. Every day just seems to stretch before me. I barely speak unless I have to. I can't even think straight most of the time. I've given up reading, and writing, because I can't concentrate on either.

I just wish the court case could be over, and I could go back home… where I belong.

∽

Ed

Hearing Tess tell Detective Daniels that she wanted to go home wasn't a surprise, but it hurt. It really hurt. And, although I know I should've stayed with her and let Sam or Ali see the guy out, I had to get away for a few minutes. Except those few minutes became an hour.

It was an hour during which I sat in the restaurant, at one of the back tables, out of sight of anyone walking by on the street, tucked away in the darkest corner. I'd like to say I was thinking, but I wasn't. I don't like thinking anymore, because when I do, all I think about is the fact that Tess will go home eventually, and I'll be here alone, with just the memories of how perfect it almost was.

Everyone's being really great. Ali and Rob are helping out in the kitchen and Petra's covering for Rob whenever she can in the evenings, so that I can spend as much time as possible with Tess. She doesn't say much and, most of the time, we just sit and watch movies, or listen to music, but I like her to know I'm there for her.

We're still sleeping together as well. Well, where the hell else am I gonna sleep? We haven't made love, or been even vaguely intimate, and I'm not sure we ever will be. When I really think about it though, I'm not even sure I want us to be. I know she's gonna leave again as soon as the court case is over, and that's gonna be hard enough as it is. I don't need to make it harder by admitting to her – or myself – that I want her more than I ever did. Obviously, I still get aroused pretty much all the

285

time, but I do my best not to let her be aware of that. That's not as difficult as it might sound; Tess is in a daze most of the time, and I'm not sure she's aware of anything much.

She's still having nightmares too. She wakes up at least once, and sometimes twice a night, usually screaming or yelling. Sometimes she hits me and struggles against me, and I don't stop her or try and hold her back. I daren't do that; it'd only make things worse for her. I let her do whatever she needs to, until she realizes it's part of her nightmare, and that it's me she's hitting and not Bryan, and then she gets upset. It can take an hour or so for her to calm down completely, so she's exhausted most of the time too. The last few evenings, she's even started to dread going to bed, so we've just been sitting up half the night on the couch until she falls asleep and then I carry her through to the bedroom.

What worries me more than any of that though is how disconnected she's becoming. As the days have gone by, she's withdrawn even more into herself and sometimes I feel like I can't get to her at all. It's getting really bad and I have to say, I'm growing more and more scared for her.

"Talk to me," Sam comes over and stands in the doorway of my section of the kitchen.

I'm working this lunchtime and Ali's upstairs with Tess. To be honest, I needed the break, so I asked her if I could work. It's not that I don't wanna be with Tess. I do. But I just needed to get out of the damn apartment for a couple of hours.

"I don't know what to say." I turn to look at him.

He comes in and leans against the countertop. "Neither do I. But you can talk to me."

"I know," I reply.

"She's lost, isn't she?" he says.

"Yeah. That's a good way of putting it. She is. She's completely lost. And I don't know how to help her find herself again."

"Maybe you can't… help her, that is. Maybe it's something she has to do for herself."

"You think?" I focus on my hands, because I don't want to look at him.

"I don't know," he says. "We've never been in her position. But maybe only she can find the answers."

"I don't even know the damn questions, Sam."

He steps closer. "Stop beating yourself up." He nudges into me. "You're doing a fantastic job with her. I mean that. We can all see what a rock you're being for her, and I'm sure she can too, deep down."

"She doesn't need a rock. She needs a soft place to lie down and sleep soundly, and feel safe."

"You're that too," he says.

"In that case, why does she keep having nightmares?" I raise my voice. "Why is she so damn scared to go to bed I have to wait for her to fall asleep and carry her there, because she won't go of her own volition anymore?"

He puts his hand on my shoulder. "I don't know," he says. "Just try and hang in there, and keep doing what you're doing… and hopefully, once the court case is over, this will pass. And remember, you're not on your own."

"Then why do I feel so lonely," I manage to say as the tears prick my eyes.

"Fuck," he murmurs and pulls me into a hug. "You're not alone, Ed. We're here for you. I'm here for you. You know that. I'll always be here for you."

He's right. He has always been here for me. And I've never needed him more.

I swallow hard and blink back my tears. "Thanks," I mumble.

"Don't thank me," he says quietly.

We muddle through the next few weeks with Ali and me taking it in turns to either work or sit with Tess, and finally get to Thanksgiving. The only good thing that's happened is that Tess finally has a date for the the court case. It's been set for next week. I'd hoped that getting the date might help, but if anything, she's worse, which I suppose must be because she's gonna have to relive the whole thing again in court, in front of strangers.

The restaurant is closed for the day and Rob's coming over with Petra and April. We talked it through and decided that it'd be good for Tess to have the distraction of a small family gathering, so Petra's mom and her boyfriend David are spending the day at their place with his kids and their families.

"It's a bit like Christmas, isn't it?" Tess whispers as Sam and Ali set out the food. Everyone else is sitting around the table, which is overflowing as usual at this time of year.

"In what way?" I turn to her. She rarely instigates a conversation these days, so I'm keen to encourage her.

"The food." She nods to the enormous turkey that Sam's just about to start carving. "It's like Christmas."

"Oh, I see. Yeah, I guess so." I smile at her. She smiles back. "Tell me about Christmas in England," I suggest.

She shrugs. "We have a big tree," she says quietly, "which has to be real…"

"Naturally," I interrupt, and she smiles again. I feel like this is progress.

"And we have roast turkey, and all the trimmings." She looks back at the table. "A bit like this. And then afterwards, we go for a walk on the beach."

"So you have Christmas at your house by the sea?" I clarify.

"If we can, yes. Although last year, we went to St Lucia for ten days."

"Did you like it?" I ask her. I'd be surprised if she did.

"It was okay. Ali had been through a rough patch and she needed to get away…" Her voice fades to silence. "I missed home though," she adds suddenly.

I place my hand over hers in her lap and leave it there. She looks up and there are tears in her eyes. I want to hug her, but I know she won't appreciate me making a fuss in front of everyone, so I just smile and squeeze her hands. She just about manages a smile back before Sam announces we should start eating.

"We've got some news," Rob says, helping himself to roast potatoes, which Sam cooked with garlic and rosemary.

"Which is?" Sam asks.

"Petra and I have set the date… at last."

"For the wedding?" Sam pauses with a slice of turkey halfway toward his plate.

"Of course for the wedding," Rob replies.

"So the you-know-what came through?" Ali asks. None of us mention the word 'divorce' in front of April. We're not sure she fully understands about her mom's past, and Petra seems to like it that way. She says she's gonna explain it when April's old enough to understand, but she doesn't like the idea of April feeling rejected by her real father.

"Yeah. Yesterday," Rob says. I help Tess to some potatoes.

"So when's the wedding?" I ask him.

"December 22nd," he announces.

"Right before Christmas?" Sam's surprised.

"Yeah. I like Christmas," Rob explains.

"I know you do… but it's a busy time of year."

"And I'm only gonna do this once… so live with it." Rob's obviously made his mind up.

Sam looks at me for a moment, then shrugs. "Okay. I guess we'll be closing the restaurant for the day, then," he announces, smiling.

Rob grins. "Thanks," he says. "And I was wondering if you and Ed would take care of the food…?"

Again, Sam and I exchange glances. "Well… I'm not sure you can afford us," Sam teases.

"It's gonna be a real small wedding," Petra says quietly, speaking for the first time.

Sam laughs. "You can make it as big or as small as you like," he says. "We'll cater it for you, if that's what you really want."

She smiles up at him. "Yes, we do. Thank you."

"So, how small is small?" I ask. "We all know how big our family is…"

"We're not inviting the whole family," Rob says, holding Petra's hand in his on top of the table. "We've decided we just want it to be the three of us, and you guys, Petra's mom, and David… and Mom and Dad." He stares at me for a long moment. "I've spoken to them already, this morning, before we came over here. They're gonna fly up on the Friday afternoon."

"And stay for the wedding?" Sam asks, also looking at me.

"They've decided to stay for Christmas and maybe a few days afterwards," Rob says.

Sam pauses, then says, "I've had an idea... why don't we close the restaurant between Christmas and New Year? We could shut down for Rob and Petra's wedding and open again on New Year's Eve... that's a busy night for us, so we're gonna want to be back open then, but I think we could all do with a break, don't you? And besides, Rob and Petra won't be here for that week, so it'll save us having to think about how to manage the restaurant without them."

"I knew it," Rob crows. "I knew you couldn't cope without me."

"You're eminently replaceable," Sam jokes. "It's Petra I was thinking about."

We've never closed down before, other than when Ali refurbished the restaurant earlier in the year, and Sam made a huge fuss about it at the time. I guess this must mean he's decided there's more to life than work, which makes a change.

I don't reply straight away, and Sam looks at me, raising his eyebrows. I just give him a single nod. I'm not entirely enthusiastic. Of course I want to spend time with everyone – even though our parents probably won't speak to me while they're here – but by that time Tess might well have gone home, and the thought of being alone, of not having her here to talk to, to hold, to sleep with, to spend time with, is more than I can contemplate. If I don't have work to keep myself busy and preoccupied, I don't know what I'm gonna do.

Chapter Sixteen

Tess

I'm due to give evidence in court today.

I didn't sleep much last night. Ed held me and we talked. I might have dozed a little, but the advantage to not sleeping is you can't have nightmares, which was a blessed relief, despite my exhaustion this morning.

I get up and shower early, and Ed uses the bathroom after me. When he comes back into the bedroom, I'm still sitting on the bed where he left me twenty minutes ago, wrapped in my towel, my damp hair loose around my shoulders. All I've thought about in the intervening time is how I'm going to feel when I have to face Bryan in the court room.

"What's wrong?" Ed asks.

I look up at him with a start and notice he's got a towel wrapped around his hips, water droplets still glistening on his chest. "Um... I don't know what to wear," I murmur, getting up.

"Okay." I'm not sure he's convinced by my answer, but he comes over and opens the wardrobe doors. "I'd say you should just wear something smart," he says, and reaches for a black skirt.

"Not that." I shake my head. "I used to wear that to work... I can't."

He rifles through my clothes more carefully. "What about this?" he suggests, pulling out a dress – one of the ones we bought when we went on our first shopping trip together.

"I could put it with my blue jacket," I suggest. The dress is really a spring or autumn weight, and it's quite cold at the moment. "That should make it warm enough.

"And we'll be getting a cab, not walking," he adds, taking the dress off the hanger. "You look really nice in this." He lays it on the bed. "Do you want me to help you?" he asks.

"I feel pathetic." My shoulders drop and he steps forward, grabbing hold of me.

"You're not pathetic. You're incredibly brave, going through with this."

I look up at him. "I wish I didn't have to."

"I know." He pulls me closer and I rest my head against his bare chest, while he strokes my hair for a while. Eventually, he pulls back. "We need to get a move on," he says. "Do you want to dry your hair?" he asks.

"No. I'll braid it. It'll be quicker."

I sit down and plait my hair, tying it with a band and then a navy ribbon that's fairly close in colour to the jacket I'll be wearing.

While I'm doing that, Ed gets dressed, in black trousers, a white shirt and a pale blue tie. I imagine he must have been back to his place to collect his suit; but that thought just reminds me that he and I haven't been there together in ages. I haven't wanted to go – not because I don't want to be alone with him, but because I know it won't be the same. Not any more. I'm saddened by that thought. Those were our special times, and they're gone now.

Once he's ready, he throws his jacket on the bed and comes over to me again.

"Let's find you some underwear," he says, holding out his hand, and taking me over to the chest of drawers, where I find some white lace knickers and a matching bra. He doesn't say a word, but pulls the towel away, and I stand in front of him, completely naked. He kneels down and holds out the knickers, letting me step into them, and then pulling them up. I wiggle into them, getting comfortable and then he puts on my bra, moving behind me to fasten it. Again, I make the final adjustments myself, and then he stands in front of me again.

"Everything really has changed, hasn't it?" I whisper, tears filling my eyes.

"How do you mean?" he asks, softly.

"You used to undress me. Now you're dressing me. I used to turn you on. Now…" I can't finish the sentence, but he reaches out and touches my cheek with the tips of his fingers.

"You still turn me on," he says.

"But I sleep with you, Ed. I notice…"

He sighs, letting his hand fall again. "You do still turn me on, Tess," he persists. "I've just gotten real good at hiding it from you."

"Oh. Why?"

"Because I don't want you to feel like anything has to happen between us. It doesn't. I know you're not ready, and you maybe never will be… and I'm really, honestly okay with that. But that doesn't mean I don't want you. I do. I'll always want you."

I look into his eyes. "They've gone," I say quietly.

"What?"

"The fireflies. They haven't been there ever since you came to England to find me."

He swallows hard. "Because I'm sad, babe," he whispers.

"About me?" I ask.

"Of course about you."

I place my hand flat on his chest. "Don't be sad, Ed. I don't want that."

"You're hurting. Of course I'm gonna be sad." He pauses and then opens his mouth to say something else, but is interrupted by a knocking on the door.

"Are you two ready?" Ali calls. "We need to leave in ten minutes, and you haven't even had a coffee yet, let alone breakfast."

Ed looks at me. "We'll be there in a minute," he says, raising his voice.

"Did you want to say something else?" I whisper, quietly enough that Ali won't hear.

"Nothing that won't keep," he replies and goes over to the bed to pick up my dress.

The courthouse is big, much bigger than I'd expected, but Ed has steered us into a quiet corner where we can wait for me to be called into the courtroom. He's holding my hand and hasn't let go since we left my bedroom, and Ali's sitting on the other side of me, nervously fiddling with the clasp on her handbag.

All of sudden, Ed squeezes my hand and I look up. Detective Daniels is walking towards us, accompanied by another man, who's much smarter, wearing a dark suit and tie.

"Miss Bishop," the detective says, holding out his hand. I stand, with Ed, take it and he gives me a gentle handshake. "This is Colin Porter. He works for the DA's office."

I nod to the man who's standing beside Detective Daniels.

"I'm really sorry to mess you around," Colin Porter says. His voice is quite high pitched and I'd imagine it could get annoying fairly quickly. "Mr Oakley has changed his plea."

"What does that mean?" I ask, because I don't understand what he's saying.

Detective Daniels takes a step forward. "He's been pleading not guilty," he says softly. "In fact, he's been shouting his innocence to anyone who'd listen… right up until about thirty minutes ago, just as the case was about to start. And now, all of a sudden he's decided to confess."

"He's confessed? To… to what he did to me?"

Daniels nods his head. "Yeah. And to the other women too."

"So… so, I don't have to testify?"

"No." He smiles. "No, you don't."

"And I can go home? I can go back to England?"

He nods again. "Anytime you want."

Ed lets go of my hand and I turn to him. "I'm sorry," I murmur, lowering my head. I didn't mean to hurt him. I feel his finger beneath my chin, and he raises my face to his, looking deep into my eyes.

"It's okay," he whispers, but I can see from the look on his face that it's very far from okay.

Ali steps forward, standing next to me. "Can I ask a question?" she says, looking at Mr Porter.

"Of course." He tilts his head to one side.

"Is Bryan Oakley still going to go to prison?"

He smiles. "Oh, yes. We offered him a reduced sentence, if he pleaded guilty, and initially he declined, because he was determined to prove his innocence, but I guess he's decided that nine months is better than five years."

"Nine months?" Ali's as shocked as I am. "That's all he's going to get?"

Detective Daniels turns to Ali. "It's classified as a Class D felony," he explains. "Your sister's over sixteen years old, and he didn't rape her…" He stops talking and lowers his head.

"Look on the bright side… At least you didn't have to testify." Colin Porter seems almost triumphant.

"Shut up, Colin," Daniels mutters under his breath.

"That's meant to help, is it?" Ed says, ignoring the policeman and pulling me into his arms. "That asshole gets nine months for what he's done. Tess has gotta live with what he did to her for the rest of her life…"

Porters shrugs. "That's the system, I'm afraid."

"Then the system sucks," Ali replies.

"Can we go… please," I murmur. I just want to get out of here. I want to be as far away as possible from this place and these people.

"Sure," Ed replies. None of us says anything else, and we just turn and leave.

We have a silent cab ride back to the restaurant. I don't think any of us really knows what to say. I know I don't.

Petra's covering the front of house because Jasmine's little girl has a hospital check-up, and when we arrive, she's just supervising the set-up for the lunchtime service. It's only just gone eleven. The restaurant doesn't open for another hour.

"You're back early," she says, smiling and opening the door to us.

"Yeah." The tone of Ed's voice sums up how we all feel, I think.

"It… it didn't go well?" Petra locks the door again behind us and we head through the restaurant.

"That's putting it mildly," Ali replies over her shoulder.

We make our way into the kitchen and, although I'd rather just go upstairs, I do understand that they've all been worried, and they want to know what's happened. The kitchen's busy, with everyone getting ready for opening.

"Sam? Rob?" Ed calls as we go in. "Can you come upstairs for a minute?"

Sam looks up and nods, coming over. Rob's in Ed's section at the back, and walks towards us too.

"Keep working, guys," Sam calls out, as we leave the room and all traipse upstairs, including Petra.

Once we're in the living room, Ed sits me down at one end of the couch and takes a seat beside me. Ali and Sam sit in the corner, and Rob perches on the other end, with Petra on his lap.

"What happened?" Sam asks. "I didn't expect to see you until much later."

"He changed his plea," Ed explains. Ali's still pale and shocked. I'm not sure she's any more capable of speech than I am.

"He pleaded guilty?" Rob speaks next and Ed turns.

"Yeah."

"Well, that's good, isn't it?" Rob asks.

"In a way, yes. It meant Tess didn't have to testify."

"But?" Sam says. "What aren't you telling us?"

Ed holds me closer, right next to him. "In return for pleading guilty, he gets a reduced sentence…"

"How reduced?" Rob asks.

"Nine months…"

"What?"

"Nine fucking months?" Rob and Sam both speak at the same time. "For what he did?" Sam continues.

"Yeah. Evidently, because Tess is over sixteen and he didn't rape her, the most the guy would've got is five years, but because he pleaded guilty, they reduced it to nine months."

"That fucking…"

"Please, Sam," I murmur, barely able to control my shaking limbs. "Don't."

He stops immediately, lets go of Ali, gets up and comes over, crouching down in front of me.

"I'm sorry," he says. "I didn't mean to yell."

I bury my head in Ed's chest and sob, and he brings his arms around me, stroking my hair and holding onto me.

After a short while, I look up. Sam's moved back to sit with Ali, but they're all still looking at me.

"How do you feel?" Ed says, asking the question on behalf of all of them, I suppose.

"Numb," I reply truthfully. "I thought I'd feel vindicated, but I guess I just feel cheated."

"That makes sense," Petra says softly. "He's not getting what he deserves. You're bound to feel cheated by that… by the system."

I nod my head.

"What are you going to do?" Ali asks me.

"When? Now? I was thinking of having a bath and trying to get some sleep."

She smiles at me. "No, I meant in the longer term…" She glances at Ed, and then back at me again.

"Oh. I don't know." I look over at Rob and Petra, clasped together at the other end of the couch. "I think I'll probably stay for the wedding, if that's okay, and also for Christmas, and then go home the next day. I know there's no such thing as Boxing Day here, and if I leave then, by the time I get home, Christmas will be over and I can just get on with things…"

Ed shifts, his hold on me loosening just slightly.

"Why don't you stay for New Year?" Sam suggests. "We're closing the restaurant after Rob's wedding. You could hang out with us for a while."

I give him a smile, because I don't want him to feel guilty. "I can't," I say softly. "If I stay for New Year, then Ali will suggest I stay for her birthday, and then it'll be Easter… There'll always be something. I'm sorry, but I have to go. I need to."

I feel Ed move. "Excuse me," he mumbles and gets up.

I turn just in time to see him going out of the door and I hear him running down the stairs.

"Shit," I hear Sam murmur under his breath.

"I'm sorry." I turn back to him. "I'm not trying to deliberately hurt him. But I can't stay here."

He gives me such a sympathetic look, it brings tears to my eyes. "I do understand," he says.

Suddenly, it's all too much. I get up and run out of the apartment and down the stairs. There's no sign of Ed, but then he's probably left. I imagine he wants to get as far away from me as he can.

"Tess!" Ali's right behind me. "Tess! Stop!" I get to the corridor, by the door to the office, when she grabs my arm and pulls me back. "Stop," she says, more softly.

She turns me. I'm crying my eyes out and she puts her arms around me, hugging me.

"I'm sorry," I whisper.

"Don't be. We all understand," she says.

"Even Ed?"

"Especially Ed." She sighs. "I haven't said anything until now, because you had the court case hanging over you, but it was Ed who explained to me that you never wanted to be here in the first place, even before Bryan…" she says, leaning back and looking down at me. "Why didn't you tell me?"

"Because you were so happy. I didn't want to take anything away from that."

She smiles. "You muppet," she says softly. "How can I be happy when you're miserable? If home is where you want to be, then that's where you should go. It was a mistake to make you come here."

"No. No, it wasn't. You weren't to know what would happen. And, if I hadn't come here, I'd never have met Ed. Who knows? Maybe if Bryan hadn't done what he did, I might have got used to it here… eventually."

She takes a step closer. "You need to try and see how this feels from Ed's point of view," she says.

"I do. I know he thinks I'm just being selfish, and wanting my own way. He's been so kind, so patient and helpful and understanding, and I've thrown it all back in his face... I don't deserve him. But I do need to try and talk to him. Well, I do, once I've worked out what on earth I'm going to say to him."

Ali smiles and nods her head. "I've been thinking," she says, a little wistfully, "if you're determined to go back to England, would it help with we took Waterside off the market, and you lived there?"

I feel a spark of life deep inside, like someone lit a candle and it's burning, just faintly, showing me the way home. "I—I was going to use some of my money to buy somewhere, but to be honest, I'd prefer to live at Waterside." I look up at her. "I'll buy you out, of course."

She shakes her head. "I don't want you to," she says. "You belong there, Tess. The house is yours... I think it probably always was."

Ed

"You belong there, Tess," I hear Ali say. "The house is yours... I think it probably always was."

I've heard every word they've said to each other, because I'm in the office. It's where I ran to when I left the living room. I couldn't go into the kitchen or the restaurant; there are too many people. It didn't feel right to leave altogether, because Tess is in a bad place right now, so I need to be here, but I also needed just a little time to myself to take on board that she's really, truly going.

The fact that I can hear everything means I also heard Tess saying that she believes I think she's selfish and that she just wants her own way. I don't believe anything of the sort and part of me is tempted to go out into the corridor, take her in my arms and tell her that. But I don't... and the reason I don't is because she's said she's gonna talk to me. I want to give her time to do that, to work out what she wants to say to me, and to say it. That way, she won't be responding to me, she'll be telling me how she *really* feels. And I need to know that more than ever.

I don't know how long I'm gonna have to wait for her to work it out, but I hope she does it before she goes home… which I now know will be the day after Christmas. Just under four weeks away. It's not enough time.

It'll never be enough time.

When I get back upstairs, everyone's disappeared, except Ali and Tess.

"They're all down in the restaurant," Ali explains, noticing me looking around, I guess. I check the time. It's gone one, so I'm not surprised.

"Oh. Okay."

Tess is fiddling with the button on the front of her dress, not looking at me, and Ali gets up. "I'll go and see if I can help out down there," she says, moving past me and patting me lightly on the arm as she does.

I sit down beside Tess. "Are you okay?" I ask her.

She looks up and nods. "I'm sorry," she says.

"Don't be. We both knew what would happen. We both knew you only came back for the court case…" I can't say anymore.

She opens her mouth, and then closes it again and looks away. I guess whatever it is she wants to say, she's not quite ready yet.

I get to my feet and hold out my hand. "Come with me."

"Where?"

"Just come with me."

She puts her hand in mine and I pull her up and lead her down the stairs. "Wait here," I tell her, leaving her by the kitchen door, while I go inside and tell Sam that we'll be out for the rest of the afternoon. He's fine with my plan and tells us to take the evening too, if we want to.

Back in the corridor, I grab Tess's hand again, and we go out through the restaurant and onto the sidewalk.

"Where are we going?" she asks me, pulling her jacket around her.

I'd forgotten how cold it was out here, so I pick up the pace a little. "You'll see," I say. "It's not far."

It doesn't take us long to reach our destination.

"The art gallery?" Tess stops and looks up at me.

"Yeah. Come on. It's cold out here." I pull her toward the door and she follows willingly, and we spend the next few hours looking at paintings. We make point of going back to see the Courbet.

"Does it still remind you of home?" I ask her, as she stares and looks up at it.

She nods her head, and then turns to me, putting her arms around my waist and resting her head on my chest.

"Thank you for this," she says. "It was just what I needed today."

I kiss her head. "You'll be there soon," I tell her, although it's a real struggle to talk, and the thought of her not being here is killing me.

When we're finished at the gallery, I take her to the smokehouse for dinner. She's not quite as relaxed as she was when we first came here, but she's more cheerful than she's been in ages, and we talk about some of the paintings we've seen, and the lives of some of the more well-known artists. It's a good way to spend the evening.

On the way back home, I put my arm around her, partly to keep her warm, but mainly because I want her close to me for as much of the time as possible.

"Do… do you still want me to sleep with you?" I ask her, just as we're crossing the road. I've been building up to asking her since we got to the smokehouse, but she seemed in a better mood there and I didn't want to spoil it.

She looks up at me. "Yes." She sucks in a deep breath, and then lets it out again, real slow. "I know I'm being selfish, but I need you."

I smile. "You're not being selfish, babe. I know you need the reassurance, and if I'm being honest, I need it too."

"You do?" She's staring at me, surprised.

"Yeah. I like feeling you close to me."

We're almost back at the restaurant, and she stops on the sidewalk and turns to me.

"Can I ask you something?" she says, looking into my eyes.

"Sure."

"Why did you take me to the gallery today?"

I shrug my shoulders. "To cheer you up, I guess."

She smiles. "Well, it worked. Thank you."

"Don't thank me."

She leans forward, so her forehead rests on my chest. "You…" she mumbles, "you weren't trying to persuade me to stay… by reminding me of happier times?" she asks.

I reach down and raise her face to mine. "No. I know I can't make you stay. And I don't want to. I know you're unhappy here, and I'd never do anything to make you unhappy." She nestles into me and I hold her. "But I am trying to make memories," I confess, and she leans back again. "For myself. I want to make some memories of our time together… things that I can cling onto when you're… when you're not here anymore." My voice cracks on the last few words and I pull her in tight so she won't see the tears gathering in my eyes.

We're lying in bed when she suddenly turns to me.

"You were going to say something this morning," she says.

"I was?" This morning feels like a lifetime ago. "What about?"

"I don't know."

I smile and turn to face her. "Well, what were we talking about?"

"We were in here, getting dressed and I'd said that the fireflies had gone from your eyes, and you said that was because you were sad," she replies with her usual frankness. "And then I asked if you wanted to say something else, because it looked like you did, and you said you did, but it would keep."

"Oh." I remember now. "Yeah."

"What was it?" she asks.

I reach over and pull her into a hug, and she lets me. "I was gonna say that, just because I'm sad, doesn't mean I won't do the right thing."

"The right thing?" She leans back and looks up at me.

"Letting you go home." I swallow hard. "It's gonna break me, Tess. But it's the right thing to do."

She blinks and tears fall from her eyes, and then she leans her head on my chest and puts her arm around my waist and clings to me.

I'm surprised that Rob and Petra chose to have such a quiet wedding, but I guess she's done all this before, and I think Rob just wants to be married. I don't think he's overly fussed about how they get there. They have a really simple ceremony at the town hall, and then afterwards the reception is held at the restaurant, which is now closed until New Year's Eve, exactly as Sam suggested. That said, New Year's Eve is fully booked and is going to be horrendous, but at least we've all got ten days off first to build up our reserves of energy.

Because there are so few of us, Rob and Petra asked if they could have a sit-down meal, so Sam's prepared a grilled seafood salad to start, followed by pappardelle with meatballs. That sounds odd for a wedding dish, but it was Rob's favorite as a kid and Sam's jazzed it up a bit as a kind of 'homage' to our brother. I've made a couple of desserts. One's a coffee and ricotta tart, and the other is a strawberry gelato, especially for April, served with lemon cookies – another of Rob's childhood favorites. Sam and I did give the menu *some* thought.

The food is a huge success and the happy couple look… happy. Actually, they look more than happy, and I'm really pleased for them. It hasn't been easy getting here, and they deserve this… both of them. My parents have managed to ignore me all day, which has probably hit me harder than ever before, given my situation, especially as they're talking to Sam now. Actually they're doting on Sam, and they're clearly head over heels in love with April and Petra. I couldn't be any more on the outside if I tried.

I feel Tess's hand in mine. "Can we talk?" she asks, coming and standing beside me.

"Of course." I look down at her. "Do you want to go somewhere else?"

"We can just go to the back of the restaurant, can't we?" She nods toward the quieter part of the room. "I don't want a fuss."

"Okay." I let her lead the way and we sit opposite each other at one of the tables along the back wall.

I don't say a word, but wait for Tess to start talking. It takes a while and a little fidgeting, but eventually she looks up at me and I know at once that she's worked out what it is she wants to say to me. Part of me wants to tell her to wait, to make sure she's got it right, but I can't…

"I'm sorry," she says, her voice so quiet I have to lean forward to hear her. "I'm so sorry things have worked out the way they have. I wish it could be different for us… I wish I could stay."

She leans forward and reaches out, touching my cheek. I don't reply, because I sense she's got more to say.

"I came to America for Ali," she continues and swallows hard, blinking back the tears that are welling in her eyes. "But you're the only thing… the only person I'd stay for. I just… I just wish I could." Her tears start to fall, and she sucks in a breath. "I'm sorry Ed," she repeats. "I'm more sorry than you'll ever know, but I don't belong here. I thought I could make it work, and if Bryan hadn't done what he did…" She wipes her cheek with the back of her hand, and opens her mouth to speak again. I can't let her…

"Stop," I say softly. "You don't have to say anymore. I know you're sorry. And I know you're right. I've hated seeing you as unhappy as you've been since you came back here and, while I know a lot of that has been to do with the court case, I also know that some of it is just because you don't wanna be here anymore." I brush her tears away with my thumbs. "I love you so much, Tess. And because of that, I want you to be happy. And that means I want you to be in the place that makes you happiest… and that's not here." I stop and take a breath. "I'll miss you more than I can ever tell you, but now I've seen you in the place where you truly belong, I could never ask you to live anywhere but there again."

She lets her head fall into my hand and I hold it there for a minute, and then I get up and pull her to her feet, holding her close to me as she sobs into my chest.

Letting her go is the right thing to do. I know that. It just hurts. So damn much.

304

Chapter Seventeen

Tess

"Buon Natale!"

Ed's parents come into the restaurant, larger than life and twice as loud. I feel myself flinch and Ed puts his arm around me. I think in the last couple of days, since Rob and Petra's wedding, he's been even more protective and attentive than before, if that were possible. Because the restaurant's closed, he hasn't left my side, and he's clearly determined to make my last few days in America as easy as he can.

"Happy Christmas," Sam replies.

"In Italian," his father scolds.

"We're in America now, Pop," Sam replies.

Petra, Rob and and April are here already, and Petra's mum Thea and her boyfriend David are also coming to lunch once they've visited his two children, because they decided they didn't see Petra on Thanksgiving, so they were going to spend Christmas with her. Also, Petra and Rob are leaving to go on their honeymoon very early tomorrow morning, so Thea and David are taking April home with them, while Petra and Rob spend the night at Ed's apartment. Considering the unearthly hour that they're going to have to get up, they decided it was easier than risking waking April, in case she gets upset that they're leaving.

Because there are so many people here, Sam's decided to cook in the restaurant kitchen, and we're going to eat down here too. It's just easier than trying to squeeze everyone in upstairs.

Ed's father, who I learned at Rob's wedding, is called Giovanni, goes over to Rob and starts talking to him and I feel Ed stiffen.

"He's still not talking to you, is he?" I ask him in a whisper.

"No." He shakes his head and shrugs. "I don't know," he adds, "I guess I hoped for too much."

"Why? What did you hope for?"

"I hoped that Rob's wedding might make him see sense… might make him remember he's got three sons."

"And your mum?" I ask him.

"She won't go against him," he replies. "She smiled at me at Rob's wedding, but that was it."

His mum smiled at him… For heaven's sake. Don't they realise what they're doing? Even as Ed turns away from his parents and looks down to the other end of the restaurant I resolve that somehow, I will try to do something about his situation before I go home… which gives me today.

Sam and Ali are both sitting at a table and Sam says something to her, shaking his head, then he gets up, looking at his father for a moment. I sense he's equally frustrated about the situation between Ed and his parents. "Ed?" he calls over. "Can you give me some help in the kitchen?" Sam clearly wants to prevent Ed from having to witness any more of his parents' prejudicial behaviour.

"Sure." Ed turns to me for a moment. "Will you be okay?" he asks.

"Yes, I'll be fine."

"You can go and sit with Ali, can't you?"

He's obviously worried about me being out here with his family, by myself.

"I'll be fine, Ed." I smile up at him and shoo him away. He gives me a brief grin and disappears into the kitchen.

I wait for the door to swing shut and clench my fists a few times. I may not get another chance like this, so I have to put my nervousness to one side. I take a deep breath and walk across the room to where his parents are still standing, with Rob and Petra.

"Excuse me? Mr Moreno? May I have a word with you please… in private?"

Everyone stops speaking and stares at me. Even Rob.

"Um… certainly, young lady." Mr Moreno looks around and says, "Shall we sit over there?" He nods towards the back of the restaurant.

"Okay." I let him lead the way and when we get to the table, he holds out the chair, and lets me sit, pushing it back in for me, before taking a seat opposite me. Of his three sons, he looks most like Sam. He's certainly got his dark eyes, which are currently staring at me.

"What can I do for you, young lady?" he asks.

"Please, call me Tess," I suggest. I can't abide being called 'young lady', it makes me think I'm being told off for something.

"Very well, Tess. What can I do for you?"

Now I've got him here, I've got no idea how to start the conversation, but I have to, don't I?

"I—I'm leaving in the morning," I say, because that seems like the best place to start, at least to me.

"You are?" He seems surprised. "I thought you and Eduardo were… together," he says.

"We are. I love your son, Mr Moreno. I love him with all my heart, but I can't live here. I don't belong in America. He does. He belongs right here in Hartford, with his family – especially with Sam and Rob – and I could never ask him to give that up, any more than he would ask me to give up being in the place where I belong."

"So, you're going home to be with your family?" he asks, leaning forward a little, like he's interested.

"No. Ali is the only family I've got. And she's staying here with Sam. She belongs here now too."

"You have no family?" he enquires. "What about your parents?"

"They died."

He lowers his eyes. "I'm sorry," he whispers. "I didn't know."

"They… they were killed in a house fire when I was eight years old," I explain. I don't want to tell the story, but I think it's the best way to get him to understand. "Ali was away at the time, so it was just me and them in the house. Our mother succumbed to the smoke quite quickly, but our dad came to find me in my bedroom, and he… he lowered me out of the window to a neighbour." I feel the tears forming in my eyes, but carry on anyway. "Dad told me… he told me that he loved me and that I shouldn't be scared, and then he went back inside the house."

"Why?" he asks. "If your mama was already dead? Why did he do that?"

"Because he didn't want to live without her," I tell him. "He went back to their room, and he lay down on the bed and he let the fire and the smoke claim him too."

He reaches out his hands and puts them over mine. "Mio caro bambino," he says softly.

I pause, swallowing down my emotions as best I can. "I don't know you," I continue eventually. "But I do know Ed. He wanted to be a certain kind of chef and he's done that… and he's so good at it; he's amazing. He really is. He followed his heart, Mr Moreno. That's what I'm doing and Ed's letting me, because he loves me, unconditionally." I take another breath. "Please, please try to remember that your time with your children is limited. I always felt like our father abandoned us, and at times I've found it hard to forgive him, but I would still give everything I have for another five minutes with him."

"Why do you want those five minutes?" he asks me, a frown forming on his face.

"Not to ask him why he left us, if that's what you're thinking. Not to tell him how angry I am with him sometimes, or to make him feel bad. No…" I shake my head. "I'd just want five minutes with him, to feel his arms around me one more time and to hear him tell me that he loves me, and to be able to tell him that I love him too. Because I still do, and I always will. I can never have that time, Mr Moreno, but you can. Please don't leave it until you've only got five minutes left to make it right with Ed. You have so much to be proud of in him, and you're missing out on all of it… And I can promise, you won't get it back."

I've said enough now. I've probably said too much, and I get to my feet.

He stands quickly and, as I go to turn away, he pulls me back and leans down, then kisses my cheek and, when he pulls back, I notice there are tears in his eyes.

Just like we did for Rob and Petra's wedding, we all sit around one big table, which is actually made up of several smaller ones, placed together and covered with a large white cloth. We're not having turkey, I suppose because they do that for Thanksgiving here, but Sam's cooked an enormous piece of roast beef. He's sitting at one end of the table, with Ali beside him and all through the meal, they keep whispering to each other. I'm too far away to hear what they're saying, but I don't need to worry as, once all the food has been dished up, Sam gets to his feet, his wine glass in hand and says he has an announcement to make.

He looks around. "Ali's not sure we should be saying anything yet, but I can't keep this quiet any longer… we're gonna have a baby." He's beaming with delight and everyone cheers. Once the noise has died down, he continues, "We've known for a couple of weeks, but Ali wanted to wait until she was three months gone before saying anything…" He smirks. "Guess that didn't happen." She slaps him playfully on the behind. "I just wanted to wait until after Rob and Petra's wedding, so we didn't steal their thunder."

"Like you could," Rob interrupts.

"I could steal your thunder in my sleep," Sam replies.

"When's the baby due?" I ask, because I know they could keep up their banter for hours if someone doesn't stop them.

"The beginning of August," Ali says, looking at me. "I wish you were still going to be here." Even from here I can see she's upset and Sam leans down, giving her a hug.

Ed reaches over and holds my hand in his and everyone falls silent. I'm going to miss being here too.

"Well," I say, trying to put a brave face on it, "I will come and visit, and my nephew or niece won't be short of uncles and aunts. He or she has even got a ready-made cousin." I give April a wink and she smiles back as Thea explains what a cousin is. Everyone soon starts chattering again and I turn to Ed. He smiles, and then looks away and I know I've upset him again.

"I'm sorry," I whisper, leaning towards him. "But what can I do?"

He turns back. "Nothing," he replies, his voice flat. "There's nothing anyone can do."

We eat lunch and everyone apart from Ed and myself seems to really enjoy it. We enjoy the food, but we can't get away from the fact that my flight's tomorrow afternoon, and time's slipping away from us.

Once everyone's finished, Ed offers to help clear away the dishes and he's on his way back from the kitchen when his father gets up from the table, and walks right up to him. He says something very quietly to Ed and then they both throw their arms around each other. Everyone's completely silent, staring and I hear a slight sob from Ed's mum and glance over to see she's crying, her hand to her mouth. Thea goes to her and puts an arm around her and Sam stares, his eyes wandering from Ed and his dad, to his mum. He's shocked. It's almost like he's never seen her cry before.

After a few minutes, Ed's dad pulls away from him and looks into his eyes.

"I've been stupid," he says. "I've been a stupid old man." Ed doesn't say a word and, keeping hold of his son, Mr Moreno turns around to face the rest of us. "And it took a beautiful English girl to make me realise it," he adds. Ed looks over at me, tears falling from his eyes and the look I see breaks my heart in two.

Thea and David decide not to leave too late, because April's had a tiring day and they don't want her getting upset that Rob and Petra aren't going home with them, so they go around six in the evening. Ed's parents aren't far behind. Mr Moreno has spent a lot of the afternoon talking to Ed, catching up on the years he's wasted, I hope, and their mum has been chatting to Ali, presumably about her pregnancy. I'm glad that Ali's going to have such a big family surrounding and supporting her. It makes me feel slightly less guilty about going home. But only slightly.

Ed and I have been avoiding each other since lunchtime, I think because we know how little time we have left and we don't want to face the reality of it ending, but as his parents go out of the door at the end of the evening, Ed turns to me.

"What did you say to my dad?" he asks simply, and everyone looks at me.

"I told him about our dad," I explain. "I told him what happened… about the fire, and how Dad went back for Mum and left me, and how I wish he hadn't. I told him that I'd give everything I've got to have five minutes more with my dad, just to feel his arms around me one last time." I hear Ali sniff and am aware of Sam moving closer to her. "And I told your dad not to wait until he's only got five minutes left to be with you, because the time we have is so precious… that's all…"

"That's all?" He moves forward, so he's standing right in front of me looking down into my eyes. "You told him your story… your secret… to bring him back to me?"

"Of course." I rest my hand on his chest and he puts his over the top of it.

"Thank you," he whispers. "Thank you so much. You know how much my family means to me… and you put us back together."

"I didn't do anything," I tell him. "I just told him that real love is unconditional. You love me enough to let me do what's right for me, rather than keeping me here and doing what you want."

He lets go of my hand and pulls me into his arms. "Yeah, I do," he says, then he leans back. "I'm sorry," he murmurs, his voice cracking.

"Why?" I don't understand.

"I can't stay here tonight."

I feel like my broken heart stopped beating. "Why?" I repeat.

He closes his eyes, then opens them again, tears glistening in the candlelight. "I can't," he repeats. "I know I've stayed with you every night since… since you came back, but I can't. Not tonight. You're leaving tomorrow morning, and it's too much. It's breaking me already, Tess. I can't do it…"

Tears are falling down my cheeks before he even stops talking.

"It's okay," I manage to say. "I understand."

He pulls me in close again, holding me tight against him. "I'm sorry, Tess," he whispers. "I love you too much to say goodbye." And then he pulls away and walks straight out of the restaurant. Rob follows quickly, with Petra and I see Rob catch up to Ed and put his arm around him as they walk past the front window in the direction of Ed's flat.

Luckily, he doesn't look back, because my legs give way and I crumple to the floor.

I'm vaguely aware of being lifted by someone strong and when I look up, I see Sam. He's holding me in his arms.

"Lock the door and get the lights, Ali," he says, and the restaurant's plunged into darkness as he carries me between the tables and we go down the corridor and through the door that leads up to the apartment.

Once upstairs, Sam turns to Ali, with me still in his arms.

"Bedroom?" he says and she nods, and he takes me along the hallway and through my open bedroom door, depositing me on the bed. "I'll leave you guys alone," he adds, and turns to leave the room, although he pauses on the threshold. "What you did for Ed... with our dad," he says. "Thank you for giving him that," and he leaves the room.

Ali sits on the edge of the bed. "Let me help you," she says.

"I'm fine."

"No, you're not. You're upset."

I look at her. "Of course I'm upset."

"Then let me help you."

"There's nothing you can do, Ali... and I'd like to be alone for a while. I'd like to think."

She looks down at me. "Are you packed?" she asks.

"Yes. I finished packing yesterday." I nod towards my case by the door. I feel like an automaton... and, as much as I love her, I wish she'd go away.

She sighs. "You're sure you don't need me?"

"No. I'm fine." She stands up. "Ali?" I say.

"Yes."

"Congratulations... about the baby. I'm really happy for you both."

"And you'll come back to visit?"

I nod my head, and giving me a last smile, she leaves, closing the door quietly behind her.

Of course, every time I come back to visit Ali and the baby, I'm going to have to see Ed again. That's going to be hard, especially as I have no doubt he'll find someone else at some point. God... the thought of him with another woman... I turn over and sob into the pillow.

I don't know how much time passes before I hear voices in the hallway. Ali and Sam are clearly going to bed... They're whispering, but I can still hear them.

"... I'm absolutely certain they're not doing the right thing," Ali's saying.

"Maybe not, but what else can they do?" Sam replies. "They belong together, but on different continents."

"I feel like I should take Tess home," Ali says. "Maybe spend a couple of weeks with her and get her settled in."

And then what? I wonder... Can't she see, there's no point in prolonging the inevitable break?

"It's her decision, Ali. You've gotta let her do this. And besides, if she wanted anyone to take her home, I think it'd be Ed, not you... and that's what makes it so damn heartbreaking. I'm sorry, baby, but all we can do is pick up the pieces. You belong here now... with me. You and our baby."

I hear their door open and close, and hope that Ali listens to Sam.

I know she means well, but Sam's right. If anyone was going to come home with me, I'd want it to be Ed. But now that he's got his family back together again, I know that would be an even bigger ask... and it's not one I'm ever going to make. Family means too much to him to expect him to sacrifice it, besides which, there's his job, his business, his life and everything he knows.

I wish I could be as strong as Ali, and forge a new life in a country that feels so alien to me. I wish it didn't have to be like this... but above all I wish Ed could be here, just for one last night. I want to feel him, to touch him, to make love with him. I didn't think I'd want to, but I do... and I really wish I hadn't left it too late to work that out.

Ed

"I'll… I'll go to bed," Petra says the moment we walk through the door of our apartment. She gives Rob a quick kiss, nods to me and disappears down the hallway toward Rob's bedroom.

"You can go with her, you know." I turn to him. "I'll be fine by myself. And you've gotta be up real early in the morning."

"It's okay. I'll stay out here with you for a while."

I go into the living room and flop down into the recliner chair. Rob sits on the couch and stares at me, his elbows resting on his knees.

"Are you okay?" he asks after a little while.

"No." I don't bother to lie, or even look up. I just focus on the corner of the coffee table.

"Tell me," he says.

"I feel like my life's over." I can't think what else to say, because that sums up exactly how I feel. "I don't feel like I have any kind of future. Tess will always be Ali's sister, and now Ali's having Sam's baby, Tess is going to be a recurring feature, isn't she?" He doesn't reply, because we both know I'm right. "Even if she doesn't wanna live here, she's bound to come over to visit from time to time, to see Ali and her nephew or niece, and when she does, I'll be reminded of what we so nearly had."

"It's gonna be tough," he murmurs.

"It's gonna be worse than that." I lean back and stare at the ceiling. "I don't think I can do it. I think, when she comes over, I'm gonna have to go away somewhere. I can't face seeing her, especially as she's bound to meet some other guy, eventually and probably bring him with her."

"You think she'd do that? After everything that happened with Bryan?" He seems surprised.

I shrug. "Not straight away, no. But once she's settled in at home, who knows? Maybe she'll meet someone who'll help her forget…" As much as I want her to be able to put what Bryan did behind her, the thought of anyone other than me helping her through that makes my heart ache. "God," I say out loud, "the thought of her with another man…"

"Whoa," Rob says, holding up his hands. "You're getting way ahead of yourself here."

"Am I?" I look at him. "You think if you and Petra split up, you could cope with seeing her with another guy?"

"No."

"But at least if you did break up, it'd be a clean break. I don't have that. Because our brother is married to Tess's sister, so she's always gonna be there, isn't she?"

He nods. "Yeah. I guess a clean break would have been easier."

I shake my head. "No. No break would have been easier." I let out a long sigh. "Don't get me wrong, I know it wasn't perfect between us before, I know she was never completely comfortable here, but she was getting there, I know she was. She'd agreed to spending part of the weekend with me here."

"Away from Ali?" he queries.

"Yeah. That felt like a real breakthrough, like she really trusted me."

"So what happened?"

"That was the same weekend that Bryan attacked her."

"Shit," he whispers.

"And nothing has been the same since."

"But you've still been sleeping with her, right?" he asks, moving a little closer and lowering his voice, although I'm not sure why.

"Sleeping, yeah."

"Oh." He looks away for a moment.

"We haven't had sex since it happened," I explain.

"I guess that's understandable," he says, turning back to me again.

"I know. I know it is. I get it. And I haven't pushed her."

"I didn't think you would've done." He moves up to the corner of the couch, so he's right beside me. "Do you still love her?" he asks, simply.

"Yeah, of course I do."

"Then what the fuck are you doing here?" he asks, his voice still quiet and gentle, despite his words.

I pause for a moment, because I don't want to lose it with him. "I explained," I say eventually. "You heard me, didn't you? I told her in front of everyone that I can't handle sleeping with her tonight. Spending another night with her is just too damn hard."

"And this isn't?" He raises his hands, like he doesn't understand. "Right now, she's ten minutes away, Ed. Five, if you run. Tomorrow she's gonna be three thousand miles away. I'm no expert on love, but I can guarantee you that you will regret it if you don't go back there and spend one last night with her. You'll regret it for the rest of your life. Don't do that to yourself… and don't do it to her either."

I stare at him for a moment, and think about what he's just said. Tomorrow she'll be gone and we'll be over. Do I really want to spend those last few hours lying in bed by myself, wondering what might have been? I know it's gonna hurt like hell tomorrow, but I have to be with her.

"You're right." I jump to my feet and take a step toward the door, but he gets up and grabs me, pulling me back into a hug.

"I know I'm going on my honeymoon, but I'll keep my phone turned on. If you wanna talk after… well, after tomorrow, just call me. I'll pick up."

I manage to utter a quick, "Thank you," and then he lets me go and I run out the door.

I run all the way back to the restaurant and let myself in, going straight through and up the stairs, into the apartment and along to Tess's bedroom. The door's closed but I let myself in.

"Tess?" I whisper.

"Ed?" In the moonlight, I see her turn over in bed and sit up. "You're here?"

I go over to stand beside her. "Yeah. I had to come back, to spend one last night with you… If that's okay with you, of course."

"Oh, God… yes," she sobs and I kneel on the bed and pull her into my arms, holding her close and letting her weep.

"Why are we doing this to ourselves?" I whisper into her hair.

She leans back. "You know why," she sobs. "I can't live here. And I can't ask you to move. You've got too many connections here…"

"But…" She puts her fingers over my mouth.

"Please," she murmurs. "Please don't make it harder than it already is. I've gone over and over this in my head. I wish there was some other way, but there isn't. No matter how much we talk it through, we'll just end up back here again, and we'll have wasted our precious time together, getting nowhere." She looks up at me. "And… I—I'd rather spend our last night together making love."

My heart stops. "You want to make love?" I brush a few stray hairs away from her face and hold her still, looking into her eyes.

"Yes," she says, clearly. "I want the memory of you. Even if that's all we have."

I really wish she hadn't said that, but being as I want the memory too, I nod my head. I can't speak right now, but I don't think I really need to.

She's wearing a t-shirt and I reach down and pull it over her head, exposing her perfect body and lowering her back down onto the soft pillows. I kiss her, my tongue invading her mouth, and she brings her hands up behind my head, knotting her fingers in my hair and holding me steady. She moans softly into my mouth and I groan in reply. I'm bone hard and eventually I break the kiss, get up and quickly undress, before getting into bed with her and kissing her once more. Our bodies touch and we come alive, touching and caressing each other. I move my hand down and she parts her legs, letting me feel her intimately, raising her hips to my touch.

"You're so wet," I whisper, inserting a finger into her.

"Because I want you."

"I want you too."

She looks up at me. "Then take me. Please. Please just make it right again." She's blinking back tears and, without a word, I move between her legs, parting hers with my own and, very gently enter her. I pause, the tip of my cock just inside her.

"You are still taking your birth control pills, aren't you?" I ask, looking down at her.

She nods, and I slowly edge forward, until my whole length is surrounded by her velvet smooth, wet walls.

"You feel so good," I murmur softly.

"So do you." She swallows hard. "I'd forgotten."

"I hadn't." I lean down and kiss her. "I've never forgotten."

She reaches up and touches my cheek with her fingertips. "I'm sorry," she says.

"What for?" I still inside her.

"For all the wasted time. For not letting you come near me for all these weeks and months."

"Hey." I balance on one arm and cup her face in my hand. "I understood. I still do understand. And if you wanted me to stop right now, I would."

"I don't," she says.

I start to move again, taking her as deep as I can, but keeping my strokes long and slow, memorizing every second, every sound, every touch. She tips her head back slightly and I lean down and kiss her neck, which makes her shudder. I can feel the beginnings of that familiar fluttering inside her and I know she's close. And this time, more than any other, I want us to come together. I thrust deep inside her, once, twice more and, as she lets go and detonates quietly around me, I fill her, pouring my love into her one last time, ignoring the tears that are forming in my eyes.

As she calms, I notice she's crying and I turn us onto our sides, pulling her close into my arms.

"Don't cry," I whisper.

"How can I not?"

"Because I love you. And even when we're not together, I'll always love you."

She nestles into me. "Thank you," she murmurs. "Thank you for everything."

"Don't thank me, babe."

"Stay with me all night, won't you?" she asks.

"Of course. I'll be right here, holding you. I won't let you go." *Not until I have to.*

I wake suddenly and my eyes focus on the window and the view outside.

It's raining, which seems somehow appropriate for our last day together. Taking a deep breath and steeling myself for the emotional turmoil that I know the day will bring, I turn over, to find I'm alone.

"Tess?" I call out softly, climbing out of bed at the same time.

But even before I get around to the other side, I realize she's already gone. Her suitcase, which was by the door, isn't there anymore.

I stand, naked, my head in my hands. She left? Without even saying goodbye? Without letting me take her to the airport? This is too much, too unexpected, and I fall to my knees, clutching my arms around my midriff, and let out a silent howl, bending over and sobbing, my body shaking with emotion. I can't handle this... I can't. I need help. I need... Sam.

I scramble to my feet and go over to the door and, at the last minute remember I'm not wearing anything, so I turn back, grabbing my jeans from the floor and pulling them on.

Then I go out into the hallway and across to Sam and Ali's room, knocking on their door.

"Just a second, Tess." I hear Ali's voice from inside, and then some movement, before she opens the door, wearing one of Sam's t-shirts. "Ed?" She looks at me, confused. "Are you okay? Where's Tess?"

"She's... she's gone," I manage to say.

"Gone?" She looks behind me, like she doesn't believe me.

"Ed?" Sam comes over, wearing a pair of shorts. "What's going on?" He looks at me. "Jeez man, what happened?"

"She's gone," I repeat and he reaches forward, taking my arm and pulling me into their bedroom. He leads me over and sits me on the bed, sitting beside me, while Ali gets back in and pulls the comforter up, covering her legs.

"Tell us what's happened," Sam urges. "We didn't think you were gonna stay here last night."

"I wasn't. Rob convinced me that I should spend every last second with Tess, or I'd regret it, so I came back." I wipe my cheek with the back of my hand, and Ali reaches over to the other side of the bed, where there's a box of Kleenex. She hands me one and I thank her, feeling embarrassed.

"And?" Sam urges.

"And I spent the night. I'd thought we might have breakfast together, and maybe she'd let me drive her to the airport, but when I woke up this morning, she was gone." I shrug my shoulders. "I guess that tells me everything I need to know."

"How's that?" Sam asks and I turn to look at him.

"I'm not enough, am I?"

"That's rubbish," Ali says sharply, leaning forward. "That's just Tess's way. If she can't handle something, she goes quiet. It's like when our parents died, she didn't talk for two years then." She smiles at me. "She couldn't handle saying goodbye to you, so she didn't." She looks from me to Sam and back again. "I'm not saying she was right to do that, but Tess isn't great with big emotions."

"I get that," I point out. "I really do. I even get why she wanted to make love again last night, of all nights."

"Sorry?" Sam looks puzzled.

"We haven't," I explain. "Not since Bryan attacked her. She hasn't wanted to."

"Until last night?" Sam asks.

I nod. "She asked. I didn't offer," I clarify, before he gets the wrong idea. "And, like I say, I get why she wanted to, but the thing is, what the hell am I supposed to do now? I mean, the thought of a life on my own, which is all I've got to look forward to, while Tess pops over every so often to visit Ali and the baby, that fills me with… well, total fear and dejection, if I'm honest."

They both stare at me and it's clear that neither of them knows what to say.

"I just don't know what to do." I say eventually, looking up at the ceiling. "Obviously, I'm tied to this place. I've never known any other life but the one I have here, with you and Rob, and everything I know is here, but…" I leave the sentence hanging.

Sam puts his arm around my shoulder and leans into me a little. "I wish I knew what to do," he says, and I turn to him.

"You've always helped me out in the past. Help me now."

"How?"

"Ask me the questions."

He looks at me for a moment, and then leans back. "Okay… Can you imagine your life without her in it?" he says, keeping his eyes fixed on mine.

"No," I reply straight away. "No life that I wanna live, anyway."

He nods and takes a breath. "And what would you be prepared to give up for her?"

"Everything. I'd give up everything I have. Everything I know. Literally. All of it." I stand up and look down at him. "The thing is, I don't know how."

He nods his head very slowly. "Okay," he says. "Whenever you've come to me in the past, I've asked you those questions and then I've always left you to deal with the solution by yourself. And you've done it. But this time, I'm actually gonna help you out."

"You are?" I take a step toward him.

"Yeah." He reaches over to the nightstand and grabs his phone. "Because that's what big brothers are for…"

Epilogue

Tess

New Year's Eve

It's a windy day again today, but then it's been this way since the day after I got back here.

I hired a car at the airport and drove down here, and then once everywhere was open after Christmas, I plucked up my courage and went to a local car dealership and bought a new one. It's going to be delivered in a couple of weeks, so I'm hanging on to the rental until then. I've been shopping a couple of times and stocked up the kitchen, and I've instructed the agents to take the house off the market. The rest of the time, I've spent walking and reading.

And missing Ed.

I still feel guilty for leaving without saying goodbye to him, or to Ali and Sam, but it was more than I could handle. It was hard enough parting from Ed in the restaurant, but then he came back, and we made love so perfectly, and it was such an emotional connection, I knew there was no way I was going to be able to cope with going through the whole 'goodbye' thing again, especially if Ed wanted to take me to the airport, which I thought he might… so I left. Call me a coward if you want to. It's completely accurate.

It's late afternoon now and I've just got back from a walk on the beach. I've been soaking some Cannellini beans overnight and now I'm starting to make a Tuscan bean soup. I didn't used to cook that much. I suppose there was always someone else to do it for me; either granny, or Ali, or Ed, but since I've been back here, I've cooked every day, and I've cooked nothing but Italian food.

I have to brown some bacon – it was meant to be pancetta, but the supermarket had sold out – and then add some onion and garlic, and the soaked beans, and lots of water and let that simmer for a couple of hours. That's good, because I can go and hopefully finish the book I started yesterday.

Once the lid is firmly on the pan, I go through to the living room, switch on the table lamps, and pull the curtains closed, shutting out the wind. I've got it fairly warm in here now, although it was cold when I arrived. I won't light the fire, for obvious reasons, but the heating's been on for a few days and the residual chill has worn off – or at least I don't notice it anymore – even though it's around zero degrees outside.

I pull the patchwork quilt off the back of the couch and put it over my legs, pick up my book from the coffee table and settle down.

It's hard to concentrate today. With it being New Year's Eve, my mind keeps drifting back to the restaurant. I know they'll be opening up again today, probably around now actually, and that it's going to be a busy day for them. I can picture Ed in his little corner of the kitchen, grating chocolate and chopping nuts, happy in his own environment, where he belongs.

This is so much harder than I ever thought it would be. I'm not saying I made the wrong decision. I know I didn't belong there. But I do miss Ed. I miss pretty much everything about him, but especially his hugs, and his kisses, mostly at night, when I feel so alone. I haven't slept well since I got here, and I know that's why. He's not here to hold me.

I sent Ali a text when I got here, to let her know I'd arrived safely. She said I was forgiven for running out on them, and that she understood my reasons. Of course that doesn't mean Ed's forgiven me, but it's good to know that Ali's okay about it. We batted a few messages back and forth, and I told her I would contact her again on New Year's Day, which is tomorrow. I know I could call her anytime, and she made a point of telling me that, but I also know she spends a lot of time with

Ed, and I don't want to make things difficult for him by calling her all the time. He needs to get on with living his life, not be constantly reminded of me. And besides, I can't keep relying on Ali. So, I'm going to try and limit my calls to her to once or twice a week. And I'm going to try really hard not to ask how Ed is every time I speak to her, even though I'm desperate to know that he's okay.

I read a whole chapter without realising that I haven't actually taken in a single word. Nothing's registering with me today, because I'm so focused on Ed and what he's doing. Maybe tomorrow will be better. Maybe tomorrow, I'll start trying to write my novel again. It'll give me something else to think about.

The knock on the door makes me jump out of my skin. But then I calm quite quickly. Beatrice, the lady from the house next door, came in yesterday at around this time, and we had a lovely cup of tea together, and a gossip about what's going on in the village. She must be seventy-five years old and I've known her since forever. She's good company, and seeing her was a nice break to the day. I think she enjoyed it as much as I did, so I imagine she's probably come back for more of the same.

I throw off the quilt, put my book on top of it, and go over to the door, pulling it open.

This can't be happening. I gasp and put my hands to my mouth.

He doesn't say a word, but pulls my hands away from my face and leans down, covering my lips with his and kissing me, really hard. Our tongues meet, and it's like we've never been apart. His body is hard against mine and I can feel his arousal pressing into me. I'm breathless in an instant. I want him. I want him so much, I ache. This has got to be a dream. I must have fallen asleep on the couch, and I'm dreaming that Ed's here. *Please let me be wrong. Please let it be real.*

He breaks the kiss and I lean back.

"Can you pinch me, please?" I ask him.

"Sorry?"

"Pinch me. I'm convinced I'm in a dream. Please… just pinch me."

He smiles and very gently pinches my arm through my jumper. "It's not a dream. I promise. I'm very real. And I'm here."

A gust of wind catches my hair. "Come in," I say at last, remembering my manners and standing to one side to let him pass.

"It's freezing out there," he remarks as I close the door, like we haven't just spent the last week apart, on separate continents, but he's just been to the shops or down to the postbox.

I just stare at him, still in shock.

"You haven't lit the fire," he adds.

"Well no. I don't. I mean, I can't."

He looks embarrassed. "Sorry. That was a dumb thing to say." He moves closer. "Can I light it? This place needs a fire to complete the picture."

"Yes. As long as you're here, and as long as you put the guard round it once it's going." I indicate the folded metal fire guard that sits to one side of the hearth. "I get scared that sparks will catch on the rug."

"That's fine." He reaches out and cups my face in his hands. "I'll make sure it's safe."

He takes off his jacket, putting it over the back of the chair, and goes over to the fireplace and starts screwing up sheets of newspaper from the stack beside it.

"Can I ask you a question?" I sit back down, staring at him.

"Sure," he replies, continuing with his task.

"Why are you here?"

He turns, smirking. "Because I made a decision."

"Oh?"

"Yeah. I decided I'm not gonna live without you," he says, and he smiles.

I feel tears forming behind my eyes. "But... but I thought you understood, Ed. I can't live there. I can't go back again."

He throws the screwed up ball of paper into the hearth and crawls over to me on his knees, looking into my eyes.

"I know. And I'd never ask you to. What I decided was that, if being with you means I have to move here, then I'll move here."

I suck in a breath and a tear falls onto my cheek.

"But you can't... your family... your home..."

"Is wherever you are," he says finishing my sentence in a way I hadn't intended. "After you left, I realised I couldn't live without you. I couldn't face the prospect of you coming over to see Ali and the baby, knowing what we could've had. That wouldn't have been any kind of life worth living, Tess. So, that was when I worked out I'd do anything, I'd give up everything, to be with you… because I love you."

I shake my head. "That's too much to ask, Ed. Your whole family is in Hartford, and your business, your career. You can't just move to England."

He takes my hands in his and rests his forehead against mine. "Yeah, I can. Well, I kinda already have. I'm in the process of buying a business here already," he says.

"You're what?" I can't hide my surprise. "What business?"

He lets go of my hands and gets up, going over to his jacket and pulling out a piece of paper from the inside pocket. "This place," he says, coming back over and sitting down beside me.

"What place?"

He unfolds the page and I look at a familiar picture of the restaurant that used to operate in the village.

"You're going to buy Jane and Matthew's old place?"

"If their surname is Henderson, then yes. That's the name of the people selling."

"Yes, it is. But, Ed, it's been up for sale for over a year. They couldn't make a viable business out of it."

"Yeah, I know. That's why I got it for a knock-down price."

He gets up and goes back over to the fireplace, continuing to screw up pages out of the newspaper.

"But don't you see what a bad business idea that is?" I ask him.

He shakes his head. "That kinda depends on what I'm gonna do with it, doesn't it?" He turns and smiles at me. "Don't look so worried. I got some real good advice before making my decision."

"From whom?"

"Ali and Sam." He reaches into the basket for some kindling and makes a pyramid of twigs around the bundles of newspaper. "After you left," he says softly, while he works, "I went to see Sam. I told him how I felt and he offered to help me out."

"How?"

"He called Rob." He strikes a match and sets light to the newspaper, which quickly catches the wooden twigs aflame.

"Wasn't he on his honeymoon?" I ask, staring, mesmerised at the fire.

"No. He was still at the airport, luckily." He piles a couple of logs onto the flames and, getting up again unfolds the guard, positioning it around the hearth, and comes over to me. "Hey," he says, noticing the direction of my gaze. "It's fine. It won't hurt you. I won't let it."

I stare up at him and feel safe. He sits down beside me and pulls me close in his arms. "So what happened?" I ask him.

"We all talked," he explains. "It was obvious I was gonna need money, and a lot of it, if I was gonna move over here, so Rob and I agreed to sell the apartment."

"That takes time though, doesn't it?"

"Yeah. So, while that'll bring me in some cash, I won't have it for a while."

"So, how are you buying this place?" I pick up the piece of paper with the particulars printed on it and hold it up.

"We all agreed that I would sell my share of the business," he says. "But Rob couldn't afford to buy out half of my share, even though Sam could, not without selling the apartment first, so for a while it looked like we were in a deadlock."

"But?"

"Ali said she'd buy my share in its entirety."

"She did?" I stare at him.

"Yeah. It's the perfect solution. Ali's gonna take over the pastry section of the kitchen, at least until the baby's born, and then they'll probably get another chef to come in, but her owning a third of the place means it's still in the family, and there's someone there to keep the peace between Sam and Rob."

I smile. "Ali's good at that."

"Yeah, she is."

"So that gave you enough money to buy the restaurant?"

"I didn't even know about the restaurant then. I just knew I wanted to come over here, and get to you. I was expecting to work out what I'd do afterwards. Then Ali told me about the restaurant, and before I knew it, she'd helped me wade through all the red tape and I'd put in an offer."

"It's in a bit of state though. Do you have enough money from selling your share of Rosa's to fix it up?"

"No."

"Then let me help you."

He pulls me in close again. "That won't be necessary, babe. But thank you for offering."

"But, I don't understand… how are you going to pay for it? Are you going to wait for the money to come through from selling your apartment?"

"No. I don't need to. Sam called our dad," he says, his voice dropping to a whisper.

"Oh. Have they gone back home then?"

"Yeah, they left the day after you did."

"I see. So what did your dad say?"

"He agreed to give me the money I need."

I lean back in his arms. "He did?"

He nods his head, his eyes glistening. "Yeah. He spoke to me. He said he knows it doesn't make up for his mistakes, but he wanted me to accept his offer, as a gift, and not a loan."

"Wow."

"I know." He's clearly touched by his dad's gesture. "He had one condition though."

"What was that?" I ask him.

"He said he'll only give me the money if he and Mom can come and visit. Dad said he can't wait to see you again. He said you're his caro bambino."

"He called me that, on Christmas Day, when I was telling him about my dad," I say quietly. "I've got no idea what it means."

"It means you're his dear child," Ed explains. "Although the way he was saying it, a nearer translation would be 'dearest child'."

"Oh." I blink quickly as the tears sting my eyes. "The thing is," I say, sitting up a little and looking at him, desperate to change the subject. "This place… it's a failed restaurant. And there's a reason for that…"

"Yeah, I know. There's the pub in the next village, where we went for dinner, and a hotel out on the main road. Too much competition for too few people, especially during the winter."

"In which case…"

"Why have I bought it?" I nod my head. "Well, other than that it gives me a reason to be with you, Ali suggested that I turn it into a tea room. She kinda had to explain to me what that was, but once I'd got my head around it, I think it's a much better fit for me anyway." He sighs. "I never really had much to do with running Rosa's; Rob and Sam did that, and the thought of running a restaurant by myself is kinda scary, but I think I could handle this. It's more in my line, and the hours are a lot less troublesome." He twists in his seat and turns to face me, taking my hands in his. "I think you'll prefer a tea room to a restaurant," he says. "We'll be closed by five in the afternoon, and although I'll have to spend some of my time working on recipes and baking, we'll have most of our evenings together."

His enthusiasm is boundless.

"You do know there's a flat above the restaurant… well, tea room, as it will be?" I ask him.

"Yeah, it's included in the sale," he explains, turning over the piece of paper I dropped onto my lap a while ago. "There are two bedrooms, a kitchen-diner and a living room, plus bathroom."

I'm not sure how to ask this question, but I need to. "Are… are you going to live there?"

His eyes widen. "No. Not unless I have to. Ali suggested I rent it out to holidaymakers. I thought about renting it out long-term, but the experience you guys had with this place kinda put me off that idea. And besides, Ali said we can probably make more money with holiday lets, as she called it." He moves a little closer. "I want us to run the place together, Tess," he murmurs, looking at our still-bound hands. "Ali's helped me to draw up some quick plans and, if we can get started fairly soon, we should be able to have the tea room open for Easter."

I can feel my mouth drop open and I know I'm staring.

"Of course, if you don't wanna do it," he says, suddenly less sure of himself, for the first time since he got here.

I pull one hand away from his and touch his cheek. "I want to do it," I tell him. "I want to help you."

He smiles. "We'll run it together… as a team."

"And live here?" I ask him.

"If you're okay with that?" He looks uncertain again. "This is your house, Tess. I know you weren't ready for us to live together in the States, and if you're still not ready, then I can live in the apartment above the tea room for a while."

I stare at him and then a smile starts to form on my lips. How can he think I wouldn't want him here with me? I want to try and explain to him how different it is, now that we're here, but he pulls me into his arms.

"Are you okay with the plans?" he asks.

I nod my head.

"You definitely wanna run the tea room with me?"

I nod again, and there's a slight pause.

"And can I move in here with you?" I sense he's holding his breath and I nod my head once more. He sighs out a long breath.

"Can you speak?" he asks.

I lean back a little. "I love you," I whisper.

"I love you too," he says, and kisses me.

Ed

"What are you cooking?" I ask her, breaking the most perfect kiss. I was nervous as hell on the flight over here, and the drive down from the airport. I thought Tess would be okay about seeing me, but whether she'd go along with my plans was another matter. But it seems my fears were unfounded, and right now, I don't think there's a single thing in the world that could wipe the smile from my face. Even the smell that's permeating the house is amazing.

"Tuscan bean soup." She looks up at me, her lips swollen from where I've been gently biting them, her eyes wide and a little doubtful.

"Tuscan bean soup?" I repeat.

She nods her head. "I found the recipe online." She looks down for a moment, focusing on a spot somewhere beneath my chin. "I've been cooking Italian food ever since I got back here." She says it like a confession and that makes me smile even more.

"What stage are you at with your Tuscan bean soup?" I ask her.

She looks at her watch. "Actually, I should probably go and check it," she says, getting up.

"Can I help?" I offer.

"Only if you want to."

"If it means being with you, I want to."

I follow her down the few steps into the kitchen, and she flicks on a light and goes over to the stove, where a large pan is bubbling away. She switches on her iPad and reads.

"You need to drain that," I tell her.

"You do know that no-one likes a smart-arse, don't you," she says, a smile forming on her lips.

"Do you know?" I reply, wandering over to her, "I think that's the closest you've ever come to swearing."

She shrugs. "I think your brothers have cornered the market on that anyway."

I laugh. "Yeah."

"So, I'm meant to drain this?" she asks.

"Here, let me." I grab a large sieve from the hook on the wall. "I'll need another pan," I tell her, and she reaches into a cabinet and brings me one over, so I can drain the liquid from the beans.

"Now what do we do?" she asks.

"I thought you had a recipe?"

"You're more fun than following a recipe," she teases, and I have to kiss her.

While I finish making the soup, Tess heats some bread in the oven and lays the table, and then we sit together, holding hands and eating at the same time.

"This is really good," she says after the second spoonful.

"Only because you cooked the beans so well," I tell her, smiling. "Although I think we've got enough soup there for about a week."

"Hmm, I'm not very good with portion sizes," she says. "I didn't notice that the recipe served six."

"Well, we can have it for lunch tomorrow, and then freeze whatever's left," I suggest.

She nods and takes a slice of bread. "I don't know if you're aware," she says, pulling the crusts off, "but the UK kind of closes down a bit for Christmas and New Year, so we'll have to wait until next week before we can start sourcing suppliers and contractors to start work on your tea room."

"*Our* tea room," I correct her.

"If it's our tea room, then you've got to let me contribute financially."

"You're letting me live here, and you'll probably be supporting us for a while, until I can start to earn a living, so you will be contributing."

She nods her head. "Okay… but if you need anything, you've only got to ask."

"You've already given me so much, Tess." She looks confused. "You've given me your love, which is the most precious gift of all, but you also gave me back my dad… my family. I—I can't do that for you, but I can promise you that, now I'm here, I'll never leave you. I'll stay by your side, always."

She leans across the table and I meet her halfway, kissing her tender lips.

When we've finished eating and cleared away, I bring in my suitcase, which I left in the car on my arrival. I didn't want to assume too much.

It's getting late already, and I'm feeling tired.

"Can I sleep with you, Tess?" I ask her as she starts switching off the table lamps in the living room. "We don't have to do anything…" I leave the sentence hanging. "But I haven't slept properly since you left."

She switches off the last lamp, leaving us with just the glow from the fire to light the room, and comes over, standing in front of me. "I'd like that," she says softly, her hand resting on my chest. "I haven't slept very well either. I've missed you too much." She doesn't say any more. She doesn't need to. I take her hand and lead her up the stairs and into her bedroom at the back of the house.

We slowly undress each other, leaving our clothes on the chair by the window, and then we climb into bed and I pull her naked body into my arms, feeling her soft skin against mine. Exhausted from the day, and everything that's happened, as well as not sleeping properly for the last week, we both drift off to sleep within minutes.

I wake a few moments before Tess, and as soon as she opens her eyes, a smile forms on her lips.

"You didn't have any nightmares," I say and she shakes her head.

"No. First time in ages. And I slept right through."

"Me too." I turn onto my side and pull her into my arms. "This feels like a new beginning."

"It does, doesn't it?" She looks up at me.

We stare at each other for what feels like a long while. I think we're both a little amazed that what seemed destined to end in heartbreak for so long, has actually ended in happiness.

"Do you want to make love?" I ask eventually.

"Yes," she says, smiling and kinda shy.

I roll her onto her back and settle between her legs. We've got the rest of our lives to do whatever we please with each other. For today, I just wanna hold her and look at her, and watch her come apart, and enjoy every second of knowing we're back together.

"Do you know?" she says, just as I'm about to enter her.

"What?"

"We forgot to say 'Happy New Year' to each other last night."

I smile. "I actually forgot it was New Year's at all," I tell her, and slowly push my cock inside her. Just like before, she gasps as I stretch her and I give her a moment to get used to the feeling. "This is the best possible start to the new year," I whisper. "And to our new life."

After breakfast, we showered together. I want to shower like that again. Every. Single. Day. What's more, now we're back together, I can. And when Tess had finished screaming my name, we both laughed, because there's no-one here to hear us. And that feels great.

We got dressed eventually and went out for a walk. We went to see the restaurant, which is kinda run down, but definitely has potential and now I've seen it in the flesh, I'm even more excited about what we can do with it in the future. When we'd finished there, we went back to the beach and started walking along the shore. It's still windy, but the sun's out today and while it's cold, it's also beautiful.

"Is that the pathway that leads up to the clifftop?" I ask her pointing to a narrow, steep-looking track over to one side of the cove.

"Yes," she replies, looking at me. "How did you know?"

"Because you described it in your book. You had the guy walking up it, and you described how long it took, and what he saw on the way, and the view from the top."

"You remembered that?"

"Of course. You write really well, Tess."

She looks kinda sad for a moment. "I haven't written anything since…" She doesn't need to say since when. "I was hoping, being here might help."

"It will," I say, trying to make her feel more optimistic. "You'll get back to it, babe. I know you will."

"Hopefully," she replies and looks up at me, smiling again.

"You belong here, you know," I tell Tess, holding her gloved hand in mine. Her hair's blowing all over the place and as we stop, I capture it and pull it back behind her head so I can kiss her. "And if you belong here," I continue, once we've broken the kiss, "then so do I."

She doesn't say a word, but smiles up at me.

"When I was in Sam and Ali's bedroom, the morning you left, and we were talking with Rob at the airport," I say, hoping I've timed this right, "my brothers made one condition to me leaving the business and moving here to be with you."

"What was that?" she asks.

"They said they wouldn't do it, until I agreed to return to Hartford regularly – and bring my wife with me." I hold my breath, waiting.

"What wife?" she asks.

I laugh. "You, of course. I want to marry you. I mean, I think we'll have to get married in the US, because my family is way too big to expect them all to travel to the UK, but we can keep it low-key if you want. We don't have to invite all the cousins and aunts and uncles. We can just keep it to immediate family, like Rob and Petra did. So, I'm gonna have to ask you to go back to the US again, but then we'll live here, and we'll renovate the tea room, and work together and be happy… and in the wintertime, when it's quieter, we can shut down for a couple of weeks and go back to Hartford on vacation, to visit my family, and maybe take a few days down in Florida to see Mom and Dad…"

Her fingers come up and cover my mouth, silencing me.

"Wait a minute, Ed. I haven't said 'yes' yet."

I pull her closer in my arms and smile down at her. "Okay. Say 'yes' then."

She bursts into tears and for a brief second, my whole body becomes ice, filled with cold fear… but then she nods her head.

"Are you saying yes, Tess?" I ask her. After that reaction, I need to be sure.

"Yes," she mumbles, her tears slowing.

"Can you do something for me?" I ask her and she nods her head. "Can you pinch me?"

She laughs and pinches my arm.

"Okay. Now say 'yes' again."

"Yes," she says, looking shy.

"You're sure?"

"I've never been more sure. I know you love me and I know you'll take care of me. You're moving to a different continent and changing your whole life for me."

"Wait. Don't say yes out of gratitude." I don't want that.

"I'm not," she replies quickly. "I'm really not. I'm saying it out of love… and need. I need you Ed."

"Nowhere near as much as I need you, babe. Speaking of which, do you think we could go back to the cottage?"

"Back to the cottage?"

"Yeah. I want to make love to you."

She blushes. "I think I'd like that too," she whispers, and she looks up into my eyes. "Oh. They're back," she says, smiling.

"What are?"

"The fireflies. They're back in your eyes."

"That's because being with you makes me happy."

I take her hand in mine and lead her back up the beach toward the beautiful house where it seems we both belong.

"You make me happy too," she says.

"Good, because you're mine," I whisper, leaning into her as we turn into the hazy, winter sun.

"Yes, I am."

"And I'm yours."

"Promise?"

"Promise."

"No matter what?"

"No matter what."

The End

Keep reading for an excerpt from Suzie Peters' forthcoming book
Believe In Us
Part One in the Believe in Fairy Tales Series.
Available to purchase from December 14th 2018

Believe In Us

Believe in Fairy Tales: Book One

by

Suzie Peters

.

Chapter One

Lottie

"You sure this is the right address?" The cab driver pulls to a halt outside the enormous gates.

"I'm positive. If you pull forward a little further, you can swipe my entry card to let us in." I hand it to him and he takes it, inching closer and lowering the window beside him, which lets in a blast of cold December air. "Just run it from top to bottom," I explain and he obeys my instructions, then hands my card back as the little light on the entry system turns from red to green, the gates hesitate for a moment, and then start to open inwards.

"Jeez," he murmurs under his breath, raising the window again and starting to move onto my father's property. I call it my father's property, but it isn't really. Not anymore. It's my stepmother's property now and this is the first time I've been back since my father's funeral, just over four months ago. To be honest, I wasn't entirely sure my entry card would still work, or whether Catrina would have had the access codes changed. Nothing that woman does would surprise me.

"Dear God." The words leave my mouth before I can stop them.

"Well, that's sure lit up," the driver says at the same time, and I stare out the window at the monstrosity of coloured flashing lights that cover the entire front surface of the house. "I guess it's festive," he adds, trying to sound positive.

"That's one word for it." I can think of several others. Cheap. Gaudy. Vulgar. They all spring to mind, and yet they all feel inadequate for the ostentatious show of tasteless flamboyance that lies before me. "What do I owe you?" I ask the driver as he pulls up right outside the front door.

He checks his meter. "Call it forty," he says, rounding down the numbers.

He's obviously noticed that, despite the showy surroundings, I'm not the best-dressed person in town and I guess he's taking pity on me. Or maybe it's just the Christmas spirit kicking in a few days early. I give him fifty and tell him to keep the change. I've worked a few extra shifts myself in the last couple of weeks and can afford to pass a little on. And besides, the Christmas spirit works both ways, doesn't it?

He gets out and opens my door. Luckily, because some of my clothes are still here, I've travelled light and only have my rucksack, which I pull out behind me and sling over my shoulder. "Thanks for the ride," I say to him.

"My pleasure," he replies. We've spent the forty-five minute journey from the airport talking about all kinds of things, but mainly his kids, and although I've only been able to see his eyes in the rear-view mirror, his pride and pleasure in talking about them has been obvious, not to mention refreshing. Working in the retail sector in the lead up to Christmas is pretty much guaranteed to leave you feeling jaded, and I'm sure it's no different for cab drivers, but this guy is more interested in the time he's gonna spend with his kids than anything money can buy.

"Enjoy the holidays," I say to him as he gets back into the cab.

"You too, ma'am."

He gives me a wave and turns the car around, going back down the long driveway and disappearing from sight. I wait until he's gone before turning and looking up at the building which, if previous Christmases are anything to go by, should have a simple tree outside, decorated with white lights. My father – and my mother when she was alive – never went in for anything ostentatious, and their Christmas decorations reflected their modest tastes. Instead of that though, I'm looking at a flashing, rainbow colored building, with almost none of the actual fabric visible, other than the windows, and the intermittent flashing of the lights is enough to make my eyes ache. So, as much as I'd like to stay out here and prolong the inevitable meeting with my supposed family, I climb the steps to the front door and insert my key.

Inside, the decorations are just as bright, the wide marble-floored hallway having been filled with fairy lights. There's also a life-size Santa Claus model at the far end beside the stairs, which is bad enough, except it's also illuminated and is rocking back and forth.

"Oh, good Lord," I murmur to myself.

"Hello?" A familiar voice sounds from the direction of the kitchen, and I move toward it, smiling, and then start running and throw myself into the arms of Mrs Hemsworth, who returns my greeting, hugging me tight. "I thought it might be you," she says, eventually pulling back and looking me up and down. "You've lost weight," she adds and takes my hand, leading me back to the kitchen.

"A little… maybe."

She shakes her head and I sit up on one of the high stools at the wide breakfast bar, dropping my rucksack at my feet. This has always been my favorite room in the house. Dad had it remodeled about three or four years ago, and it's very sleek and chic now, with every modern convenience you can imagine, but that's not why I like it in here so much. I like it because Mrs Hemsworth makes it feel so homely. Every day, when I finished school, I used to come back here and have a glass of milk and a couple of her home made cookies, or a slice of cake, and we'd sit and talk about my day. Then my mom would come home from the foundation she used to run about an hour later and she'd join us and, while I did my homework, they'd cook our evening meal together, like two old friends. Dad always did his best to get home in time to eat with us, even if it meant he had to carry on working afterwards in his study. That was one of the best things about my parents. Despite their wealth and how busy their lives were, they never forgot the value of family time.

"Eating too little, or working too hard?" she asks, opening the oven and pulling out a lasagna.

"A bit of both," I reply. "Is that for me?" I can hear my stomach grumbling already.

"Sure is," she says, smiling. "Your favorite." She cuts into it and the heady aromas of tomato, Italian herbs and cheese assail my nostrils.

"That smells so good," I tell her truthfully as she places the plate in front of me, and fetches a bowl of salad and some cutlery, before taking a seat opposite and looking over at me. She hasn't changed at all, but then I suppose it's only a few months since I last saw her, standing holding my hand at dad's funeral. At least she's not wearing black now, but she's in her usual smart skirt and blouse, an apron tied around her waist. I've never known how old she is, and never been brave enough to ask, but I imagine she's in her mid to late fifties. She's got brown hair with a fair amount of gray running through it, and pale blue eyes that always seem to know when I need someone to talk to…

"Well… eat up," she says, smiling.

The way the lasagna is calling to me, I don't need telling twice, and I cut through the crispy cheese topping to the rich meaty sauce below.

"Where's everyone?" I ask, taking my first delicious mouthful and closing my eyes in appreciation of one of life's finest things.

"They're all out," she replies. "The twins have gone to a party, and her ladyship went out for dinner." She rolls her eyes. "Again," she adds.

"You'd better not let her hear you calling her that," I warn. "And what do you mean 'again'?"

"I think that's the third time this week she's gone out…" She gives me a knowing look.

"You think she's got another man… already?" Although I hate my stepmother with a passion, I can't help the emotion from seeping into my voice. The thought that she can have forgotten my father so quickly is appalling.

Mrs Hemsworth shrugs. "I don't know," she says. "Let's face it, she was never around that much, even when your daddy was alive, not once she'd persuaded him into marriage, anyway. But you've seen what she's like with Jack. She was all over the poor boy today…" She lets her voice fade and we both smile now, but then it's hard not to. Jack is the gardener and handyman. He comes in three times a week, usually on Mondays, Wednesdays and Fridays and whenever he's around, Catrina does her best to attract his attention, wearing the skimpiest clothes imaginable, even in the middle of winter, fawning over him like a lovesick teenager, complimenting his impressive physique and generally making a fool of herself. The reason we're smiling is because Mrs Hemsworth and I know something that Catrina doesn't… namely, that it would have to be a very cold day in hell before Jack would ever be interested in 'her ladyship'. That's because he's already in a relationship, with an equally attractive lawyer, by the name of Alex, which is short for Alexander.

"Is he responsible for decorating the house?" I ask.

She nods. "Yes, but she didn't give him a choice, and he didn't like doing it. Your step mother had all the lights delivered last week and it's taken poor Jack all his time to put the darn things up, which is why she's got him coming in tomorrow as well as Friday, to make sure the garden looks just right for the party on Saturday…" her voice fades again and she looks across at me.

I pause, my lasagna-loaded fork poised mid-air. "Excuse me? Did you say 'party'?"

Mrs Hemsworth nods her head, then rests her elbows on the countertop, letting her chin fall onto her upturned hands. "You know how your father always used to have a Christmas party?" she says thoughtfully.

"Yes."

"Well, Catrina's decided to do the same thing."

"But I don't understand… why does it matter what the garden looks like? Dad always held his parties at a hotel, not at home." Dad's Christmas parties were legendary, but he never held one at our house. This was always a place that was private… for us to be alone, away from it all.

"She's holding it here…"

"She is?" I can't disguise my surprise. "And did you say it was going to be on Saturday?" She nods. "This Saturday? But Christmas Day is only next Wednesday. It's too close…"

"Yes."

"But…" I'm stunned into silence. That was something my dad would never have done. His appreciation of family time wasn't limited to us Hudsons. He'd never have held a business function like this on a weekend so close to the holidays, because he knew people had their own family commitments. They had relatives to see, shopping to do, children to be with. The last thing they needed was to have to attend a business party, even if it was being thrown by a man who'd done a lot to help them and their community.

"I know," Mrs Hemsworth replies and I know I don't need to explain to her.

"Why's she doing it?"

"I have no idea." She gets up and goes over to the coffee machine, filling it with ground coffee from the container that sits beside it, and then going to the sink. She turns around to face me again. "But she told me to tell you that she wants to talk to you tomorrow."

"She did?"

"Yes. She said she's got something in mind, and she needs to talk it through with you."

"That sounds ominous," I reply, suddenly feeling nervous. When Catrina says she's got something in mind, it's usually time to be worried, because I know it's going to mean work for me. Even before my father's death, she dropped not very subtle hints – out of his earshot, of course – that, once I came back from university, I needn't think I could live at the house rent free. She told me in no uncertain terms that I'd have to earn my keep if I thought I could continue to live in luxury. That rule doesn't seem to apply her twin daughters, Christa and Chelsea, who swan around, doing whatever takes their fancy. But with that thought in mind, I dread to think what she's planning for me.

Paul

I stare at the invitation in my hand, trying to make a decision.

I've been to this particular Christmas party every year for the last ten years, but this time around, it feels wrong. Charles Hudson only died a few months ago, so for his widow to be throwing the customary Hudson Investments annual Christmas party feels a little inappropriate, to put it mildly. I check the date again. The party's this coming Saturday, which is really close to the holidays, and although I'm supposed to have replied by now, I've been putting off making the decision. I mean, I know I'm supposed to have gone back to them by the end of the day – one way or the other – but being as it's only just after five in the afternoon, it's not the end of the day yet. Not my day, anyway.

I put the invitation down again and check my emails, answering one from my newest potential game designer. He's based in Detroit and, so far, we've only communicated by email and Skype, but I'm supposed to be flying to meet him in the New Year. In his message, he details out a couple of questions about the draft contract I sent through to him earlier in the week, which I refer to the legal department, just as there's a knocking on my door.

"Come in," I call out.

"What's going on?" My friend Fin Price comes into my office, looking around, with a surprised expression on his face.

"Sorry?" I stare over at him, feeling confused.

"I expected to find you running around, in a state of panic, your share price tumbling through the floor, the bottom having fallen out of the market…" He comes over and flops his six foot three frame down into the chair opposite me.

"What the hell are you talking about, Fin?" I sit forward.

He leans over and rests his arms on my desk. "Since when do you ignore my text messages?" he asks. "I assumed there had to be some kind of national emergency going on…"

"You sent me a message?"

"Yeah… about Friday night."

Fin and I have known each other since high school and we usually meet up for a quiet drink after work at least once a week. Mostly it's on a Friday, but sometimes we'll change the evening, if we have to. I guess this is one of those times.

"I've gotta pull a late shift on Friday, which on the upside means we could play golf in the morning, if you want to, but it means I won't be able to come out in the evening, so I was suggesting we could maybe do something tonight… except you didn't answer my text."

I check my phone, which is on silent and look up at him, sheepishly. "Sorry," I murmur.

"So you did get the message then?"

"Yeah. I just didn't realize."

"And you call yourself a chief executive," he mumbles, rolling his eyes. "It's a good thing I have to drive past your office to get home," he adds.

"I've been distracted," I point out. "So shoot me."

"Why would I wanna do that? I'd only feel obliged to fix you up again." He shakes his blond head at me. "So, what's been distracting you?" he asks, leaning back again and crossing one long leg over the other. He's well-dressed, in a sharp suit, although I know he'll have spent his day in scrubs, being as he works as an Emergency Room doctor in the city hospital. "It's not a sexy new secretary," he continues. "I recognized Maureen the moment I walked in."

"Yeah… and she's the only one who'd let you walk in here unannounced," I reply. She's been with me for nearly five years and feels more like a mother than a secretary sometimes. "And besides, you know I never mix business with pleasure… unlike some doctors I could mention."

"It was once," he replies, rolling his eyes. "Just once. And in my defense, she was the sexiest theater nurse I've ever seen." He smiles, clearly remembering something I'd probably rather not know. "But, like you, I prefer to keep my personal life and my professional life separate."

"Except when you find a particularly sexy theater nurse, evidently," I joke.

"Yeah… except then." He folds his arms across his broad chest. "You still haven't told me what was distracting you," he says, looking across at me.

"Oh, it's this," I reply, tossing the invitation across the desk at him.

He leans forward and picks it up. "Hudson Investment Corporation," he murmurs. "Isn't that the guy who first invested in you?"

"Yeah," I confirm. "Charles and I met at a conference when I was just finishing university, we got talking over a beer and Charles said he saw something in me. It just kinda blossomed from there really." I can't help remembering that meeting, in the hotel bar, and how he'd listened to my young and occasionally naive dreams, not in a critical or judgmental way, like some of my lecturers, nor in a jokey, disbelieving way, like many of my peers, but in a supportive and helpful manner. A few weeks later, Charles called me up and arranged to meet me again, and told me he wanted to invest in me, to give me a head start in forming a computer gaming company. I've never looked back.

"So, how much did he invest?" Fin asks, still looking down at the invitation.

"Half a million," I reply.

He lets out a soft whistle.

"On a kid he didn't know?"

I nod my head and Fin locks eyes with me. "You could probably buy Hudson Investment Corporation several times over now, couldn't you?"

"Yeah. If I wanted to."

He smiles. "So, how much *are* you worth?"

"I don't know really," I reply honestly. "It changes every few minutes. Last time I checked, I think it was about two point eight…"

He looks surprised. "Million?"

"No… billion."

His jaw drops and the surprise becomes shock. "Holy shit, Paul. I had no fucking idea…"

"It's taken more than ten years of hard work to get here, but I'm here." I glance across at him, noticing the invitation he's still clutching. "And no matter how much I'm worth, it still doesn't help me make a decision about the goddamn party, does it?"

"What's stopping you from saying 'yes'?" he asks.

"I've gone to Charles' Christmas parties every year since I first met him," I explain. "It's something he always did, bringing together all the people he'd invested in so he could catch up with us all and see how we were getting along."

"But?"

"But he died in the middle of August, and this feels…"

"Too soon?" he prompts.

"Yeah. But it's more than that. It feels inappropriate, especially as he won't be there, and the whole point of these parties, as far as I was concerned, was to see him." I pause for a moment. "But at the same time, I feel that if I don't go, I'm dishonoring his memory."

He nods his head. "The invitation's from Catrina Hudson," he says, looking down at it. "Is that his widow?"

"Yeah." He must be able to hear the distain in my voice, because he raises his eyebrows and tilts his head to one side. "They were only married for about a year before Charles died," I add, "and this feels like a fairly typical, and cynical ploy of hers."

"You like her then," he says.

"Yeah. I'm a huge fan."

"Hmm. I can tell." He smiles at me. "Well, maybe she just wants to carry on the tradition, or perhaps she's looking for some moral support from the people he helped over the years?" he suggests.

I shake my head. "No, that's not how Catrina operates," I reply. "She couldn't give a damn about tradition, and I've never met anyone who needed moral support less."

He leans forward again, putting the invitation back on my desk and looking hard at me. "Whatever you think of her," he says softly. "Charles obviously loved her, or he'd never have married her, would he? Maybe you should remember that?"

"I'd love to. I really would. But I'm not convinced he did love her. I think he married her because he was lonely."

"Really?" He leans a bit further forward, clearly interested.

"Yeah. Charles was married to his first wife, Olivia, for years. He told me they were childhood sweethearts and she was the love of his life." I pause and think for a moment. "It was odd, you know, he was a fairly hard-nosed businessman, but he was complete mush when it came to Olivia." I always remember feeling kinda jealous of that, knowing I'd probably never have anyone like that in my life. I'm just not that kinda guy. I can't imagine myself being in love, or even coming close to it.

"So what happened?" he asks, interrupting my train of thought.

"She died about three years ago. She ran a foundation which helped disadvantaged children, and was working really hard, so she missed the early signs…" I let my voice drop.

"Cancer?" he asks.

"Yeah. By the time they caught it, it was too late. She died within a couple of months. I was out of the country at the time, doing some work in Europe, but I went and saw him when I got back. He was in pieces, being fawned over by Catrina."

"She was on the scene even then?"

"She was his secretary," I explain. "And she obviously wanted to be more."

"If he and his first wife were so close, how did she manage to convince him?"

"I think she played on his loneliness," I reply. "And of course, there was Lottie…"

"Lottie?"

"Yeah. Charles and Olivia's daughter."

"They had a daughter?"

"Yeah. And Catrina had a couple of kids too… twin girls, if I remember rightly. I think she convinced Charles that she'd take care of Lottie and be a mother to her."

"Well, maybe that wasn't such a bad idea," Fin says.

"Maybe not, in normal circumstances. But I don't think Catrina has a maternal bone in her body. She's the last person you'd want to mother your child. I guess Charles wasn't thinking straight at the time and, after a year or so of her wearing him down, he asked her to marry him. She jumped at the chance and the rest, as they say, is history."

"So, the daughter is now living there with the stepmom and the twins?" he asks.

"No. I think she was going off to college when her mom died. As far as I know she did so, which is probably a good thing. At least she escaped Catrina's malevolent influence."

"Sounds to me like you should avoid this party," he says, tapping the invite with his fingertips.

"Except I kinda feel I owe it to Charles to go… not just to pay my respects, being as I missed his funeral, but also to make sure Catrina's not ruining his company and taking his good name down with her."

"Then go," he says, sitting back again, seemingly a little exasperated.

I reach across and pick up the invitation again.

"It says 'To Paul Lewis and guest'," I remark and look up at him. "What are you doing on Saturday evening?"

"Um…"

He fumbles around mentally for an excuse. "You're free? Great. You can come with me." I check the email and start typing out my reply, giving them Fin's name as my guest.

"You're kidding, right? You must have a list of women who'd willingly accompany you. Let's face it, most of Boston's finest young ladies are positively gagging to be seen with you, and your billions."

"Yeah, but none of them will watch my back like you will."

"Will you need to have your back watched?" he asks.

"I might. It depends on what Catrina's done to Charles' company, and what her real motives are for throwing this party."

He stares at me for a moment. "I guess I'd better find my tux then, hadn't I?"

I smile at him and press 'send'.

... to be continued.

Printed in Great Britain
by Amazon